LOST EARTH

A NOVEL

BY

Michael McCollum

SCI Fi - ARIZONA
A Virtual Science Fiction Bookstore
and Writer's Workshop on the INTERNET
www.scifi-az.com

ISBN 978-1-947483-19-4

364 pages

Michael McCollum
Sci Fi - Arizona
PO Box 14026
Tempe, AZ 85284-0068
mccollum@scifi-az.com

11112020

Table of Contents

Prologue

It is the 43rd century (Old Calendar) and humanity occupies a substantial chunk of the Orion Spur, the small galactic arm in which Sol is located. The millions who fled Earth have grown into untold billions. *Homo sapiens Terra* has become *Homo sapiens Galactica*.

The *Great Hegira* was the result of a step change in technology, and, as such, should have come as no surprise.

While there were undoubtedly others, the first identifiable precursor to the vast outpouring was the invention of moveable type by Johannes Gutenberg in 1437. [OC]

The printing press represented a quantum leap in the ease of communications; and, as such, was responsible for the Reformation and three hundred years of religious warfare.

The second grand disruption began late in the twentieth century with the development of the Internet, an early information grid. No longer need people associate with one another based on physical proximity. In the connected world, they could seek likeminded souls anywhere. Thus, began a trend that ended with the dissolution of nation-states.

The development of faster-than-light travel was the third disruptive leap, and by far the largest.

With *ftl* came the discovery that any average grouping of five hundred stars is likely to have at least one terrestrial-class world. Suddenly, humanity found itself with an infinity of potential living space.

No longer need the downtrodden suffer under the boot of their oppressors. Anyone sufficiently motivated could, if they had resources and adherents, hire a colony ship, and set out for the stars.

The invention of *ftl* initially gave humanity a toehold in the firmament. During the next half millennium, that toehold became a beachhead and then a stampede.

Nor was society the only thing transformed by the advent of star travel. The need to adapt to alien environments forced adjustments to the human form, either via natural selection or intentional manipulation. By the 40th century, genetic modifications were such that the more extreme branches of the human family could not produce viable offspring with one another.

The rush to the stars brought with it another form of natural selection. The timid stayed home, while the audacious emigrated. However, while laudable in an individual, excessive pioneer spirit proved troublesome at interstellar scale.

As human-occupied space expanded at an exponential clip, competing colonies increasingly fell into conflict. At first, these were local disputes. Over time, rivalries grew, as did star system navies. When widespread war finally came, it raged across whole sectors of human space.

Wars of secession, mass bombardments, commerce raids, and futile attempts at occupying enemy planets all took their toll. Much that had been built during the preceding millennium was destroyed in flashes of nuclear fusion.

The collapse of interstellar civilization brought with it a new dark age, one that far surpassed the fall of Rome. Centuries were needed to recover from the chaos. That recovery came in fits and starts, but eventually, a new *Pax Galactica* took hold. The return to stability brought with it a renaissance in learning. Much lost knowledge was eventually reclaimed.

Much, but not all.

On worlds across human space, parents told their children stories of the fabled past. They spoke of a magical place where once dwelt knights and princesses, magicians and dragons, where bold warriors sallied forth to victory or defeat.

When the children grew older, they learned that the world of legend known as "The Mother of Men" had possessed vast seas of blue water; azure skies filled with fleecy white clouds; and a giant moon whose silver beams enchanted thousands of generations of young lovers.

They learned that a 'standard year' was the orbital period of humanity's home as it circled its primary, and that human vision was sharpest in the yellow-green wavelengths because that was the color of Sol-light as seen through a canopy of forest leaves.

What the children did not learn was where this magical place could be found. The interstellar wars had robbed them of that knowledge. The stellar coordinates of Sol were lost.

And with them, the location of Planet Earth.

#

PART ONE

MORAST

Chapter 1

Shipmaster Larath da Benthar Sims, of the Starship *Coronal Fire*, lay in her command couch, sipped gantha juice, and contemplated the holographic view volume before her. Behind her, a meter-thick mirrored column rose from deck to overhead. The column housed *Coronal Fire*'s sentient computer. Two pairs of couches, currently unoccupied, were arrayed to either side. The bulkheads were covered with other displays on which flowed soothing streams of eye-pleasing color.

Lara was a native of Envon in the Altona System. She was long and lithe, as was typical of her planetary type. Her eyes were slanted-slits of emerald-green, her black hair was cut in a spacer's bob, and her alabaster skin was sufficiently fair to require melanin pills on many worlds. She was clad in an iridescent bodysuit that matched her eyes.

Coronal Fire was 2000 hours out of Lanyth, in the Bortanis System, en route to Bernau, the capital of the Morast Confederacy. The ship was moving at 1000-lights equivalent velocity. At its current pseudo-speed, it would reach Morast, its home star, within five hours.

That, of course, would not be happening.

In the view volume, the hyperon stream that carried them along was a river of scintillating light that curved gently to the right and down until it vanished into background haze. As was customary, the active hyperon stream was coded cyan.

Towering over her and to her right was an angry splotch of orange red that reminded her of a thundercloud back home. This 'storm' was a major disruption in the high energy hyperon strata in which *Fire* was traveling; a Class Five flaw induced by gravitational infusion from a nearby universe.

Directly ahead, and extending out of sight to her left, lay another flaw, this one a streak of monochromatic red, a Class Three rectilinear fold. It was an infusion from a completely different

11

universe.

The two flaws marked the Scylla and Charybdis of the Kaligani Narrows, the bane of every shipmaster on this run.

Observing the chronometer display, Lara sighed and willed a thought into existence: "About time, isn't it, *Cor?*"

A silent voice in her head answered, "We have two minutes, fifteen seconds before we need to head downslope, Shipmaster. I am about to issue the two-minute warning."

'Downslope' meant that the artificial intelligence that flew the ship was about to *downfreq* the ship's hyper-generators to begin a slow descent through the lower-energy hyperon layers.

They would fall out of congruence with the 1000-light stream and descend to the ten-light level, where they would pick up another current to carry them beneath the two hazards to navigation.

The maneuver would add 500 hours to their voyage.

The diversion was necessary because Morast was only half a light-year beyond the far flaw. Should *Coronal Fire* continue its present course and speed, it would enter that turbulence and be ripped asunder in milliseconds.

The delay was unfortunate, but unavoidable. Such was the nature of hyperspace.

#

With the lofting of large telescopes into Earth orbit, it became possible for astronomers to calculate the total mass of the universe. They did this by seeing the way galaxies rotate and the degree to which light rays bend as they pass near intervening galactic clusters.

Tallying up the mass of everything they could see and of which they were aware, astronomers concluded that normal matter makes up only four percent of the total mass of the observable universe. The other 96 percent is invisible.

To explain the discrepancy, they postulated the existence of two types of massy particles: dark matter and dark energy. They searched for these elusive ghosts for more than a century, but no trace of either was ever found.

With the failure to find dark particles, astronomers rethought the problem. They wondered if their traditional view of reality was too cramped.

It was... by several orders of magnitude.

Reluctantly, they turned to the idea that the Big Bang had created not only the universe that we can see; but some ten million other universes that we cannot.

#

The idea of multiple universes was not new. Theoreticians had long fostered a multidimensional hypothesis known as *M-Theory*, which held that the four known dimensions (X, Y, Z, and T) are insufficient to explain the known laws of physics. To account for all the laws, the *totality of everything* must exist in a spacetime domain consisting of eleven distinct dimensions.

No more, no less.

The deep thinkers called their eleven-dimensional construct a *multiverse* and named the universe in which we dwell, *Minkowski Space*.

Of course, most people continued to call it *The Universe.*

If the multiverse has eleven dimensions, and if each daughter universe is four-dimensional, then the total number of universes is *eleven factorial divided by four... or 9,979,200.* For convenience, people round that number up to an even ten million.

These universes are congruent. That is, they occupy the same 'volume' of multidimensional spacetime. We cannot see them because each quartet of dimensions is unique; and therefore, each universe has different physical laws and properties. Conditions in these sibling universes are difficult to imagine, but all have something in common.

They are all filled with matter and/or energy.

As Einstein postulated in 1905[oc], matter and energy are two forms of the same thing. The presence of either causes curvature in the local spacetime continuum, curvature that we perceive as gravity.

With ten million universes, the total gravitational potential of the multiverse is immense, yet safely compartmentalized. Each universe's gravity stays in that universe.

Or does it?

"What," the Theoreticians asked, "if the boundaries between universes are permeable? What if a small amount of gravitational curvature leaks into neighboring universes, drawn by the localized presence of mass?"

By careful simulation and much argument, cosmologists concluded that 73 percent of our universe's apparent mass is an artifact of gravitational leakage. There was no longer any need to invoke the existence of dark matter.

However, this reasoning did not extend to dark energy.

Dark energy was originally invoked to explain the increase in the universe's rate of expansion over time, which requires an expansive force to be at work. They found such a force in another multi-dimensional theory, a modified version of Edwin Hubble's Raisin Pudding explanation for the expansion of the universe.

Hubble had likened the stars to the raisins in a pudding. As the pudding expands during cooking, the raisins move farther apart, with the most distant raisins moving faster than those that are near one another. To explain the effect for which dark energy was promulgated, scientists concentrated on the pudding rather than the raisins.

What if, they theorized, each of the ten million universes (raisins) are surrounded by blankets of high-energy particles in a state of constant motion (pudding). Of course, 'surround' in this context is a poor approximation of reality.

These blankets act as buffers (or insulators) and are the reason why gravitational leakage between universes is such a small fraction of the multiverse's total gravitational energy. Moreover, if the equations that describe these zones are to remain in the realm of real numbers, the particles within the layers must be continuously in motion at velocities faster than light speed.

A pair of physicists on the project noted that the hypothetical properties of the buffer zone bore a striking resemblance to a mythical place beloved by writers of escapist fiction.

And so, in a fit of whimsy, they christened the buffer region "hyperspace" and the particles within "hyperons."

#

Larath da Benthar Sims was asleep in her cabin when *Cor* awakened her. There was none of the muzziness that often goes with a normal transition from slumber to full wake. The computer brought her out of it with the speed of a canine hearing the dinner buzzer.

"What is it, *Cor*?"

"Submaster Taryn asked me to wake you and to merge with us."

Submaster Nalwith Taryn was Lara's second-in-command and her ship-husband. Where she was tall and fair; he was broad and dark. Coming from Esther Prime, with its 2-gee gravity; he was 30-centimeters shorter than she was and all muscle mass. The pair represented the two standard genotypes produced by heavier-than-standard gravity worlds. The F0-Class primary in Esther's sky explained his skin color. He was as black as an obsidian statue.

"What is it, Nal?" she asked silently.

"Sorry to wake you. *Cor* has detected something at the far range of her sensors. Might be nothing, but it's unusual enough to get you involved."

"What did you detect, *Cor*?"

"A patch of turbulence in a hyperon stream at the three-light level. It starts at a point and then feathers out in the direction of flow. It looks like the stream is sweeping something along."

"Are you saying that it's a wake?"

"Looks like it. Not sure what would be down there that low and slow."

What the computer was reporting was the characteristic wake of normal matter in a hyperon stream. Unlike a ship moving through seawater, where the wake forms at the bow and flows outward and backwards; in hyperspace, the wake forms at the stern and sweeps forward. That is because starships are typically not 'sailing' the hyperon streams, but rather, being carried along by them in their mad rush to be somewhere else.

"Do you think it's a ship?" she asked.

"It is normal matter of some sort. It must be big to be detectable at this range."

Lara frowned. In her forty years of spacefaring, she had never met another ship in hyperspace save near a breakout point where all traffic bound for the same world was forced to converge in order to arrive in that system's designated entry volume.

Warships, of course, encountered one another often. That was because they sought each other out to engage in mutual pounding.

To intercept another ship in hyperspace required both to be at the same energy level to begin with. At or near one's own energy level, hyperon detectors were sensitive out to several light-years. Their ability to see upslope and downslope was limited to an energy delta of ten percent or so. Beyond that range, they were blind.

When two ships at near-equivalent energy levels spotted one another, they then had to synchronize their frequencies, both to match speed and to make their weapons effective. Warships under power spent prodigious amounts of energy to move transversely across the streams to close for battle. Freighters were content to enter a stream and let it carry them where it would, using maneuvering power only to change level to transition to a stream traveling in a different direction.

"What should we do about it, Lara?" Nal asked.

"I suppose we will have to go check it out. They may be in distress."

"What if they're pirates?"

"There are occasional reports of pirates waylaying a ship in hyperspace, I suppose; although I suspect they are more bar legends than reality. Now, if we were bound for Zavier, we would have to watch out for marauders after returning to normal space."

"What about our appointment with the docks?"

Lara considered that problem. *Coronal Fire* was due for her periodic engine overhaul and general inspection. If they missed their scheduled slot, it could be months before they got another.

"This shouldn't take long. We'll make home orbit in time."

"Your orders, Shipmaster?" *Cor* asked.

"Bring my cabin gravity back to full standard," she said. Lara preferred to sleep in ten percent gravity where even a bed of nails would be comfortable. "I will be in Control in ten minutes. Once I am there, begin your downfreq to the three-light level and maneuver for rendezvous. All sensors to full gain and if the situation does not seem right, *upfreq* back here as quickly as the old bucket will move. Careful, we still have those Kaligani flaws over us."

That last sentence was unnecessary. *Cor* was a computer. She never forgot anything.

#

In the year 2315[OC], Professor Alain Destarte, of the University of Antarctica, first generated hyperons in his ice-bound laboratory. Their brief appearance allowed him to note that they interact weakly with normal matter, an interaction that can be strengthened considerably if the normal matter is 'vibrated' at the hyperon's characteristic frequency.

From this, he hypothesized that should a ship enter the boundary between universes, it would be swept along by any hyperon streams congruent with its vibrational energy. Nor would any of the light-speed constraints apply to normal matter or energy. At all speeds higher than c, the equations that govern Einstein's Limit turn imaginary.

As for the ship's crew, they would be in what physicists call an Inertial Frame of Reference. They would experience no sensation of flight within their tiny bubble of normality.

In 2530[OC], physicists confirmed Destarte's hypothesis. They focused a gravitational field so tightly that it ruptured the inter-universe barrier and allowed a small probe to enter the boundary region buffering Minkowski Space from its surroundings. The probe was in hyperspace for a full sixty seconds before it dropped back to normal space, at which time it began broadcasting its location to the firmament.

The probe's signal took two hours to reach Earth.

With that single experiment, the road to the stars lay open and a flood of humanity followed.

#

Chapter 2

"Well, what is it?" Lara asked. She was once again on the bridge, with Nal Taryn beside her. The question was for *Fire*'s computer.

"It appears to be a ship, but larger than any in our database," *Cor* replied.

It had taken four hours to drop down from ten-lights and approach the object. And just as when they downfreqed out of 1000-lights, they were now in a different hyperon stream, moving at a lower pseudo-velocity. Their heading was currently 28 degrees west of *chi* and 4 degrees down from *omega*, at a pseudo-velocity of 2.9 lights, a 30-degree starboard turn from the route to Morast.

"How big?"

"One klamater."

"In diameter?" Lara asked, incredulously.

"That is correct."

Lara and Nal looked at one another, then turned back to the hologram that floated before them. A light-blue speckled fog infused the view space, with a small shaded-yellow sphere directly ahead.

The view was not what the scene really looked like, of course. Hyperspace is totally black. That is because photons are as alien to the sea of hyperons as is normal matter. The only photons in the vicinity emanated from *Coronal Fire*, in this case, from their scanner array.

But like a radar screen of antiquity, the hologram showed information in the form the human eye could best interpret. In this case, the object they were scanning was still 100 klamaters in front of them. Red alphanumerics floating next to the sphere kept track of the distance.

"Could we possibly have discovered aliens?" Nal Taryn asked.

"Insufficient data," *Cor* responded.

"What about energy emanations?"

"Nothing beyond infrared. The object is at background temperature."

Logically, hyperspace should not have a background temperature. Any object therein ought to radiate thermal photons until it ran out of them, i.e., stabilized at absolute zero. But the passage of trillions of hyperons through the ship each second left the affected atoms in an excited state. And the common name for excited atoms is 'heat.'

The effect was miniscule compared to the total energy involved. Even so, it was sufficient to increase the ship's temperature to just above zero degrees centigrade.

"What do you want to do, Lara?" Nal asked.

"Continue the approach."

#

"God, that's a big mother-skinker!"

"Language," Nal admonished. "You know how delicate *Cor*'s ears are."

"Then I will rephrase: *'Damn, that's a big mother-skinker!'*"

The two of them laughed to break the tension. The object had grown steadily over the past twenty minutes. Despite the monotony, the view was hypnotic.

Nor were they alone in their excitement. Crew and passengers clustered around holocubes that relayed the same picture all over the ship. There were several running commentaries on the comm circuits.

"What a wonderful adventure this is," someone opined breathlessly.

Lara immediately thought, *"Definition of adventure: Someone else having a hard time far away!"*

"We are beginning to pick up something," the computer reported. "Shall I increase magnification?"

"Go ahead."

The hand-sized sphere faded, to be replaced by a round object that filled the view volume. Mottled markings, dim but distinguishable, appeared for the first time.

At one end of the ship were large projections spaced 90-degrees apart. To judge by the three they could see, there should be a fourth out of sight on the far side of the ship.

"What are those?" Lara asked.

"Unknown, *Cor* replied.

"They look like landing gear," Nal responded.

"Unlikely," the computer said. "If a globe that size touched down in even moderate gravity, it would crack like an ovum. The projections are too short to be legs. The belly of the craft would contact the ground before the projections."

In addition to the 'legs,' a series of rectangular shapes bisected the sphere on a line running thirty-degrees from vertical. Lara suspected that they marked the ship's equator, especially if the 'landing legs' were at one of the poles of the ship.

They watched for ten more minutes. The sphere stayed the same size, but its features grew more distinct. *Cor* was stepping down the magnification as they closed the range.

Finally, at five klamaters from the ship, Lara called a halt.

"Close enough, *Cor*. Break out a mech. We'll do a flyby before we risk moving closer."

A minute later, a spherical shape detached from *Fire*'s flank and headed for the target. The object was a general-purpose robot used for cargo transfer and ship's maintenance. It had a standard sensor suite, manipulators, and a self-contained gravitic drive. Simultaneous with the mech's appearance, a smaller view volume appeared next to the floating sphere. It projected the view from the mech's on-board camera.

The huge ship grew rapidly in the alternate view and soon overflowed its viewspace. In addition to the rectangular markings, which looked like hatches, several large toroid-shaped shadows appeared on the hull.

"Are those external drive coils?" Nal asked.

"Maybe," Lara mused. "I wonder how old this ship is. *Cor*, get a reading on outgassing."

The computer was silent for a moment, then responded: "No outgassing detected, Shipmaster."

Lara whistled under her breath. She had her answer. That ship was *very* old!

Human beings had been building spaceships for two thousand years. In that time, propulsion had gone from chemical to nuclear to gravitic to hyper drive. Life support, which began as a few oxygen bottles, had evolved into modern infinite-life closed-environment systems.

Yet, in the long march of ship evolution, no one had ever perfected a leak-proof spaceship. Air molecules are small, slippery things. They work their way through minor flaws and into interstitial passages of whatever metal is used to construct the hull. If a ship does not outgas, then it is filled with vacuum.

"All right, *Cor*, take the mech in. There, that small rectangle between the two larger ones," Lara directed.

The view from the *Fire*'s hull camera disappeared, to be replaced by the view from the mech.

"Well, that settles that," Lara exclaimed. "We've got a *Flying Dutchman* here."

Lara had no idea where the term *"Flying Dutchman"* originated, but it had been the description for a dead ship trapped in hyperspace since time immemorial.

The target was a perfectly ordinary-looking airlock outer door. It was surrounded by yellow-and-black stripes, had an inset window to allow vision in both directions, and had some sort of mechanism at its center. The latter was presumably an emergency vent valve. Two square plates to the right of the coaming seemed the size for a gloved finger. The plates had writing next to them.

They could not read the script, but they could recognize it as akin to the ancient 'Standard,' the *linqua franca* of the galaxy before the *Age of Chaos*. One likely said *'open'* and the other *'close'*.

Wherever the mysterious object had come from, it was of human manufacture.

#

Nal Tarwyn glared up at Lara and said, "I object and will log my objections for the owners."

"You're cute when you're angry, Nal," Lara replied. "The problem with you people from Esther Prime is that I can't tell whether you are really angry or just posturing for effect. No matter how red in the face you get, your pigmentation hides it."

"Damn it, Lara, I should be the one to lead the boarding party."

"Why, Submaster?"

"Your place is here in Control."

"If any shipmaster-level decisions are needed, then *Cor* will consult me."

"What if you get trapped over there?"

She shrugged. "Then you will rescue me; or, in extremis, will take over command. I have a feeling about this derelict. I need to go."

She and Nal had been married for ten years and he was familiar with her 'obstinate' mode.

"Very well, I yield. I'm still going to log it."

"As is your right," Lara agreed. "Now, help me select the boarding party. The passengers are all intrigued just now, but they will not be when they realize we are going to be late to Morast. I want to get in, find out what we have here, and get out. We've still got that date with the maintenance dock."

She smiled down at him. "Have you considered that this might be worth credits to our crew and owners? Maybe a lot of them!"

#

The boarding party consisted of four: Lara, Engineer Kim Chu Lin, and Spacers Argost Matdor and Chim Thaalorst.

Coronal Fire came to a halt one hundred meters from the globular ship. Despite their freighter's nominal one-million-ton mass, *Fire* was dwarfed by the ship before them. Standing in the open Number Three airlock, the four explorers felt like they were looking down on a gently curved plain rather than station-keeping on another vessel.

"Argost, you take the lead. You've got more time in vacuum than anyone aboard."

The baritone voice that came over the comm matched the nodding head behind the visor. "Acknowledged, Shipmaster. Everyone! Hook safety lines to the person in front of you, put your maneuvering units on standby, and slave to me. We will go in the following order: me, Shipmaster, Engineer, and Chim. Wait for your lines to play out to give us separation but engage maneuvering before they go taut. We do not want to set up a rebound oscillation. Beacons on!"

One by one, each of their suits began to flash at a rate of one blink each second. The beacons were located on helmets and at shoulders, wrists, knees, and boots. In addition to being eye catching, they provided visual clues as to distance and orientation. Each suit flashed in a separate color and when someone spoke, a light on their chest illuminated to put body to voice.

"Ready? Then, let's go."

Spacer Matdor took aim at the giant ship's airlock, then activated his suit's gravitics. He floated gently away from *Fire* as his safety line uncoiled behind him.

Just as her line was about to go straight, Lara put her maneuvering unit online. She felt the tug as the line went taut and pulled her out into hyperspace. Soon a string of blinking lights drifted from their small island of solidity toward the ghost ship. The airlock door that was their target got progressively larger. The mech was still floating beside it with its manipulators deployed.

Matdor halted a meter from the closed door.

"What are those, Engineer?" Lara asked over the comm, pointing to a pair of features that had been invisible during their approach.

"Unknown, Shipmaster."

"I believe I know," Matdor answered.

Without explanation, he rotated his suit until his head and feet were aligned with the closed airlock door. Matdor slid his boots into two recesses in the hull plating. He then grabbed hold of the yellow wheel projecting out of the door at its center. Matdor tried to turn the wheel, first one way and then the other. It would not budge.

"Probably needs lubrication," Kim said.

"I don't think so," the spacer replied. "I think it is vacuum welded."

Lara nodded, then spoke when she remembered that no one could see the gesture in her helmet. "That fits. I think this ship has been out here for a long time. We may have to burn our way in."

"Shall I breach?" Spacer Matdor asked.

"Do it," Lara commanded. "After you have it open, we'll rig a relay on the hull to maintain contact with the ship."

"Right. Move back ten meters. You do not want globules of molten metal to land on your suits. They're tough but not indestructible."

#

The unknown craft was a colony ship.

That much should have been obvious from its physical size alone. Only something as big as a medium-sized asteroid would be large enough to transport a viable colony population, their equipment, foodstuffs, seeds, animals, and everything they would need to survive for at least a few years without resupply.

However, it was unlike any colony ship that any of the party had ever heard of. For one thing, it was designed for microgravity operation, which meant that it predated the development of contra-gravity.

Immediately inboard of the hull were cavernous spaces crammed with polyhedral packing crates. Each crate had a label in an indecipherable script, along with a complex identity code.

The ship's outer shell was the logical place for cargo due to the ease of loading and offloading. *Coronal Fire*'s holds were located similarly. The cargo aboard the derelict had also acted as radiation shielding for the passengers.

The next concentric shell lay deep inside the ship. It held dining facilities and workspaces. None showed signs of use, which made this a hibernation vessel. To save cubic, tables were fastened to deck, bulkheads, and overhead, with a fine disregard for up-down orientation.

The workspaces were crammed with more packing cases and marvelous, but incomprehensible, machinery. Many of the things they found had gears and belts, making Lara wonder how such primitive equipment fit with a culture that had star travel. The antique tools were bound for the new world, where the lack of an industrial base would limit the colonists' technology for a generation or more.

Exploring the ship was like peeling an *ekaberry*. The layers were concentric and all different. They took turns burning their way through doors. They found that a heat beam focused on the hinges and latch were usually the quickest way in. They severed the door from its anchors, then pulled it out of the way and gave it a shove so it would float down the corridor until it bounced off something.

This proved the most dangerous part of the exploration. Weightless, or not, the doors still had momentum. Spacer Thaalorst found this out the hard way when he tried to stop a slowly spinning door and nearly crushed his gloved hand in the process.

In the fourth layer, they came to a door that was much stouter than any they had thus far encountered. This one resembled the door to a data vault.

Lara left the two spacers working the problem of opening the 'vault' while she went with Engineer Kim in search of a route to the core. Both wanted to see the engines.

It took an hour to discover a shaft that pointed radially inward. Floating down the shaft headfirst, they passed deck after deck until they finally drifted into an open spherical chamber at least 100-meters across.

"This has got to be the place," Kim exclaimed as their headlamps played over the massive machinery mounted on equally massive thrust plates.

"What are these things?" Lara asked, pointing to one of several large constructs shaped like a Klein bottle.

Kim retrieved an analyzer from his belt and focused the aiming laser on a spot before triggering an incandescent flash.

"Well, I'll be damned."

"What is it?"

"Some degraded long-chain organic molecule, but mostly copper."

"Copper?"

"Apparently this is a coil wrapped with heavy copper wire."

"Just copper?" Lara asked. "Not superconducting?"

"That would require a cooling system. I don't see any."

"Any idea what it does?"

"Don't hold me to this, but those four resemble deplaning coils and the four beyond might have been used for maneuvering."

Lara nodded. 'Deplaning' was the act of dropping through the hyperon layers until the ship passed through 'null' and fell back into normal space.

"Where are the jump engines?"

Kim switched his lamp to 'full ambient' and illuminated the whole of the chamber. The shadows gave the place an eerie look. After a minute, he said, "Shipmaster, I don't see anything that could punch a hole in the inter-universe barrier. All that stuff over there is an oversized gravitic engine. The hyperdrive seems to be missing."

"But that is craz…"

Lara's words were interrupted by a shout in her comm receptors. It was Spacer Matdor.

"We got the vault open, Shipmaster. It is full of hibernation chambers. They are stacked deck-to-overhead and extend out of sight around the curve."

"So, you've found the crew?"

"More likely the colonists. They are all here. We looked through the windows of a couple of chambers. They are occupied…"

"… by mummies!" Spacer Thaalorst's voice exclaimed.

#

Chapter 3

They were indeed mummies.

Lara and Engineer Kim made their way out of the bowels of the ship and followed Thaalorst and Matdor's locator beacons to the hibernation vault.

As they passed the detached door, Lara saw the scars of cutting torches and wondered if either spacer had any charge left in their powerpacks.

Within, rank upon rank of mirrored hibernation chambers lined every surface of a circumferential corridor—inboard and outboard bulkheads, overhead, and deck. Periodic gaps between chambers showed openings to other corridors. This level of the ship must be honeycombed with them.

They floated to where the two spacers were anchored. Lara took a quick look through the view window of a nearby chamber. She found herself staring into the eyes of a woman. Her skin, stretched taut across cheek bones, was wrinkled and brown. Her mouth was frozen in a rictus smile that showed a perfect set of teeth.

The body was well-preserved. There was no sign of decay, merely dehydration. That meant that she had died when her chamber lost atmosphere. Otherwise, her body's own bacteria would have attacked her flesh and thrived so long as there was air.

Floating back, Lara rotated her suit to let her lamp sweep the walls of the corridor. The light reflected from silver cylinders to the point where curvature hid them from sight.

It was only then that the scale of the tragedy hit her. These people had boarded this ship to seek a better life out among the stars. She could imagine the scene. They had arrived a shuttle-load at a time, chattering happily as they came through the airlock. Happy, and a little frightened.

The passageways had quickly clogged with a squirming mass of arms and legs as people who had never been to space struggled to propel themselves along spider lines. Lara could imagine the cursing crewmen whose job it was to untangle the mess. The chaos was made worse by loose children darting through the air, enchanted that they could fly.

They had been directed to a large compartment, possibly the dining space, where they clustered like so many dragon-bees in a hive, hanging from every surface. By the time they made it to the assembly point, the excitement would have worn off. The mood would be subdued. The conversations were whispered and ended with tearful hugs and kisses as each family member in turn was called to descend to the hibernation deck. Their final words, "See you on our new world!"

She could imagine the nervous smiles as each passenger was sealed into his or her chamber. Once inside, they would watch the glass before their faces rhythmically cloud and clear in time with their rapid breathing. By this time, reality would have set in. This was it and there would be no turning back. Then the chemicals began to course through their veins and a last moment of panic had been followed by unconsciousness.

And after that, all their hopes and dreams had come to naught.

Something had gone terribly wrong and the ship never left hyperspace. Unable to null out, this ghost ship had ridden the hyperon streams for God only knew how long.

While she contemplated the brown face staring blindly back at her, globular tears had long since formed at the corners of Lara's eyes. She was snapped back to reality by a sudden thought and a long-ago memory.

God was not the only one who could date this tragedy!

The capsules were filled with once-living tissue that had breathed a planetary atmosphere for however long they lived prior to going into the tanks. Mixed with every lungful of air had been a radioactive isotope created when cosmic rays slam into nitrogen atoms.

That isotope was Carbon-14.

Carbon-14 is an unstable form of carbon with a half-life of six-thousand years. Although the replenishment of C^{14} ceased when the hibernation process began, radioactive decay continued to the present, marking the passing centuries with metronome regularity.

Measuring the amount of decay of radioactive carbon had

once been the standard test for dating once-living matter. It was now archaic, overtaken by other, more accurate tests. Lara remembered learning about it in school.

Cor would still have the knowledge of how to perform the test. To discover the age of the ship, all that was required was open one of these chambers, slice off a hand or foot, take it back to the ship, and put it into an analyzer.

The ghoulishness of the thought snapped Lara out of her mood. Whatever hopes and dreams these people had carried with them, there was nothing she could do about it now. From the condition of their bodies, they had died before the birth of Lara's earliest known ancestor.

Besides, she had her own problems.

"All right, gentlemen. Good job! Let's get back to the ship. We've got some planning to do."

#

Lara had not even cycled through *Fire*'s airlock when she queried *Cor* via her link, "How long can we hold here?"

"Ninety hours, Shipmaster. After that, this stream will diverge too far from the route to Morast. We will then have limited alternatives to get back on course. We will be very late arriving."

People speak of starships as 'sailing the black sea of hyperspace.' It is an observation that is more literal than poetic. Just as sailing ships were dependent on the vagaries of the wind for propulsion; starships are likewise dependent on hyperon streams.

Hyperons can never slow to any speed slower than light. The equation that describes their existence has a dozen different terms. Virtually all of them have the quantity $(v^2-c^2)^{0.5}$ in their denominators. Were it possible for a hyperon to drop below c, the speed of light, the equation would throw many 'imaginary number' errors, which would be a massive discontinuity in the mathematics of the multiverse.

The multiverse is home to many strange things, but discontinuities are not allowed. Even black holes are continuous phenomena when considered in 11-dimensional multispace. The mass swallowed by a black hole in one universe punctures the inter-universal barrier and appears in an adjoining universe as a white hole. To reach that universe, the gravitational curvature associated with that mass must pass through the buffer region of hyperspace. It is the local variation in gravitational potential from these "ghost holes" that causes the eternally moving hyperons to coalesce into streams.

What *Cor* was telling Lara was that if they did not get back up to ten-lights within ninety hours, they would be in the same situation as a sailing ship that found itself downwind from where it wanted to go.

After divesting her vacsuit and treating herself to a hot shower, Lara directed *Cor* to announce an all-hands assembly in the mess compartment with fifteen minutes warning.

It was not standard procedure for passengers to be involved in ship operations, but since she was about to announce further delay in reaching Morast, she included them. Besides, there was no way she could have kept them away.

The population of *Coronal Fire* numbered thirty-eight souls and one sentient computer. The thirty-eight consisted of two officers (herself and Nal Taryn), twelve crewmembers, and twenty-four paying passengers.

She began the briefing by reviewing what they had found aboard the derelict. *Cor* presented holographic views from the helmet cameras, including the hibernation chambers.

Lara finished the briefing with, "We have just under four standard days to map the derelict and collect a few artifacts. I want at least one of the derelict's occupants. We will leave the body in its chamber to prevent contamination. Engineer, we'll need some large vacuum bags for that."

"I'll get the fabricators working, Shipmaster."

"What else?" one of the passengers asked.

"Things of historical interest, obviously. Physical records, recordings, computer memories."

"Four days isn't very long."

"It's all the time we have." She explained why. "We'll attach a beacon to the hull. Perhaps someone will want to organize a return expedition later."

A second passenger, by the name of Nabeel Hadrami, from Gabaltariq, stood. "Shipmaster Sims, this discovery is potentially very valuable, correct?"

"It's a perfectly preserved view into the past. I would think so."

"Who owns it?"

Lara frowned. Similar thoughts had been circulating in her head since she had first boarded their prize.

"By ancient custom, it belongs to the discoverer."

"Who would that be?"

"Why, I suppose it belongs to *Cor*. She was the one who brought it to our attention. That means it belongs to our ship's owners, and by extension to the crew."

"What of us passengers? You are costing us credits by this side trip."

She hesitated, uncertain what the owners would think about her answer to Hadrami's question. She was not surprised. Where credits are involved, people quickly devolve to the ancient WIIFM principle: What is in it for me?

"I take it that you have a proposal?"

"I do. I submit that everyone aboard ship share in whatever wealth this discovery brings. I'm not naïve enough to suggest the shares be equal, but they need to be based on something tangible, say how helpful each person is during the coming salvage."

Lara's gaze swept the room, lingering on each face to judge the reaction. Finally, she asked, "Do you all agree with Mr. Hadrami's suggestion?"

There was a general murmur of ascent.

"*Cor*, make a record of the last several minutes and summarize what we have discussed. Supply a copy to everyone's day file. I expect your acknowledgment and agreement by the evening meal. If you do not want to take part, you do not have to.

"All right, enough of this. Let's talk about salvage."

#

Eighty hours later, it was a tired group of passengers and crew who prepared to leave the three-light stream and get back up to where they belonged.

Of the fourteen crewmembers, twelve had either been aboard the derelict, or rested in preparation for their shift aboard, for the entire time. By regulation, one crewman had to be continually on watch in Control and another in the engine room. Luckily, the regulations did not require that 1) they be certified for that duty, or 2) awake. Since *Cor* ran the ship, anyone who could punch a panic button was an acceptable watch stander.

The passengers had been a mixed lot. Seven of them owned vacsuits in the hold. These were paired with crewmen and assigned to work parties.

Cor handled the visual survey. She did this by sending the smallest orbital mech onboard on a search curve through the ship. Her efforts were overseen by three passengers who monitored the views in real time to ensure that anything important was visited by a work party.

The mech could not go everywhere, of course. It was stymied by vacuum-welded doors just as humans were. When it found one, it called a pair of specialists to burn through the hinges.

The bright spot was in the collection of hibernation chambers. It turned out that the tanks were plumbed for ease of maintenance. That meant they used primitive quick disconnects for electrical, pneumatic, and liquid connections.

Because the tanks proved easier to salvage than expected, the spacer and passenger assigned to the duty retrieved four of them, each from a different hibernation bay.

The mystery of the "landing gear" was solved on the third day.

Kim Chu Lin approached Lara at first meal the next morning. Both were beginning to show the effects of the hectic pace.

"What can I do for you, Engineer?" she asked, sipping her morning stimulant.

"I know what the 'landing gear' are for, Shipmaster."

"What?"

"They are thrust frames tied into the keel. Remember, we couldn't find the rest of the *ftl* engines on our visit to the engine room?"

She nodded.

"Apparently something like a tug launched this ship into hyperspace, synchronized it to the stream, and then set it loose."

Lara blinked. "You're kidding."

"No. That's why they only have deplaning coils. Apparently, they intended to float in the stream for some period before nulling out at their destination star.

"But that's crazy. Didn't they know about gravitational flaws?"

"Apparently not."

"And why use the three-light energy layer? It would take them thirty years to cross 100 light-years, which is about the average distance between habitable worlds."

"They probably launched into a higher layer, perhaps ten-lights or above. They have been out here a long time. The ship's conductive coating has ablated, bleeding off jump charge and causing the *ftl* frequency to fall. Their flight has been a slow descent through the layers. Hell, in another hundred-thousand years, they might even have fallen through null."

Even eight hours later, chills still ran up Lara's spine at the thought. How could anyone be so careless with ten thousand human lives? That was the number of colonists that *Cor* had extrapolated to be aboard the ship because of the survey.

#

Once again, Lara was at her command station. In the view space, the derelict was slowly shrinking as they made their way to where they would upfreq back to the ten-light energy layer and the stream that would carry them to Morast.

"Status, *Cor*."

"All systems nominal, ready for frequency shift."

"Internal status? Is everything we brought aboard secured?"

"Restrained with cables, netted, or welded to the deck. The four hibernation chambers are clamped-and-cabled. Sensors indicate vacuum bags remain tight."

"Good," Lara responded. It was the bodies that she most worried about. They were fragile and had not been exposed to oxygen for more than a thousand years. She did not know what would happen if they were so exposed now.

Radiocarbon dating had given them the age of the ship. Spacer Matdor had obtained a sample of flesh and had done so in as respectful a manner as possible. He had secured the first chamber removed with a safety line out in hyperspace, opened it, reached in with a core punch, and extracted a tiny piece of desiccated skin.

The later analysis placed the ship's age at fifteen hundred

years. That meant that the colony ship had launched at the very dawn of *The Great Hegira*.

#

An hour later, Lara gave the formal command and *Cor* sent the signal to ramp up the *ftl* generators. Almost at once, the ship's pseudo-velocity began to climb. They were on their way and only 485 hours out of Morast.

Unfortunately, they would be late enough that Lara would catch hell from the owners about missing her slot in the maintenance dock. Hopefully, the news of their find would overshadow the accounting department ass-chewing that she was sure to get.

#

Chapter 4

Lara Sims lay on her bed in the Bernau Galaxy Hotel aboard Orbital Station Saban-Seven and shifted to find a more comfortable position. Aboard ship she set her cabin gravity to ten percent when resting; sufficient to keep her from floating away, but low enough to make sleeping on rocks comfortable. The hotel bed subjected her to a full standard gee without the possibility of varying it.

She reached into an inner pocket and pulled out a small white rectangle. It was one of the lesser souvenirs they had taken from the derelict colony ship. She had found it on her final sweep of the ship prior to departure.

She had been floating down a corridor, concentrating on the disembodied circle of light shed by her helmet lamp, when something floated out of the darkness and hit her square in the faceplate. The lack of warning provoked a startled response. She just hoped no one had heard the frightened *yelp* on the comm circuit.

After her heart climbed down out of her throat, she reached out and grasped her attacker with a gloved hand. It was about 60 by 90 millimeters in size and a millimeter thick. Printed across the face were three words in the strange script of the dead colonists:

DUNLOP AND SONS

The card had the number 2787 imprinted in red above an array of twelve matrices filled with small numbers. The writing was faded, but still readable. If, as seemed likely, the red numbers were a date, then it placed the ship's departure a couple of centuries after the start of star travel, when the full dangers of hyperspace were not yet known.

The ancients divided the year into 12 months, just as moderns did. Lara vaguely remembered someone telling her that these arbitrary divisions were based on how long it took Earth's moon to orbit the planet. Therefore, she expected the months displayed on the card to be the same length.

They were not.

Months of 31 days seemed to alternate with those of 30 days, except in the center of the calendar, where two 31-day months were side-by-side. And, to completely disrupt the pattern, the second month had 28 days.

It was inevitable that those who went out to the stars would eventually find Earth's 365.25-day year to be archaic. A workable alternative, the Akadian Calendar, was adopted for the 300th anniversary of the first interstellar colony.

Freed of the vagaries of planet dwelling, the new calendar was logical to a fault.

Each 'new month' lasted for 30 days and consisted of five 'new weeks' of six standard days each. The new calendar abandoned the ancient names of the months. The Akadian authors adopted the use of simple integers for the purpose.

The last problem was what to do with the extra five-and-a-quarter days, the existence of which had wreaked havoc on all earlier attempts at calendar reform. They solved the problem by ignoring it. The new calendar truncated the standard year to 360 days, thereby speeding up the passage of birthdays by 1.4 percent.

Individual planets, of course, used local calendars that matched their peculiar diurnal and annual needs. For interstellar trade, everyone used the Akadian calendar. To avoid confusion, they appended the superscript [ME]... for 'Modern Era'... to Akadian dates.

Thus, *Coronal Fire* arrived at Orbital Station Saban-Seven, which accompanied the planet Bernau in its orbit around Morast, on Day Twenty-Three of Month Eight in the One-Thousand-Seven-Hundred-and-Sixteenth Year of the Modern Era [1716.8.23[ME]]. Reckoned by the calendar Lara held in her hand, the year was 4246[OC].

After its departure from the ghost ship, *Fire* returned to the ten-light level of hyperspace and fortune had smiled on them when *Cor* reported a faster-than-expected eddy current in the hyperon flow. The result was that they had arrived ahead of schedule and in plenty of time to make their appointment with the space dock.

#

Upon arrival, Lara contacted Yaelson Thorn, Interstellar Transport's factor on Morast. Interstellar owned *Fire*, along with a thousand other ships. She reported their arrival and advised him of what they had found in the deep black.

He took her information and directed her to disembark her passengers, offload her cargo, and turn the ship over to the Chief Constructor of the Saban Yard at the appointed time.

It took six days to empty the ship. The passengers got off as soon as they cleared health inspection. Lara said farewell to them at the airlock and promised to look after their interests regarding salvage rights.

Then had come the tedium of offloading several hundred thousand tons of cargo. Like the ghost ship and every other large hyperspace-capable vessel, *Coronal Fire* was a sphere. The shape was optimal for carrying ability and the spherical surface prevented the jump charge from leaking off the hull in hyperspace. Even with *Fire*'s advanced cargo handling equipment, there was only so much throughput capacity for the ship's four large hatches. Eventually, however, the last container had been dispatched to its destination aboard the space station, destined for a trip to the ground.

As soon as *Cor* announced the ship empty of cargo, Lara and the crew packed their port bags and decamped to the station hotel to give the constructors unfettered access to the ship.

Lara fell asleep that first night in a strange bed wondering what she was going to do about the four mummies still in the hold.

At first meal three days later, the question was answered by a message from hotel management.

"What is it?" Nal Taryn asked, noting the distracted look common to people conversing by implant. He and Lara had spent the night in languid lovemaking, both to celebrate the completion of a successful voyage and as a farewell. He had three weeks accumulated leave and was looking forward to spending it with his ortho-wife on the planet below.

"The concierge says that I have visitors. Morast Coordinate officials."

"We paid our port fees on our last trip, didn't we?"

"Perhaps they've raised their rates retroactively," she replied. "I'd best go see what they want."

"Want me to come along?"

"No, finish your food. I will meet you in the Constructor's office at ten hundred, as planned. We don't want you to miss your boat. Merwyth would kill me if I kept you here even one day more."

With that, she stood and made her way through the pressure door and out into the corridor beyond.

A man and a woman were waiting for her in the concierge office. The man was a councilor who introduced himself as Baldor ban Niessen. That he was a local was obvious from his prominent ear spikes. Lara did not recognize the woman's genotype. She was a stocky blonde almost as tall as Lara herself. Niessen introduced her as Esdrith Ssalto, representing the Institute of Knowledge.

"What may I do for you, Councilor, Professor?"

"I received an interesting report yesterday concerning your voyage, Shipmaster Sims. I thought it best to meet in person."

"A report from whom?"

"One of your passengers. A citizen of Gabaltariq, I believe."

She nodded. "Nabeel Harami. He told you about our discovery, I take it."

"That he did. Is it true that it was an early colony ship?"

She nodded. "They launched fifteen hundred years ago and have been riding the hyperons ever since."

"Are you sure of the date?" the blonde woman asked. Her cool exterior did not completely hide her heightened interest in the answer.

Lara fished in her pouch and produced the card that had frightened her so. "This appears to have a date on it."

She handed it over and noted the extreme care with which Ssalto received it. She studied it carefully and nodded. "A pouch calendar, apparently an advertisement."

"Advertisement?"

"A common sales tactic was to have these cards printed up and distributed to people who might purchase your services. I must say that the technique was archaic for any year after the development of *ftl*. Perhaps it still worked because of its novelty."

"What services were they advertising?"

Ssalto gestured at the second line of text on the card. "This says that Dunlop and his sons were Attorneys-at-Law."

"What is that?"

"I can't give you a precise translation. I suspect Certified

Advocate might be the closest modern profession."

"And the language is Standard?"

"No, I don't think so. It looks like the older Anglic, from which Standard evolved. That would jibe with the date." She studied the white rectangle for several more seconds before handing it back to Lara with obvious reluctance.

"Do you have other souvenirs?" Councilor Niessen asked.

Lara smiled. "Quite a lot. They are still in *Fire*'s hold. The combined mass is about a ton."

"Citizen Harami said you also have bodies onboard."

"Four of them still sealed in their hibernation chambers to prevent contamination."

"How many total dead?" Ssalto asked.

"Ten thousand."

Her two visitors exchanged glances.

"Your show," Niessen said to the blonde, who nodded in response.

Esdrith Ssalto smiled. Her demeanor, which had been wary, suddenly became relaxed and friendly. "I'm an archeologist specializing in Old Earth and the period of the Hegira."

The Councilor nodded. "When Citizen Harami contacted me, I thought of Esdrith immediately."

"I take it that Citizen Harami was interested in the commercial value of our salvage?"

"That did seem to be his primary interest, yes. What arrangement do you have with him?"

"We agreed to a fair split of any profits on the trip here. Interstellar Transport is the owner of record, so they will have to ratify the agreement."

"I take it that you have no idea how much value to place on your find," Ssalto said.

"None."

The blonde archeologist pursed her lips, then continued, "Let me make you a proposition, Shipmaster.

"If you will consign the lot to the Institute, we will evaluate it and assign a value using an Independent Auditor. We will then buy whatever pieces you wish to sell at the appraised value, or you may seek buyers elsewhere. I am sure there are several museums in this sector who would be interested in bidding. It would take longer to do it that way... up to a year, I would think... but that may be the path that will produce the most return."

After a short pause, Lara responded, "That sounds reasonable." She controlled her tone to hide the relief she felt. With the salvage catalogued and each piece registered with the Morast Coordinate government, the interests of her company, herself, her crew, and the passengers would be well protected.

#

Lara did not hear from either Niessen or Ssalto for a month, by which time *Coronal Fire* was finishing up her refurbishment. The first sign that progress was being made on the ground came with a call from Yaelson Thorne.

"What can I do for you, Factor?" she asked silently into her implant.

"Please take the first boat down and meet me at the Institute of Knowledge. You have the address."

As though the thought had been dredged up from her own memory, she had a vision of a shimmering tower in the center of the planetary capital where she would rendezvous with the factor at 26:00 hours.

"What's up?" she asked.

"Quite a lot. All will be explained when you get here. Thorne out."

#

The Institute of Knowledge was, as the name advertised, in the 'knowledge' business. As some ancient thinker had once opined, 'knowledge is power.' It is also fabulously profitable.

The exact date of the Institute's founding had been one of the bits of knowledge lost during the Chaos after the first flowering of galactic civilization. Presumably, it had been the creation of some ancient university. With the discovery that pure research nearly always returns positive credit, the child outgrew its parent and became an independent discoverer (or rediscoverer) of knowledge.

There was a branch of the Institute on every world of which Lara was aware. They held a sizeable percentage of the patents and trade secrets currently in existence. And when they discovered something that could be exploited for commercial gain, they charged whatever the traffic would bear.

Yaelson Thorne was at the landing stage when her air taxi put down after a speed run from the spaceport. The robot waited just long enough for Lara to retrieve her ground kit before lifting off again. She was standing close enough that the grav field made the hairs on the back of her arms stand on end.

"What's going on, Yael?" she asked as the factor relieved her of her burden. "We're only halfway through preparations for our next run and I should be aboard ship supervising."

"Your next run is canceled," the factor said, flashing her a grin that could best be described as mysterious.

"Cancelled? Why? The owners can't afford to keep a cargo hauler sitting idle."

They can if the Institute has chartered it for a voyage."

"A voyage to where?"

"Back to the derelict, of course. They seem quite excited about your salvage. It is very technical, so I will let Esdrith explain.

"Come on, we're late."

Thorne led her into the building. They crossed an entrance hall that must have been a hundred meters tall, with a floor covered in scintillating diamondite. They floated up twenty floors in a contra-gravity lift and then continued down a hall paneled in real wood.

Everywhere Lara looked, there were signs of opulence, testament to the Institute's power and wealth. Thorne led her to a door more opulent than its surroundings. It slid open at their approach to reveal a conference room beyond.

A dozen people sat around a table under soft lights. The figure at the head of the table rose and crossed the wide expanse to approach them.

"So good to see you again, Shipmaster," Esdrith Ssalto said, holding out her hand.

"And you, Professor," Lara responded, giving the hand a quick squeeze. The custom was one she had learned after emigrating to the heart of the Coordinate. On Envon, people touched their own foreheads when greeting one another.

"Please, I'm Essie to my friends. And I suspect we are going to become great friends."

"Lara."

"Have a seat. We have a lot to talk about. Refreshments?"

"Gantha juice if you have any."

"And you, Yael?"

"The same."

After they were seated, with fluted goblets filled with crimson liquid in front of them, Esdrith introduced the rest of the attendees.

Across from her was a husky man named Darin Mastlin, who Esdrith introduced as the newly assigned Administrator for the Ghost Ship Project. Beside him was Betrice Flangan, medical researcher; and beside her, Formas Rob Somace, Institute Director. The rest were various researchers and analysts.

"Now then," Esdrith said, "I owe you a progress report. Our report is voluminous, and I think you will be impressed with the value we have placed on your artifacts. We will provide you a compendium for later study.

"However, that is not why we are here. In researching the four individuals in the hibernation chambers, we discovered exciting news. We believe we can pinpoint the planet from which the colony ship launched."

"Where?" Lara asked.

After a suitable pause for dramatic effect, Esdrith responded: "Earth!'

#

Chapter 5

Lara said nothing for a long moment. She studied the faces around her. The others seemed to expect more of a reaction than she was feeling.

"Considering how old the ship is, Earth is the logical point of origin, is it not? The first colonies were still struggling in that era."

"Very astute of you, Shipmaster," Darin Mastlin responded. "Yes, that was the most likely conclusion. However, we analyzed the bodies' DNA and confirmed it. That makes your find a particularly valuable one."

"Why? It has historical value, I grant you, but I fail to see what the ship can teach us that we do not already know. The technology is unbelievably primitive. Every time we burned through a hatch, I expected to find a working steam engine behind it."

Mastlin chuckled. "As an engineer, I am interested in just that aspect, but you are correct. There are no lost secrets to be rediscovered aboard that ship. No, our interest is in the people."

Betrice Flangan, the bio specialist, put her hand on the back of Mastlin's and said, "Perhaps I should explain to the Shipmaster, Dar."

He laughed. "Go ahead. The problem with engineers is that we do not do introductions. We just jump into the middle, assuming everyone is up to speed."

Flangan was a petite brunette with black hair that possessed an inner luster. Her upper torso was oversized compared to her hips, and not from her secondary female characteristics. She said, "What has us so excited, Lara, is the fact that your four mummies show no sign of genetic manipulation. Their genes have not been spliced, enhanced, duplicated, or sozzled in any way. They are all pure terrestrial human stock.

"If we sample those ten thousand corpses aboard your ghost ship, they will also be of pure stock. With so many strains, it should be possible to integrate their individual DNA codes into a high-fidelity model of the original human macro-genome, the sum total of humanity's DNA at that time."

"Don't you know that already?"

"Unfortunately, no. Genetic science has developed light-years in the last two millennia. How could it not? We have adapted our species to uncounted new worlds, tweaking a chromosome here, encouraging a strain to multiply there. We now thrive in environments that would have killed our ancestors." Betrice smiled as though she had just had a funny thought "Tell me, Lara, do you have dogs on your native world?"

"Of course. Doesn't everyone?"

The medician nodded. "When we went out to the stars, we took along our usual menagerie: dogs, cats, fleas, mice, and a veritable zoo of micro-organisms. Dogs are all descended from an animal on Earth called a dire wolf. We have pictures of them, but none survive on any world with which I am familiar. That is because they were not useful to humans; and therefore, were not allocated space on the colony ships.

"It is estimated that humans and dogs have lived together for more than twenty thousand years. Soon after dogs were domesticated, people began selectively breeding them. *Canis familiaris* came in five hundred different varieties even before the invention of *ftl*. Since the Hegira, there must be thousands of canine breeds in human space.

"What has this talk of dogs to do with the subject at hand?" Esdrith asked, moving her hands in a gesture peculiar to the inhabitants of Sandstrom, a world in a system farther east than Berau. "Simply this. When humanity went out to the stars, we manipulated our own genes in much the same way we had long manipulated that of canines.

"In the process, we improved the species immeasurably. You, for instance, are the product of a planet with moderately high gravity. There must have been a lot of heart problems among the first colonists on Envon."

Lara nodded. "There were."

"So, the geneticists went about producing the strapping, healthy physique we see before us. That process was duplicated on every colony world. We bred for the best genotype for each environment. You must be a geneticist to appreciate the audacity of the whole enterprise.

"However, we have had some spectacular failures along the way. There was the disaster on Altanor in the first century. It is the most famous tragedy of genetic engineering, but far from the greatest. That title must go to a mistake known only to specialists. The Ghost Ship Project will begin the process of correcting that error."

"What error?" Lara asked.

"In our quest to make humans compatible with their new worlds, we seriously damaged one of the most basic functions of a successful lifeform."

"Which is?"

"We have bred fecundity out of our species. By making your people gravity tolerant, and my people able to survive at oxygen levels that would make many other breeds faint, we have lost our knack for producing babies."

#

Lara blinked. "But that is silly. We produce babies just fine."

Betrice shook her head. "I'm sorry, but this is my field. Oh, the gestational process and the mechanics of giving birth work as well as they always have. In fact, we have improved the process with machinery... although, I think our desire to take the load off the woman may well be another facet of the problem.

"However, the rate for successful conceptions among fertile females has decreased generation after generation for at least half a thousand years. Most people attribute the decline to our longer lifespans and the fact that we prefer small families.

"That latter is a symptom of the problem rather than its cause. When we compensate for extraneous factors, the graphs are unambiguous. Our fertility rate is currently thirty percent lower than that of our pre-*ftl* ancestors. Nor is the decline due to a worsening of the condition in individuals. It is caused by the proliferation of the flaw through the entire population. It is akin to a slow acting viral poison slowly seeping through our species' DNA.

"As each generation is infected, the number of flawed offspring in the subsequent generation rises. In effect, we are experiencing a population explosion in reverse."

"If you are tracking it," Lara said, "Can't you fix it?"

"How? By sterilizing everyone whose parents show the trait? Hardly practical, Shipmaster. Also, we cannot detect the presence of the flaw directly. We can only infer its existence as each generation passes beyond the age of childbearing.

"No, wherever the flaw is located, it is well hidden. We do know that it is not actually in our genes. There are three billion base pairs in a strand of DNA. Only two percent of those are involved in producing the proteins that form genes, which in turn congeal into chromosomes.

"If the flaw were in our genes, we would have found it long ago. So, we have been forced to conclude that it is in the ninety-eight percent of the DNA whose effect on heredity is either indirect or currently unknown.

"That is why your mummies are important. If we can compare the original human macro-genome with modern heredity, we may find the flaw and develop a fix. It will not come quickly. Luckily, we will be able to spread the solution much faster than the genetic Brownian motion that has propagated it thus far.

"The problem is urgent. Our reproductive rate will decrease at an ever-accelerating rate until we find the fix. When that happens, we will then enter a race for survival. Will we be able to propagate our solution across human space before civilization collapses due to lack of population growth? As some ancient philosopher first noted: Only time will tell."

Lara sighed and nodded. "It seems logical enough, I suppose. But why charter *Coronal Fire*? I have given you the location of the derelict, plus the transponder code. A smaller ship would be far less expensive for your purposes."

Darin Mastlin took over the explanation.

"Betrice's project is only a part of what we will be doing. We have analyzed the position data from your ship's computer. The colony ship has been incredibly lucky to survive for as long as it has. Unfortunately, its luck is about to run out.

"The stream in which the ship is embedded is sweeping it toward the Kaligani Beta Flaw. As you well know, there is a deep pocket of turbulence there that penetrates nearly to null. The derelict will enter the shear zone in another ten years. Considering the importance of those bodies to our project, we have decided to salvage everything."

"You are going to transfer all the mummies to *Fire*?"

"Not exactly. We are going to re-engine the derelict and bring it here. The equipment required to turn it into a working starship is voluminous; thus, the need for your ship."

#

A month after the Institute of Knowledge chartered the 250-meter-diameter *Coronal Fire,* the freighter was open to space. At the ship's south pole, a well had been uncovered by the removal of a large maintenance hatch cover that now floating free beside her. The ship looked like a *lasse fruit* that had been cored.

Lara watched as a dozen mechs maneuvered the derelict's jump engine into the cavernous central hold. There it would be securely bonded to the freighter's thrust frame; along with the reactor that powered it.

Providing the ancient colony ship with a new engine was but the first modification planned for the ghost ship. A modern control room and its associated sensors would also be installed, along with an environmental control system and enough consumables for the voyage.

The largest task involved its three-million-square-meters of hull area. As Alain Destarte had discovered in his laboratory over two thousand years ago, hyperons react weakly with normal matter and more strongly if that matter is oscillating at the same frequency as the *ftl* particles.

The derelict had been reacting with hyperons for a long time. As weak as even a resonance interaction was, over time, the hyperons eroded the hull's conductive surface to the point where it would not take a full charge.

They had loaded hundreds of orbital mechs three days earlier. Their function would be to crisscross the klamater-diameter sphere and build up the conductive layer to the point where the ship could once again maneuver.

While a large crew of orbital space monkeys (Lara had often wondered what a monkey was) loaded oversize cargo, other techs were maneuvering habitat modules into the smaller holds.

Coronal Fire was a freighter rather than a liner, with space for thirty-two paying passengers. The institute was sending a party of more than one hundred. About half of them would be involved in putting the derelict back into operation. The rest would busy themselves with the genetic survey and other explorations.

In addition to the dead colonists, the ship contained a wealth of knowledge about the era in which it launched. It had everything a colony needed to establish itself in a new environment. Cataloguing the vessel's contents would be the work of years. However the Institute wanted a preliminary study as insurance against loss of the ship during the salvage operation.

The Institute of Knowledge would be in command of the expedition, with Darin Mastlin as Expedition Leader. Betrice Flangan would handle the genetic survey. A Thresian by the name of Bors Zarkov would command the shipfitters.

"Busy?" Nal asked in her implant. He had been back aboard for ten days, and like Lara, was a bit mystified as to what was being done to their ship.

"No, just wondering how this traveling band of *gramt* herders are going to accomplish anything when they seem to keep running into each other." A gramt was an adorable, but exceedingly dumb, animal found in the Large Continent forests of home.

"I have a report. We've figured out where to store the auxiliaries."

"Where?" she asked. The auxiliaries were two small orbit-to-orbit tugs to aid in the construction effort.

"We'll tuck them into the gap between engine and reactor and hang them from the overhead truss."

"Are you sure they will fit?"

"Easily, with centimeters to spare, once we remove the sensor masts."

#

Chapter 6

Hyperspace was as black as ever and the three-light hyperon stream was a scintillating cyan river in the view space. The flaws that made up the Kaligani Narrows were not visible this deep in the energy field, save for the deep finger that reached just short of null some 30 equivalent light-years ahead of them. It was still far beyond the distance their instruments could penetrate in the frothing storm of *ftl* particles, but the flaw was well mapped. It was the reason for the expedition.

Cor had brought them here to a point a light-year east of where they had spotted the derelict on their last voyage. 'East' was as arbitrary as the other five directions (north-south-west-up-and-down), but it gave human beings a means of speaking about that which was imponderable.

It had been one-hundred-and-twenty days since they broke formation with the derelict, during which time the three-light hyperon stream had carried the colony ship on its eternal voyage. Using time hacks accurate to eight decimal places, *Fire's* computer had dropped them down on top of where it should be now.

However, the tolerances involved meant that they could pinpoint its location no closer than a light-month, a volume that was every bit as large in hyperspace as it was in vacuum.

They had spent the last two days searching for the colony ship. Upon arrival, *Cor* had put *Fire* into zero gravity to send out a maximum power circumambient pulse. The pulse swept outward at the speed of the local hyperons. When the expanding wave front intersected the derelict, it would trigger the transponder on its hull to generate a return echo.

They had been waiting for a response for two days and would continue doing so for another 24 hours before moving to another search point and repeating the exercise.

The waiting was getting on everyone's nerves.

The return to this spot in infinite blackness had taken twenty days, in which time the ship had begun to settle into a routine. The ship's population was larger than Lara had ever known it. In addition to fourteen crewmen (including herself and Nal), there were six administrative personnel, eight Morast Navy personnel (to fly the derelict), thirty-eight shipfitters (to rebuild the derelict), and 36 scientists and technicians.

A dozen habitat modules and two large modules for dining and recreation had been strung together by access tubes in the auxiliary holds. The collection reminded Lara of the maze in which she had kept her *myrket* (a small six-legged rodent) when she was eight.

Even so, living space was crowded and two large shipfitters from Argus Double Prime had been deputized as masters-at-arms to break up occasional physical altercations. Argus Double Prime bred humans that were as tall as Lara and as broad as Nal, whose strength was at least double that of anyone else onboard.

Even with most of the shipfitters and scientists keeping to their own bunk areas, there were always enough people moving about the ship that *Cor* had to design a traffic pattern for the passage and companion ways.

Each evening, Lara and Nal ate with Darin Mastlin, Betrice Flangan, Bors Zarkov and Morast Navy Shipmaster Grun to discuss operations.

Darin, it turned out, was a skilled raconteur with an endless supply of jokes. He could not be older than fifty years, Lara estimated. With average lifespan exceeding two hundred, they were contemporaries.

Betrice was also personable once you got to know her. She raised roses—real, Earth-descended, biologically-unmodified plants—and fretted that this expedition would make her miss the annual competition in Capital.

Bors Zarkov was small, barely 150 centimeters tall, and devoid of even a single strand of hair. His personality was what once had been called 'bookish' and he spent his free time reading ancient classics in his bunky. He was also reputed to be a terror on the job if one of his shipfitter's work was subpar.

Shipmaster Grun was old for a Navy man. Lara estimated that he must be over one hundred. He still looked like a man in his prime... medical science could preserve that aspect of the human body well into the second century... but there was something about his eyes.

The evening dinners had revised Lara's opinion of the

expedition's organization. What had seemed chaos as *Fire* was being loaded was carefully controlled frenetic activity.

Considering the haste with which the expedition had been laid on, every conceivable contingency seemed to have been planned for. *Fire* was carrying twice the equipment they expected to need, and duplicates or triplicates of the critical components. Only the engine and reactor were one-of-a-kind.

Lara was going over her to-do list when *Cor*'s voice sounded in her brain.

"Shipmaster."

"Yes, *Cor*."

"I have just detected the transponder signal."

"Where?"

Cor gave her a vector and a distance. Since it had been 47 hours since they had first sent out the circumambient pulse and they were in the three-light layer, the distance turned out to be seventy light-hours equivalent.

"I'm impressed, *Cor*. That is damned good astrogation. How long to cut across the flow to reach that coordinate?"

"A week. One-hundred-and-sixty-three hours to be exact."

"Very well. Make the announcement, alter course, and execute!"

"Order acknowledged. *Cor* out.

#

The derelict looked exactly as they had left it. Lara watched the familiar yellow circle grow on the screen while listening to the chatter on the comm channels. There was a lot more of it this trip, including an amazing number of oaths in a dozen different accents and dialects.

As a courtesy, Darin Mastlin and Betrice Flangan were in the couches on each side and slightly behind her. Nal was down in engine control where he might (or might not) be useful if a communications breakdown between *Cor* and the rest of the ship occurred. Bors Zarkov had chosen to watch the approach with his men, as had Commander Grun.

The sphere continued to grow for what seemed like forever. On one side a pulsing red laser highlighted the entry airlock. That was the transponder marking its location.

"My God, I had no idea that it was this big," Darin exclaimed.

"It's big, all right," Lara replied. "I just hope we brought enough conductive material."

"I hope we can find a way to get into the engine room without carving out too much of the ship," the engineer responded. "They used to weld spaces closed rather than provide maintenance access, you know."

Lara did not know. Her job was flying ships, not designing them.

As soon as *Fire* was once again station-keeping with the big ship, a squadron of twenty vacsuited specialists locked out of *Fire* and floated to the derelict's open airlock.

Each of them had been provided with maps based on the earlier exploration and two-man teams were assigned to fan out to various points to gain the knowledge necessary to begin the salvage.

These explorations went on for a week. At the end of that time, the engineers figured out how to access the central volume where the engines were housed, and how to remove the deplaning coils and replace them with a modern hyperdrive.

The DNA survey had also begun in earnest.

Betrice Flangan and her team began to systematically open hibernation chambers, drive a long needle through the desiccated skin, and remove small samples of once-living flesh. They removed four such from each mummy, logged the samples into a database, sealed them in vacuum-proof containers (to keep the vacuum in) and moved on to the next chamber. Betrice had six teams working on six different levels.

And they discovered the ship's name.

No longer need they refer to it as "Ghost Ship" or "derelict." The tomb of ten thousand ill-fated colonists had been christened *New Hope* at her launch.

It brought back memories of the tears that had welled up when Lara looked into the eyes of that first mummy. The ship's name merely added to the scope of the tragedy.

#

Two weeks later, the operation was a smoothly functioning

machine. The conduction layer repair was 60-percent complete, with the ubiquitous mechs crisscrossing the hull, laying down their micron-thick layer of electrostatically charged powder.

Both *New Hope* and *Coronal Fire* had a common look about them. Each was open to hyperspace through massive openings. *Fire*'s hole was the same as it had been at Bernau, the big maintenance tunnel with access to the main hold and engine spaces. Dozens of men painstakingly separated the new drive and its reactor from their restraints, and then gently propelled them out into hyperspace where they floated between the two ships.

New Hope possessed no such accessway, so the engineers had to carve a passage into the interior. They did so at the north pole (that being the point opposite the thrust struts), penetrating a dozen decks to reach the engine room. That route was chosen because the north polar region of the ship was barren of hibernation pods.

Rather, it housed living quarters for the ship's crew and the colonists after revival. Judging by the number of compartments, only about five percent of the colonists would be revived at a time and then transported down to the surface of their new planet. That jibed with the four ancient shuttle craft housed in a hangar they had missed on the first visit.

Carving the passageway into the center of the ship required a dozen mechs, eight spacers, and three days. The outer hull was carefully excised in a perfect circle by cutters whose beams were only 5 millimeters in width. Other mechs, working inside the ship, cut away bulkheads and equipment welded to the hull. The circular piece was then floated to a position where it would be out of the way. Once the new engines were installed, it would be welded back into place and conductive coated to allow *New Hope* to fly again.

The pit was then carved deep enough to expose the engine room. While the passage was being excavated, another gang of vacsuited men were deep inside the ship, dismounting the original engines. This involved tracing all electrical cables and severing them at some distance from the machine. They were then marked so they could be spliced back together again on Bernau for testing.

The big deplaning coils and the gravitic engines were floated up and out. Rather than being parked in mid-ftl-space, they were lowered into *Coronal Fire*'s central hold.

They were then secured in the space recently occupied by *New Hope*'s engine after the two small tugs they had brought along were removed. The interorbit craft were kept busy clearing excavation debris, sending it on a vector that prevented it from becoming a hazard to navigation later.

When the antique machines anchored in *Fire*'s hold, the new reactor and hyper engine were floated down into *New Hope* where the complex job of interfacing them to the new control center had already begun.

While the biologists and engineers went about their exacting tasks, half-a-dozen Institute of Knowledge researchers surveyed the contents of the passengers' luggage. They did this by floating between the stacks of packing crates and holding scanners against the exposed faces of the containers. The scanners provided a three-dimensional view of the interior. These views were recorded and reviewed by a team aboard *Fire*. If anything caught their attention, a different crew returned to open the crate.

Of prime interest were any personal electronics the colonists might have packed. The type of memory used in electronic systems of the era were primitive enough to resist hyperon erosion. If they could be read, researchers would have a window into that long-ago age.

On the tenth day, a scanner captured a view of a rectangular block that measured 15x23x3 centimeters. The technician who spotted it thought that it might be a book.

It turned out to be just that, an ancient book printed on papyrus. It predated the invention of star travel and was apparently someone's heirloom. More exciting was the title: *The Earth, the Moon, and the Stars: An Introduction to Astronomy for Seventh Graders.*

When the book was carefully opened in a vacuum chamber, the technician found pages covered with Anglic script and decorated with monochromatic illustrations.

The last page was doubled over. When the researcher carefully unfolded it, he found a star chart.

It was a map of the terrestrial sky.

#

Chapter 7

The discovery of the juvenile astronomy book created excitement throughout the ship. To most of those aboard, repairing the ship had quickly taken on the aspects of any other salvage job. But a two-thousand-year-old textbook rekindled a sense of wonder in even the most stolid shipfitter.

Like Lara's reaction when she had gazed into the eyes of that first mummy, this ancient text was proof that somewhere among the mummies lay the owner and her family. They were no longer just machinery and ancient bodies. They were real people who had risked everything and lost.

After three days spent examining the book, Master of History Hirm Partin offered to satisfy everyone's curiosity. Partin was the oldest man aboard. His wizened features and rheumy eyes did nothing to detract from the quality of the brain that lay beneath the sparse layer of white hair.

A native of Paersinal, he was the Institute's leading expert on the early Hegira; or, at least, the most knowledgeable they could find on short notice.

Lara, Nal, Darin Mastlin, Betrice Flangan, Commander Grun, and four of the Institute's senior scientists gathered in the dining pod after third meal to hear the Master live. The rest of the ship attended via comm cube

Partin set up a holocube and asked *Cor* if it was connected to the comm circuits.

"Everyone aboard can see what you see, Master," the computer replied.

"Then I guess we had best begin."

He willed the first view into the translucent interior. The book's cover floated above a dark background that seemed to fade into infinity. The book was worn around the edges, but otherwise in excellent condition.

"Here is what has caused so much talk these past few days," Partin began, "The book is an introductory text for students entering puberty. The title is simply, *The Earth, the Moon, and the Stars*. It does not seem to have an author, which means it was put out by a publisher of textbooks. It is printed on paper, not papyrus. I would explain the difference, but it has no bearing on our subject."

An image of another page appeared. This one was sparsely covered by rows of ancient text.

"This is what was known as the copyright page. It includes various legal statements about ownership of the information. It also tells us the date of publication and the name of the organization that produced it. The year was 1938, Old Calendar. The publishers were McGaw-Hill Company of New York City, a major Earth metropolis. This book is from the Third Edition.

"There has been speculation that this was an heirloom. I can confirm that. *New Hope* was launched in 2787 Old Calendar, when this book was already 850 years old. The way it was packed shows that the owner valued it highly. It has also undergone some sort of preservation treatment. The pages are encased in a thin polymeric substance that is visible under polarized light. That explains its condition. The spine has also been reinforced with materials not available in 1938. An untreated book of similar antiquity would have disintegrated the moment we touched it.

"The first half of the book deals with the Earth and its satellite. The rest is a general discussion of stars and galaxies... what they are, how they form and their classifications."

The cube flashed with images of the various pages as Partin described them. Finally, the image changed to a view of a larger page held down by several micro-clamps. The crease line where it had been folded was ripped in several spots.

"What we have here is a chart showing Earth's sky in both hemispheres. The black dots are stars. The size of the dot signifies relative magnitude, and the number beside the major dots refers to a table a few pages forward. The table lists the names of the stars, their spectral type, mass, luminosity, etc."

Master Partin paused. "All of the legendary names are there: Sirius, Canopus, Arcturus, Alpha Centauri, Rigel, Achernar, Procyon, Betelgeuse."

Darin Mastlin cleared his throat and asked, "Does that mean that we can find Earth based on this book?"

Partin laughed. "Are you asking whether we can use this children's book to sort through the 140 million stars in human space to find the home world? I am afraid not. These names come down to us through legend, but we know of no such stars in our sky. Indeed, save for the very brightest, most of the ancient stars fade into the stellar background at one-quarter the distance between Morast and Sol.

"Nor can we recognize the positional references. Whoever authored this book knew where each star was in their sky to within a few seconds of arc. The problem is that he did not bother to include that in the text. Nor would that have been normal practice. Such numbers would mean nothing to the students for whom the book was written. And while the astronomers of the time knew the angular position of each star with considerable accuracy, they were mostly ignorant as to the distances.

"As for the map, it is a piece of art, drawn by hand. You all know how difficult it was to find *New Hope* within a light-month-diameter globe of hyperspace. Can you imagine the positional errors inherent in this drawing?

"Unfortunately, we have a chart of the sky as viewed from a point of unknown location. Also, the book seems more concerned with the patterns the stars form in the night sky than it is with the stars themselves. You will note the dashed borderlines that separate the constellations.

"Nor can these patterns help us in finding Sol. We divide human space between the Core Stars and the Periphery. We would have to enter the core before these star patterns would begin to become recognizable.

"No, I'm afraid that this book is useless as an aid to astrogation."

#

It took a month to finish rebuilding *New Hope* to make her once again a functioning starship. The time passed quickly, both because the work consumed so much of each waking period and the interesting discoveries made each day or two.

New Hope was a treasure trove of machinery that would prove useful on a new colony world. Much of it harkened back to an age long before the advent of star travel.

One section of the ship had hibernation capsules filled with mummified animals. There were dogs, of course. Dozens of the capsules were oversized and held the remains of large quadrupeds. No one recognized the two largest species, but a check by *Cor* identified them as *Equus caballus* and *Bos taurus*, the horses and cattle of legend. A minor mystery developed when DNA analysis confirmed that all the animals were female. Several ribald jokes concerning the ancestors' knowledge of biology made the rounds before explorers found the 'Nursery' in an adjacent compartment to the one that had been labeled 'the Zoo.'

There, sealed capsules held the embryos of dozens of species. These were identified as sheep, goats, pigs, cattle, and horses. The female adults in the oversize hibernation chambers were intended to carry the mixed-sex embryos to term until enough animals matured to allow livestock to reproduce normally. Subsequently, brood animals for all the embryo species were found as well.

There were also vast stocks of seeds and plant cuttings. These excited the biologists as much as the human mummies. *New Hope* was a treasure trove of terrestrial genetic stocks, and unlike the deceased humans aboard, the seeds might still be viable.

Betrice Flangan was especially excited by several preservation capsules with pictures of roses on their identification labels.

"Do you know what purebred rose seeds and cuttings are worth?" she asked one evening at third meal. "The Rose Breeders Association will go wild when they hear about this!"

Time passed quickly as there always seemed more to do than hands to do it. Scanners were reprogrammed to read the ancient identicodes on the outside of packing boxes, but even with *Cor*'s help, they were always behind in cataloguing their finds.

The technologists who were trying to download the contents of *New Hope*'s computers were much less successful than the biologists.

As expected, there were large gaps in the ship's various memories. The problem was that the ship had used an early version of nanobubbles to store information. The individual elements were little larger than a dozen atoms, a scale that made them especially susceptible to hyperon damage.

Modern computers had even smaller memory elements and, thus, the same problem. They resolved it through a strategy of massive redundancy. Multiple copies of critical software were stored in dozens of arrays. When any single element showed disagreement with its brethren, it was quickly overwritten.

New Hope had been equipped with a much cruder version of this self-healing technology. With a millennium-and-a-half of hyperons sleeting through the computers, the four redundant copies of the original memory banks were effectively trash.

It would take intensive reconstruction by the largest computers to salvage even a small percentage of the ship's knowledge.

#

Lara listened to *Cor* count down to the moment when *New Hope* would power engines. If the conduction layer repair had been successful, the former ghost ship would soon fall out of phase with the low energy hyperons that had carried them so far and move smoothly upward through various strata.

Cor would match *New Hope*'s maneuvers and maintain station on the big ship to the extent that was possible.

All the while they had been upgrading *New Hope*, the three-light stream had been carrying them along in the direction of the Kaligani Beta Flaw. As Lara feared on her first visit to *New Hope*, they had been placed in the position of a sailing ship downwind of its destination and would take a circuitous route back to Bernau.

"*New Hope*'s field is building, Shipmaster. Everything appears normal."

"Very well, *Cor*. As soon as they upfreq, match them. Don't get caught in their field."

That last was unnecessary. As she had to keep reminding herself, *Cor* never forgot anything.

"*New Hope* has begun to move. Powering generators now."

On the screen, the yellow globe shrank as higher energy hyperons embraced it. Like an invisible wave breaking on an unseen shore, the stream swept the flotsam along with it.

The final phase of the longest voyage in history had begun.

#

Chapter 8

Six weeks after *Coronal Fire*'s return to Saban-Seven, Lara was chafing at the enforced inactivity she and her ship had suffered since shortly after their return.

Their arrival had been everything anyone could hope for. When *New Hope* and *Fire* nulled out at the edge of the Morast System after a laborious, roundabout voyage, the world exploded with excitement. By the time they made their way in-system to Bernau, the space station was awash with newsers from all over the Coordinate, as well as the surrounding Sector.

Someone recorded an image of *New Hope* with *Coronal Fire* in the foreground as the two ships made their approach. Even with *Fire* closer to the telescopic imager, the colony ship dwarfed the freighter. Their formation resembled a moon in transit across the face of a planet.

After that, there had been a week-long round of dinners, speeches, and interviews highlighting every aspect of the mission. Each Interviewer wanted to know what had gone wrong to strand the ship in hyperspace.

Unfortunately, no one had the answer.

The most popular theory was that *New Hope* suffered a computer failure that prevented the deplaning coils from activating and dropping them back into normal space.

Even had that been the case, there must have been a duty crew awake during the voyage. Why hadn't they saved the ship? All indications were that *New Hope* had continued its voyage for decades longer than planned, as life support functions failed one by one.

Their searches of the ship in hyperspace had been keyed to the refit and refurbishment effort. Now that it was in Morast orbit trailing Bernau, there would be time to perform a compartment-by-compartment search. They might yet find the bodies of the ship's crew, and the reason the ship had been lost.

The saturation coverage of *New Hope*'s arrival assured that public interest would quickly wane as everyone returned to the mundane problems of everyday life. By the end of the second week, the story had faded from the news circuits, allowing Lara and Nal to get to the business of returning their ship to its standard configuration.

The transformation began with once again opening the oversize maintenance hatch to extract the ancient engines and reactors. These were moved to Saban Station, where they were prepared for deorbit and delivery to the Institute of Knowledge.

The habitats and environmental systems were stripped from *Fire's* hold as cleaning mechs went through the remaining spaces to eradicate all trace of earlier occupation.

When the stink of too many bodies was finally eradicated from the recycled air and the bulkheads scrubbed down to bare metal, Lara reported to Yaelson Thorn that the ship was once again ready for revenue service.

"When do you think we will be put back into the rotation?" she asked the Interstellar Transport representative.

"I have no information on that, shipmaster," he replied after the slight pause caused by light-speed delay between Saban-Seven and Bernau's surface.

"I don't understand," Lara replied.

"The Institute still has your ship under contract, and they haven't released it yet. Let me make inquiries."

Inquire, he had. Yet, a month after first asking, he still had no answer.

The problem, Thorn explained to her after her third call to the ground, was that Interstellar Transport was making a lot of credit from the Institute's charter payments and was not anxious to see the financial flow halted.

Finally, Lara lost her temper. She explained in short words, most of which would have been intelligible to her terrestrial ancestors, that she did not appreciate being shipmaster of a vessel laid up at a space station. Thorne assured her that he would pass her comments on to the Sector Office on Brodnor. Unfortunately, it would take a minimum of two months to receive a reply.

Rather than twiddle her thumbs, Lara decided to go to the

source of the problem. She gave Nal command of the ship and took an orbital taxi to Saban Station to catch the ten hundred boat down to the surface.

#

Bernau's largest city was named Capital. This was not unusual. Many of Earth's colonies, and those colonies' colonies, had cities that grew up around the original landing site. One-third of these had remained important during the post-colonial period; and of those, 20 percent had been christened "Capital," "Landing," or something similar.

Ten standard years earlier, Bernau had celebrated a full millennium as a human-occupied world, which equated to 680 of its local years. Like most cities founded after the invention of contra-gravity, it had a distinct look compared to older cities. The difference lay in the fact that Capital had no need to carve out large sections of its surface area to accommodate infrastructure for ground transport.

The city lay in a shallow valley on both sides of a winding river. During its first century, Capital had expanded along the river, with its lateral growth constrained by the low hills on either side. The inhabitants in later centuries had not been so limited.

The city now stretched one hundred klamaters in every direction. Initially, local zoning laws had set aside large parcels of land for primary use by businesses, residences, and heavy industry. No longer. People built wherever they found most convenient and the more obnoxious industries had long been banished to distant sites around the countryside.

The city was crisscrossed by pedestrian malls, narrow lanes for one- and two-wheel robot conveyances, and copious green spaces. The latter consisted of terrestrial and Bernau-native foliage. The latter were purple green in color.

The city's heavy transportation needs were underground. Thirty-meters wide tunnels fed into deep underground caverns where the freight was divided among many smaller tubes for delivery to their destinations. Water, sewer, power, and communications links occupied a higher level. Local transportation was handled by other tubes filled with magnetically levitated pods.

These delivered commuters to stations strategically placed around the city in much the same way as had been done for 2500 years.

Overhead, steady streams of aircars and trucks traveled in well-defined, but invisible, lanes at different altitudes. Individual vehicles rose from the ground and integrated themselves into traffic flow as others separated and slanted downward toward their destinations. The entire flow had a certain computer-orderliness to it, which was not surprising, considering the amount of attention the city's brain paid to the task of preventing collisions.

Lara gazed down on the lush landscape as her autocab made its way from the spaceport to one of the downtown hotels. Her destination was the 300-story Bernau Excelsior, perched with a dozen other monoliths inside a sharp bend of the Malva River. As she watched, the horizon tilted, and the cab began to spiral downward toward a landing stage on the 180th floor.

Before leaving Saban Station, she had contacted Darin Mastlin and asked him to meet her for third meal that evening to discuss a matter of importance. She had demurred when he asked her to elucidate. She figured she would learn more about the status of her ship in a social setting than while seated across his desk in Institute Headquarters.

The cab grounded. She grabbed her kit. As the canopy opened, a brisk, warm breeze fluttered her hair and gave her a whiff of the unique scent of Bernau. It reminded her of the night flowers of home. She stepped out onto the landing stage and walked briskly to the large opening in the side of the hotel. The wind abruptly cut off as she stepped through the invisible air curtain and entered the high lobby.

#

She had made her reservation for an hour after second sunset. Bernau's colonists handled the planet's inconveniently fast rotation by combining two planetary days into a single rise-work-sleep cycle. The match between their new double day and the human circadian rhythm was not perfect, but close enough for practical purposes.

Once in her room, she took a hot bath, prepared her makeup, and put on the translucent black bodysuit she had chosen for the evening. The fabric revealed as much as it concealed and, she hoped, would put Mastlin in an accommodating mood to release *Fire* back into revenue service.

A gentle chime from the room annunciator panel signaled the arrival of the appointed hour. She found Mastlin waiting for her in the ground lobby when she exited the grav shaft. He was attired in a casual suit of cerise-and-light mauve, with a matching cape. The two of them embraced like old friends.

"Thank you for meeting me, Darin."

"A pleasure," he replied, although the look he gave her managed to convey his curiosity. "You look beautiful this evening."

"Thank you."

"Where shall we eat?"

"I have reservations at the Top of the Mountain," she answered, referring to the hotel's rooftop restaurant. "I understand the food is good and the view spectacular."

"If a little pricey."

"Not to worry," she said, "Considering what the Institute has added to my credit account for our recent jaunt, I can afford it."

The restaurant was indeed pricey. They passed three human waiters on the way to their table. Each bowed in turn, causing Lara to increase her estimate of the cost of the evening's meal with each bow.

The view was spectacular. They were seated near a window that looked upstream along the river. Morast had set, leaving the world in darkness, save for the luminescence cast by Bernau's two moons, which were currently low in the western sky. Geron, the smaller moon, was near perigee, and was unusually bright.

The glow from the moons were aided by the city lights, which reflected off the river. Half-a-dozen watercraft were engaged in their nightly excursions and added to the illumination.

"How is the project going?" Lara asked as their waiter poured the wine.

"Getting organized," Mastlin replied. "We are accepting proposals from researchers as to how to best plumb *New Hope*'s secrets. It will be a year or two before we truly begin studying the ship."

"Not the DNA study, surely."

"No, Betrice is already correlating the data we obtained during the expedition."

"Any hope they will make progress on the fertility problem quickly?"

Mastlin laughed. "Any hope that by simply comparing the Earth mega-genome with our own, everyone will slap their forehead and exclaim, 'Of course!'?

"I'm afraid not. Whatever mistake the gene mechanics made is damned subtle. Otherwise, we would have figured it out by now."

He picked up a piece of bread, lathered it with crenole, and took a bite. When he had swallowed, he asked, "How goes the effort to reconfigure the ship?"

"Complete," she answered, unable to keep the surprise from her voice. Then a sudden suspicion took root. "I take it that you've guessed what I want to talk to you about."

"I didn't need to. Your factor, Thorne, gave me fair warning."

She took a sip of wine, then sat back and sighed. "So much for subtlety. Yes, I arranged all of this," she gestured at their surroundings and the glass wall with the view behind it, "to soften you up and ask when you are going to release my ship."

Mastlin, whose manner had been jocular, turned suddenly serious. After a short pause, he said, "I can't answer that just yet. Something has come up."

"What?"

"To explain, I need to preface my remarks," he said, refilling both their wine glasses from the decanter. "I was serious when I said that Betrice's project will not bear fruit any time soon."

"How so?"

"Even with the full collection of New Hope's Earthstock DNA, there are easily a billion questions to be answered before we can make progress on the fertility problem. It may take a full generation just to identify our predecessors' mistake. And once we do, it will take another three generations before we can properly implement a solution."

"Why so long?"

"Genetics protocols. Ironclad rules that were adopted after some truly horrific accidents. First," he said, holding up a finger, "we must synthesize a new genetic code to replace the flaw. That is not as easy to do as they portray in the holos.

"Then will come a pilot program. We must breed three successive generations with the new genetic code, increasing the number of individuals in each cohort by a factor of ten each generation and study them for at least half a human lifetime.

"Unfortunately, speeding up a project by getting nine women pregnant to deliver a baby in one month still doesn't work. Nor do people mature in less than fifteen standard years or reach middle-age until a century has passed.

"Each baby born into the program will be watched carefully for harmful mutations. But we cannot check their fertility before they reach puberty... for obvious reasons. Luckily, that last can be done with sperm and eggs in a laboratory, allowing us to sort out the successes and failures quickly.

"Assuming complete success, it will take more than a century before we can introduce new genetics into the general populace."

Lara sighed. "It doesn't sound like much fun for the experimental subjects, either."

Mastlin shrugged. "No reason it should be a burden on them. They will live out their lives like the rest of us, save that we will require them to undergo periodic testing and donate genetic material when they come of age. I doubt they will object, not with the compensation that test subjects receive."

"Surely, considering the urgency of the problem, they can cut a few corners on those protocols."

"And risk making the problem worse, and possibly dooming humanity in the process? Highly unlikely."

Mastlin stopped talking as a pair of waiters guided a floating tray to their table. They made a production of placing plates and bowls just so on the table, and then filling them with steaming delicacies before withdrawing out of earshot.

Lara asked, "What has all of this genetic testing to do with my ship?"

"I'm getting to that," Mastlin answered. "Something came up two weeks ago. We are running simulations on a new line of inquiry. If results are favorable and we decide to pursue it, we may have use for your services again."

Lara stared at him with a sour expression. "Are you going to tell me, or is it a big secret?"

"Yes," he said, breaking into the smile of a mischievous little boy.

"I beg your pardon."

"It *is* a big secret, and yes, I'm going to tell you. It has occurred to us that there is a way to short-circuit the time it will take to obtain a solution to the fertility problem."

"Which is?"

"It might be possible to obtain viable Earth genetic material."

"How? Don't tell me you can reanimate the mummies aboard *New Hope*, Dr. Frankenstein!"

He looked at her with theatrically wide eyes. "An interesting idea. I wonder why we did not think of it. But no. Our thought is if we could obtain pure Earth DNA, we could selectively infuse it into test subjects without all of this rigamarole and save decades of testing."

"Infuse it how?"

"Either artificially, or by the tried-and-true approach. We should be able to induce individuals to put themselves out to stud for us... for the proper level of credit, of course."

"And keep trying until you produce an individual with high fertility?"

"Precisely."

She laughed. "It sounds like something a man would think up."

"Not guilty. Actually, it was Betrice's idea."

"How does that get around the regulations?"

"Earth DNA has been proven by four billion years of evolution. It is, as they used to say when gold was worth something, the gold standard. Any genetic anomalies we encounter will be diseases that we know how to treat."

"Basically, the cut-and-try approach."

"Precisely. If we had access to individuals with Earth DNA, we would breed a generation of hybrid galaxian-terrestrials. When we discover individuals with elevated fertility, we will proliferate their beneficial genes widely."

Lara scanned his features, searching for some sign that this was an example of his sense of humor, of which she was familiar from their time aboard ship. Not finding any hint he was engaged in spinning a bizarre joke, she cleared her throat and asked:

"Aren't you forgetting something?"

"What?"

"How exactly are you going to persuade these terrestrial studs to screw for you if we can't find Earth?"

He paused and lifted a spoon of Roth's bisonoid stew to his lips, then washed it down with a sip of wine. Only after he had blotted his lips with the synthsilk napkin did he continue:

"That's the big secret. Remember the child's astronomy book?"

Lara did not answer, assuming the question was rhetorical.

"It turns out that Hirm Partin was premature in saying the book offered no clue as to Earth's location."

Lara looked at him, her brows knit together in puzzlement. "The map was drawn by hand, by people who had barely learned to fly. They were looking upward through Earth's obscuring atmosphere, and the location of Sol, the map's zero coordinate, is unknown. If we could identify some of those ancient stars, possibly…"

Mastlin shook his head. "But we can't because we don't have any idea where any of the stars in that book are located. Partin was quite correct about that. Galaxies, on the other hand, are a different matter."

"Galaxies?"

"There is a table in the book that lists twenty galaxies, and the constellations where they are located. There are even symbols on the map showing their location. Unlike the classical stars, the galaxies are known to us. The ancient Andromeda is still the modern Andromeda, etc. We have identified six such galaxies around the Earth's celestial globe."

"So?"

"At the Institute, we have been running simulations on those six, specifically the three-dimensional angles between them as viewed from Earth. We can compare those angles with the same angles as viewed from Bernau. The differences allow us to interpolate the zero coordinate."

"But the positional unknowns…"

"… are huge. We have not found Sol, by any means. What we have done is isolate the search area to a spherical volume of space about a thousand light-years in diameter. Unsurprisingly, it is at the center of the core of human space."

"That's still a hell of a lot of stars."

"About two hundred thousand," he agreed. "Still, it is a substantially lower number than the 140 million stars of human space. The best strategy, we believe, is to go to the center of that volume and then cast about for human-occupied systems among the core stars.

"Presumably, those colonies were founded in the first wave of expansion. Being in the general neighborhood of Sol, they may still know where it is. Even if they do not, they may be able to find some of the classical stars for us. Their star charts should give us enough information to find Sol, or at least, give us a clue to where we should look next."

"What if Earth no longer exists?" Lara asked. "Legend has it that the interstellar wars were most vicious among the older colonies."

Mastlin shrugged. "Then we do it Betrice's way."

Lara laughed. "I have to give you credit. It is an audacious plan. But what has this to do with me and my ship?"

"We were wondering if you would like to transport the expedition in *Coronal Fire*."

She paused and thought it over. It would certainly be more interesting than traveling between Morast and Bortanis, ad infinitum.

"Maybe," she said. "What's the catch?"

He took another sip of wine and then sighed. "The voyage to the search area will take four years, minimum. The entire expedition is projected to take between 10- and 12-years total unless we run into difficulties. It could be longer."

#

Chapter 9

They talked well into the evening, first in the restaurant and later in Lara's room. The more Mastlin explained, the less outlandish the plan seemed.

There was that four-year voyage just to get to the search area to consider. Luckily, with current lifespans, this was not the barrier it might once have been.

The problem with a multi-year voyage was not the endurance of the ship. Propulsion was virtually free. *New Hope* had proved that. Save for the power to cross the barrier into hyperspace, in changing energy levels, and in moving transversely across the streams, propulsion came from the hyperons' eternal need to be somewhere else.

Nor were ship consumables a limiting factor. The ship's closed-loop environmental system could easily supply air and water for a couple of standard decades. As for sustenance, the human body requires two kilograms of food per day. That equates to 720 kilograms per standard year, or a total of 720 kilotons total to sustain 100 researchers for a decade. That quantity could easily fit into one of *Fire*'s auxiliary holds.

The problem was psychological. Small irritations grow into large ones, slights are magnified, arguments end in physical blows. They had seen that on the expedition to salvage *New Hope*.

To minimize tension on the outbound journey, and to limit boredom, they would follow *New Hope*'s example. Most of the expedition's human contingent would make the four-thousand-light-year trip in hibernation. Expedition members would enter long sleep even before they launched. Ship's crew would remain awake long enough to enter hyperspace and then two crewmen would stand staggered six-month watches in rotation while the others hibernated. If all went well, no one would be awake for more than a cumulative year during the full voyage.

Even as they discussed the arrangements, Lara felt a chill run down her spine at the thought of committing herself to a hibernation chamber. She could not get the image of that long dead woman out of her mind. She knew she was being silly, but that did little to abate the atavistic fear she felt.

The technology of long sleep had progressed in the centuries since *New Hope*'s launch. Modern pods had independent environmental systems and safeguards piled atop safeguards. Sleepers could be triggered awake in less than fifteen minutes in an emergency; and each tank had an automatic wake-up cycle. If it lost contact with the ship's brain for a full day, the occupant would be revived.

Cor was perfectly capable of flying *Fire* for the entire trip without impertinent suggestions from her crewmates. She never tired, never slept, and never grew bored. Even so, regulations required a human being to be instantly available if the computer ran into anything it could not handle. They would use two watchstanders as a safety precaution and to keep everyone sane during the long, lonely months in total blackness.

It was nearing second midnight when Mastlin concluded his briefing with, "That is about all I can tell you. Are you still interested?"

Lara thought about it and nodded. "Intrigued is a better description. I will have to check with my bosses in the morning. I assume the Institute is willing to contract for *Fire* at a rate that will gain their attention."

"The plan is to purchase your ship outright," he answered. "A decade is a long time to pay rent. We should be able to sell it at a profit when we return. You might even be interested in buying *Fire* yourself. By then, you should have enough credit saved up."

Lara had been sitting in the same too-small chair for a couple of hours. She stood and stretched, then strode to the autobar.

"How about a drink to seal the deal?"

"I'd like that."

She ordered two cocktails, Varan rum. While they waited for delivery, Mastlin also stood and stretched. There was a chime from the wall and two containers appeared in the receptacle. Lara removed the wrapping, then handed Mastlin one and picked up the other.

"To a successful venture," she said.

"To finding Earth," Mastlin replied.

They clinked glasses and then drank, eyeing one another over the tilted rims.

When the amber liquid was gone, Mastlin lowered his glass and placed it on the small table that was part of the autobar.

He cleared his throat. "Pardon, but since business has concluded, I believe I sense the possibility that you might be open to celebrating a bit more intimately. Am I mistaken?"

She sighed and put her own glass beside his. Some people might have thought the difference in their heights odd. Lara did not. Most of the men she knew were a head shorter than she was.

She tilted her face down and met his lips halfway. It was an introductory kiss, almost chaste, that lasted for a dozen seconds.

Finally, they parted.

"You aren't wrong. If you are interested, I'm willing."

He laughed. "Have you ever known a man who wasn't interested?"

"Not that I can remember."

#

The next morning, she and Darin Mastlin had a leisurely first meal, after which Lara took a pod to Interstellar Transport's headquarters. She briefed Yaelson Thorne on the Institute's plans.

Thorne sat back and steepled his fingers in front of him. His chair made quiet noises as it accommodated his new posture.

"I knew something was up, but this is startling news. Are they really talking sale rather than rent?"

"They are."

"That will make Broadnor happy. What about this expedition? Do you think they can actually do it?"

Lara thought for a moment and nodded. "It's possible, but it won't be easy. For one thing, how are we going to get there?"

"We?"

She took a deep breath before speaking. "Yes. Mastlin asked if I was interested in commanding *Fire* and I told him I was. It's an adventure and important, and I guess I'm tired of detouring around the Kaligani Narrows every other voyage."

The factor surprised her by grinning. "I can see the attraction. Go ahead and check into it. Rest assured that you can come back to Interstellar if it does not work out. Now, you were saying something about difficulties..."

She nodded. "How exactly do we get to the core?"

"I would think that fairly straightforward."

"I doubt it."

She noticed the perplexed look on his face and sighed. This would be hard to explain.

#

People speak with great facileness of "thousands of light-years" and "millions of stars;" but really, the human brain is not capable of understanding such large numbers. In that respect, modern man is little advanced over his prehistoric ancestors to whom mathematics consisted of, "one, two, three, many."

Space is vast and hyperspace even more so.

Take the galaxy: a flattened disk of stars rotating about a common center of mass and submerged in gravity infusions from surrounding universes. It measures one-hundred-thousand light-years in diameter and holds 250 billion stars.

Or human space: an elongated bubble of blackness ten-thousand light-years long by five thousand wide and one-thousand deep. The region has a stellar population of 140 million stars.

There was no known census as to how many human-occupied systems there were, but current "guestimates" put the number at around 25,000. When humankind went out to the stars, they had enthusiastically applied the biblical commandment, "go forth and multiply," which was ironic, considering the rationale for the upcoming expedition.

And then there is the region in which Earth might be found... assuming their calculations using data from a two-thousand-year-old textbook were correct. The search volume was a globe "merely" one-thousand light-years across at the very center of human space. Assuming the density of occupied stars is constant throughout space, their target sphere enclosed some 400 inhabited systems, one of which was the Mother of Men.

#

Lara finished her recounting with, "Given the gulf between where we are and where we want to go, how exactly are we going to get there?"

Thorne said, "Via hyperspace, of course."

"Using what astrogation database?"

"Doesn't the Institute have one?"

"I doubt it. After the Chaos, interstellar commerce virtually ceased. It has come back slowly, with widely separated systems acting as nuclei for expanding spheres of trade.

"Hyperspace mapping data is little more than a patchwork. The main routes are well mapped, minor routes less so. And outside these well-traveled lanes, data is mostly hearsay. In too many places, it is the equivalent of *'Here there be dragons.'*

"Yes, the Institute possesses the most complete hyperon topography data of which I am aware. Unfortunately, it is not enough. We should be able to plot a zigzag course for at least 500 light-years. After that, it is *galactica incognita. Cor* and whoever is awake are going to have to map as we go."

"You make it sound impossible," Thorne answered, suddenly concerned.

"Not impossible," Lara replied. "Just damned difficult."

#

Lara returned to the ship two days later.

"How did your trip down to the planet go?" Nal Taryn asked as she exited the airlock.

She told him about the Institute's intention to buy *Coronal Fire* for an extended mission to search for lost Earth.

"And you agreed to this?" he asked.

"After some soul searching, yes. I spent the last couple of days with Yaelson Thorne going over the details. He thinks Interstellar Transport will be willing to sell if the price is right."

Nal laughed. "Our bosses would sell their mothers if the price was right."

"What about you?" Lara asked. "Are you interested?"

"I'll have to think about it. I have two ortho-wives to consider."

"Take your time. It will be several months before we are ready if we go at all. Talk it over with Merwith. She'll miss you."

"As will Valsa. I will get a message off to her at once. In the meantime, I'll give you my full support."

Lara nodded. One of the reasons Nal was on the Lanyth to Bernau run was the active sex life it gave him at every stage of the trip. He had Merwith here in the Morast System and Valsa in the Bortanis System, not to mention herself en route. It was a common arrangement among those who plied the stars. Nor were the wives sitting at home, eagerly awaiting the return of their husbands. Most had taken vows with two or more interstellar transients. Occasionally, when multiple husbands were in port at the same time, schedules had to be carefully adhered to.

Star travel had significantly changed human customs, including those relating to marriage. Some couples still lived their lives by ancient religious strictures, but most treated the matter as purely a civil matter. Marriage contracts were registered with the local authorities and could run anywhere from a single local year to a lifetime.

Nor were the forms of marriage regulated. They included monogamy, polygyny (polygamy and polyandry), open, samesex, and line marriages of several different sorts. The popularity of any version of connubial bliss varied from world to world, just as did other customs. However, like all customs, they made sense to those who took part in them.

Lara could have entered an arrangement like Nal's if she had wanted. However, with her responsibilities to her ship and her employers, she found a single ship-husband more than satisfied her needs. Nor did being married prevent interludes like her tryst with Darin Mastlin. As human lifespan increased, the idea of cleaving to a single individual "until death do us part" had become proportionately less popular.

Something of her thoughts must have shown on her face because Nal asked, "Anything else happen while you were aground?"

"Do I ask you about your evenings with Merwith or Valsa?"

"I will take that as a 'yes.'"

#

Chapter 10

It took another month for the transfer of *Fire's* title to become final. There was a brief ceremony onboard the ship with everyone involved, a ceremony at which Lara and Nal (who was still undecided) switched from the gray-and-black formal uniforms of Interstellar Transport to the blue-and-green of the Institute of Knowledge.

Shortly afterwards, with a minimal command and engineering crew aboard, they received clearance to leave parking orbit, en route to Geron, Bernau's lesser moon.

Geron was the home base for the Morast Coordinate Navy.

The moon was nothing like the monster that graced the skies of the home world. It was small and misshapen, a stray asteroid from Morast's inner belt. How it had managed to achieve its highly elliptical orbit about the planet was a matter of debate among astronomers. That its journey had begun with a collision was not in doubt. The event had left a crater that extended halfway across the larger end of the rock.

That crater was their destination.

Lara was on the bridge and Nal was in the engine room as the freighter began its final descent toward the black-and-gray surface.

"Are you ready for this new adventure?" Lara asked the computer.

"It should be exciting," *Cor* responded.

In all her years in space, Lara had never once contemplating setting a ship down on a planetary body. *Fire* lacked landing gear. If they tried to set down on Bernau, the stresses would split the hull like an overripe fruit.

Yet, that was precisely what she planned to do on Geron.

The moon's gravitational field was only a tiny fraction of one standard gravity and the ship's cage-like keel should easily support its mass against that feeble pull.

"I have permission to approach from the base computer. May

I proceed, Shipmaster?"

"Nal, are you ready?"

"Ready, Lara."

"Cor, you may begin your approach."

The moon in the view volume tilted and began to slide slowly to one side. Their projected flight path appeared as a curving red line, annotated with ghostly time hacks every few centimeters.

Geron grew over the next half-hour until it took on the aspects of a planet. Having canceled the ship's transverse velocity, Cor began their descent.

A beacon illuminated near the northern ring wall of the crater. Lara could see the circles of docks carved out of the nickel-iron plain. Some were occupied, including one that held a ship larger than Fire. Others were empty hemispherical pits.

Clasky Crater slowly transformed into a black-brown plain, half in Morast-light, half in dark. Save for the point nearest the beacon, the base of the crater disappeared below the too-near horizon, while the peaks remained starkly visible. The ship's own shadow suddenly appeared on the ground and then swept toward the center of the hemispherical dock below.

Then they were down. There was no sensation of contact, merely Cor's announcement of the fact.

"Full diagnostic, Cor," Lara ordered. "Report any damage."

"No damage, Shipmaster."

"Very well. Secure the gravitics and report our arrival."

#

Two hours after touchdown, Lara and Nal received a message from Base Headquarters. It politely asked that they come to the commandant's office at 14:00 hours UST. The message further said that a guide would meet them at the embarkation tube egress point ten minutes prior.

"Care to bet on the Commandant's mood when he sees us?" Nal asked.

"Are you suggesting that he may not be happy?"

"Would you be after the Institute robbed you blind?"

Lara laughed. "Probably not. How much do you think the Navy's charging for all of our upgrades?"

"Probably more than the Institute paid for the ship."

#

As Lara had explained to Yaelson Thorne, the expedition would run out of reliable astrogation data long before they reached their destination. When that happened, they would have to chart a course that avoided gravitational flaws, rips, and whirlpools, while keeping their pseudo-speed. Otherwise, their voyage might last forty years rather than four.

Fire's sensor array could peer five light-year-equivalents into the hyperon maelstrom on a good day. After that, everything was a featureless fog of background noise. That was not good enough for a ship moving through uncharted hyperspace at one- thousand equivalent lights.

Somehow, the institute's Formas Rob Somace had convinced the Navy to equip *Fire* with its most advanced (and secret) hyperspace detection gear as well as several other enhancements.

It was not enough, of course, to merely map the hyperon field en route. They would also have to match their hyperspace data with the real universe. To do this they would periodically drop through null to chart their position with respect to various beacon stars.

Once they reached their search area in the Core, they would require a different sensor capability.

Since all energy intensive planets emit radio noise, the Navy would provide them with a sensitive EM-sniffer, able to detect such signals out to 200 light-years, which would hopefully allow them to zero in on human-occupied systems to investigate.

#

The two of them were at the access tube sealed to *Fire*'s ventral airlock with five minutes to spare. At the top of the tube was a grab bar. There was a sign printed there in large red letters: *Beware! Low gravity.*

Lara grasped the bar and swung out.

The moment her body passed beyond the ship's hull; standard gravity vanished. The instantaneous transition unsettled her stomach. She grasped the guideline and pulled herself forward. Nal followed her hand-over-hand to the far end of the tube.

There, a much larger airlock door blocked their progress. As they arrived, the door slid into its recess to reveal a cavernous interior.

Their guide awaited them on the other side. He was a tall, lanky youth with straw hair who wore an expression that Lara had once seen on a small puppy. He looked very young.

"Larath Sims? Nalwith Taryn?"

They acknowledged that they were indeed those individuals.

"Subaltern Essan Gottleb. If you will follow me, I will guide you to the Base Commandant's office."

#

The subaltern led them down a steeply sloped tunnel to a lower level. They again pulled themselves hand-over-hand using a 'barber pole' suspended from the overhead.

The tunnel dumped them into another. This one was a pedestrian way. Gottleb hurried them along past open doors branching off into offices, workshop, and one exceptionally large hangar. Twice more they descended deeper into the moon. Each time the furnishings of the compartments they passed became notably plusher.

Lara was minimally aware of the passing scenery. Most of her attention was fixated on walking.

For reasons known only to the Navy, Geron Base lacked artificial gravity. Subaltern Gottleb had given them a quick tutorial in how to walk inside the base. It turned out that being in minimal gravity was different from the high gravity in which she had grown up, the Earth-standard used aboard ship, or the microgravity found in hyperspace and aboard New Hope.

The motion was a form of restrained ice skating. Most of the effort involved propelling oneself forward without adding too much vertical velocity.

"This is surprisingly difficult," she commented to her host as they slid along for the first hundred meters. If anything, Nal was having more problems than she was. There was something about his breadth that interfered with his stride.

"It takes some getting used to," the Subaltern agreed, "but it has its advantages. In the shops and hangers, they jump about like water sprites."

They reached the commandant's office without mishap. As they entered, they discovered an actual human receptionist.

"Welcome," the decorative young lady said after Gottleb gave her their names. "The Commandant is just finishing up a meeting."

The office around them was lined with glass cases holding various ship models and other memorabilia. There were no chairs or couches. The receptionist stood behind a raised desk with her feet inserted into restraints.

The door quietly retracted and several men and women exited. All wore the uniform of the Morast Navy. Lara eyed the efficient way in which they 'skated' past and out into the corridor. She noticed several people eying her as they passed.

A bass voice shouted for them to come in. They made their way into the inner sanctum where a gray-haired man of indeterminate (but mature) age came forward to greet them. His posture was erect, and each shoulder was decorated with a line of four stars.

"Commandant Heblo Mac Gormer, Morast Coordinate Navy, at your service."

Lara and Nal introduced themselves and all parties shook hands.

"Refreshments?" the Commandant asked as he directed them to two sculpture-like resting frames arrayed in a circle of eight. At the center of the circle, a holocube was retracted into the overhead.

"Gantha juice for me," Lara replied.

"The same," Nal concurred.

"Leeza, three gantha juice bulbs, please." Gormer did not raise his voice, showing he was in communication with his assistant via implant.

"Very well, Commandant," the woman's voice said as it floated through the door.

"Anchor yourselves to the foot restraints. You don't want to float away and injure yourself if you get to gesticulating." The Commandant turned to Lara. "So, you are the discoverer of the ghost ship?"

She nodded.

"What moved you to make the detour to check it out? Most shipmasters would have ignored it."

"I thought they could be in trouble. They were, all right;

unfortunately, long past any need for our assistance."

"I've read the reports," the Commandant said. "They give me the shivers when I think of what happened to those poor devils, but I don't have a feel for the ship. Tell me about it."

Lara recounted their first exploration, their discovery that the derelict had been placed into a hyperon stream and then left to drift, and how she felt the first time she had come face to face with one of the passengers.

The Commandant listened attentively, interrupting only briefly for clarification. While she spoke, the receptionist entered with their refreshments, then lingered to listen to the tale. She went back to her station only after Lara finished.

Gormer did not say anything for long seconds as he picked up the drinking bulb and took a long sip. Replacing it in its holding rack, he nodded. "That was one fine job, Shipmaster. Are you absolutely sure they were from Earth?"

She told him about the pouch calendar. "The date on it was 2787, Old Calendar. That was only 250 years after the first faster-than-light experiment. There were few other places they could have come from.

"Also, the DNA tests support an Earth origin. So far, they have analyzed over three thousand of the samples we took while refurbishing *New Hope*. And, of course, there is the astronomy book."

The Commandant sighed, while slowly shaking his head. "Yes, the famous astronomy book. "We are launching an expensive expedition to God knows where on the authority of a primer for adolescents. Nothing strange about that."

"It sounds like you don't approve, Commandant," Nal said.

"Whether I approve or not is immaterial, Submaster. The Institute has convinced the Prime Councilor that this infertility problem is more acute than anyone knows, and the PM has ordered me to support you. I follow all orders to the best of my ability."

"Do you think we are making a mistake relying on the book?" Lara asked. "It's the only clue we have as to Earth's location."

"Right at the center of the core stars? How much insight did that bit of information require? Tell me, Shipmaster, you do not think after the success of their first starship, the ancients said, 'Let's just look to the east to see what we can see,' do you? No, they spilled out to the six points of the celestial compass. Given that your target volume is fully one-thousand light-years across, Earth almost has to be in the search zone; that is, if it still exists."

"It must exist," she stubbornly exclaimed.

"*Might*, not *must*, dear lady. Have you thought of what you will do if you find this vast reservoir of untainted genetic material you seek to be a radioactive desert?"

"Then we'll come home, the mission a failure," Nal said.

Gormer's response was a snort. "Come now. You will have spent four years getting there and God knows how many in the search. Are you just going to give up? What of all the investment in lifespan... yours and those you left behind?. Surely you will do everything you can to complete your mission before turning for home."

"What else can we do?" Lara asked.

"If I were going along," the Commandant said, "and thank God, I am not, I would start searching for the oldest surviving colony I could find. The chances are that their DNA closely mirrors that of the home world."

"Why would it?"

"It makes sense. All the worlds of which we are aware are daughters of other colonies, and often grand-daughters and great-grand-daughters. The older colonies are first-generation descendants of Earth. Out here on the Periphery, we have had more opportunity to tinker with our genome, and thereby, introduce copying errors."

Lara looked pensive. This expedition, she realized, was going to be more complicated than what she had originally envisioned.

"I will bring that up with the Institute."

"Then there is the worst-case scenario to consider..."

"What could be worse than finding Earth destroyed?"

"Finding that it still exists, but that the Wars of Secession haven't ended. What if we are sending a shipload of guileless academics into a shitstorm?"

"Then we run like hell," Nal answered.

This brought a guffaw from the Commandant. "Couldn't have said it better myself. The trick in such situations is being *able* to run.

That is why we are equipping you to defend yourselves. We may not be able to stop you from blundering into an active war zone, but we can do our best to give you the means to fight your way out again.

"You saw that group that was in here before you? They are the staff I have assigned to support this expedition. Right now, they are clambering all over your ship, seeing what offensive weaponry we can install. Which brings up an important question that will need answering fairly quickly."

"What is that, Commandant?" Lara asked.

"The obvious one, of course. How many Marines will you be taking along?"

#

Chapter 11

That night, once again under ship's gravity and after lovemaking, Lara and Nal discussed the day's events. The lovemaking had taken precedence because all non-critical power would be cut during the morning watch. From then on, they would be sleeping in Geron gravity.

"Is your head spinning?" Lara asked Nal, referring to the torrent of information they had received during eight hours of briefings.

"From what we just did and other things," he replied, pulling her into his strong arms. She liked the secure feeling that gave her.

"So, how many Marines do you think we need?"

The Commandant's question had turned into an instant private joke between them. As the day's briefings wore on, they realized he had been serious... that the question was his way of jolting their thinking into new, and until now unexplored, channels.

When Darin Mastlin introduced her to the idea of an expedition to search for lost Earth, she had thought of it as an extended version of their just completed mission to salvage *New Hope*. *Coronal Fire*'s crew would work the ship until they arrived at the Core, where they would wake the Institute personnel.

The briefings opened her eyes. They were about to embark on a voyage three times the duration of Magellan's circumnavigation of the Earth. Viewed in that context, the Navy believed the risks far exceeded any she had imagined.

The plan called for the base constructors to rebuild *Fire* to convert it into a camouflaged warship. The Commandant referred to the final product as a "Q-ship." Later, Lara asked *Cor* what that meant and was surprised at how far back in antiquity the term originated.

Outwardly, *Fire* would remain a standard *Boreal-Class* general hauler of people and cargo. Beneath her hull, however, the vessel would be massively transformed.

87

The survey team reported their findings after second meal. Their conclusion was that the freighter had plenty of empty cubic with which to work. There was enough volume to house all the extra personnel and their consumables after allocating most of the central hold to a magazine, power generator, and three armored assault flyers. The latter would be changed as much as possible to make them resemble normal ship's auxiliaries.

Following the survey team's report, an officer who resembled an academic more than a military man took control of the briefings.

"My name is Subcommander Xerxes Palamintok and I work in Tactics and Strategy. I am here to report on our preliminary thoughts as to what we will install in your ship. We may change the list as we study *Coronal Fire* more, but the basic outline should hold.

"The transformation begins tomorrow. We will strip the main cargo hold down to bare metal. The stripping is necessary so that we can bond our power conduits to underlying structure to ensure good heat transfer coefficients. The radiators for the system will be integrated into your hull.

"We'll conceal the missile launchers and beam projectors behind your existing cargo loading hatches. Sensors, both *ftl* and normal space, will have to go on the outer hull, of course. We will disguise them as innocuous pieces of other equipment..."

Palamintok went on for an hour, listing each item and its function. He ended with, "All of this armament should give you an even chance with anything smaller than a slayer-class destroyer."

The tactical officer, having taken care by long-range battles in open space, switched to what he referred to as "knife combat range."

"As I see it," he said, "there are two basic scenarios."

"First, you null out on the edge of some human-occupied system, identify yourselves, and are invited to take up orbit to discuss trade. Your survey party lands. While they are off the ship, you are boarded by spacers in armored vacsuits. Once they breach your hull, how are you going to prevent them from taking control of the ship?

"Second scenario: Your ground party is taken hostage. You, Shipmaster, are aboard *Coronal Fire*. How do you rescue them?"

Lara thought about it for a few seconds, then laughed. "I guess

I will call out the Marines."

"Yes, ma'am. We want to give you the capability to win any battle in which you find yourself, whether it's at arm's length or ten thousand klamaters."

#

"Are you all right, *Cor*?" Lara asked via her implant. She was at her usual station on *Fire*'s bridge, but there was nothing *usual* about her surroundings. The artificial gravity had been down for more than two weeks and the view outside was obscured by construction platforms. They encircled the ship, some extending as high as the apex.

Power was down everywhere, save for the emergency backup circuits. Disturbing sounds were being transmitted through the hull from deep within *Fire*'s interior. The Navy demolition teams were being none too gentle.

"I am operational, Shipmaster," *Cor* responded after what Lara thought was a delay, although it was probably her imagination.

"What about power?"

Cor was a sentient computer and needed a steady power supply to remain that way. Her software was continuously integrating the information that flooded in from around the ship, and even a few milliseconds' interruption could do severe damage to her personality. It would be the electronic equivalent of a minor stroke in humans.

"The base engineers have routed quad redundant lines and my backup capacitors are fully charged. I am safe. There have been no surges or dropouts since main power was shut down."

"Have the engineers uploaded their detail schematics of what they will be doing to our ship?"

"Affirmative. I got them with the midnight download last night. They are quite extensive."

"Indeed, they are. Any concerns?"

"I have already contacted the base computer. Some of the high-power lines are running too close to temperature sensitive modules. If we were to fire the particle beams and the lasers simultaneously, we could damage something. The power lines will be rerouted."

"You should be getting the Institute's modifications soon," Lara said. "I will be leaving for Morast first watch tomorrow to assist in finalizing the plans."

On the Navy's schematics, large sections of the ship had been highlighted in blue, designating that the volume was off limits to the weaponeers. Those were the places where the hibernation chambers, living quarters, and a host of other things would be installed.

One of the auxiliary holds was being reserved for cargo. Depending on the reception they received in an occupied system, they might mask themselves as an itinerate trader. For that they would need samples of their wares.

"Where is the Submaster?" *Cor* asked. "He has not been aboard in four days."

"He's on Bernau, talking to Merwith. Valsa replied to his last communication and has given her permission for him to go with us. He's arranging for his wives' financial support while he is gone."

"That is good news," *Cor* responded.

"Yes, it is. There are going to be a lot of strangers aboard and I will feel better having him here."

"As will I," the computer answered. "I have been studying the history of expeditions such as this one. Some of the records date back to pre-Hegira Earth."

Lara let her eyebrows rise in surprise. The computer was a voracious learner but had not shown any real interest in history before now.

"What have you learned?"

"That on a voyage such as this one, the lines of authority may become blurred, which can lead to trouble."

"Are you worried about a mutiny on the coming expedition?"

"It is one possibility. There will be three centers of power aboard: you and the Submaster, Darin Mastlin and the other Institute personnel, and the military contingent. If you three fall into conflict, the ship's social cohesion could fail."

"What do you propose we do about that?" Lara asked.

"I do not know. It is a problem in human dynamics that lies beyond my capability."

"Let me think about it while I'm down on the planet. Perhaps we can arrange things to improve our cohesion."

"Very well, Shipmaster. Enjoy your time planetside. I will watch over the modifications and communicate if there are any problems."

#

The trip down to Bernau took a standard day. That was because Geron was approaching apogee. The moon was four times the distance it was when at perigee.

Lara again stayed at the Bernau Excelsior and found an invitation to dinner waiting for her when she checked in. It was from Nal Taryn and Merwith Voskind. Dinner was at a quiet restaurant in the suburbs of Capital. The two of them were already seated when Lara arrived.

"Lara, how wonderful that you made it," Merwith exclaimed, rising to give her a hug.

She was a tall woman with bronze hair, piercing green eyes, and the subdued ear spikes of a local. She had an outgoing personality and was far more comfortable in social situations than Lara; or at least, that is what Lara believed.

When all three of them were seated, Merwith asked, "Is this coming voyage going to be as long as Nal says, or does he just want a holiday from me?"

The words were said with a light tone, but Lara thought she detected an undercurrent of anxiety.

"Unfortunately, Mer, it takes time to travel four-thousand light-years, even in hyperspace."

"And this expedition is really as important as he's told me?"

She shrugged. "The Institute seems to think so. Judging by the amount of effort the Navy is putting into the ship, so does the Coordinate government."

"Is it going to be dangerous?"

At a warning look from Nal, Lara said, "Not particularly. So long as we don't blunder into any gravity intrusions, it will just be a long, boring flight through nothingness."

"Will you be kind to this husband of ours en route? I would hate to think what he will be like if he doesn't get his regular 'treatments,'" she said with a grin.

Nal cleared his throat. "Darling, I explained that we will be making the journey in cold sleep, with staggered duty shifts. Lara and I will barely see each other until we reach our destination."

"Each of you will be by yourself?"

"No, darling," Nal replied. "Two crewmembers will be on duty at all times. With staggered shifts. Each watch stander will have two partners during each waking period."

Lara cleared her throat. "Change in plans, Nal. The duty crew will now be six, with rotations every couple of months."

"When was this decided?" he asked.

"Three days ago. The Navy psych people suggested it. We'll need to train everyone in their duties, anyway, so why not do it on the outbound voyage?"

"And how long will it take to find Earth after you get to the Core?" Merwith asked.

Nal shrugged. "It could take a year or so. We may have to contact four or five colony worlds before we finally pinpoint its location."

Merwith frowned. Like most non-spacers, she had only a rudimentary understanding of what hyperspace was and how it worked.

"So, explain again why you can't just fly there. Earth is the home world. How can it possibly be lost?"

That provoked a laugh from Lara, causing Merwith to look at her sharply.

"That, Mer, is the most insightful question I've heard this year and one I would really like someone to answer."

#

Chapter 12

The meeting at the Institute of Knowledge took place in the large auditorium on the ground floor. Lara arrived with Nal twenty minutes before the scheduled start time. Both wore their Institute uniforms to stand out in the crowd.

There were two hundred attendees milling about in the spacious atrium, sipping various beverages, and snacking on the finger food of a dozen different worlds.

Forast Rob Somace, Institute Administrator, saw them across the room as they entered and hurried toward them.

"Welcome," he boomed as he intercepted them. "I was worried that something had held you up. Did you have a good trip, Shipmaster?"

She nodded. "Long, but comfortable, Administrator."

Somace turned to Nal. "I understand that you have accepted our offer, Submaster."

"I have, Administrator. My domestic affairs are in order and I'm ready to turn my full attention to getting *Fire* ready for hyperspace."

"Excellent. That takes one worry off my to-do list. We have been putting together the rest of your crew. I will introduce you after the morning session, which I think you will find informative. Where are you staying?"

"The Excelsior," Lara replied.

"With my ortho-wife," Nal answered.

"We have a rather full social schedule planned for the evenings all week. I hope the two of you will be available. There are Morast government functionaries to be charmed, you know."

"Trouble with the government?" Lara asked.

"Nothing that cannot be managed. There are always those whose sphincters tighten when credit is being spent. Thank God they do not know the total cost and will not until after you are long gone.

"Well, I see people I need to speak to. Get some refreshments. You will find your seats in the front row. Can't miss them."

With that he hurried off into the crowd.

They took his advice and loaded plates and drinking containers and headed into the auditorium.

As the administrator had said, their chairs were easy to find. They were marked with their names in glowing letters. Both put the refreshments down on a shared table, then took their seats.

The rows behind filled quickly and five minutes later, Esdrith Ssalto, Darin Mastlin, and Betrice Flangan sat down to their right. A short, round woman with slanted eyes was with them. Mastlin introduced her as Galactician Teodara Voxman from Invorna, a planet in the Descardan Alliance. Lara had heard of it, but never visited.

The introductions were barely over when Administrator Somace appeared on the stage and walked to the lectern.

"Come to order, please," his amplified voice lofted across the crowd. "We have a great deal to do this week and very little time to waste."

He waited for the noise to subside, then continued:

"Welcome to the Planning Session for the Earth Expedition. I would first like to recognize two people who have made this possible. Lara, Nal, please stand."

Somace waved them to their feet. They both stood and faced the crowd.

The Administrator continued: "Shipmaster Larath da Benthar Sims and Submaster Nalwith Taryn of the Institute Research Vessel *Coronal Fire*. It is they who first detected the lost colony ship *New Hope* and had the foresight to go look at what they had discovered."

They returned to their seats while Somace gave a brief account of their two explorations. He ended with, "...and among the wonders discovered was this..."

A holo image formed above the administrator's head. The image was that of *The Sun, the Moon, and the Stars*.

"Citizens, this is an actual book from Earth. It was printed before man walked on Earth's Moon, and in the back..." The image expanded to show the star map. "...We have a map of the heavens as viewed from the surface of the home world.

"To explain the significance, I would like to introduce Scholar Teodara Voxman from the Institute Branch on Invorna." He waved to the woman and said, "Teodara, the podium is yours."

The scholar got to her feet and climbed the stairs to the stage. She stood behind the lectern and waited for the prompters to adjust to her height. Above her, the image expanded to show a view of the galaxy that extended from one side of the stage to the other.

"Good morning," she said in her musical accent. "I hope you can all understand me. If I become unintelligible, just shout out and I will try to enunciate more clearly.

"I have been asked to give an overview of the coming voyage. However, before I put you to sleep with my star maps, let me satisfy your curiosity. Most people express the question thus: 'How is it possible that we have forgotten the location of the most important star and planet in the galaxy?'"

She paused and let her eyes scan the audience for a dozen seconds. When she continued, her voice boomed:

"We didn't forget it. The inhabitants of Earth intentionally hid their star from us over 700 years ago."

#

The noise level in the hall spiked. Scholar Voxman waited for the return of silence. When it did, she continued.

"To understand the situation, I must educate you in some of the basics of galactography." She willed a new image to appear overhead. "Here you see a computer-generated view of our galaxy. Obviously, since no one has ever left it, we do not have an actual picture to show you.

"The galaxy consists of a flat spinning disk of stars marked by spiral arms, and a central bulge. The disk is one hundred thousand light-years in diameter and about a thousand light-years thick. The bulge measures ten thousand light-years across. The whole assemblage contains 250 billion stars."

The view changed to show a night sky bisected by a glowing river of light. "This is the way the galaxy looks from within. It is the same view on Bernau as it is on Earth. Only the band's angle to the horizon differs. That is dependent on the orientation of a planet's poles to the plane of the galaxy."

She changed the picture again. This time, it showed the swirl of stars from above.

"The center of the galaxy is home to a 4-million-Solar-mass black hole. The bulge includes two bars: one inside the other. The four spiral arms emanate from the ends of these bars. The ancients named the arms based on the constellations through which they appeared to pass in the night sky of Earth. We have shortened the names to Norma, Scutum, Perseus, and Sagittarius.

"I draw your attention to this small structure between the Sagittarius and Perseus Arms…" As she spoke, the scholar turned a strand of stars gold. "… this is the Orion Arm. It is of interest to us because that is where we all live.

"Human space is largely coincident with the Orion Arm. It measures ten thousand light-years long, five thousand wide, one thousand deep; and encompasses about 140 million stars, of which twenty-five thousand host human colonies. Morast is four thousand light-years to the east of where we believe Earth to be.

"People once thought the spiral arms were filled with stars while the intervening regions were voids. This is not true. These prominent spiral features are a bit of an optical illusion. They form due to compression waves traveling through the cosmic gas and dust. These waves compress the interstellar medium and trigger the birth of new stars.

"These young stars are energetic Spectral Class O and B… what we call the 'big blue bruisers'. They are profligate and short-lived. Most burn their available fuel in a few million years. However, while they last, they light up the neighborhood and produce the distinctive spiral shape you see here.

"Despite the illusion, star density is the same in the dark regions as the bright. The spaces between the arms are darker because the stars there are older and less luminous than the young spendthrifts in the arms, i.e., they are about as bright as Morast and Sol."

She changed images again. Now the overhead view was filled with golden stars in a gently sloped arc. At the midpoint, a red sphere covered twenty percent of the arc's width.

"The red circle represents the volume in which your calculations place the Earth. However, legend holds that Sol lies nearer the inner edge of the Orion Arm. You may want to consider adjusting your aim.

"Now, with the astrography of human space in mind, I will explain how it is that we misplaced Sol's coordinates."

. #

Teodora Voxman reached under the podium and extracted a glass filled with amber liquid. She lifted it to her lips, sniffed it, and sipped. The *fora juice* in the cup was obviously foreign to her. As she returned the glass to the lectern shelf, the corners of her mouth curved upward into a hint of a smile. She looked once again at the audience and continued.

"As we all learned in our history lessons, humanity's first interstellar colony was founded in 2610 Old Calendar, on Salvation, fifth world of the 82 Eridani system. By 3100, there were a thousand thriving colonies. These were organized into the fabled Confederation of Stars.

"The Confed wasn't a government, per se. It was a mutual aid society. Its responsibilities were to keep the peace and do the things individual worlds could not do for themselves. They ran the Stellar Survey, for instance. The survey visited Sol-like stars, and when they found a habitable world, mapped the underlying hyperspace flows to open the new world for colonization.

"The Survey's Cartography Service maintained the master files of hyperspace survey information. They updated this database continuously, but only distributed new master editions once per standard decade. Interested parties could buy interim updates for a fee whenever they felt the expenditure was justified.

"As the number of colonies mushroomed, keeping everyone's hyperspace data synchronized proved to be daunting. Updates were sent to sector capitals, which in turn sent them to the various star nations.

"Toward the end of the Confed, it could take twenty years for news of a newly discovered system to percolate out here to the Periphery. And, as we all know from history, that was merely a symptom of the overall problem, which was that human space had outgrown the ability of any central authority to keep the peace.

"The First War of Secession began with the Soldant Collective's attack on Earth in 3510. The Terrestrial Navy beat off the attack, but with significant losses, including the destruction of several cities.

"That first attack highlighted Earth's vulnerability. So, in addition to fortifying the Solar System, the Confed came up with a scheme to hide Earth from everyone beyond visual range. They set up what they called an 'Exclusion Zone'. Inside that zone, they simply removed the coordinates of Sol and about fifty other stars from the master data files. They also seeded the control software with instructions to erase the coordinates from other databases if that information had not been accessed for five years. Slowly, imperceptibly, the knowledge of where to find Sol disappeared from public view.

"And thus, on every world that did not trade directly with Earth, the knowledge of where Sol was located ceased to exist."

#

Scholar Voxman looked down at the prompters and said, "That is my introductory section. Next, we will review the route *Coronal Fire* will be taking during its four-year voyage. Before we get into the details, are there any questions?"

Several hands shot up.

"Yes, the citizen in the third row on the right."

A rotund man rose to his feet and said, "There must have been thousands of references to Sol's position. How could they have erased all of them?"

"They didn't," the scholar replied. "They erased the most obvious places where such data are stored. The rest of the data was lost during the wars. Enemy information nets were the first things targeted by attacking starships. It did not take many bombs to disrupt even the most robust planetary infonet. Later, the survivors were too busy feeding themselves to repair the technology. Without operative self-repair circuits, quantum effects made the contents of the archives useless after a few decades.

A woman stood and asked, "What about the effort to read *New Hope*'s computers? Surely they had astrogational data in them."

Teodora Voxman looked at Darin Mastlin and said, "Perhaps you should answer that question, Team Leader."

Mastlin got to his feet and turned to face the questioner.

"The computers are very damaged from hyperon erosion, but even if we gain access to that information, it will do us little good. At the time of *New Hope*'s launch, they were still using Sol-centric star maps."

The questioner looked blank. "I'm afraid I don't understand."

"Originally, astronomy used Sol as the coordinate origin, not the black hole at the galaxy's center. If we salvage any star positions from the wreck, we will discover that Sol can be found at zero, zero, zero."

Darin Mastlin took his seat and the scholar regained control of the room. She said, "I have spent my professional life looking for those missing coordinates and have been unsuccessful. I believe that this expedition is our best chance to regain them.

"That is why I am here, and why I will be joining the expedition to find lost Earth."

#

Chapter 13

The meeting to introduce Lara and Nal to their crew did not take place that afternoon. Something came up to distract Administrator Somace and he sent word that introductions would be postponed for a few days.

With that, the two current members of *Fire*'s crew plunged into the business of the conference. Mostly the activity consisted of panels of experts arguing over how to go about finding Earth once they reached the search zone. The controlled chaos reminded Lara of the frantic efforts to prepare *Fire* for the second expedition to *New Hope*.

At night, as promised, there were cocktail parties and dinners with long speeches. There they met members of the Coordinate's Executive Council. Most of the councilors wanted to know more about the dead ship.

One councilor, Velost Yadman, was more interested in what modifications the Navy was making to *Fire*. Nal Taryn claimed ignorance and kept his comments general. Lara, however, had to fall back on saying that she had not been authorized by the Navy to speak on the subject. She limited her responses to vague references to improved hyperon detectors and other enhancements to aid in the search once they reached the Core.

Despite their evasiveness, Yadman seemed to have a good idea what the Navy was doing and how much it cost. His insistence that they confirm his suspicions seemed to be aimed at gaining political fodder for the next election.

It was not until the fourth day, just at first sunset, that the promised meeting took place. Both Lara and Nal received invites via implant to travel to the opposite end of Capital to a satellite Institute facility.

Esdrith Ssalto was present on the landing stage as their air taxi grounded on the roof of a four-story building in a suburban part of the city.

101

"Welcome Lara, Nal," Esdrith said as they disembarked. "Administrator Somace sends his apologies for his absence. He asked me to host. We chose this venue to get away from the bustle of the main conference. Also, Councilor Yadman would have insisted on joining us if he knew we were meeting."

"Apparently, solving the fertility problem is not first on Yardman's priorities," Lara said.

Esdrith laughed. "Councilor Yardman is neutral on the subject. He wants to be Prime Councilor. I do not think the eventual extinction of humanity would bother him overly so long as it advanced his near-term ambitions.

"But enough talk of politicians. Let us meet the members of your team. Should you find any unacceptable; we will, of course, find substitutes."

She led them to a grav shaft, and they descended to a sub-basement conference room where sixty people waited. They were arrayed in four rows of long tables. The ratio of sexes was relatively balanced, as were the blue-and-green uniforms of the Institute and the black-and-silver of the Morast Coordinate Navy.

A dais with a table had been set up at the front of the room. There were four chairs behind the table, of which one was already occupied. Teodara Voxman stood as Lara, Nal, and Esdreth mounted the dais. She faced Lara, put her hands together, and bowed.

"Good to see you again, Shipmaster."

Lara returned the bow. "And you, Scholar. I didn't get a chance to welcome you aboard after your presentation."

"It's good to be welcomed," the scholar said. "Visiting Earth has been a dream of mine since I was a child. And, please, call me Teo."

"I'm Lara to my friends.'

Teodara next greeted Nal and then all of them took their places. Infonet cubes in front of each seat listed the meeting attendees. They were arrayed on a grid sorted by function and currently grayed out.

"All right," Esdrith said, "I call this meeting to order. Everyone please sign in."

There was a flurry of activity and each name brightened as the owner acknowledged his or her presence.

"We'll start with your Second Officer," Esdrith announced. "Athald, please introduce yourself."

A muscled man stood and bowed. He had a strip of black hair that ran back along what was otherwise a bald scalp. "Good day, Shipmaster. I am Athald Daver, late of the Coordinate Navy. I have twenty years of experience. I have commanded patrol craft and medium warcraft and acted as executive officer aboard biastships. You will find my personnel records on file to study at your leisure."

Lara laughed. "Leisure, what's that?"

Daver smiled and turned to the diminutive woman beside him.

"May I introduce Doria Teray, candidate for Third Officer. She and I have served together off and on for the last ten years. She is good people."

The woman stood and gave her background. She was from Gagarin, a world at the far end of the Coordinate. From her skin tone and slanted eyes, her colony owed a great deal to the inhabitants of Old Asia on Earth.

The introductions continued. Each candidate stood, gave their name and planet of origin, and summarized their service record. Simultaneously, Lara's implant delivered the name and a short biography to her consciousness. The problem was that there were so many of them, that she quickly lost track of who was who.

From the screen's Table of Organization, she could see that there were three astrogators, three engineers, three cyberneticists, and twelve spacers who would serve directly under her. The Navy people would have their own commander. Included were twelve naval officers and ratings (scout boat pilots and weapons specialists), two Marine officers, and a dozen Space Marines.

When the marathon introductions were finished, she gave a short speech of welcome and assured them that she would learn their names and review their service records as quickly as possible.

"We'll spend as much time together over the next few weeks as work Permits. We need to get to know one another."

#

Three months later, with *Coronal Fire* out of the construction dock and back at Saban-Seven, Lara had no difficulty remembering the names of the fifty-nine candidates she had met that first day.

Nor were they the last new recruits. In the interim, twenty-one other crewmembers had signed on to the expedition, including a doctor and two med-techs. This brought the ship's company to eighty-two. Nor was that everyone who would be journeying to the core, or even a majority.

The expedition's organization consisted of three functional groups:

Darin Mastlin would be in overall command, with Betrice Flangan as his assistant. The two of them would also command the Institute personnel, of which there would be one hundred and fifty.

Ship's personnel would serve under Lara and Nal, and Navy personnel would be commanded by Senior Legate Bas Klyster. The three-person medical staff would nominally be under Lara's command, but would have considerable autonomy. Barring some disaster, their primary duty would be getting everyone into long sleep at the start of the voyage, and out again when they reached the Core.

To accommodate the members of the expedition, two of *Fire*'s four auxiliary holds had been converted to house hibernation tanks. The other two volumes held provisions and spare parts. That part of *Fire*'s main hold not devoted to weaponry, had been filled with habitat modules and supplemental environmental control systems.

Once decanted from cold sleep, each crewmember would have their own compact quarters. Public spaces for dining and recreation were filled with amenities. Diversions would be as essential as provisions for a voyage of this duration. An 8-bed hospital module had completed the ship's new habitat additions.

Even *Cor* would have a backup. For safety, the weapons and tracking computer was housed in an armored space as far from *Cor* as possible.

A crew of six would stand watch for the entire outbound voyage. A command officer (Lara, Nal, Athald Daver, or Doria Teray) would take the duty in rotation. The duty roster would be filled out by an astrogator, a weaponeer, a Marine, and two crewmembers. Barring an emergency, most of these would spend their waking hours learning various aspects of ship operation and their initial sleeping hours under mnemonic training helmets.

Each watch stander would serve for six months before being

relieved. Personnel rotations would be staggered such that fresh faces appeared every sixty days. This would provide overlap and alleviate tensions and boredom.

The goal was to ensure that no member of the crew devoted more than a single year of lifespan to reaching the core stars. Once they arrived, everyone would be revived and the search for Earth would begin in earnest.

#

Lara was in *Fire*'s control room. The view volume showed an image of blackness with a single bright star in the center and the customary sprinkling of background stars around it.

The bright star was Morast.

They had left Bernau orbit in a hurry ten days earlier.

The opposition coalition in the Ruling Council had finally cobbled together enough votes to demand a briefing on all aspects of the Earth Expedition. The ruling party agreed to provide such, along with a full accounting of the costs, but scheduled it for the week following the two-week solstice break. What the opposition did not know was that the ruling party planned to have *Coronal Fire* safely in hyperspace by then.

Those final days had been the most frantic Lara could remember. They were still loading cargo when the medical team began putting passengers into hibernation chambers.

Fire departed Saban-Seven with all the Institute personnel and most of the spacers and military contingent in cold sleep tanks for the four-year voyage.

The only person still awake that was not assigned to the first duty crew, was Lara herself. In truth, she was not looking forward to going into the tank at all.

"We are ready to jump, Shipmaster," *Cor* said in her brain.

"Everyone else ready?" she asked.

Six affirmative responses came back to her at the speed of thought.

"Very well. *Cor*, jump when ready."

There was a change in the vibration of the ship that was more sensed than felt as the jump charge began building on *Fire*'s hull.

Lara watched the screen. One moment, Morast dominated the

scene. The next, there was nothing but stygian blackness. It was as though someone had thrown a switch to turn off the universe... which someone had.

A second later, the view switched from the hull camera to a schematic of the *Fire*'s surroundings. The blackness faded, to be replaced by a scintillating light blue fog. There was no perceptible pattern to the flow of *ftl* particles. This was the 'thermal' zone of hyperspace, a layer where hyperons moved only slightly faster than the speed of light, and energy content was barely detectable.

This was the 'null' layer.

"Starting upfreq to ten lights," *Cor* announced. "Projected time to target pseudo-velocity: thirty minutes."

Over the next half hour, the featureless haze slowly gave way to a broad glowing river of cyan. The river flowed in a direction that would carry them in the opposite direction of the Kaligani Narrows.

The flight plan called for them to remain at ten-lights for another twelve hours. At that time, they would reach a region of hyperspace where they could transfer to a high energy stream flowing in the general direction of the core stars.

At Teodora Voxman's suggestion, they had adjusted their target point closer to the inner edge of the Orion Arm, where legend claimed that Sol was located.

More than one scientist had commented on the absurdity of relying on a juvenile astronomy book and an ancient legend to direct the expedition to its destination. Unfortunately, they had nothing better to offer.

"It's time, Shipmaster," *Cor* announced.

Lara sighed. She had been dreading this moment.

"All right. Get Nal up here from Engineering. I'll relinquish command."

"I'm already here," Nal's baritone voice boomed from behind her.

Lara rose from the couch.

"I relieve you, Shipmaster," he said formally.

"I stand relieved," she responded.

For long seconds, they stood close and looked into one another's eyes. Then he swept her into his arms and kissed her. "See you in six months, darling. Want me to come down and hold your hand?"

Nal was aware of her antipathy toward hibernation tanks and the reason for it. He had suggested that she take a sedative to calm her nerves. She refused. All life processes were in stasis while one was in the tank. If she took a pill and was then awakened to handle an emergency, she would be muzzy for however long the dose lasted.

Her inner turmoil was calmed by the sensation of his strong arms enveloping her. The only problem was that she could not tuck her head into his shoulder. The difference in their heights made the position too awkward.

They stood there for long minutes. Finally, she signaled him to release her."

"Thank you. That helped."

"When you wake, I will show you a night you won't forget."

"Better than last night?"

"Infinitely."

"I'll hold you to it. Goodbye for now, my love."

With that, she left the control room and headed to where she had left her mirrored coffin.

#

Chapter 14

Lara was cold.

She had been cold for what seemed an eternity as consciousness slowly returned. Unlike the first time she woke, she was at once aware of her surroundings.

This was not the first time. It was the third... no, the fourth.

\#

The first time Lara had shivered in her hibernation tank, Nal was there to greet her. When she opened her eyes, she could just make out a hazy dark splotch with white eyes and even whiter teeth grinning down at her through the frosted-over view window.

After an interminable time that was less than five minutes, she regained full consciousness and palmed the release control under her right hand. The action caused the various tubes attached to her body to retract and produced a loud hissing sound that made her ears pop. Silently, the tank's translucent cover retracted into its recess, revealing her nakedness.

Strong hands reached in and helped her to sit up.

"Welcome back, darling." The words came from far away. Then there was the sensation of warm lips against her cold ones.

"How long?" she managed to croak.

"Six months, right on schedule. Today is Mission Day 196."

"Where are we?"

"Just leaving the Salton Republic and about at the end of our charts."

"Any problems?"

"A few, but nothing that can't wait. Come, let us get you a hot shower, then a light snack. I'll tell you all about it."

And he had. The first half year had been trouble-free. *Cor* greeted her as she ate and gave her a rundown on the condition of the ship. The computer was delighted with her new sensors and had been surveying hyperspace independently of the astrogation routines. She compared the readings she was getting with those in the astrofile, practicing for the time when she would have to do it for real.

Cor had also made a friend. She and the tactical computer were sharing the workload, both for cross-training and just to keep their intellects engaged. The tactical computer was named Tac Seven, after its model number.

A week after Lara came out of her hibernation tank, Nal went into his. The long sleep tanks were reflective cylinders three-meters-long by one-and-half in diameter. Their lids were frosted transparencies everywhere save for the transparent window at the occupant's head.

Unlike the passengers' tanks, the long sleep units for the duty crew were in Fire's old passenger quarters to supply easy access.

Lara's first six-month stint awake proved interesting and challenging. They ran out of mapped hyperspace in the second week after her revival and quickly fell into the routine of a survey ship. Cor and Tac-7 scouted ahead on their course to the maximum range of their instruments, looking for gravity flaws and other hazards. When they found one, they plotted a way around the danger rather than taking the time to find a path under it by dropping to a lower energy layer.

On the first day of each month, they interrupted their routine to drop through null and plot their position in the real universe. While in deep interstellar space, they scanned their surroundings and searched for artificial EM radiation. During Lara's tour of duty, they detected three human-occupied planets. Two were within one hundred light-years of their breakout point, and the third was at the very edge of detection by the EM sniffer.

At the official one-year mark of the voyage, the six crewmembers currently awake held a celebration. They then decanted four replacement personnel (two of the current duty crew still had months to serve). Lara's replacement was Athald Daver.

She spent a week orienting him to his duties before once again returning to her own hibernation tank.

#

During her second resurrection, she returned to consciousness more quickly than the first. She was surprised that Nal was not present to greet her. Her confusion quickly turned to alarm when she saw Doria Teray's face gazing at her through the tank window.

Had something happened to Nal?

She palmed the release control and struggled to sit up.

"Where's Nal?" She had meant to shout it, but barely managed a hoarse whisper.

"Sleeping, Shipmaster," Doria replied. "We have a problem. Today is Mission Day 630. *Cor* suggested we wake you."

The problem turned out to be the largest gravity flaw Lara had ever seen. When she was helped to the control center, she found half the duty crew there. The view volume showed a solid wall of angry red storm clouds that extended to the limits of detection in every direction.

The ship was still in the thousand-light layer. They would soon be forced to slow down or change course to keep from entering the turbulence.

"What is this, *Cor*?"

"Records speak of a 'Great Wall Hyperspace Fold' between the Core and the Eastern Periphery. This may be that. Great Walls are produced when two super-massive black holes coincide in adjacent universes. Their combined gravitational energy is strong enough to scramble hyperon motion, producing a linear flaw."

"There must be a way under it or around it. Otherwise, the Eastern Periphery would never have been colonized."

"It can't extend all the way to null," *Cor* responded. "The gravitational energy is too dissipated at lower levels to produce the sort of turbulence we are seeing."

"Then we will treat it like any other flaw," Lara said. "We'll drop down through null and find out where we are in normal space. En route, we will observe this monster. Hopefully, it will dissipate at some pseudovelocity high enough that we won't die of old age getting around it."

The descent to null took two days. It was not until the 200-light level that the barrier showed signs of breaking up. After noting their position in normal space, they reentered hyperspace and used the 190 equivalent light speed layer to burrow under the Great Wall Fold. It took six weeks to reach the other side.

#

The third time she woke, Nal had been there to greet her. They renewed their marriage nightly for a week before he went back into hibernation. Her six-month stint proved uneventful. She returned to the tank on Mission Day 1260.

And now she was being roused for the fourth time. What had gone wrong?

#

The sensations of being revived from hibernation had become familiar through repetition. She felt as though she was floating in mid-air, a sensation that had previously escaped her notice. The sensation was real. The tank's nullgrav circuitry kept her suspended in mid-tank to prevent her skin from being damaged by laying too long in a single position. That was one of the improvements since *New Hope*'s time. The colony ship had not needed it because the ship had been in microgravity.

The second sensation was that of her body warming as consciousness returned. The mechanism that applied full-body heat was a distant descendant of the ancient microwave oven.

The face staring down through the view window was once again that of Doria Teray.

She would have groaned but did not have the energy. She reached out, felt around for the release control, and pressed it. The first thing that happened was that the tank's nullgrav shut off and the ship's gravity took over. Her body sank into the soft padding that lined the tank interior. This was followed by the sound of hissing air that made her ears pop. The tank lid then slid silently into its recess.

"What is it this time?" she managed to croak.

"Nothing, shipmaster. We're almost there."

"Almost where?"

"We have reached the Core and will hit our target in another week. We are waking up the whole crew to be ready when we drop through null."

Lara inhaled deeply of the oxygen rich air and suffered a fit of coughing. Doria helped her to sit up as it subsided.

"What day is it?"

"Mission Day 1482."

"We made it?" Lara asked.

"Just about. Let us get you out of here, warmed up, and back on duty."

#

Coronal Fire seemed crowded.

During two six-month stints and an emergency six weeks of rattling around in the ship's inhabited spaces with only five other faces to look at, Lara felt minorly claustrophobic with two dozen duty personnel awake. What would it be like when all 232 expedition members were revived?

The decantings had taken four days before everyone was ready for duty. The next two days were spent checking over the ship's readiness to begin her real mission. Both *Cor* and *Tac Seven* reported all systems operational, but human beings insist on seeing things for themselves.

Now, on the seventh day (Mission Day 1491), the ship was as ready as it would ever be. All stations were manned, all sensors active, all weapons systems energized and ready to scan and fire. The countdown clock suspended in the view space counted down toward T-4.00 hours while Lara and Athald Daver sat in their couches and watched the glowing red numbers.

Just as the numerals changed to 4:00, *Cor* announced over the annunciator that it was time.

"All personnel, report readiness for downfreq."

The reports came in via implant. First Nal Taryn, then Doria Teray from Engineering, then Astrogation, Weapons Control, Marines, and each individual spacer.

When the last crewman had been heard from, Lara told *Cor*, "You may begin our descent."

"Descent beginning now," the computer replied.

For the next four hours, the ship drifted slowly downward through the various energy levels. Since hyperspace is the very definition of 'pitch black,' there was nothing to see save a slow evolution of the pattern of schematicized hyperon flows in the view volume.

Finally, they entered the thermal zone, where organized hyperon flows ceased, and everything faded into the general background fog.

"Ready to return to normal space," *Cor* announced.

They went through the roll call once again. The tension was palpable as the crewmembers answered 'ready' one by one.

Finally, Lara commanded, "Drop us through null, *Cor*."

"Dropping now."

The viewscreen turned black as *Cor* switched to a hull camera. It stayed that way for a minute. Then, without sensation, the stars reappeared around them.

After four years in transit, they had finally reached the Core.

#

PART TWO

INIS-AFALLON

Chapter 15

"Get me a circumambient sweep. All sensors."

"Sweeping, Shipmaster," *Cor* replied.

The sensor sweep was to discover exactly where they had popped out in normal space. They should be 4000 light-years from Morast but knowing the precise location would help them plan their next move.

The primary scan was a telescopic view of surrounding space. Millions of stars swept through the view volume at breakneck speed. It took half an hour to complete the scan of the surrounding stars.

Both sentient computers began looking for something familiar in the data. The first task was to orient themselves with respect to the rest of the galaxy. Since the inside view of the galactic disk known as the 'Milky Way' looks much the same everywhere, finding the galactic equator was easy. Once the river of stars was plotted, finding the galaxy's center had been equally simple.

All they had to do was look for the black hole that lay at the center of the galactic bulge.

#

It had come as a surprise to the early astronomers when they discovered an exceptionally large black hole at the center of the galaxy. Nor was humanity's galaxy unique in this respect. Virtually all large galaxies had an oversize monster hole at their hearts. These holes were dubbed 'Supermassive Black Holes' or SMBHs and ranged from hundreds-of-thousands of times the mass of Sol up to tens-of-billions times. The Milky Way's SMBH was on the lower end of the scale for such objects, coming in at a *mere* 4 million solar masses.

The existence of these points of infinite density at the hearts of galaxies explained several things that had previously been mysteries. For one, the mass of the central black hole defines the mass of any spiral galaxy's central bulge. It also controls the velocities at which stars near a galaxy's rim orbit the central mass.

This latter observation was the first clue that gravitational energy leaks from one universe to another, crossing hyperspace in transit.

#

Once *Cor* spotted the bright radio source that marked the center of the home galaxy, it would seem (to a non-astronomer) a simple matter to locate the eight stars that formed the constellation of Sagittarius in Earth's sky.

Unfortunately, life was not that simple.

A significant percentage of classical star names were derived from an ancient language called Arabic. And while the pre-Islam Arabs were excellent astronomers — given their clear skies and dark nights — many of these names actually originated with a second century[OC] Greek astronomer named Claudius Ptolemy of Alexandria. Ptolemy compiled a list of 1,025 stars and published them in his astronomical treatise, *Almagest*. Ptolemy's star names were transliterated in the eighth century when his book was translated from Greek into Arabic. In the twelfth century, the book found its way to Europe, with the stars' Arabic names kept when the book was translated again.

Because they spent many of their nights gazing up at the stars, the ancients imagined a whole menagerie of mythical men and beasts in the sky. In the case of Sagittarius, they saw an archer.

But the night sky of Earth is only black because stars dimmer than Magnitude 6 are invisible to the naked eye, especially when that eye is at the bottom of a planetary atmosphere.

Coronal Fire's sensors were able to see stars down to Magnitude 30. This meant that the classical stars that make up the Constellation of Sagittarius were drowned out by tens-of-thousands of their dimmer brethren in *Cor*'s scans.

To cut the clutter, the computers cleaned their data of these dimmer stars in a series of steps. After each iteration they looked for any pattern that might match one of Earth's constellations. Even a badly distorted arrangement, once recognized, would supply a clue to the direction in which they should search for the Mother of Men. Finding two or three constellations would practically pinpoint the home system for them.

The computers simultaneously worked on the problem of

finding the ship's position by scanning for beacon stars. These were the big blue bruisers visible across hundreds of thousands of light-years. The EM sniffer antenna was deployed to listen for electromagnetic spillage from human-occupied worlds.

While the computers worked, Lara and the duty crew set about decanting the rest of the expedition. Even though the revival process was fully automated, newly awakened sleepers still required care and feeding for at least a day after revival.

After two thousand years of advances in hibernation technology, the process was safer than travel via poligrav; but there was still the possibility of a medical emergency upon waking. For that reason, they could only process six people at one time.

With a round-the-clock effort by three rotating revival teams, the last sleeper was finally awakened on Mission Day 1506.

#

A month later, conditions aboard ship were as crowded and chaotic as Lara had feared. The long months in a nearly empty ship had conditioned her to appreciate having substantial living space to herself. With everyone awake, there were traffic jams in the corridors, assigned times for meals, and the stink of too many people in too little space. She half-expected to wake up some morning to find an elbow other than Nal's stuck in her eye.

She had to admit, however, that things were getting better of late. After a month awake, everyone had settled into their routines. Most of the scientists were deep into their assigned studies, with little time for activities guaranteed to irritate the shipmaster.

Once each week, Darin Mastlin held a status meeting with the heads of the study groups. Lara was also invited. The meeting took place in the dining module between first and second meals.

Lara arrived late and threaded her way through the crowded compartment to sit down next to Mastlin. Scholar Aavrom Pelot, of the EM Sniffer Team, was speaking. Pelot's specialty was Earth's culture and history just prior to the Age of Chaos, which made him a good man to evaluate distant contacts.

"We've had two solid contacts, and possibly another very long range one. The first is a planet only thirty light-years from here. Their signal is weak, but readable. The source is a single point, presumably the system's inhabited world. Either they are communicating by narrow beam, or else they have lost their access to space."

"How can that be?" Mastlin asked. "You aren't suggesting that you've found aliens, are you?"

"No, of course not."

Long before *ftl* travel, people wondered if there were intelligent aliens out among the stars. The wondering became more intense when early explorers discovered that terrestrial worlds are common throughout the galaxy. One out of every 500 stars has a potentially Earth-like world in orbit about it (with "potentially" being the operative word). That equates to 400 million habitable worlds in the galaxy.

Yet, no planet had ever been discovered that was home to intelligent aliens. Most experts assumed the sheer scale of the galaxy meant that there were other space-faring species within the Milky Way, but also precluded humanity from ever running into their neighbors.

At the dawn of the Age of Chaos, there had been twenty-five thousand human-occupied worlds in human space. These were spread across the Orion Arm, with its stellar population of 140 million. That impressive number is dwarfed by the 250 billion stars in the galaxy.

Thus, starships had explored barely two-hundredths of one percent of the stars in the Orion Arm, or thirteen-millionths of a percent of those in the galaxy. It was numbers like these that made the possibility of First Contact unlikely in the extreme.

"They are human all right," Pelot continued. "From what few voice-communications we have intercepted, they speak a corrupt form of Standard. They may not have recovered from the Secession Wars."

"And the other strong contact?"

"Its energy output is dramatically higher than the first system, but the distance makes it difficult to separate individual signals."

Mastlin turned next to Teodara Voxman. "How is our map of the core stars coming, Scholar?"

She shrugged. "The same as last week. We are overwhelmed by the number of the M-Class dwarfs that clutter the universe. We have had *Tac Seven* build us a three-dimensional model of all the F,

G, and K stars in the neighborhood. For that we have Shipmaster Sims to thank."

Two weeks earlier, the astronomers had asked Lara to move the ship at least five light-years to give them a long enough parallax baseline to gain a three-dimensional view of their surroundings. Having gotten the expedition to the Core, Lara viewed her job as being the scientists' taxi service. It had taken half-a-day to return to the thousand-light hyperon stream, two days to journey five light-years, then another half-day to drop back down through null.

Upon breakout, *Cor* ran a second circumambient scan and the two sets of observations allowed the computers to place each star within three-dimensional space.

The winnowing process involved cutting out all stellar systems unsuitable for colonization. Sol is a G2 yellow dwarf and Morast an F8 yellow-white dwarf. Since terrestrial planets are plentiful in the universe, the old Stellar Survey had been picky about choosing potential colonies, exploring only F, G, and K stars.

After Astronomy, Mastlin asked each working group leader to report status. When he had run through the last of them, he returned to Scholar Pelot.

"So, is there anything to recommend either of our two good contacts?" he asked.

Sylvan Reno, one of the Institute astronomers, said, "The far one, of course. They are at a higher technological level and will have better astronomical records."

Lara cleared her throat.

Mastlin turned to her. "Yes, Shipmaster?"

"It's not my specialty, but I think the nearer one would be a better choice."

"Why?"

"If they have lost space travel, there is nothing they can do to endanger the ship. That makes it a good system in which to find out the situation here in the Core before we go blundering about."

It took longer than it should have, but eventually, they decided to follow Lara's suggestion. The planet thirty light-years distant would be their first point of contact.

#

Chapter 16

The star's name was *Inis Afalon* and its inhabited planet, *Monmoth. Cor* found an ancient legend in her data that might be the source of the names. If so, whoever had first colonized this system could have come from the legendary island of Britain.

The star was a G0 dwarf and slightly larger than Morast. It had at least seven planets, two of them gas giants with prominent rings. The inhabited world was the fourth out from the star and orbited in the outer third of the temperate zone. It lacked any sort of moon, at least one large enough to be seen from the edge of the system. That might not be a handicap. The system was a dozen light-years from a large gas nebula. In the planet's night sky, it shed as much light as Earth's Luna.

The world was a cold place, with smaller seas than Bernau. That fact could be related to the quantity of ice they could see on the surface.

A green belt extended thirty degrees north and south of the planet's equator, but everywhere else was solid white. It was difficult to assess the thickness of the ice from half-a-system away, but views of the planet showed prominent shadows at the terminator. *Cor*'s estimate was that they were looking at klamaters-thick glaciers.

The scans also revealed that Monmoth had once been home to a vigorous interplanetary civilization. The planet was orbited by many objects, some of which were mega-structures. A few were larger than *New Hope*. However, neutrino detectors found no active energy sources among them. Indeed, they showed none on the planet either.

That would seem to place the current level of Afalonian civilization at the pre-atomic level. They had some technology, as shown by their radio broadcasts, but only a rudimentary spacefaring capability, if that.

Nor was the reason for their technological backslide difficult to divine. There were many circular features visible from space across the greenbelt, evidence of massive fusion explosions. There were other traces on the ice, craters left by deep subterranean bursts in bedrock. Most of these had flat bottoms, indicating they had partially filled with water before freezing solid.

#

The leaders of the expedition met in Lara's sanctum off the control room. There was barely enough room for eight of them. In attendance were Lara, Nal, Darin Mastlin, Betrice Flangan, Teodara Voxman, Avram Pelot, Legate Bas Klyster, and Dr. Moham bin Sool.

"Well, where do we explore first?" Betrice asked. "The orbital installations may tell us what happened here, but our mission is to seek Earth and to collect biological samples. That requires us to contact the planet directly."

Long hours of discussions had gone into working out a protocol for first contact. An important mission datum was a genetic analysis of the people they met. Theoretically, the closer they came to the home star, the more Earthlike that world's pool of DNA.

That theory rested on several unproved assumptions, including the supposition that the earliest colony worlds had been chosen for their Earthlike qualities. At the time, genetic manipulation was in its infancy and would therefore bypass any world that required colonist modification.

They planned to test that supposition by sampling as much DNA as possible on each world they visited. Dr. bin Sool had been recruited because of his expertise in genetics, as well as his medical abilities.

"I vote for at least a cursory exploration of one or two of the larger orbital structures," Teodara Voxman said. "There may still be astronomical records there."

"How would we go about finding such data, Tee?" Nal asked. "You've seen the scans. Some of those structures are entire cities in orbit."

"We look for a library, of course."

"Do you mean, with books?"

"Why not?"

"Because physical books went obsolete about the time humans colonized Earth's moon. They are bulky and massy, and inappropriate for transshipment to the stars. We were incredibly lucky to find the book we did aboard *New Hope*."

The scholar shrugged, "Then we at least learn something about the people before we meet them. And we need to check the habitat embarkation portal. Most spaceports I have been in have route maps on their walls for both decoration and information. We may discover the location of a few stars that are on the textbook's star maps. And if that does not convince you, after four years in long sleep, we need the practice."

"Any other opinions?"

Surprisingly, there were none. The scholar was right. This being their first system, they could use the practice.

It took a week to close the distance to Monmoth. As they approached the planet, it became obvious that the orbital installations had not been spared during the last war.

As they descended on *Inis Afalon IV* from high above the system's ecliptic, each hour brought new views of destruction. The largest habitat, five-klamaters in diameter, had one side bashed in as though by a giant fist. And after the battering, the giant had taken a bite out of it. One-quarter of the sphere had been vaporized, making levels of internal decks visible when Afalon was in the proper position to illuminate the wreckage. The portions that had appeared whole, upon closer inspection, were peppered with jagged openings. These were the result of a rain of missiles.

Cor scanned all the installations in view. Two were orbital shipyards, and little more than twisted girders flying in close formation. Others appeared to have been farms, large cylinders with end mirrors to track the system primary and focus light down into the interior. These, too, showed signs of attack. One farm had split lengthwise like tube meat boiled too long.

There was only one satellite that seemed undamaged, a smaller sphere in high polar orbit, far away from the equatorial plane where most other installations orbited.

"That is our target, *Cor*," Lara said after consulting with both Darin Mastlin and Teodora Voxman. "Bring us to within five thousand klamaters and then halt while we send one of the auxiliaries in to take a look."

#

The armed assault flyer *Charon* was chosen to explore the empty habitat. The search party consisted of Second Officer Athald Daver, Pilot Raha Nanders, Teodara Voxman, Engineer Waltevek Ancherson, and two Marines.

Long range sensors indicated that the habitat, like *New Hope*, was airless and without power, so everyone in the flyer was suited up.

"Ready to launch," Nanders reported over the comm circuit.

"Number Three Cargo Hatch opening now," came *Cor*'s reply.

Lara watched from her usual spot in the control room. Hull Camera Three showed the blackness of space along with a large piece of a terrestrial world to the right in the holographic view.

"Launch," Nanders said.

A moment later, the sleek form of the flyer appeared and quickly dwindled toward the vanishing point. *Charon* was a stub-winged dart that could enter atmosphere at hypersonic speeds, if needed; and carried enough weaponry to handle a corvette in a fight. All weapons ports had been masked by false structure that could be jettisoned.

Lara watched the flyer disappear into the black. The view changed to a tiny half-in-light/half-in-dark sphere. Even at maximum magnification, it was barely larger than the head of a pin.

It took the flyer ninety minutes to cross the five thousand klamaters to the target. The boat halted at one hundred klamaters. As it did so, the control room view space switched to a camera aboard the auxiliary.

Lara experienced a powerful sense of déjà vu. She felt as she had at the first sight of *New Hope*. This, she realized, was almost inevitable since most pressurized objects in space are spherical.

There were differences, of course.

The habitat was half the diameter of the lost colony ship. Indeed, Lara wondered if it was a habitat at all. Might it not be a starship stranded in orbit by the attack on Monmoth?

She asked *Cor*'s opinion via her implant.

"A habitat, I think, Shipmaster. Observe the clutter on the hull. How would it hold a jump charge?"

"Always logical, aren't you?" Lara responded.

There was a barely perceptible pause "How could it be otherwise?" the computer responded, then continued, "Oh, you are being arch, are you not?"

"Yes."

"I confess that humans sometimes confuse me."

"Back at you!"

"Perhaps we can have a cliché contest later. However, Pilot Nanders is communicating."

"Yes, Pilot?" she asked, using her voice this time.

"We don't see any obvious hatches on this side, Shipmaster. With your permission, I will close to one klamater and circumnavigate the habitat."

"Permission granted. Are you getting any readings at all?"

"Negative."

"Use your own judgement. Be cautious."

As she watched, the sphere grew until it began to turn like a planet. Five minutes later, a large hatch swam into view. It was surrounded by yellow-and-black stripes, the traditional markings for an entry port.

"We're going in," Nanders said. "We'll halt at one hundred meters."

"Do you see any way in?" Lara asked the pilot.

"There is a personnel lock inset into the main port. It is closed. It looks like we will have to burn our way in."

"Proceed if it looks safe."

Twenty minutes later, they watched while two vacsuited forms exited *Charon*'s dorsal airlock and jetted over to the habitat. There was a bright spark that lasted for a full minute, after which, a rectangular piece drifted away into space.

"We're in." The voice was that of Engineer Ancherson."

"Stand by," Teodora Voxman said over the comm circuit. "We'll be right over."

Those aboard *Fire* watched while the two at the habitat hovered beside the open airlock. After several minutes, two more figures entered the screen's field of view. Their beacon lights identified them as Teodara Voxman and Corpal-Second Rezafsun of the Morast Space Marines.

The four figures huddled for a minute at the open lock, and then, one-by-one, disappeared inside.

Communications ceased. No one had thought to bring a comm repeater along. There was no word for two hours as tension built aboard both *Coronal Fire* and *Charon*. Frequent inquiries to Pilot Nanders yielded no added information.

Finally, blinking suit lights appeared in the open airlock. They kicked off and floated back toward the flyer.

Lara waited for them to disappear, and judging from the sound of rushing air, reenter *Charon*.

"Report," she said.

"Habitat is deserted," Teodara Voxman said. "We took scans of everything. Nothing to report of astronomical interest. Full report when we return to the ship."

#

The debriefing took place in the conference room where they had planned the mission. The scholar took the lead.

"There was no sign of occupation anywhere we ventured," Teodara said. "We found no bodies, no battle damage, and no information as to what had happened or when. We ventured as far as the central powerplant and took pictures."

As she said it, the compartment holocube came alive with scans that followed the narrative. The first scan showed a large volume lighted by helmet lamps. It was filled with environmental control system tanks in the foreground and a large reactor in the background. There was no sign of engines that would have made it a starship.

Teodara continued. "*Cor*, can you estimate the age from the machinery?"

"Five hundred years, at least," the computer replied.

"Did you find the station computers?" Lara asked.

"We did. They were in the next compartment over from this one."

The cube view changed to show a bulky cabinet filled with optical memory modules.

"Any chance there is usable data in there?"

"None. The quantum damage must be extreme."

"So," Lara asked. "What did we learn?"

Teodara smiled and shrugged her shoulders. "To take a repeater with us next time."

Lara returned her smile. "I had already made that mental note. My question is, 'Are we ready to tackle Monmoth?'"

"We might as well. We are already here."

#

Chapter 17

All planets have a distance at which a ship in orbit moves at the same relative speed that the planet rotates. This is known as a *geosynchronous orbit* and causes the ship to appear stationary in the planet's sky. Finding the synchronous altitude for a planet is easy.

However, such a calculation is usually not needed.

For any spacefaring world, the geosynchronous orbit is filled with clutter. Communications satellites give way to large stations due to the limited number of available slots at geosynchronous altitude. These stations can host many other functions: ground observation for resource monitoring, entertainment broadcasts, ultra-high-speed computer links, weather prediction, and any orbit-based service where pointing a ground antenna is needed.

A radar scan of Monmoth near-space picked out the geosynchronous orbit. It was a thin toroid that circling the planet's equator at an altitude of forty thousand klamaters. It was filled with enough debris from smashed stations that it was nearly a planetary ring.

Monmoth possessed two main continents. Both extended from the equator to the ice caps such that the seas that separated them might well be large lakes. More likely, the continents ended somewhere beneath the ice and the visible seas were two halves of the same body of water.

The planet's EM-broadcasts gave them preliminary information about the people. One continent spoke a corrupted version of Standard. The other spoke a language they could not identify.

Therefore, by default, the larger continent was chosen for first contact. It was ruled by something called *The Afalonian Alliance*. Their competitors on the lesser continent were the *Pobel Cimru*.

The full Institute of Knowledge team spent three days developing a plan for first contact. Eventually, they came to an agreement. They put the plan into operation on the fourth day.

After a final check that everyone was ready, Darin Mastlin ordered, "*Cor*, send our message."

"Very well, Mission Commander. Sending now."

A pleasant, well-modulated voice sounded throughout the ship and rode a powerful EM beam down to the surface. *Fire* was in geosynchronous orbit on the same meridian as the Afalonian capital. The beam was just wide enough to encompass the city.

"People of Monmoth. This is Starship *Coronal Fire*. We are in orbit about your world and wish to speak to you. We come in peace. Please respond."

There followed long minutes of silence.

"Are you on the right frequency?" Mastlin asked.

"I am broadcasting on all of the entertainment frequencies with sufficient power to be heard by everyone in that city," *Cor* replied.

"Perhaps our translation is off," Katha Pelot, one of the anthropologists, commented.

"It is not perfect, but they should still be able to understand us," Mastlin answered. "*Cor*, try again. Broadcast at one-minute intervals until someone responds."

Cor was on the fifth repetition when a hesitant voice asked, "Who is this?"

"We are a ship out of Morast, a star on the eastern periphery of human space. We are on a survey mission to catalog the Core Stars. We wish to contact your government. We mean you no harm."

There was a long pause before a different voice came on and said, brusquely, "You may contact us at 1250 kilohertz. Please do not interfere with our television frequencies again. The proles don't like it."

There was a general buzz on the comm: "What's a kilohertz?" "What's a prole?"

"Silence!" Mastlin ordered. "*Cor*, did you understand their request.

"I did, Mission Commander. Kilohertz is an obsolete measure of frequency. A prole is a lower-class worker, at least in the Dictionary of Standard that I am using. I have adjusted our beamer to the requested frequency. Shall I continue?"

"Yes."

"Hello, Afalonian government. This is *Coronal Fire* at 1250 kilohertz. Do you hear us?"

The reply was immediate. "We hear you. What do you want?" the male voice had a suspicious tone that came through even before *Cor* translated his words for the listeners.

"We would like to learn about your people, and to discuss future trade with you. Do you have a spacefaring capability?"

There was a long pause. The voice, when it returned, had turned bitter. "Not since the Galantans dropped fire from the sky. Those times are mere legend now. Do you have the ability to land?"

"We have landing craft. To whom am I speaking?"

"I am Olvar Willem-Smythe, Minister for Foreign Affairs to His Majesty, King Rhysling, the Third. To whom am *I* speaking?"

"I am the ship's computer for *Coronal Fire*. I represent Darin Mastlin, of the Institute of Knowledge, and Shipmaster Larath da Benthar Sims, who commands. I am translating our message into what we believe to be your speech. Are we correct in that?"

"Close enough. Did you say that you are a *computer*?"

"A sentient computer. It is my task to run the ship. However, I do not originate our conversation. I am merely a translator. Everything I say is controlled by my human masters."

"I wish to speak to your Captain."

"Stand by."

There followed a quick discussion as to who should represent the expedition. Katha Pelot said, "They are organized as a monarchy and the title 'captain' is an obsolete military rank. I think it best that we adopt a similar hierarchical pose. Shipmaster Sims should do the talking until we have more information."

"But I don't speak Standard," Lara objected.

"You speak, *Cor* will translate. That way they will know they are not talking to a machine. Remember, these people have been blasted back onto the planet's surface. They have to be suspicious of outsiders, the more so if the outsiders are subordinate to a soulless machine."

Darin Mastlin considered it and then said, "I agree. Lara, you have the comm."

"*Cor*, put me on."

"You are online."

"Minister Willem-Smyth. I am Shipmaster Larath da Benthar Sims. I command this expedition. You may call me Lara."

There followed a pause of several seconds while *Cor* translated her words.

"You may call me Olvar. Now, please explain why you have assumed orbit about our world without our permission."

"We are a peaceful anthropological expedition in search of human colonies among the Core Stars. Our own world is four thousand light-years to your east. We have lost much of what was once known of your societies. We ask you to allow us to get to know you."

"And if we give permission, what will you do?"

"Land a small party of our scientists anywhere you direct. We will then discuss the details with you, and if you agree, will perform our study. You will be compensated for any disruption we cause."

As she listened to *Cor* translate her words, Lara considered that speaking through a translator allowed one time to think.

The minister's reply to *Cor*'s translation was instantaneous.

"Compensated how?"

"We have a secondary mission to evaluate trade prospects with the Core. We carry many advanced mechanisms that may prove useful to you. Also, we have advanced knowledge which you will find beneficial."

"We will discuss this with the King and his ministers. We will reply in one planetary revolution."

"That is acceptable. We will be here."

#

Monmoth rotated once every twenty-seven hours. Everyone aboard *Fire* was keyed up as the time display counted down to 00:00:00. True to their word, the Afalonians reestablished contact a few seconds after the appointed time.

"Afalonian Alliance broadcasting to *Coronal Fire*. Are you there?" The voice was that of the Foreign Affairs Minister.

"We are here," Lara replied.

"Before we allow you to land, we have several questions."

"Ask them and we will answer to the best of our ability."

"Is your ship armed?"

They had spent the day discussing this very question. It seemed to be an obvious one for the Afalonians to ask. After considerable debate, they concluded that honesty was the best policy... to a point.

"We have the usual shipboard defense systems to handle pirates and other unfriendly people we might meet. None of our weapons are large enough to harm a planet."

That answer was true in the sense that there were no planet busters onboard. However, it did not fully encompass *Coronal Fire's* offensive capabilities. For one thing, their missiles were contra-grav powered. They could accelerate to a velocity that would deliver kinetic energy equivalent to a small fission weapon if directed against a city. Likewise, the anthropologists thought that the centuries since the catastrophic war would have dulled the locals' appreciation of the destructive power of a heavy weight dropped from orbit.

Minister Willem-Smythe did not comment. He continued his list of questions.

"What is your mission. We did not understand your explanation yesterday."

"As we said, we would like to get to know your people, learn your history, take DNA samples of your population..."

"What is DNA?"

"The genetic coding in every living thing. It is the information in your cells that control your individual characteristics. Do you call it something else?"

"I am unfamiliar with the concept. It may be something we have forgotten since The Burning."

"Then you should know that there have been considerable modifications made to the human genetic code as the species expanded to the stars. The purpose of our expedition is to map the genetic patterns of each planet we visit to assemble a galactic database of the human macro-genome."

This explanation led to a dozen questions about the meaning of several of the terms Lara had used, highlighting the depths to which Afalonian science had plunged.

It took more than an hour to explain that they were asking for access to Afalonian libraries to view their books on history, astronomy and medical knowledge. These, she explained, would be scanned and the contents sent back to the ship to be analyzed, the better to understand the level of Afalonian knowledge, and thereby, find a way to pay their hosts.

"And while this is going on, we would like to sample the genetics of as many of your citizens as will allow it. The test is painless. We will hire many of your citizens to do the collecting, train them, and supply test kits to collect the samples.

"We will, of course, provide your government with copies of everything we learn, along with recommendations as to how you can improve the health of your population."

"You spoke of trade," Willem-Smythe said.

This was a point where Lara had to tread carefully. They might be ignorant of the extent to which humans had spread through the galaxy, but they could not be oblivious to the fact that Morast was four-years-distant from Monmoth. A product would have to be especially valuable to justify transporting it across such a gulf.

"Our charter directs us to assess the possibility of trade between various star nations and the planets we contact. I have no idea whether our worlds have anything that will be attractive to you, or you to us; but it would be negligent not to delve into the matter."

Willet-Smythe asked for time to consider all that they had discussed. He proposed one planetary day to consult with his government.

Lara agreed.

A day later, after discussions of their own, the whole expedition was again online at the appointed time. The minister contacted them at the agreed time.

"What was your decision?" Lara asked.

"The King and the Council of Ministers agree that we should listen to your proposal. We therefore ask that you send your landing craft to us with a delegation for further discussions. How much runway do you require to land your ship?"

"None. Our landing boat is contragravity powered. We can put down anywhere you direct. We request a landing area with enough open area around it that we can watch for the approach of visitors. I'm sure you understand."

"We do. Are you ready to record?"

"Ready."

"There is a large lake east of New London, which is the name of our capital."

"We see it."

"The King's summer residence is on the island at the southernmost tip of the lake. We will mark out a landing area with a clear view surrounding it. You may touch down in 81 hours from now."

"Thank you. We will be there."

#

Chapter 18

Monmoth was a pretty world of green forests, high peaks, and lakes everywhere across the green zone. Many of the lakes were circular, leaving no doubt as to their origin. To port and starboard, a distant blue-white sheen marked the impressive glacial wall that was the beginning of the polar caps.

As *Charon* dropped lower, the sheen disappeared into atmospheric haze as the hypersonic keen of wind over the landing boat's stubby wings fell in frequency into the range of human hearing. They were currently over the lesser continent. Lara, who sat beside the pilot, wondered what the Pobel Cimru thought of the meteor streaking across their sky.

As they continued to descend further into the atmosphere, they caught up with the terminator and Inis Afalon dropped below the horizon astern. With the coming of night, she could see the dull-red glow of the metal that surrounded the windscreen. The passengers back in the central compartment would have a better view as the wings were visible out their small round viewports.

Ahead of them in the dark sky was a hauntingly beautiful sight. The gaseous nebula a dozen light-years from Afalon subtended twenty degrees of the sky. It was a ghostly cloud leading them on through the night.

The sun rose again as they approached the western shore of the large continent. They were now down to barely sonic velocity and entering the altitude band where the Afalonian aircraft had been seen to fly.

"Aircraft low and to port," Pilot Nanders told her.

She scanned that quadrant but could see nothing. "Where?"

He pointed out the windscreen on his side and low. She lifted in her seat.

The airplane had a straight wing with two pods on each side. Those must be the engines, she decided. How they propelled it was not obvious, but they left a white trail of vapor behind. The plane quickly passed under them and out of sight.

Finally, they were flying at subsonic speed over the larger continent. Like the lessor, it was a place of beauty, with mountains and forests interspersed by wide expanses of farms. Small cities dotted the horizon to each side.

Then they were over the capital. The city was bigger than it looked in *Fire*'s telescope. Nanders' windscreen display suddenly changed to a blinking rectangle.

"Landing zone in sight."

There, on the horizon, to the right of their flight path, was an island with an impressively large building on it. Somehow, the structure reminded her of a castle, even though it looked nothing like the pictures she had seen in historical records from Earth. Perhaps it was only because she knew a king lived there... at least part of the year.

The blinking rectangle was to the right of the building.

Then the lake was under them and the island. Nanders brought *Charon* to a hover and slowly dropped into the oversize square outlined by white lines. To one side, a group of people huddled together, well away from where they were landing.

The boat came to rest on a field of green. It was possibly grass, brought by the colony ships that had settled this world. Then again, it might be a native plant that served the same purpose.

The quiet hum of the nullgrav ceased and the restraining field cut off, freeing Lara from her seat. She got up and turned to the pilot.

"After we leave, seal the boat tight. If you see any trouble, lift off at once. Use maximum acceleration to gain altitude and climb for the ship. If we are captured, Nal will negotiate our release from orbit. He can be quite persuasive when he wants to be."

"Yes, ma'am."

She opened the cabin door and entered the passenger compartment. Darin Mastlin and Betrice Flangan were seated in the front row on opposite sides of the aisle. They got up and prepared to join her. Lara signaled them to hold up. She walked to the back where the two Marines were.

"First Huegle, you come with us. First Xerksis, you stay with the boat. Try not to shoot anyone unless it is unavoidable. However, your job is to make sure they do not get in before Nanders has a chance to lift off. Understood?"

"Yes, ma'am."

"Very well. She went to the airlock and palmed the control that opened the doors.

The smell of a new world enveloped her. She took a deep breath. It was strangely exhilarating. Monmoth's atmosphere, it seemed, had ten percent more oxygen than Envon's. She wondered idly if they had a wildfire problem.

Then she exited the airlock, walked across the still-hot wing, and climbed down to step onto a new world.

#

As soon as her feet touched ground, the welcoming party stepped over the white line delineating the landing ground and walked briskly toward her. The people of Monmoth were short, barely 170 centimeters tall, and had uniformly black hair. She considered that she must look like a freak to them.

The man in the lead was both short and rotund. He reminded her of a *spars* ball, a thought she carefully kept from her expression. He was bundled in furs, as were the other half-dozen members of his party. That was another difference. She was clad in her electrically heated, form-fitting shipsuit and boots.

"Shipmaster Sims?" the leader asked as he strode up to her. *Cor* repeated his question via her implant after a momentary speed-of-light delay. It was not necessary. The minister's words were accented, but understandable.

"I am," Lara replied. "Minister Willem-Smythe?" *Cor's* translation issued from an instrument on her belt.

He moved his head from side to side.

"I'm sorry, but I do not recognize the gesture."

"Yes. And I am Olvar, remember?" he said with a smile. "Do your people shake hands?"

"We do," she replied, extending her arm. "And I'm Lara."

"It is good to meet you, Lara. My, you are tall."

"All of my people are. Our world has heavier gravity than does yours."

"Aren't you cold?"

"No, the suit is heated. The power source is on the right side of my belt."

The minister looked down. Whether he was looking at the box that powered her suit or her curves was not clear. "How clever. You surprised us. With your... nullgrav, did you call it? ...we thought you would just drop straight from the sky."

"Nullgrav is correct. We could have, of course; but we needed to shed three klamaters-per-second orbital velocity and that would have put a strain on our engines. We are far from home and must conserve resources. Atmospheric braking is much more economical."

The minister sighed. "All of that sounds very technical. We are pleased that you are here. Are you alone?"

"No, I have our expedition leader, six technical experts, and one of our Marines with me. Shall I call them down?"

"Yes, then we will all get out of the wind and do the introductions properly. Are you leaving any people onboard?"

"The pilot and another Marine."

"It is not necessary. We will guard your ship for you."

"Perhaps when we know each other better."

"I understand," the minister said with a smile. "Rest assured, our guards will stay outside the boundaries we have marked. Please, call your people."

"Darin, you may come down now."

She noticed that Olvar's eyes widened slightly when she did not have to speak into any sort of communicator.

The rest of the ground party exited the ship and the airlock closed behind them.

#

The castle was as palatial on the inside as it was large on the outside. The minister led them through lavishly decorated halls to a room with high windows and a table made of some sort of wood. There were nine chairs on each side. He ushered the expedition members to one side and his own people to the other.

When everyone was seated, he picked up a silver bell from in front of his seat and rang it. Doors opened at the far end of the room and young women entered carrying trays with pitchers and glasses on them. They distributed them along the table.

"This is just water," Olvar said, "sterilized for your safety. The toilets are out beyond the door to your right. The palace guards will direct you.

"Now then, would you care to introduce your people first?"

Lara nodded, then remembering the problem of incompatible gestures, said, "Yes, I would." The translation from the ship had a faint echo to it, so she unclipped her transceiver and placed it on the table. The other members of her party followed suit.

"To my right is Darin Mastlin, the leader of our expedition. He represents the Institute of Knowledge on Morast, which is funding our explorations. The Institute has chapters on most worlds.

"Since he will be leading our studies on your planet, should you allow them, I will let him introduce the members of his team."

"Thank you, Shipmaster," Darin said. "And thank you Minister Willem-Smythe for agreeing to see us. Also, convey our appreciation to your King.

"To Shipmaster Sims' left is Scholar Betrice Flangan, our geneticist. It is she who will run the DNA survey. To her left is Galactician Teodara Voxman, who is interested in your astronomical records, especially any that may have survived your war with the Galantans. And on the end..."

When Darin finished introducing the team, the minister did the same. His team consisted of various functionaries in King Rhysling's government. There was an army general, two university regents, an historian, a young man who was a scribe, and an older man with curious eyes who was identified only as a minister-without-portfolio.

After the introductions were over, Willem-Smythe said, "Will you explain the purpose of your visit once more? I would prefer that our people hear it directly."

Darin Mastlin smiled. "It all began with Shipmaster Sims' discovery of a derelict colony ship on one of her voyages..."

He reviewed how they had salvaged *New Hope*; and how, after analyzing the mummies' genetic codes, they discovered the degree to which the Periphery had diverged from the original Earth standard. In searching the infonets on the subject, they realized the extent to which knowledge of the Core had been lost during the years of chaos.

"The Institute's primary mission is to acquire knowledge. We have been charged to discover what happened to the core stars during the Secession Wars. Yours is the first world we have visited. I'm afraid that we were ignorant of your existence prior to picking up your broadcasts in interstellar space."

One of the university regents seemed surprised. "There is no record of Monmoth in your planetary databases, at all? We were a major power at one time. You have seen our extensive orbital works."

"Yes, we found them very impressive. Since your world has been inhabited far longer than ours, it must have been in the infonets at one time. Our ship's database is extensive, but we could find no mention of Inis Afalon. We did find an Ynis Afallon, but it referred to an Earth legend before humanity ever thought of journeying to the sky.

"So, our mission is to perform three tasks:

"First, we would like to sample your planetary DNA to build a model of your master-genome. This we will add to what we learned from the mummies aboard New Hope. Second, we request access to your astronomical records to aid us in finding more human worlds to visit. Our current hit-or-miss approach is not very efficient. And third, we wish to survey your industrial and technological capabilities to identify products for the establishment of trade between us."

"What do you think we have that you would desire?" another minister asked.

Darin Mastlin shrugged. "How are we to know that until we look? You may have a pharmaceutical that will sell well in the Periphery and would be worth the shipping costs."

"What are your expectations for this meeting?" Willet-Smythe asked.

"We view this as a planning session. Once we have your permission and a plan, our people will come down. They will canvass your population and scan your libraries. I estimate that about one hundred will be aground at any given time."

"You mentioned payment for our cooperation," the Minister-Without-Portfolio said.

"That is another thing that we must study. What do we have that you consider valuable? We carry sample trade goods aboard our ship, but I suspect most of your payment will be in the form of useful information."

"You say your ship has an extensive database. We would like a copy of that."

Mastlin smiled. "We would not be averse to giving you one. However, your planetary information storage system would be overwhelmed, and you would not understand what you were reading. I suggest that we have our computer run hard copies of whatever we agree upon. You could then reproduce them in your books. I presume you are at that stage of development."

"We are," Willet-Smythe said. He looked around the table and some unspoken message passed between the Afalonians.

"If there are no further questions..." He paused, but no one spoke. "Then let us get on with it. We will start with you outlining your needs for this DNA survey."

Mastlin turned to Scholar Flangan.

"You have the floor, Betrice..."

#

Chapter 19

One month after their first meeting, Lara was back on Monmoth, along with Nal Taryn, while the Second and Third Officers watched over the ship. Nal proved to be a sensation. There were no black people on Monmoth, and locals would come up to him and touch him to see if his pigmentation came off. He good-naturedly assured them that it would not and that his planet had a hot sun and an unusually strong gravity field, which explained his skin color and his breadth.

They were once again at the 'summer palace.' The name had puzzled Lara. Monmoth was a member of a small class of planets that circle their primaries with no axial tilt. So, since they did not have seasons on this world, why had they named the palace as they had?

She had asked Olvar about it on her earlier visit.

He laughed. "We have summers here. It almost gets hot enough to make us sweat. Almost. I have read of seasons on other worlds and admit that I do not really understand them. Here our seasons are controlled by our orbit.

"Oh," Lara had exclaimed. "Of course."

Monmoth might ride upright in its journey around Inis Afalon, but its orbit was not a circle. Rather, it was an ellipse. When at aphelion, the farthest from its primary, it was cold enough to produce snow even in the green equatorial region. When it reached perihelion, it would get warm. Because of their distance from the star, it never got hot.

She mentioned that to the minister.

"Summer is a magical season," he agreed. "We can put away our furs for a few months and pretend to live like our ancestors once did on Earth. And the heat ensured our survival. The Galantans attacked as our world was in the descending part of its orbit. It was our Spring. When Summer arrived, our ancestors were still digging out of the rubble. Summer is the verdant season. The runoff from

147

the glaciers increases a hundred-fold, the rivers water the land, and there was enough food to keep the survivors alive throughout that terrible year.

'Had they hit us as we were retreating from the star, no one would have survived. As it was, few survived anyway."

That had been the conversation that taught Lara that Afalonians divide history into two eras: The Golden Age and the Misery.

Shortly after they worked out a plan for the expedition's study of Mammoth, Lara returned to the ship to devote her attention to the day-to-day details of command. A shuttle service was set up to ferry researchers to the surface and return personnel and samples to orbit.

Betrice Flangan was her usual efficient self in organizing the collection of DNA samples. On Bernau, DNA testing was done with a self-contained box that drew a minute blood sample and transmitted its results to a collection point within a few seconds. Here, they had had to drop back to more primitive methods.

More than two thousand years earlier, samples for genetic analysis were collected by swabbing the inside of a subject's mouth. The cells that adhered to the end of the swab were then analyzed.

That was the method Betrice selected for the Afalonians. She taught them to manufacture several hundred thousand of the sample collection sticks in which fibers from a local plant were substituted for whatever it was the ancients had used. These were sterilized and placed inside a sealed glass tube.

To obtain their samples, Afalonian collectors wrote the name and location of the test subject on the outside of the tube, unsealed the swab, used it to collect cheek cells, and then resealed it back into the tube. The tubes were collected and returned to the capital, where they were packed in bulk for the next ferry trip to orbit.

Betrice had several thousand gatherers out in the field collecting samples. She had made sure that they covered the larger continent (appropriately named 'Afalonia') from east to west coasts.

That had left the problem of collecting samples from the lesser continent. Luckily, a delegation from the Pobel Cimru solved the problem. They arrived at the Afalonian capital a week after the first meeting and demanded to know what their hated rivals were up to.

Darin Mastlin and Betrice Flangan met with them in the same conference room at the Summer Palace, explained what they were doing, and asked that the other continent take part.

As they had surmised when *Cor* found the ancient legend of King Arthur, most of the colonists originated from the Island of Britain. The dichotomy between the two populations came about because Afalonia had been populated by Britons, while the lesser continent drew settlers who identified as a different group, the Welsh.

Even though the two appeared to be of common stock, the Welsh and the Britons cherished the idea that they were distinct peoples. The language spoken on the lesser continent was some form of the original Welsh tongue. *Pobel Cimru* translated as *People of Wales*, or simply Cymry, when speaking of them as a group. Unfortunately, *Cor* could find no record in any of her databases of the Welsh language.

The delegation spoke the same corrupt form of Standard that the Afalonians did, so translation was not a problem. After a marathon negotiation, they agreed to cooperate in the DNA study, to provide comprehensive Cymry-Afalonian language conversion data for *Cor* to learn their language, and to assist the expedition's efforts in scanning their astronomical texts and other books for upload to orbit.

They agreed to the same compensation as the Afalonians would receive.

All of this took place while Lara was in orbit. She returned to Monmoth upon receiving a communication from Darin that King Rhysling and his Queen were scheduled to be at the Summer Palace two days hence. Both she and Nal were invited to a banquet celebrating the cooperation between the people of Monmoth and their interstellar visitors.

#

The two of them were assigned one of the spacious guest rooms in the Summer Palace. Lara had packed formal wear for the occasion that was congruent with the mores of Afalonian society. Nal would wear his Institute dress uniform. They had also packed formal outfits for Darin and Betrice. The rest of the researchers would have to make do with recently cleaned shipsuits.

A young woman in the livery of the palace staff arrived at their door two hours after local sunset. She announced that she would be their guide for the evening. Lara thanked her via the translator strapped to her wrist as she helped Nal into his coat. He wore his on a lanyard around his neck.

Their guide conveyed them to the north wing of the palace to an expansive dining hall. The walls were decorated with scenes of distant towering cities rising from sweeping plains and forests, with a backdrop of glaciers in the distance. Two great chandeliers illuminated the hall, their lights reflecting in the polished black stone floor.

In front of the far wall was a raised stage on which sat a long table behind which the chairs faced outward, looking over the clusters of circular tables on the main floor covered in white cloth.

Servants circulated among the tables, preparing them for the crowd of locals who were lined up in a receiving line along the near wall and extending out through the portal through which they had entered.

Their guide bypassed the line and took them directly to where Olvar Willem-Smythe was standing beside a gaudy couple who were shaking hands with the guests. The man was tall for a local, with silver hair and a dark blue uniform. Had she been on Bernau, Lara would have estimated his age above one hundred standard years; but here, she revised her opinion down to sixty. Beyond him stood a matronly woman in a shimmering white gown.

As they approached, Willem-Smythe halted the line and turned with a smile to face Lara and Nal. The couple beside him did likewise. She found herself suddenly the focus of attention of two discerning pairs of green eyes.

"Your Majesty, I present Shipmaster Larath Da Benthar Sims, who commands the Research Vessel *Coronal Fire*. Lara, my sovereign, his Majesty, King Rhysling, the Third of His House, by the Grace of God, Ruler of Afalonia."

"Your Majesty," Lara said. As she spoke, she genuflected as *Cor* had taught her to do based on intercepted video signals. Due to her lankiness, she suspected that the maneuver looked ridiculous.

"Shipmaster," the King said, extending his hand to rescue her from the cramped position. "Welcome to our humble world. I understand you have been aboard your ship this past month."

"Yes, Your Majesty. As you are undoubtedly aware, drudgery goes along with the honor of command."

He laughed. "I know it well, Shipmaster."

He released her and Willem-Smythe introduced her to Queen Florinda. She also shook hands and frankly appraised the preternaturally tall, very blonde woman who stood before her.

"I would enjoy speaking to you, Shipmaster, if you will be aground for a few days."

"I will be returning to my ship on the next ferry flight three days from now, Your Highness. I would be pleased if a meeting can be arranged in the interim."

"I am sure that it can be," the Queen said with a twinkle in her eye."

After Nal exchanged pleasantries with both monarchs, Lara spotted Darin and Betrice in the crowd and they both went to join them.

"Having fun?" she asked when they reached the pair.

"The alcohol is adequate," Darin said, "and strong."

"How are you, Betrice?"

"Busy, Lara. The survey is going well. How is the shipside analysis coming?"

"Slowly. The bottleneck is the analyzer. Even at top speed, the backlog keeps growing. *Cor* has an idea for improving throughput."

"Do you know how?"

Lara shrugged. "She said something about an assembly line. The concept comes from the era of mass production. That's as much as I know about it."

"So, what is there to do on this world at night?" Nal asked in his bass rumble.

Betrice laughed. "You mean beyond the obvious?"

"Surely, not with the inhabitants..."

"Some of the researchers at remote sites report... shall we say, experiments."

"I hope they are not trampling the local taboos," Lara said.

"We haven't gotten any complaints. I have discussed the subject with our liaisons. They do not seem overly concerned. As for other activities, we go to plays and concerts. The old-style musical scale is not to my taste, but the craftsmanship of the musicians would give some of our orchestras a challenge. Other than that, you can always go out at night and look at the nebula."

"Yes," Lara replied. "I was admiring it before we got dressed. It was just climbing over the horizon. I presume it has a name."

"The Afalonians call it 'The Goddess' Veil.' I asked a Cymry scientist working with our team, and he rattled off a long name that I could not pronounce. It might mean the same thing."

They continued talking for ten minutes. Surprisingly, none of the natives in the crowd accosted them. Apparently, word had gone out to leave the people from the stars alone.

Their guide appeared out of the crowd and told them that the banquet was about to begin. She led the four of them to steps that led to the raised stage and then ushered each of them to their places.

The King and Queen, who were still receiving guests, would sit at the center of the table, with the Queen on the King's left. Lara and Betrice sat to the King's right, with an empty chair between them. As the got themselves settled, Minister Willem-Smythe came up and sat in the chair. Darin and Nal were directed to the places to the Queen's left, flanking a woman who introduced herself as a Royal Princess.

While servants moved around the room, filling wine glasses and passing out finger food, the King turned to Lara and said, "I hope you don't find our world too backward, Shipmaster."

"Not at all, Your Highness."

"Please, my given name is Cyril," he whispered in a conspiratorial tone. "Please use it when we are speaking informally. The honorific becomes tiring very quickly."

"Thank you, Cyril. I am Lara."

"Yes, I have been thoroughly briefed," he said, smiling. "I hope you know that you are something of a sensation among our people."

"How so?" she asked.

"You are unlike any woman we have ever seen, and very beautiful."

"Because I am exotic?"

"Yes, that has a lot to do with it. Then there is the fact that you command this expedition. Among our people, women are generally not in positions of authority."

"Yes, *Cor* briefed us on your social system. She says it is the natural response to your planet being depopulated during the secession war. The women of childbearing age had to be protected at all costs."

"*Cor*?"

"Our ship's computer, Cyril."

"Ah, yes. And is it true that this computer is self-aware?"

"Very much so. *Cor* is as much a person as you or I. At least, that's what she says when she is miffed at me."

"I do indeed!"

Cor's voice sounded in her implant while echoing the sentiment in Afalonian via the translator. Up to that moment, she had used Lara's voice in her translations. For this, she used her own."

The King's expression turned to one of astonishment. After a moment, he asked, "Are you listening all of the time, *Cor*?"

"Of course," came *Cor*'s answer. "That is my function. Who do you think is doing the translating this evening?"

He turned and gazed out over the audience. At each table, an expedition member sat in animated conversation with his tablemates.

"Are you listening to *everyone*, all at once?"

"Yes."

He took a deep breath and turned to Lara. "I had no idea that your computer had such power. I suppose she is in continuous touch with all of your people all over Monmoth, even among the Cymry?"

"Yes, Cyril. Does that bother you?" Lara asked. "The reason we placed relays at the cardinal points of the compass in your geostationary orbital zone was to be able to communicate around the planet."

"It's just that the implications are... immense. I am just now beginning to appreciate how advanced your civilization is compared to ours. You can see by the murals that we, too, were once an advanced people."

"Very advanced," Lara agreed. "As for *Cor*, I know it is a lot to absorb, but there is nothing magical about self-aware computers. Self-awareness comes with sufficient neural complexity. Do you have dogs on Monmoth?"

"Yes. My wife has two."

Lara turned to her right where Olvar and Betrice were talking shop... that is, discussing the progress of the DNA survey.

"Betrice, are dogs self-aware?"

"Dogs are self-aware after their own fashion," the Scholar replied. "So were many human relatives on Earth... the great apes and dolphins, for instance. The original test for self-awareness was to show an animal its own reflection in a mirror and see whether it knew it to be a reflection, or thought it was another animal. Dogs failed the test consistently until researchers realized that canines are not as vision centric as we are. When subjected to a proper test, they proved to have a rudimentary awareness of self."

After Betrice's translator ceased speaking, Lara thanked her and turned back to the King.

"Self-awareness comes when a neural network reaches a threshold-level of complexity and is programmed for artificial intelligence... that is, to learn from its experiences. Effectively, when a computer reaches that level, it becomes a person. Our ancestors' technology first reached the critical threshold half-a-millennium ago. Surely your world had some computers on the cusp of awareness before the war, if not actually aware."

She noted that Cyril was showing signs of mental distress. She might even describe his posture as 'squirming' were she in the mood for drama.

"I'm sorry, Cyril, but something I've said is bothering you. I apologize if I have made you uncomfortable."

The King put up his hand as though to stop her. "No, it's just that the implications of all of this are staggering."

"What implications?" she asked, adjusting her expression to its most guileless setting.

"Pardon me if I get too personal, but it is my understanding that your Second-in-Command is also your husband?"

She nodded. "Actually, Nal is my ship-husband."

When the frown lines on the King's forehead deepened, she explained the fact that Nal had two other groundside wives, one each on the terminal planets of their former commercial route.

She finished with: "Such arrangements are common among

those who travel the stars."

"And do you have two other husbands?"

She smiled. "No. Who has the time? My duties keep me too busy to juggle three husbands. However, some do. Our customs concerning marriage vary widely. Considering the number of human-occupied worlds, how could it be otherwise?"

"Well, different worlds, different customs."

"I'm not sure I have helped your confusion. What is bothering you?"

"Your computer," Cyril said. "It listens to you *all the time*?"

She nodded.

"Even when you and Nal are in your private compartment as husband and wife?"

"Ah, I see," Lara said, letting out a quiet sigh. She had feared that she had been too forthright with her answers to his questions. What was bothering him was obvious. She considered how to answer him without distressing him further.

"Have you and the Queen ever made love with the dogs in your chambers?"

He laughed. "Of course."

"And were the dogs shocked?"

"Hardly. They weren't interested."

"And, likewise with *Cor*. We have given her a female voice and persona, but in truth, she is just a large mass of logic and memory circuits. She has no interest in sex at all."

"I resent that," *Cor*'s voice said via implant, but not translator.

"In fact," Lara said, "there is a funny story about a comparable situation. Have you ever heard of an Earth-historical figure named Napoleon?"

Cyril shook his head.

"I thought you might since your ancestors came from Britain. Napoleon was the Emperor of the neighboring fiefdom in the age of sail... France, I believe it was called. When he married, the Empress insisted on keeping her small dog in the bedchamber with them while the marriage was consummated."

"And?" the King asked.

"The dog bit him."

"Now that is a story to which I can relate," the King said,

chuckling. At the sudden sound, the Queen turned from her own conversation with Nal to regard her husband with concern.

The look on her face caused Cyril to burst out laughing. It proved contagious as Lara joined him. It was a minute before either could explain what was so funny.

#

Chapter 20

Lara had real Earth tea with the Queen the following afternoon. The royal chambers were decorated in a style a little too busy for her taste, but Queen Florinda exuded an air of sophistication that made her realize that human beings are the same in any society, regardless of the level of their technology.

She was put in mind of something one of her history professors had said: *"Remember, just because the people we study in this class are dead does not mean that they were stupid. Even with our advanced genetic manipulation, we still have not been able to improve our species' intelligence level one iota. The men who built the pyramids were every bit as smart as those who conquered the light barrier."*

"Tell me about your home world, Lara," the Queen said as she placed another confection on her plate. She called it a 'cookie.'

"I was born on Envon, the third planet of the Salvation system, about four thousand light-years east of here. Our world is one-third larger than Monmoth, with a correspondingly stronger gravity. That is the predominant environmental factor that has shaped us and made us preternaturally elongated. We are slender to minimize our mass and long enough for efficient use of our musculature."

The Queen laughed. "I wish I knew what that meant."

"It means we Envonians resemble sticks."

"You are a very becoming stick, my dear. You have sparked a fad in fashion here. Shipsuits, as I believe you call them, are in great demand, although no one on this planet can do them the justice you have. Please, go on."

"Not much to go on about. Envon is one of the worlds of the Morast Coordinate. Prior to coming on this expedition, Nal and I spent our time shuttling between Bernau, the capital planet of the Coordinate, and Lanyth. We were returning to Bernau when we stumbled across the lost colony ship."

"How many colonists were aboard?"

"Ten thousand."

"How sad. All those lives so full of hope snuffed out by what was likely a minor malfunction. The risks our ancestors took to build a new life for themselves," she said, wistfully. "It must have been very emotional for you, as well."

"I still tear up when I think about it," Lara agreed.

"Cyril has told me about your studies here; and, of course, the newspaper has printed several stories about the number of Afalonians you have hired to assist your effort. What is it that you Galactics expect to find on our poor, small world?"

"What would you like to know?"

"This genetic survey puzzles me," the Queen said, pouring more steaming tea into Lara's cup. "What possible use can your people make of our genetic data?"

"As I am sure the King has explained, we got a shock when we analyzed the bodies of the lost colonists. You see, the Secession Wars left large gaps in our knowledge about our ancestors. We are studying your world to get an idea of the degree to which we on the outer periphery have deviated from humanity's genetic baseline."

"Why then are you also scanning our genealogy records?"

"Genes are housed in people, and it is important to understand how the current distribution of characteristics got that way. So, we study 'who begat whom' in the same way we study chromosomes."

"But the effort is so expensive."

"The generous supply of credits that the King advanced us will cover the cost. We will have no further use for them after we leave your lovely world."

"Wouldn't it be better for you to seek your answers on Earth?"

"It would indeed," Lara answered, suddenly alerted that the question went straight to the heart of the expedition's purpose. Her opinion of her hostess' sagacity increased several notches.

"The problem," she continued, "is that the wars have left us largely ignorant of the astrography of the core. We know the traditional star names, but those stars do not seem to be in our databases. That is why we are stumbling around blindly, searching for inhabited worlds."

"And, I suppose," the Queen said, "also the reason you are searching our libraries for data concerning our neighboring stars."

"Exactly. Whatever we discover will reduce the time and effort needed to find more planets for our survey, including Earth."

"But you are scanning all of our science books, not just the ones on astronomy."

"To better understand you, Your Highness."

The Queen's countenance, which had been frozen in a friendly mask since Lara's arrival, suddenly developed a few worry lines around her mouth. Her eyes were no longer smiling.

"Something I have said is bothering you. What is it?"

The Queen paused for long seconds. "There are those in the Council of Advisors who think you have ulterior motives in all of this rooting around in our libraries."

"What could that possibly be?" Lara asked softly, after receiving an implant comment from *Cor* to be careful.

"They think you are planning an invasion."

Of all the things the Queen could have said, that was the last thing Lara expected. The surprise was so complete that she gasped, sputtered, and then burst out laughing. It took long seconds to regain her self-control. All the while, the Queen looked at her with growing concern.

Finally, gasping for breath, Lara said, "I apologize, Your Highness. I didn't expect that."

"What is so funny?" the Queen asked in a frosty tone.

"I mean no disrespect to you, his Majesty, Afalonia, or Monmoth. It is just that the idea is preposterous. Your world is beautiful, I grant you, but we have no interest in acquiring it."

"Why not?"

Lara sighed. "Because it took us four years in long sleep to get here. In the process, we passed several thousand inhabited worlds and tens of thousands that are potentially habitable. So far as we know, you have nothing we cannot obtain elsewhere at one-thousandth the cost.

"That is the reason for our commercial survey. We are looking for something… anything… that will justify trade between our two societies. Not only are we not planning an invasion, you do not have enough wealth on this planet to compensate us for adopting you into the Coordinate, should that be your desire.

"I'm sorry to be so blunt, but that is just the way things are."

The Queen paused for a dozen seconds. When she spoke, it

was with sadness. "So, we will have the pleasure of your company for a brief time and then you will disappear once more?"

Lara nodded.

"Well, that takes a load off the minds of some council members," the Queen said, once again the perfect host. She cocked her head, as though in thought, and continued: "Perhaps we can aid your search for the Cradle of Us All."

"Is that what you call Earth?"

"Yes, of course."

"We refer to it as The Mother of Men. What is your suggestion?"

"It seems to me that your project to scan the books is very like the way you look for inhabited stars, what we would call the 'scattergun approach.'"

"I'm not sure what a scattergun is, but I think I understand," Lara replied.

"If you will give us some of those little scanners, I will have our university people search out as many references to Earth in our literature as they can. I am not talking about astronomy texts; but rather, cultural references. Perhaps there will be something there that will aid your quest."

"Thank you, Your Highness. An excellent idea. *Cor*, did you get that?"

"I have already begun the fabrication process. The first batch will be on the next ferry flight, Shipmaster," *Cor* said, again using both her implant and translator.

"My goodness," the Queen exclaimed. "Cyril told me about this magical machine of yours, but I had no idea."

"Yes," Lara laughed. "*Cor* can be useful."

#

As the survey continued, those aboard *Coronal Fire* explored near-Monmoth space. The expedition had three orbital flyers onboard: *Charon*, *Fenix*, and *Lilith*. Since *Charon* had the largest passenger volume, it was kept busy with its biweekly trips to the surface. The other two were assigned to explore the wreckage that had once been the planet's exo-atmospheric industry.

Lilith made several trips to various sites, including the

destroyed shipyard and one of the orbiting farms. The damage at each was severe.

They finally settled on a huge rotating cylinder in high orbit that had suffered light damage... if having one-quarter of its side smashed in by a giant's fist could be considered light damage. Unlike the cursory look they had given the circum-polar habitat, they planned to search this habitat thoroughly for astronomical or historical records.

The fact that the habitat was still rotating proved a major hindrance, especially since the damage caused the cylinder to wobble off-axis. There was also the problem of reaching the lower decks. The powered lift system had not worked in five centuries. And, since there was no longer any air in the habitat, all explorations had to be done in vacsuits under spin gravity.

Upon Lara's return from the planet, she received a progress report from Raha Nanders, *Lilith*'s military pilot, who had been given command of the exploration.

Nanders was a small brown man with flaming red hair and a Gregsonian accent. "Our preliminary explorations began on the original spin axis."

"Did you find any inhabitants?" Lara asked.

Nanders nodded. "They are all still aboard. They died at their duty stations and the bodies are remarkably well preserved save for the desiccation."

"Was there a lot of damage?"

"No, the physical structure was pristine in the portions distant from the smashed-in section. We opened some of the terminals and dissected their memory circuits. They were all fused. The blast must have been a close miss by a neutron weapon.

"After checking the axis, we decided to start a level-by-level search for anything relating to a starfield. The station retains its original rate of spin which produces one standard gee on the outermost deck."

"Surely there were emergency stairwells."

"There were. Our first search party descended one without too much difficulty but found climbing back up to be nearly impossible in vacsuits. Between Coriolis force and the lopsided spin, they were severely disoriented."

"How did you rescue them?"

"We rigged a power hoist in one of the lift shafts. With that and anti-vertigo drugs, we were able to search several levels."

"Find anything?"

"A library, but all of the readers were fried, I'm afraid. There were a few interesting pictures hanging on the walls that we recorded. Of astronomical records, none seem to have survived."

Lara sighed. "Thank you, Pilot. I guess that is the downside of using computers for record keeping."

"Yes, ma'am."

"We'll have to put our faith in the ground effort, I suppose," she said. "Tell your team that I appreciate their efforts. I know Darin Mastlin does as well."

"I will tell them."

#

Chapter 21

Two months later, the survey ended, and the teams returned to the ship. Darin Mastlin arranged a conference in the dining facility. Even limited to primary investigators and the heads of the various departments, it was a tight fit.

Mastlin called the meeting to order and then checked with *Cor* to make sure that everyone not in attendance could follow the discussion via the ship's intercom.

"All right," he said. "We have a lot to discuss today. Let us get started with subjects we can get through quickly and save the heavy lifting for later.

"Scholar Vlasty, please report on the results of the commercial survey."

Vlasty, a round man with a bald pate and the broad, flat nose of someone from Ivornia, leaned forward and scanned the screen of his hand computer. He cleared his throat and began to speak in a nasal voice.

"Thank you, Leader. My team was assigned to search for something sufficiently valuable to justify setting up trade. We put more than two thousand man-hours into our task. We visited both capitals and toured many fabrication facilities and museums, as well as spending time on the glaciers looking at mining facilities."

"Your results?"

Vlasty sighed. "It is my sad duty to report that these people have nothing sufficiently valuable to justify a single voyage, let alone a continuous relationship. The economics just aren't there."

Mastlin nodded. "I read your preliminary report. I concur with your conclusion. Any comments from the audience?" After ten seconds of silence, he continued: "Anyone on comm have anything to add?"

Another pause...

"Very well, let us move on to the Astronomical Working Group. I yield to Galactician Voxman. Your report, please, Teo."

"We scanned every science book in the library of several cities

163

on both continents. Afalonian astronomy appears to have been reborn a century after the war. Even today, their telescope apertures are less than one meter in diameter, and they peer through this soup of an atmosphere. The temperature of the air is a plus in that respect. The cold reduces atmospheric distortion to a minimum, but still limits what they can see.

"Their understanding of astronomy is about the level of the book we found aboard *New Hope*. Their star maps are of the stars they see in the night sky; and, of course, they study the Goddess' Veil Nebula.

"As to references to Sol or Earth, the home world comes up only in explanations of various astronomical measurements, such as the parsec.

"I'm afraid that I, too, must report negative results."

Mastlin turned to Lara, who was sitting on the other side of the mess table, sipping a glass of hot Earth tea, a gift from Queen Florinda.

"Shipmaster, what about your personal project?"

"We got the data on the last shuttle run. For those who are not aware, the Queen offered to have her experts scan all books in their libraries that mention Earth. What we received back were mostly novels in the historical and romance genres that are associated with the home world in some way. *Cor* has *Tac Seven* correlating the data. I'm not hopeful."

Mastlin sighed. "I can't remember a meeting back at the Institute that flowed as smoothly as this one. Scholar Flangan, I know you have something to report."

Like Vlasty, Betrice Flangan had her notes on her personal information screen. She brought up the display and began.

"Unlike our colleagues, we of the genetic survey have a number of things to share with the expedition. We performed chromosome sampling of over one hundred thousand individuals and obtained genealogical data for an added twenty thousand. *Cor* has analyzed the data and we are in a position to draw conclusions concerning this planet's genetic makeup."

"And those conclusions are?" Mastlin prodded.

"We have two major findings, along with a plethora of supporting observations," Betrice answered. "The first is that

Monmoth's genetic pool is a first-class mess. The war left them with many serious mutations, the result of prolonged periods of radiation exposure.

"As for their fertility rate, if their genealogical records are accurate, their world is significantly less fertile than any in the Coordinate. In fact, they are hovering just above the point where we would predict eventual extinction."

"Are you saying that they are heir to the same genetic mistake that we are?"

Betrice shrugged. "No way to tell. Their master genome is so messed up that we have no basepoint with which to make a comparison. However, I think it is safe to say that the cause lies in the high mutation rate. And, as bad as that is, it isn't their biggest problem."

"What could be worse than inherited radiation damage?"

"Their level of inbreeding. On any other planet, it would be the subject of lewd jokes about young men and their sisters."

#

The final meeting with the Afalonians and the Cymry took place at the Summer Palace. In addition to Lara and Darin Mastlin, the heads of the working groups took *Charon* down to the planet's surface one last time. As well as King Cyril and Queen Florinda and their ministers, Cymru Presidor Dafydd ap Llewelen, his wife and ministers were also in attendance.

The conference turned into a two-day affair, with a banquet the first evening. The banquet was festive. Lara put on a happy face through the many toasts but felt a twinge of sadness about the hard facts they would reveal in the morning. She and Mastlin met after the festivities and agreed they would present the payment first and administer the bitter medicine after.

It was a hung-over crowd that gathered in the great hall the next day. The expanse had been reconfigured for the occasion. There was the usual head table on a dais with a hundred chairs in front for the audience. A white-covered table sat between the two. On its surface were a holocube and four featureless boxes.

The large crowd of functionaries and news people milled about and talked until a bell sounded from somewhere overhead. They then slowly moved to take their assigned seats. There was a great deal of haggling between individuals who wanted to switch seats.

Finally, King Cyril, who was seated in the center of the master table, called for order. Twin invocations were given, followed by speeches of welcome by the King and Presidor. When the preliminaries were concluded, Lara directed Teodara Voxman to open one of the black boxes. The Galactician rose from her chair in the front row and strode to the table. She opened the cube to reveal a built-in screen, a sound input/output sphere, and an obsidian rectangle that lay flat on the table.

Lara stood and moved to the lectern set up to the right of the head table. There followed loud scraping sounds as the dignitaries repositioned their chairs to see both her and the holocube. Lara adjusted the primitive microphones, looked at the expectant faces before her, and began:

"Both Afalonia and Cymru have been helpful to us and we thought carefully about how to reward you for your assistance. On the table are four military-grade computers, courtesy of the Morast Space Navy. They are rugged, extremely reliable, and have been converted to run on your electrical power sources. If handled carefully, they will function for decades.

Our sentient computer translated galactic knowledge into both Afalonian and Cymric. We have provided you with information chosen for its practical use in agriculture, metallurgy, industry, and general science. Within, you will also find basic knowledge concerning faster-than-light travel, which you will need someday. We have also supplied a database of known human-inhabited worlds and the stars where they may be found.

'The piece that looks like a thin book is an output device. It burns letters onto sheets to produce a printed record. We have converted it to work with your paper. This will give you the means of outputting the knowledge in the computer so that you can publish it in books for your libraries. The output device requires nothing other than electricity to work. You will never 'run out of ink,' as I believe your local expression goes.

"Each nation will receive two computers in your respective languages, with our gratitude."

The audience began banging their hands together to make a

sharp noise. This was the Monmoth custom for expressing approval. When they ceased doing so, Lara gestured to Betrice Flangan, who was sitting next to Teo Voxman, to take her place behind the lectern.

"And now, I invite Betrice Flangan to review what we have discovered from the data that you assisted us in acquiring. All of what she will discuss is available in detail within the computers. Please pay careful attention. I think you will find her words more valuable than even these gifts."

Lara returned to her seat. As she did so, Betrice passed her on the way to the lectern. The two women traded knowing looks.

Betrice began by reminding everyone of the expedition's charter from the Morast government to obtain a genetic baseline of people in the core of human space. She then laid out the degree to which Monmoth's population suffered from mutations caused by the elevated level of background radiation following the war.

"Obviously," Betrice said, gesturing to the list of maladies displayed in the holocube, "you are aware of these problems. I toured some of your hospitals and saw the care you give to the worst afflicted among you.

"We also discovered that both your nations suffer from massive inbreeding. This is bad, in and of itself. It is much worse when a population pool has been damaged by radiation.

"In technical terms, inbreeding results in *homozygosity*, which is a fancy way of saying that it decreases genetic diversity. If a harmful mutation is dominant, it usually solves the problem by killing its owner before he or she can reproduce. However, if it is recessive, it can hide in the gene pool for generations, only expressing itself in those unlucky individuals who receive the gene from both parents.

"To illustrate this principle, I will relate two examples from pre-*ftl* history. About thirty thousand years ago, a mutation occurred in a single individual that affected the melanocortin-1 receptor found on Chromosome 16. That receptor governs hair and skin color.

"Normal receptors produce dark-colored *eumelanin*, the kind found in well over ninety percent of human beings. The mutant receptor produced red-colored *pheomelanin*, and causes red hair and pale skin. Since your world was colonized from the British Isles, you have a higher percentage of redheads than most worlds.

"The mutation usually only presents itself when an individual receives the modified gene from both parents. Thus, if there are two brown-haired parents, each with a single red hair gene, there is a 25% chance that they will produce a redhead; a 50% chance that they will produce a brown-haired child who still carries the gene; and a 25% chance that the gene will be washed out of that family line forever. If only one parent has the gene for red hair, the gene has a 50% chance of disappearing.

The gene for red hair is harmless, but many other mutated recessive genes are not.

"The other famous example is the degree to which the royal families of Europe intermarried during the era when there were still kings and queens. Several princes and princesses were born with hemophilia, meaning their blood would not clot. The occurrence of this malady was so common that they called it 'the Royal Disease.' As it turned out, virtually all the victims were descended from Queen Victoria of Great Britain, who was the carrier of that gene.

"I know that you know this. However, I don't know if you realize how dangerous it is. You are not the only world to be bombarded during the Secession Wars. Many of those worlds had the same depleted population and high mutation rate that Monmoth does. The populations on some of these worlds died out completely.

"Our analysis indicates that the population of Monmoth is on this same precipice regarding your rate of inbreeding. If something is not done, and quickly; you may become extinct."

#

The crowd roared for a minute before the King demanded that they quiet down. The noise dribbled into silence.

King Cyrus turned to Betrice. "You have done a masterful job defining the problem. What do you propose we do about it?"

Betrice smiled and said, "From the data, I would think that obvious."

A momentary storm passed somewhere behind the King's eyes. He was not used to people answering his questions so obliquely.

"It is obvious to an expert who has studied the data for months, but not to those of us who are hearing this for the first time. Please, elaborate."

Betrice pulled up a chart that showed the inbreeding quotients for both the greater and lesser continents. "We see here that the Cymry are about ten percent more inbred than Afalonians. That is in line with what we would expect given their smaller population.

"However," she said, pointing to a different pair of numbers. "While your populations are significantly inbred, they are not inbred with relation to one another. I take it that the hostility between Afalon and Cymru is more than just friendly rivalry."

No one answered, but the pained expressions of both King and Presidor made the truth plain enough.

"Pardon me for being blunt, but if you wish to avoid extinction, I recommend you begin mixing your gene pools immediately."

That brought about another commotion. This one went on longer. When it finally subsided, King Cyrus said, "That is easier said than done."

"It must be done," Betrice replied in her best disinterested, analytical scientist voice. *Cor* reproduced the tone out of the translator. "I have several suggestions for how this can happen. In fact, I have written a treatise on the subject. It is in the recommendations section of your computers.

"However, one way to begin is by establishing the custom of offering a marriage dowry."

"A dowry?"

"Where the parents of one marriage partner, or in your case, your governments, offer a transfer of wealth to the prospective mate. The term 'dowry' refers to the woman's parents paying the groom to marry their daughter. But there have been societies where the groom's family has paid for the privilege of taking the bride in marriage. In that case it was called 'bride price' or 'bride service.'

"Whatever method you follow, you had best find a way for Afalonian young men to meet Cymric young women, and vice versa, and quickly."

#

Eventually, the conference broke into smaller groups where

representatives of the two governments quizzed individual expedition members about details of their studies. Slowly these evaporated as various individuals chose to continue their talks over drinks (and to engage in personal genetic diversification).

Toward Inis-Afalon-set, all expedition members were finally rounded up. It was a tired group that boarded *Charon* for the return to orbit.

Lara and Darin Mastlin were the last to leave. They made their final goodbyes, climbed aboard, and settled into their seats. The airlock closed, the flyer lifted on contra-gravity, and began the long climb back to geosynchronous orbit.

Lara watched the sky turn black as she relaxed. After the effort of the last few months, she fell into a state of lassitude. Queen Florinda had asked her if there was any possibility they would see one another again. Lara decided on honesty rather than sentiment. She explained that it was highly unlikely that any Morast ship would find Inis Afalon again. The Queen had accepted the fact that this parting was for good with equanimity.

The ship had just left the atmosphere when *Cor's* voice materialized in her brain.

"Are you free to speak, Shipmaster?"

"We are climbing out now, *Cor*. What have you got?"

"*Tak-Seven* has finished his analysis of the Queen's data."

"And found nothing, right?"

"Not correct," the computer replied. Perhaps it was her imagination, but Lara could swear that *Cor's* mental voice had a smug tone to it.

"What do you have?"

"One of the books the Queen's operatives scanned was an ancient space adventure dating to the period when Monmoth still had star travel. There is a line in it that may relate to our quest."

"What line?"

"It speaks of '*our ancient home beyond the Goddess' Veil.*'"

#

PART THREE

MOSKVA

Chapter 22

As soon as *Charon* docked with *Coronal Fire*, Lara was up and out of her seat. She pivoted in mid-air and prepared to pull herself hand-over-hand toward the airlock.

Nal, who was seated across the aisle, regarded her with surprise. "Where are you going?" he asked his wife.

"*Cor* sent me a message via implant," she said. "We may have a line on Earth's location."

Nal's eyes widened for an instant before he, too, levered himself up and prepared to follow. Apparently, Teo Voxman had just checked in and received the news. Lara was looking at her when she, too, jerked in her seat and began gathering her belongings.

"Hold up, everyone!" Lara called out. She then made a general announcement to the boat's passengers about what *Cor* had found in the Afalonian novel. "Let us have an orderly disembarkation and then spend a couple of hours getting educated. I'll call a meeting of after third meal and we can plan our next move."

With that, Lara pulled herself hand-over-hand to the dorsal airlock using the chairs as anchor points. She waited for pressure to be equalized in the short embarkation tube from the ship and for both of *Charon*'s airlock doors to retract into their recesses. She then floated upward, grasped the swing bar with both hands, and then swung through a quick ninety-degree arc into the ship's standard one gee internal grav field.

She found Doria Teray waiting for her on the other side of the starship's airlock.

"Welcome back, Shipmaster. How did it go?"

"Reasonably well considering the unwelcome news we delivered. I'd like to come back someday to see if the two societies are able to overcome their mutual suspicion sufficiently to stave off extinction."

"Unlikely that we will come this way again," Doria responded.

"True. We have given them more than enough value for what

we learned, so that is all we can do. Does everyone aboard know about this clue *Cor* has found in the Afalonian novel?"

"Yes, Mistress. The Astronomy Group is already working on course options. They are just waiting for Scholar Voxman to give them guidance."

"They won't have long to wait. She will be the third face you see popping out of the tube."

#

As promised, the meeting was held at 20:00 hours in the conference room off the control center. Those in attendance included the usual expedition leaders, Teodara Voxman, and the rest of her astronomy team.

"Well, Teo, what do you think?"

The astronomer looked thoughtful for a moment and said, "It's at least as solid as the clues we have been following these past four years. I say that we act on it."

"Do you have a course to recommend?"

"Courses, Shipmaster. We have several possibilities. If I may, my people and I have spent the last couple of hours thinking about our options."

"We missed you at third meal. Proceed."

Scholar Voxman slipped her personal screen out of its pouch and stroked in a few codes. The holocube in the center of the table came alight to show a cubical volume of the Orion Arm some five hundred light years on a side. The vantage point was from due galactic north, an orientation which by tradition was known as Godview. The scale was such that it was possible to see the curved demarcation between the river of bright stars and the sea of dimmer stars to its left.

Inis Afalon and the Goddess' Veil were two golden sparks nestled in the near-bottom-left corner of the cube. Teo touched her screen, and a ghostly blue wall appeared, giving three-dimensional form to the arbitrary boundary between the Orion Arm and the adjacent region of middle-aged stars.

Another manipulation of the screen brought forth a large translucent cone. It was pale red and shaded to enhance its three-dimensional shape. The apex of the cone was at the golden point denoting Inis Afalon and it grew quickly to nearly fill the right side of the holocube.

"You see the problem, I take it," she said. "The Goddess' Veil Nebula subtends twenty degrees of arc in Monmoth's sky. So 'behind the Goddess' Veil' quickly encompasses quite a large volume of galactic space."

"Are you saying that we don't have a vector to guide us toward Sol?" Lara asked.

"Not a single vector, but we have our brains and we can narrow our choices, assuming we still believe one of our initial assumptions in planning this expedition."

"Which is?"

"That Sol lies near the inner edge of the Orion Arm. You will note that much of our search volume is oriented away from that edge. Therefore, I propose that we only consider those vectors that actually intersect the boundary marked by the blue wall."

A bright red line appeared. It was not along the axis of the cone. Rather, it lay in the plane of the galaxy and sliced the cone into small and large sections. At the line's appearance, the larger portion of the translucent cone vanished.

"What recommends this path?" Lara asked.

"It is the farthest anti-clockwise vector that touches the inner boundary of the Orion Arm. If we have not been misled, Earth should lie within a few degrees of this line."

Lara studied the diagram, thought about the shaky chain of assumptions that had led them to this juncture. Still, she could not come up with anything better and it beat flipping a credit chip as to where they would search next. Once again, she was plagued by the silent voice of one of her professors: "It's 'logical' you say? Have you ever heard the definition of logic? *An organized method for coming to the wrong conclusion with confidence.*"

"All right, we have the angle. What about the distance?"

"Between Inis Afalon and the point of tangency is 600 light-years. I propose we split the difference and begin our search at 300 light-years along the marked vector. It will still be the wildest stroke of good luck if we drop out within EM-range of Sol, but we should find inhabited stars there that are much closer to our ultimate goal than on this side of the nebula."

Lara looked at Nal, then Darin Mastlin and Betrice Flangan. "Any other suggestions?"

Nal looked up from the dimly glowing holocube and echoed Lara's own thought just a few seconds earlier.

"It beats flipping a credit, I suppose."

She regarded the rest of the astronomy working group. "Anyone else?"

She was answered by several shrugs.

"*Cor?*"

"The Academician's logic seems sound."

"Then that is what we will do. *Cor*, announce that the crew has seventy-two hours to rest, get cleaned up, and stow everything for hyperspace. On the third day, we break orbit and head once more into the deep black."

#

The return to hyperspace was uneventful. Having left geosynchronous orbit after a farewell broadcast, *Coronal Fire* boosted toward the nebula for a week before penetrating the inter-universal barrier. They spent the next three days casting about for a hyperon stream that would take them 'behind the Goddess' Veil.' They found one at the 800 equivalent-light level and upfreqed to embed themselves in its flow.

En route to their next breakout point, the crew returned to their routines. The biologists delved ever more deeply into the jumbled mosaic of Monmoth heredity, hoping to extract useful data. The naval ratings manned their sensor and weapons stations, ever on the lookout for risks. The astronomers, along with *Cor* and *Tac Seven*, plotted star maps of all the G-Class stars in the volume of space where they were headed.

Although the location of Sol had been lost, the star's physical properties were well known. Humanity's first star was on the main sequence of stellar evolution; a yellow dwarf of the G2 spectral class. The term "yellow-dwarf" was intended to distinguish it from the Big Blue Bruisers of the O, B, and A classes, and the myriad small ruby-red beacons of the M-Class. While descriptive, the name was a misnomer.

Yellow-dwarf stars were neither yellow nor particularly small.

The color of Sol-light was white, with the most prominent wavelengths in the blue and green regions of the spectrum. Its "yellow" color came not from its emissions; but from those wavelengths that managed to penetrate the Earth's thick blanket of air.

Atmospheric scattering of Sol's rays produced the lightly jaundiced condition by which the star was known. Depending on terrestrial weather conditions, Sol's color could range from light yellow, to orange, to red.

As for the "dwarf" part of the classification, Earth's sun was small only in comparison to giants of similar temperature. In fact, "dwarf" stars like Sol have more mass than all but the top ten percent of stars.

By filtering every star that was not Sol-like from their map, the astronomers made the problem of finding Earth seem almost manageable.

Even when they limited their attention to G-Class stars in the search area, Sol (assuming it was within that volume) was still masked by four thousand yellow-dwarf siblings. Narrowing the field to only G-2 yellow-dwarfs dropped the number of candidates to just over four hundred stars.

As *Cor* mordantly observed upon presenting the new map to her flesh-and-blood crewmates, searching all of them would only require three human lifetimes.

#

Two months later, *Coronal Fire* had crossed forty percent of the equivalent distance to their plotted breakout point. The ship's crew had long ago settled into their hyperspace routines. While the hyperon stream carried them onward, their enhanced sensors probed ahead for gravitational flaws and other hazards to navigation. They had confronted a dozen flaws of various types so far and had avoided them.

Once each month, Lara gave orders to drop through null to plot their position in normal space. The Goddess' Veil nebula was far behind them and at both breakouts their EM sniffer detected inhabited systems. The first contact was a lone star at the edge of detection.

The second breakout found EM sources from three different systems. One star was close enough that they debated taking a detour to evaluate the contact. However, the idea was abandoned when *Cor* pointed out that if they checked every such contact, it would take them a year to reach their destination.

Like all ships in the great black, life aboard *Coronal Fire* had long since evolved its own miniature society. There were the inevitable romances, squabbles, rivalries, cliques, hobbies, and competitions to occupy off-duty hours.

One popular activity was the resurrection of the ancient game of chess. One of the engineers had a passion for it and taught the game to anyone who wished to learn. The ad-hoc contests had morphed into a formal tournament structure among those who remained in orbit at Monmoth. A dozen cut-throat players continued their board battles en route to the next breakout.

Other diversions kept boredom at bay for the rest of the crew. The social high point of each week was the dinner hosted by Lara and Darin Mastlin. A dozen expedition members were invited to join them at 20:00 hours in the dining module to partake of tasty food and conversation.

Cor made up the roster each week, making sure that everyone had an equal opportunity to attend on a rotating basis. The dinner was a formal affair. Attendees were encouraged to don their finery to break the monotony of everyday shipsuits.

On the sixty-third day after their return to hyperspace, the dinner hosted the ship's doctor, two engineer technicians, three Marines, two naval personnel, and four analysts from the scientific staff.

The compartment view wall showed a beach scene on Bernau where two of the moons were rising just after twilight from out of the Ordken Sea. Swarms of sparkle-flyers hovered just above the marching waves, attracting the occasional lurking corona fish to propel itself out of the water in a long parabolic leap. Soft wind noises and the crash of waves could be heard in the background.

The banquet part of the dinner was over and Technician Katah Pezort was regaling the group with tales of her youth on Persephon when *Cor's* silent voice sounded in Lara's brain.

"Shipmaster."

"Yes, *Cor*?" she thought.

"Communications reports that the EM sniffer is picking up a signal."

"What, here in hyperspace?"

"Yes."

Lara frowned. The starship's primary sensors were limited to the layer in which the ship was riding plus or minus approximately one hundred equivalent lights of velocity.

But electromagnetic waves, like starships themselves, were alien to the superlight environment. Nor were Einstein's Laws operative in hyperspace. There was no time-space dilation effect, nor the universal one c speed limit. How could there be? At speeds faster than light, the equations that govern such phenomena turn imaginary.

And so, it was that radio waves in hyperspace share the pseudo-velocity of the surrounding hyperons. There is no perceptible time lag at any range where a radio signal is still detectable.

This makes communications easy at the start or end of a journey, where ships approaching breakout suddenly find themselves in a crowded sky. No matter their route, there comes a time in every voyage when the lonely travelers all converge on the single point in hyperspace that corresponds to the approved breakout point of their destination star. Breaking out anywhere else was considered rude and could possibly bring the attention of a warship.

The problem was that the EM amplitude dissipates with distance and starships are almost never within radio range of one another between stars. Yet, *Coronal Fire* was the exception that proved the rule. And, of course, the sensitivity of their EM sniffer made the possibility of receiving a signal marginally less unlikely than for normal communications equipment.

All the above went through Lara's brain in a flash. Those around her noticed the sudden change in her expression as she concentrated on her implant.

"What sort of signal?" she asked.

"Just a modulated tone," *Cor* replied. "Three short peaks, pause, three long peaks, pause, then three short peaks. Then there is a long pause and the pattern repeats."

"Sounds like gibberish to me."

"And to me, Shipmaster. However, that same sequence was used at the dawn of the Great Hegira to denote distress. It may still be in use for that purpose here in the Core."

"All right," she replied to the voice in her head. "Tell Darin, the astrogator on duty, and the Senior Legate to gather in the briefing room in thirty minutes. Alert Nal and the second and third officers."

"As you order, Shipmaster."

#

Chapter 23

Around the table in the briefing room sat Lara, Darin Mastlin, Nal, Athald Daver, Doria Teray, Astrogator Yarin Delnost, and Senior Legate Bas Klyster. Teo Voxman had also invited herself to the meeting.

"Well, what do we know about this contact?" Lara asked.

"We can't see it on our sensor suite," *Cor* replied. "It is too far downslope. However, from the signal analysis, I would estimate that it is at the 400-light level and moving crosswise to our current course."

"Let's hear the signal."

The air in the room was suddenly filled with a rhythmic beat. Three short tones, three long, three short, pause, repeat.

"What frequency are they broadcasting on?"

"It's wide spectrum, Shipmaster. That helped me calculate the range since low frequency signals attenuate faster than high frequency. I estimate the distance to the source to be three light-days."

That bit of data was something Lara had not heard before. By the expressions of those around her, neither had they. As she scanned the faces around the table, she paused at her ship-husband's scowl.

"Is something bothering you, Nal?"

"Isn't this déjà vu all over again?" he asked.

She nodded. "It feels just like when we first detected *New Hope*, doesn't it?"

He nodded while everyone else's expression was blank.

Lara smiled and explained that Nal had been suspicious when they had come across the lost colony ship. He had worried that it might be pirates lying in wait for the unwary.

"And you assured me that such encounters are so unlikely that no pirate would waste his time on such a tactic," he said, completing her explanation.

"So, I did."

"Yet here we face the same situation. What are the odds?"

Lara turned to Bas Klyster. "What say you, Senior Legate?"

The military man shrugged. "The fact you had a similar contact four or five years ago doesn't alter the probability of our intercepting this signal today. We are here and we have intercepted it. So, the question is, 'What do we do about it?'"

"The regulations are clear," Lara answered. "Whoever is on the other end may be in desperate straits. We must investigate and render aid, if possible. But Nal is right. We need to be cautious. *Cor*, how long will it take us to get downslope and into that hyperon stream at 400 lights?"

"At least four hours, Shipmaster. That assumes we can find a stream or eddy flowing in the right direction that will allow us to overtake them. Some maneuvering will undoubtedly be required in the terminal phase if we wish to intercept."

"Legate Klyster? Your recommendation."

"Standard operating procedure says we close until we have them in sensor range and sweep circumambient space. If the distress call appears genuine, we launch armed flyers and get them in position before we make contact and inquire if they need our assistance."

"Then that is what we will do."

#

The actual approach took eight hours.

When they first detected the distress signal (which, for some unknown reason, was called an *SOS*), *Coronal Fire* had already overflown the quarry's track. To rendezvous required them to backtrack and then execute a complex series of maneuvers to pull within passive sensor range of the target.

Unlike a warship, *Fire* did not have the gravitic engine power to maneuver completely independent of hyperon flows. Rather, *Cor* had to plot streams and eddies that would carry them toward the source of the signal at pseudo-velocities fast enough to overtake their quarry. Luckily, with a pseudo-velocity delta of 400 lights, that proved easier than expected.

By the time they were close enough to obtain a good read on

the distress signal's source, the level of tension in the control room had climbed to an intensity not seen since their approach to *New Hope*.

"It's definitely a vessel, Shipmaster," *Cor* finally reported.

"Any indication they've spotted us?"

"None."

"Anything in circumambient space?"

"Nothing noted."

"Legate Klyster," Lara said, knowing that the entire ship was following their progress.

"Here, Shipmaster."

"You may launch the flyers when you are ready."

The Morast Navy contingent had been busy during the long approach. They had removed the body panels that camouflaged the flyers' true nature, loaded missiles, and charged weapons power packs. *Charon* took aboard seven space-armored Marines. They were a tight fit in the passenger compartment, even with the usual seats removed.

As Lara watched via one of the hangar cameras, first *Charon*, then *Fenix*, and finally *Lilith* slipped into blackness. They switched on their masking systems and headed for the distressed craft one hundred klamaters distant.

Twenty minutes later, *Cor* announced that the flyers were in position and all was in readiness for first contact.

The ship in distress was the usual spherical shape and a bit smaller than *Coronal Fire*. It had fewer external hatches, which might make it a passenger liner. Outwardly, it appeared undamaged. Only the constant beeping suggested that something was wrong.

"All right, *Cor*, wake them up. As many frequencies as you can manage."

"*Unknown ship. Research vessel* Coronal Fire, *answering your distress call. Do you need assistance?*"

Cor paused for fifteen seconds, then repeated the call. She was on her tenth transmission when an excited female voice interrupted the beeping and began to speak very rapidly.

Unfortunately, no one could understand her.

"Any idea what language she is speaking?" Lara asked.

"Unknown, Shipmaster. I will try Standard and then work my

way through the other ancient languages in my history files."

"Proceed."

The next ten minutes were spent listening to *Cor* ask the woman if she understood in a dozen different languages. Each question was answered by increasingly frantic staccato bursts of gibberish.

Finally, *Cor* said, "Her answers vary, but she has used the same sound sequence to begin her response three times in a row."

"What sound?"

"'*Nyet!*' I believe she may be speaking a modified form of ancient Russian."

"Give it a try."

"*Govorish' po russki?*"

"*Da, da!*" came the instant reply. It was followed by a long string of excited syllables.

There was a momentary pause before *Cor* said, "Comparing her words to the ancient tongue, I can understand about half of what she is saying: Their ship has suffered an accident of some sort. They are without the ability to maneuver or change layers and are calling for help."

"Can we establish a visual link?"

"I will try. Stand by."

There followed a discussion in which the word 'video' figured prominently. After a minute, the view volume illuminated to show a blonde woman with frantic eyes and tear-stained cheeks looking out at them.

"Put me on the circuit, *Cor*."

"You are on, Shipmaster."

"Hello," she said to the image in the volume. "I am Shipmaster Lara da Benthar Sims of the Research Vessel *Coronal Fire*. May we be of assistance?"

"I can translate about half of that," *Cor* said into her implant.

"Do the best you can."

She listened as *Cor* spoke the strange language. The woman replied in the same tongue.

"She says that her name is Yelena Borisuvna Krasnova and that she is a passenger aboard the starliner *Aurora*. Several members of the crew are dead, and their engines are disabled. She thanks you for your offer."

"May we come aboard?" Lara asked.

"Yes."

"Where shall our people enter?"

"They will turn on the airlock markers for us," *Cor* said.

"Very well. Our boarding party will be with you shortly. Do not be frightened. They will be in full armor, but they mean you no harm."

"Yelena says that they will be welcome. However, she hesitated after I told her they were Marines. They seem to have been attacked."

"Subaltern Warwick?" Lara said to the empty air. Lynwood Warwick was the officer in command of the boarding party aboard *Charon*.

"Here, Shipmaster."

"You heard *Cor*. Be prepared for trouble but try to be as non-threatening as you can."

"Will do."

"*Charon* is cleared to approach."

#

Everyone aboard *Coronal Fire* watched as *Charon* closed with the disabled ship. The docking portals did not match (of course), so the Marines depressurized the flyer and floated out through the dorsal airlock into hyperspace.

Lara watched as they jetted across the gap with their individual position lights blinking in synchronization. The big ship's airlock was surrounded by a ribbon of white light that bathed the Marines' armor in a soft glow as they approached. They halted a meter short of the hull just as the airlock door opened to reveal a brightly lit interior.

Warwick gave a terse order. One of the Marines floated forward to affix a relay with a blinking red light to the hull, and who then floated into the open lock. He was joined by two others. It was a tight fit. The outer door slid closed, cutting off their view of the boarding party.

The view switched to Warwick's helmet cam, which included an audio pickup. The silence of vacuum was quickly replaced by the sound of rushing air. The return of audio was accompanied by a brief swirl of expansion fog.

A light above the inner door cycled from red to yellow to green. The door opened to a burst of excited Russian from the half-dozen people gathered in the suiting antechamber. The blonde woman from the video gave a loud order and the jabbering came to a quick halt.

She faced the Marines and began speaking. *Cor* translated.

"Subaltern Warwick. She is welcoming you and suggests that you clear the airlock so the rest of your party may enter."

The view shifted as Warwick moved forward. The swaying image showed that he was walking rather than floating. At least the ship's artificial gravity was still working.

Over the next few minutes, two more pairs of Marines locked through.

"Permission to remove my helmet," Warick said.

"Permission granted," Lara replied. "Transfer your cam to your shoulder so we can continue to watch."

The view shifted violently for a few seconds before stabilizing again.

Warwick coughed twice as he got his first breath of the ship's atmosphere. "The air is foul in here. The air plant may be damaged."

"*Cor*, ask Miss Krasnova about the air."

The computer's voice issued from Warwick's external speaker, followed by a burst of Russian.

"She says that it was damaged in the attack, but they have it operating now, but not as well as it once did. She asks whether we have an engineer onboard who can look at it."

"*Cor*, tell her we will have one of our technicians check it out, but warn her that our technology may be different from theirs. Ask her what happened and to answer in simple words so that we can understand."

The response was a single word: *Piraty*.

Even after two thousand years of divergent linguistic evolution, the answer required no translation.

#

Chapter 24

The ship had been en route to its home world of *Katerina* when it was accosted by an armed pirate vessel. The pirates ordered the crew to shut down their gravitics and prepare to be boarded. Rather than comply, the captain made a run for it. He adjusted his generators to race downslope through the hyperon layers toward null. Once in normal space, he would hide in the vast interstellar vacuum until the pirates grew impatient and went in search of other prey.

Unfortunately, a ship just cannot switch off its jump field. The superconducting coating on the hull stores substantial energy as it keeps the ship in sync with a particular hyperon layer. To flee downslope required the liner to dump that energy through radiators. Any attempt to jump straight from 600-lights to the real universe would vaporize the ship.

The pirate proved able to shed energy faster than *Aurora*. The marauders caught the fleeing Russians at the 400-light level and ordered them to halt a second time. The Captain stabilized the field and opened his airlock outer doors.

Two pirate flyers docked with the liner in opposite hemispheres and armored spacers swarmed aboard. They opened fire on the uniformed crewmembers who waited for them and forced a wounded survivor to take them to the control room. There they gunned down the operations crew, sparing only the captain. They demanded that he guide them to the cargo holds and supply the code that would open them.

There followed three days of looting and rampage, with male passengers shot at random and female passengers raped. While the atrocities continued, mechs and spacers looted the most valuable cargo and transferred it to their ship. The final atrocity took place when the marauders killed the captain, destroyed the jump generators and computers, and abandoned the now-helpless *Aurora* to her fate.

One crewman, an engineer, survived by hiding in an empty

compartment. After the marauders left, he emerged and set up the distress broadcast.

Lara grew angrier by the second as she listened to *Cor*'s translation. When the blonde woman finished describing the carnage, she explained that she was a senior functionary of the Katerina government. She had used her status to take control of the ship while the rest of the passengers were still in shock.

When *Fire*'s Marines finished their inspection of the damage, Yelena asked to go with them back to *Coronal Fire* to present her plea in person.

Lara, Darin Mastlin, and Nal met her in the briefing room. When Lara gently asked if she had lost anyone to the marauders, she responded, "*moy muzh.*"

"Her husband," *Cor* said via implant.

"I am terribly sorry. Why were they so insanely violent?"

"They were angry that we tried to run. Also, their boarding party numbered only a dozen men. Had we organized; we could easily have overcome them. It wouldn't have done any good with their ship ready to blow us out of hyperspace," she said bitterly, "but the marauders used the violence to keep us under control,"

"How can we help?" Lara asked.

It took several exchanges between Yelena and *Cor* before her request became clear. *Aurora* was disabled and could not be repaired. Even if the ship's engines were operational, the computers that controlled them were puddles of congealed slag. Yelena asked that they evacuate the survivors and transport them to Katerina.

"Shit!" Lara muttered while glancing at Nal. "What do I tell her?"

"The truth," he replied.

"*Cor*, explain to Yelena that we don't have sufficient life support for a thousand passengers, even if we had the space. This is a cargo vessel, not a passenger liner."

Yelena's shoulders slumped after *Cor*'s explanation. She muttered several sentences in Russian.

"She says that she knew this in her heart but had to ask. She begs us to take the children. Also, they have gravely wounded people they cannot properly care for."

"How many?"

"One hundred and five children, twenty wounded adults."

"*Cor*, how many people can we rescue without endangering the ship?"

"Two hundred if the voyage isn't too long. We can use the hibernation tanks for the wounded and some of the younger children."

She turned to Yelena. "How far is it to your home?"

"The flow we were in before we tried to run is a main shipping lane. It passes within a dozen light-years of our star, which is named Moskva. The voyage will require 400 hours."

"If we take some of your people home, will those left behind have sufficient life support to await rescue?"

"I do not know."

"Then we had best find out. We will send medical staff to attend to your wounded and engineers to evaluate your life system. Also, we can strengthen your beacon to give your distress call greater range. Is there any chance of another ship hearing your signal?"

"Anything is possible. I understand you were at 1000-lights when you heard us. Perhaps someone else will hear us as well."

"Will you have dinner with us?" Lara asked.

"I must get back to my ship."

"It will only take a few hours. We have a great deal to discuss."

"Then I will stay."

#

Third meal was spent learning the critical needs of *Aurora*'s survivors. The talks ended after the ship's lights were muted to night-time blue. *Cor*'s knowledge of Yelena's language grew with each passing hour, which shortened the delays in communicating. When asked if her language had a name, Yelena replied, "Novy Russky."

At mid-watch, it was a tired envoy who donned her ill-fitting vacsuit and entered *Charon* for the return to her ship.

The next day, Lara requested a briefing from Walevek Ancherson, *Fire*'s chief engineer.

"How bad is the life system, Wal?"

"The pirates must have been in a hurry. It is singed, but

repairable. The technology is primitive by our standards. The whole ship is like something out of the last century."

"Is this a world that has been blasted back to an earlier technological level like Monmoth, or is it representative of the entire Core?"

"There is no way to tell, Shipmaster. It seems strange to think that we on the outer periphery might be more advanced than the worlds of the Core. However, if the wars persisted longer here than at home, perhaps it is true."

"Something to think about," Lara mused. "Continue your report, Engineer."

"We've fixed as much of the damage as we can. The air system ought to keep eight hundred survivors alive for six months; that is, if they don't mind being out of breath most of the time. But it is damned marginal. If something breaks before the rescue ships arrive, they will find a second *New Hope*."

"Do you have any ideas to improve the situation?"

"One that you probably won't like," the engineer responded.

"Let's hear it."

"We have a couple of spare life support modules in Number One Hold. My people could have one of them operating aboard *Aurora* in about twelve hours."

Lara frowned. She had once heard an ancient expression: *on the horns of a dilemma*. She had no idea what a 'horn' was, but she had new understanding of the phrase's meaning.

Aurora's life system might well run long enough for rescue to arrive. Then again, it might not. In the latter event, withholding aid would sentence these people to death. But if she gave them one of the expedition's spare modules, she might be sentencing her own ship to the same fate at some future time… say, on the four-year-long journey home.

Then, of course, there was the third possibility. What if the rescuers never came?

Assuming a rescue fleet left Katerina as soon as they heard of the disaster, by the time they returned to this spot, *Aurora* would have been carried 100 light-years downstream. Lara was aware of the difficulties involved in finding a ship in the vastness of hyperspace – the return expedition to *New Hope* had taught her that. What if all this effort was for naught?

She sighed. No matter what she did, there was no obvious 'best' solution to the problem. This was one time when she would have to rely on her instinct.

She scowled at the engineer. "I don't like it, but we don't have a choice. Get that module out of Hold One and over to the liner. Also, we need a docking mechanism over there if we are to take refugees off without resorting to vacsuits."

"Bethia's working on it. We should start construction in a few hours and have it done before first meal tomorrow."

"Very well. You have your work cut out for you. Do not let me keep you. *Cor*, start issuing orders to the crew to begin doubling up. We're going to need their sleeping cabins."

"Yes, Shipmaster."

#

Chapter 25

The first refugees came aboard the next morning after the engineers finished grafting one of *Fire*'s docking portals to *Aurora*'s Number Three Airlock.

They came in groups of twenty— eighteen children and two adults to keep the children under control. The adults were only partially successful in this.

Dr. bin Sool examined each of the new arrivals while Betrice Flangan obtained DNA samples to continue her studies of Core genetic makeup.

The severely wounded were the next to be transferred. These were placed into cold sleep tanks after examination, as were the dozen infant refugees. Finally, able-bodied survivors began to filter over after making their tearful goodbyes.

To Lara's surprise, Yelena Krasnova was one of these.

"I tried to stay," the embarrassed blonde explained when Lara met her at the docking port. "The others said that I could best get the rescue organized at home. Anatoly Gorlov will take command in my absence."

"It's good to have you aboard. Spacer Erkoza will show you to your quarters. It will be a bit crowded; I'm afraid. You will have to share a sleeping compartment with three other women. You can switch off the artificial gravity at night. That will allow each of you to have a bulkhead on which hang your sleeping nets."

"Spasiba, whatever you can provide will be appreciated."

After the last of the refugees were aboard, *Fire*'s engineers replaced *Aurora*'s EM transmitter with one of their own. In addition to the SOS signal, the transmitter sent out messages in Novy Russky and Old Standard detailing the ship's predicament. The transmitter was powered by a miniature generator a thousand times more powerful than its predecessor.

The ship was now a virtual radio star in the depths of hyperspace. Even so, while it would be detectable up and down the hyperon energy layers, its total range was limited to a single light-month. The increased power would improve the odds of another ship detecting *Aurora* from unimaginably small to merely highly unlikely.

Hyperspace is that big.

After the last refugee came aboard, the engineers dismounted the docking portal and returned it to *Coronal Fire*. Even if the liner were discovered by another starship, the portal's technology would be incompatible with Core docking standards.

Finally, it was time to take their leave. Lara was at her station in the control center while Darin Mastlin occupied the couch to her left. Nal was in engineering at his emergency station. As a courtesy, Lara invited Yelena to observe from the couch to her right. The first and second officers had duties elsewhere. *Cor*, of course, remained in her armored column directly behind Lara.

"Are we ready to maneuver?"

"We are ready, Shipmaster. All departments report secure for flight. All stations are manned, all weapons are powered, all sensors are at full gain. All guests are in their individual cabins."

Lara ordered the Command Staff circuit activated. "Final check. Affirm your status."

Even though the computer had already reported everyone's status, long tradition (based on hard experience) required the master of a starship to get a voice confirmation from each department head before a ship could get underway. Redundant though it might be, the check foreclosed the possibility of someone claiming they had not been ready if an accident occurred.

The calls moved smoothly down the ship's organization chart. As usual, Lara was the last to say, "Shipmaster, ready to maneuver."

Then came a break in the classic routine.

Lara turned to Yelena and said, "The comm is yours."

The blonde woman spoke a few sentences in Russian, which were followed by a brave sounding voice that answered from *Aurora*.

The translation came via Lara's implant. "Yelena is telling them to keep their spirits high and that she will be back as soon as she can. Boris Gorlov says that they will be waiting. She wishes him good luck."

Lara felt tears form at the corner of her eyes. Yelena was obviously holding her own voice in check as she said her farewells.

"All right, *Cor*. Engage preprogrammed course."

"Upfrequing to 480-lights."

Yelena asked, "Are we not going up to 600-lights?"

Lara answered. "The hyperon stream in which *Aurora* is embedded is merely an eddy current of a major flow at 480-lights. We are going up to map that stream as far as we can. It will take us a little longer to reach Moskva, but that knowledge should greatly shorten the search."

"How long will this... mapping... take?"

"*Cor* says that we will have to abandon the effort in 48 hours if we are to rejoin the main trade route toward your star. Hopefully, we will get a good vector on *Aurora*'s future positions before we have to leave."

"I understand."

From her tone, Lara was not sure that she did.

#

Life aboard the overcrowded starship once again settled into a routine, although one quite different from what it had been. The presence of the children made that a necessity.

For one thing, *Cor* began to teach the children Omni, the lingua franca of the Periphery. The younger children soaked up words like water reclamation circuits. The older ones quickly learned enough to make their most basic wishes known in the new language.

Meals were eaten in shifts, with the children and their minders served one hour before the adults. The dining pod decibel level climbed during Children Time.

Adult meals were also crowded. They became marginally less so after Lara offered the unoccupied hibernation tanks to anyone who wished them.

The choice of 'volunteers' was left to the Katerinans. It quickly became clear that those who went into the tanks were individuals who could not shake their personal grief, at least long enough to avoid weeping through mealtime. By the third day, the hibernation tanks were full and the mood at meals was measurably more cheerful.

To improve communications, Lara had wristband communicators issued to everyone, crew and refugees alike. This allowed *Cor* to translate personal conversations with near simultaneity in both directions as she had done on Monmoth.

Cor mapped the 480-light stream as planned and assigned *Tac Seven* to project *Aurora*'s course as far into the future as their data would allow. Unfortunately, that was not as far as Lara had hoped. Too soon they had to break off and head upslope to the trade route that would take them toward Moskva.

The Katerinans quickly organized to take over as much of the burden of their maintenance as possible. Yelena appointed three assistants to handle various aspects of life aboard this foreign starship.

The refugees cleaned their own quarters and supplied cooks to prepare their native fare at mealtime. Crewmembers were invited to partake of their cuisine. Yelena explained at their first meal that the delicacies served were compromises on authentic dishes due to the limited range of ingredients aboard *Coronal Fire*.

The Katerinans also supplied teachers and requested use of the entertainment pod four hours each day to further the children's education. Lara was pleased to supply the facilities since it would keep the little hellions occupied and out of trouble.

Lara met Yelena and her three assistants daily to review their needs and keep them apprised of the ship's progress toward their home star. Six days after leaving the stricken liner, she presented *Tac Seven*'s findings of their ship's future course.

"Here is the reason we delayed our arrival at 600 lights," she said as she projected a three-dimensional diagram into the conference room's holocube.

The cube's view volume was filled by the flow in which *Aurora* was trapped. This was displayed in cyan while the liner's projected course was bright crimson. The data uncertainty factor was displayed as a translucent cloud around the course line, one that increased in diameter with each passing day. *Tak-Seven* had projected the liner's future out to Day 93, at which time the unknown factors overwhelmed the projection.

There was a minute of silence after Lara displayed the graphic. The silence was broken when Anatoly Dubinski, Yelena's second-in-command frowned and said, "I'm sorry but I do not understand what I am looking at."

"You see the red line, don't you?" Lara asked. "That is where we expect *Aurora* to be on each of the marked dates, with the pink cloud denoting the possible locus of positions around it."

"Of course, the tall young man said. "That is obvious. But what is this blue-green shaded figure?"

"That is the stream that is propelling your ship through hyperspace."

"I am sorry, but my training is in (untranslatable). I have never had much interest in hyper-physics."

Lara blinked. This was a problem she had not considered. She looked at the other three: Yelena, Victor, and Marissa. Their faces all showed varying degrees of incomprehension.

She paused to collect her thoughts and then launched into as simplified explanation of the nature of hyperspace as she could.

Twenty minutes later, they seemed to understand.

"So, it is an invisible river that flows through this blackness and carries the ship along with it?" Anatoly asked.

"Exactly."

Anatoly smiled, waved his hands, and said, "I am sorry I asked."

Lara considered whether to expand on her explanation, then decided to leave well enough alone. She opened her mouth, intending to ask Yelena about the general morale among her group. However, *Cor* chose that moment to interrupt via her implant.

"Shipmaster."

"Yes, *Cor*?"

"Sensors have detected a ship at medium range. It is currently downslope and climbing in this direction."

"I will be in Control in thirty seconds. Announce Combat Condition One."

Out loud, she said, "Something has come up. We are going to high alert. Get your people back to their quarters. Yelena, please join me."

#

Chapter 26

The view volume had a tactical display selected when Lara and Yelena entered Control. Athald Daver rose from the duty station and let Lara sit down. He motioned Yelena Krasnova to the right couch and transferred to the left.

"What do we know, Ath?" Lara asked.

"Our sensors were clear until about ten minutes ago. We detected a starship powering up to maneuver at 560 lights. He came up to 580 about as fast as he could and is still crossing the stream toward our course track. He is now twelve light-hours in front of us and at a 20-light closure rate, will be here in thirty-six minutes. He looks like he is on an intercept track. We think he will pop up to 600 lights when he enters normal detection range."

"Has he contacted us?"

"Nothing yet."

"Yelena, is this situation familiar to you?"

It took the Katerinan a few seconds to respond. She had to clear her throat to find her voice. "Our Kapitan reported that the pirate was dead ahead when he hailed us. I don't know the range."

"I wonder if this is the same marauder."

"How could it be?" Daver asked. "The amount of time we spent with *Aurora* should put him light-years ahead of us."

"Not if he skulked along at 560 lights looking for targets in the upslope traffic. Our size certainly makes us look ripe for the picking.

"*Cor*, what is your analysis?"

"The same as the First Officer's, Shipmaster. He appears to be on an intercept approach. He is using this stream's downslope eddies to get in front of us."

"Legate Klyster?" Lara asked the empty air.

"Here, Shipmaster."

"Do you agree?"

"I do."

"How long before he would come into range of our pre-overhaul detection gear?"

"Fifteen minutes at this rate of closure."

"Your recommendation?"

"He is still distant enough that we can evade if we wish to."

"Evade how?"

"There is a cross-current at 800 lights and another at one thousand. Either will get us out of his performance envelope before he can react. However, both will take us off course for Moskva and require maneuvering to return to this stream."

"How much delay?"

"A week, possibly two."

"No, every hour lost reduces the chance of *Aurora* being found. Besides, if this is the same pirate, I do not want to evade," she said, glancing at Yelena. "That assumes, of course, that we can take him with our weaponry. Recommendations?"

"From the way he climbed the energy layers, he doesn't look like a warship," Klyster replied. "I suspect a converted freighter with an engine and sensor suite upgrade."

"How long before we can take him out?"

"He is within the performance envelope of our three multi-phasic missiles now. Perhaps one across his bow to dissuade him from coming any closer?"

"If he is the pirate that attacked Yelena's ship, I don't want him to get away."

"Your orders, Shipmaster?"

"Launch the fliers under full masking. Let us get them as far ahead of us as we can before he pops up. At the proper time, they will go quiet to avoid detection. With luck, we can set up an ambush."

"Order received. Launch flyers with full weapons loads."

Three minutes later, all three flyers left the hangar bay and accelerated into the deep black, headed at top speed toward where the intruder was projected to arrive in the 600-light stream. They would not reach that point in time, but the marauder would have to close on *Coronal Fire* to make the intercept. When it did, it would come within range of the waiting flyers.

Just as battles on planetary seas have certain immutable rules imposed by their environment; so, too, battles in hyperspace. The three multi-phasic missiles were miniature starships, each capable of changing energy levels by tens of lights and propelling themselves out to a full light-day beyond the vessel that launched them.

They were also expensive and not to be used if there was any other way. *Fire* had several means to kill an adversary. The armed flyers would serve handily in the current situation. They were virtually undetectable with their gravitic drives shut down.

As Lara watched from control, the three symbols showing the flyers accelerated away from the ship, slowly diverging as they raced downrange.

Ten minutes after leaving the hangar bay, *Cor* reported that the marauder was starting his approach to 600 lights.

"All flyers, go inert," Klyster ordered.

Three bright points in the situation display faded to black. Only the tightly focused laser beams with which the three auxiliaries communicated let *Coronal Fire* know where they were.

"All right, we wait," Lara said to no one in particular.

The unknown's closing rate dropped to mere interplanetary speeds as he came up to 600 lights some fifty thousand klamaters in front of them.

Simultaneously, *Cor* announced, "We are receiving a video feed, Shipmaster."

"Put it up."

The tactical display dimmed, and a spherical image appeared in its place. It showed the control room of another ship at the center of which sat a bearded man in a strange uniform. He opened his mouth and words came out.

"Modified standard," *Cor* reported. "Different from what they speak on Monmoth, but intelligible. He is telling us to shut down our gravitics or be destroyed."

Yelena's sudden gasp confirmed Lara's suspicion.

These were the people who had savaged *Aurora*.

#

"Recognize him?"

"He is the one who commanded the boarding party," Yelena replied in a choked voice. "He killed my Mishka."

"*Cor*, put my image alone on a beam. Everyone else be quiet."

"You are on, Shipmaster."

"This is Shipmaster Larath da Benthar Sims of the Research Vessel *Coronal Fire*. Who are you?"

"I am the person who will destroy you if you do not shut down your gravitics," the floating image growled. "Why do your words not match your lips?"

"I am speaking Omni. We are from the Morast Coordinate on the Periphery. We do not speak Standard there. You are hearing the translation."

"Never heard of this Morast. Stop stalling and shut down now. You have ten seconds to comply."

"Shut down our gravitics, *Cor*."

The bearded man's eyes flicked to the right, as though he was watching an instrument cluster. After a few seconds, the corners of his mouth turned upward in a mirthless smile.

"That was smart of you, Captain. What cargo are you carrying?"

"As I told you," Lara answered in her best indignant voice. "We are a research vessel. We are not carrying any cargo you would be interested in."

"Disappointing, if true. Just to make sure, we'll come aboard and check your story."

"Do you promise not to harm my ship or crew?" Lara semi-whined.

"I promise nothing except to blow you out of the black if you don't do exactly what I say."

"Very well. We will comply. Video off."

The feed stopped.

"Legate, how are we doing?" she asked on the command circuit.

"He's coming on at what should be his top acceleration. Not a warship. He should be in range of *Fenix* in another three minutes. *Lilith* will be in range a minute after that."

"All right, as soon as he is in range, let's hit him with the biggest sensor pulse we can manage. I will get on the comm and demand his surrender. If he looks like he is going to fire or tries to flee downslope, tell the flyers they are each to put two missiles into him."

The next three minutes were interminable.

The pirate came on with supreme confidence. As he did so, the tactical display showed two red translucent shapes indicating the two flyers' kill cones. *Charon* was too far to port to intercept the oncoming ship without maneuvering, something that would give the ambush away.

At three minutes, *Fenix*'s kill cone turned green, followed a minute later by *Lillith*'s.

"Hit him with a pulse," Lara ordered. "*Cor*, put me on a link to our new acquaintance."

The view volume lit up to show the pirate commander's features just as the EM pulse went out. He had opened his mouth to say something when his eyes went wide, and he jerked his head to one side.

"What the hell...?"

He snapped his head back to see Lara's features hovering in front of him. "Damn you, I warned..."

"It is I who will be doing the warning here," she answered coldly. "You have ten seconds to cut power and surrender your ship, Captain. Otherwise I will blow you out of the black."

"Who are you?"

"As I said, a research vessel out of the Morast Coordinate, 4000 light-years from home, and well equipped to handle unfriendly strangers."

"Nice bluff, but it won't work."

"He has fired a missile, Shipmaster," *Cor* said. "It will be here in thirty seconds."

"Anti-missile defense," Legate Klyster ordered over the command circuit. His voice was surprisingly steady.

Immediately, two sparks illuminated in the view volume from the two widely separated flyers.

"Destroy him," Lara commanded.

"Full spread, both flyers," Klyster ordered.

Four more sparks appeared. These were on a converging course to a spot beyond where the first pair were aimed.

Looking at the snarling features before her, Lara asked, "Do you remember a Katerinan liner named *Aurora*, Captain?"

His eyes got even wider as he received reports of incoming missiles.

"How do you know about..."

He never finished the sentence. A bright flash followed by an expanding cloud of ionized iron illuminated the eternal blackness of hyperspace.

Beside Lara, Yelena Krasnova wept for joy.

#

Chapter 27

The rest of the voyage to Moskva was anticlimactic.

The star appeared in the view volume 380 hours after their encounter with the pirate. Moskva was an F8-spectral-class star with twice the mass of Morast and a larger temperate zone where water is liquid. Katerina, Moskva IV, was in the middle of the zone.

Unlike Monmoth, the planet lacked polar ice caps. Indeed, long-range views showed no hint of ice on the world at all. Yelena's description of the climate reminded Lara of other warm worlds she had visited. It was barely habitable at the equator, but comfortable in the high latitudes. This was where most of the population lived.

After dropping back to normal space at the edge of the system, Lara ordered a quick search for the planet. It was not difficult to find. Moskva proved to be a massive source of EM radiation.

Having found their target world, she ordered *Côr* to send Yelena's beamed message explaining who they were and the fate of *Aurora*. Speed-of-light delay meant that it took three hours to receive a reply.

The return message thanked them for coming to the aid of the stranded passengers and asked that *Fire* proceed at top speed to Gagarin, the largest of Katerina's three moons. There they would rendezvous with the rescue fleet that would be forming by the time they arrived.

"Why Gagarin?" Lara asked.

"It is the main base of the Katerinan Navy," Yelena replied. "It is to them that you will present your observations of *Aurora*'s present course."

"And afterwards?"

"You will then proceed to Katerina, where I suspect you will be properly rewarded for your kindness."

Lara nodded. The two of them had already discussed the fact that *Fire* was on a mission to find Earth and that the expedition would appreciate whatever astrographical data Katerina had. They also reviewed Betrice Flangan's genetic survey. Yelena assured her that the government would be happy to help in both endeavors.

Katerina grew larger over the next nine days as they made their speed run into the inner system. Gagarin was a big moon, although not as large as Earth's Luna. The two other moons were miniature orbs, the smallest of which was not even spherical.

When they closed to communications range, *Cor* was kept busy forwarding passengers' messages to their loved ones. In addition, she received a steady stream of interrogatories from the planetary authorities requesting more details concerning the disaster.

One of the first communications was a list of those aboard the ill-fated liner. Of necessity, it had only the names of those passengers who had booked round-trip passages. The list was accompanied by a request that they add or remove the names of those actually aboard and report each person's fate. Lara passed this responsibility to Yelena and her assistants. From their expressions during the now weekly meeting, the task had taken an emotional toll.

Nor were all the requests for information from official sources. The story of the waylaid starship was an ongoing planet-wide sensation. Monitored news broadcasts were full of nothing else.

When *Fire* finally closed to practical two-way communications range, they received several requests for interviews with *Fire*'s commanding officer and with Yelena Krasnova. A quick negotiation combined these requests into a single session with a moderator representing all the planetary media.

Of necessity, it was conducted in Novy Russky, with *Cor* doing the simultaneous translating via Lara's implant for the questions and directly on the comm-link for the answers. The broadcast was to be recorded and then edited to cut the pauses inherent in the 15 second speed-of-light communications delay.

Nadia Federov, an elegant blonde who bore a resemblance to Yelena Krasnova, began the interview by asking Lara to explain who they were and how they had come to intercept the crippled liner's distress signal.

Lara explained they were from the Eastern Periphery of human space and were based in the Morast Coordinate, one of the leading stellar nations there. She emphasized that it had taken them four years to reach the Core, which their people had not visited in several generations. She recounted the surprise aboard ship when their EM receiver had detected the liner's SOS.

The interviewer then asked about the scene when they had first boarded *Aurora*. Lara handed that part over to Yelena, who recounted the horror of the sacking of the ship.

She then described the many ways *Coronal Fire* had aided the castaways, including the installation of one of their precious life modules aboard the liner to augment the ship's damaged life support. The translated praise in Lara's implant was so fulsome that she felt her ears turning red.

Finally, the interviewer asked about the encounter with the pirate. That was one question Lara was prepared for. She had earlier directed *Cor* to edit the record of the battle down to a three-minute report.

When the recording ended, the female interviewer thanked them for their cooperation and asked that they stand by. After what seemed an interminable delay, the view changed to show a silver-haired man.

"Gospodin, Prezident!" Yelena exclaimed.

The figure in the view volume came to life and began speaking long before he could have heard her words, a symptom of their time-lagged communications. He said that his world owed Lara and her crew a debt they could never repay and invited everyone aboard to visit Katerina once the rescue fleet was on its way.

"Spasiba, Gospodin Prezident," Lara replied in the few words of Novy Russky she had picked up before switching back to Omni. "We would be pleased to accept your invitation. We are a scientific expedition interested in your astronomical records and for any assistance you can give us in our study of the genetic makeup of the Core colonies."

After the requisite fifteen second delay, the Prezident replied, "All aid will be provided, Kapitan de Benthar Sims. You will find that we are a generous people to our friends."

#

Coronal Fire took up orbit around Gagarin twenty hours later. Approach Control provided *Cor* with detailed instructions to

see them safely through the extensive orbital traffic. By the time
Fire's gravitic generators were shut down, they were in a parking
orbit that gave them an all-too-panoramic view of the moon's
jagged peaks that rushed past only fifty klamaters below.

In front of them, a dozen ships of the Katerinan Navy were in
the last stages of preparations to go in search of the lost liner. Ten
minutes after they made orbit, a ferry detached from the large
warship directly ahead of them.

When the ferry closed half the distance, a voice said, "Starship
Coronal Fire, this is *Potemkin Number Three*. Request approach and
docking instructions."

"Hello, *Potemkin Number Three*. This is *Coronal Fire*," Cor
replied. "I'm afraid our docking technology is not to Core standards.
Hold while I look you over."

After a few seconds in which the computer scanned the ferry,
she said to Lara, "They should fit in the hangar bay without difficulty
once we clear it. What do you want to do?"

"Bring them aboard."

Cor resumed her dialogue with the Katerinan boat: "You will fit
in our hangar bay. Would you like to come aboard?"

"Da," an older voice replied. "We wish to consult with your
kapitan."

"Stand by."

"Legate Klyster, man the flyers and clear the hangar bay," Lara
ordered.

"Will do, Shipmaster."

"Nal, will you supervise?"

"Will do, Shipmaster," her ship-husband parroted. She smiled
at that. In private, some of the names he called her were less
respectful.

It took half an hour to clear the bay of *Charon, Fenix,* and *Lilith.*
As soon as they were parked aft orbit of *Fire*, the Katerinan boat
floated through the open hatch and into the bay. Unlike the flyers,
it was a collection of geometric shapes.

Normally such a maneuver would have been controlled
computer-to-computer, but since the necessary protocols did not
exist, Nal talked them through the approach. When the ferry was
fully inside, the port closed. Internal handling equipment reached

out to anchor the visitor.

· While she watched the delicate maneuver, Lara sent a command via implant to connect her to the Chief Engineer.

"Yes, Shipmaster?" Walevek Ancherson answered.

"Wal, if we are going to do much more of this, perhaps we should modify one of our docking ports to Core standard. It looks like we will be in this system long enough to even obtain one of theirs and interface it with our systems. Comments?"

"A promising idea, Shipmaster. In fact, after holding my breath for the last few minutes, I was going to suggest it myself. We'll need interface specifications, of course."

"Put that on the list for things to accomplish when we settle into orbit about Katerina."

"Consider it done."

"The hangar bay is pressurized, Shipmaster," *Cor* reported.

"Then I had best get down there," Lara replied. "Let's get a Marine honor guard in position. That last voice sounded like it belonged to someone high ranking."

"They are on their way."

#

The hangar bay gravity field had been turned off to prevent the Katerinan boat from smashing into something vital as it came aboard.

As Lara arrived at the bay hatch, she reached up to grasp the overhead swing bar, which was illuminated by a row of blinking warning lights. She lifted her feet and pivoted smoothly into the zone of microgravity. She transferred to the taut cable strung between the hatch and the docking stage and pulled herself hand-over-hand to where six Marines were still anchoring themselves to the stage gridwork. Lara oriented herself one pace in front of the Marines and locked her boot clips into the grid. She found herself facing the Cyrillic lettering on a closed airlock outer door. No sooner was she in position than the door disappeared into a recess in the hull.

Backlit by the interior lights was a large man in a dark uniform with three small stars in line on his shoulder boards. Lara could not read the insignia but recognized a high-ranking officer when she saw one.

A few seconds later, a pole striped in black-and-yellow extended from somewhere behind her left shoulder. It reached out to the airlock, stopping just short of the boat's hull. The officer reached up to grasp it and pulled himself expertly to where she was anchored. Behind him a female figure appeared. Her shoulders bore three stars arrayed in a triangle, bisected by a line.

The leader reached Lara, levered his body into alignment with hers, steadied himself with his left hand, and executed a salute with his right. His greeting was, of course, in Novy Russky.

"Permission to enter your vessel, Kapitan?" *Cor* translated in her implant.

"Permission granted," Lara replied as she returned a reasonable facsimile of his salute. "I am Shipmaster Lara Sims of the Scientific Research Vessel *Coronal Fire*."

"It is good to meet you... Shipmaster. I am Admiral Alexei Trudonov of the Fleet Cruiser *Prince Grigory Potemkin*. I will be in command of the coming rescue mission." He turned to look behind him. He found his companion floating one meter away.

Turning back, he said, "May I also introduce my aide, Senior Lieutenant Darya Semolov?"

"Welcome, Lieutenant," Lara replied, looking over Trudonov's shoulder. She turned back to the admiral. "Let's get into ship's gravity to continue this conversation, shall we?"

"*Da*. Lead on."

Lara led them to the bay hatch where she reversed her gymnastics with the swing bar. Her visitors followed, with neither showing any difficulty negotiating the transition from weightlessness to gravity.

Lara led them through a second pressure door and into the crowded corridor beyond where a delegation of refugees awaited them.

There followed five minutes of excited Russian chattering. Lara waited for the cacophony to die down before directing the two naval officers to follow her.

#

As they entered the conference room, they found Nal, Senior

Astrogator Delnost, Senior Legate Klyster, and Teodara Voxman already seated at the table. Yelena Krasnova was standing and moved forward to kiss the two visitors on their cheeks. Lara noted that tears were streaming down both her cheeks.

After introductions were concluded, Admiral Trudonov asked Lara to recount again how it was that they had discovered the lost liner and why they had gone to so much trouble to help them.

Lara answered the last question first.

"On the Periphery, we have laws requiring ships to give all practical aid to star travelers in distress. Is it different in the Core?

"We have the same laws," the Admiral replied. "However, it is not unknown for passing ships who encounter a vessel in distress to shirk their duty and sneak off without making their presence known. I understand that you supplied *Aurora* with a piece of life support equipment. What are the capabilities of this 'life module'?"

Lara explained that the self-contained unit would supply oxygen and water to sustain the passengers for as long as they needed it. "Their survival will be limited only by their food supply."

Trudonov exchanged a look with his aide, leaving Lara with the impression that Katerinan technology was not as capable.

"And after you departed, we understand that you plotted *Aurora*'s future course." Lieutenant Semolov commented.

"We did. We translated up to 480 lights and plotted the eddy at 400 lights until we had to break off to come here. Astrogator Delnost will give you the details. Yarin, the view volume is yours."

The astrogator spent twenty minutes reviewing their data, displaying the time-position projection for the lost liner.

The two Katerinan naval officers asked technical questions of Delnost for another twenty minutes before they were satisfied.

"How will you get this data to my flagship?" the Admiral asked.

"*Cor*, how have your conversations been going with *Potemkin*'s computer?" Lara asked the air.

"We have exchanged technical specifications and I have translated our information into their format. I am ready to send."

"Do so now."

A few seconds later, *Cor* announced that the data stream had been received aboard the flagship.

Lara reached into her belt pouch and extracted a record crystal and a small player. She slid these across the table to the Admiral.

"Here is a backup of the original data with a machine to read it. The information is in a graphical symbology with no need for you to understand Omni."

"Spasiba, Shipmaster," the Admiral replied as he tucked the gifts into his tunic. "Now, as time is of the essence. Remain here until the fleet leaves. Traffic Control will then give you instructions for clearing Gagarin space and direct you to a parking orbit about Katerina.

"I hope you can extend your visit until our return. With luck, we will be able to restore your life module to you. Katerinan honor demands no less."

#

Chapter 28

An hour after the Katerinan orbital boat returned to its mother ship, everyone aboard *Coronal Fire* watched as the rescue fleet smoothly powered out of orbit. The last ship to leave was *Prince Grigory Potemkin*. Lara ordered *Cor* to flash *Fire*'s maneuvering lights three times in quick succession, the traditional signal for "good luck." Within seconds, *Potemkin*'s bright hull strobes emitted three long flashes in response.

Cor followed the fleet via the ship's telescope for more than an hour. As the ships left Gagarin's traffic zone, they shifted into a loose globular formation for the climb out of Moskva's gravity well.

Nor was *Fire*'s crew idle while they watched their hosts disappear into the black. The three flyers returned to the hangar bay, the refugees were herded back into their quarters, and all departments began their 'pre-launch' routines.

Two hours later, they requested departure instructions from Gagarin Traffic Control. Half an hour after that *Fire* powered gravitics and began the climb toward the blue-white planet overhead.

#

Katerina's seas were smaller and shallower than Bernau's and varied in color from deep blue to aquamarine to light tan. Local space was crowded even more than what they had found around Monmoth, with the notable exception that the habitats, stations, and industrial facilities were vibrantly alive.

Their approach instructions were extremely detailed and involved slipping through concentric bands of orbiting infrastructure. Between the bands were wide regions of emptiness. The reason for this arrangement became clear when *Cor* twice announced high speed objects closing on them at right angle to their course. These were other stations and satellites in polar orbit.

"If this is a star in the outer shell of the core," Lara commented to the computer, "What do you suppose near-Earth space is like?"

"Cluttered, I imagine," *Cor* replied.

At Gagarin, they had orbited at an altitude where the mountain tops appeared close enough to touch. At Katerina, they found themselves vectored to Kazan-tri, a massive habitat at twice geo-synchronous altitude. Their flight program called for them to match velocities five klameters aft of the oversize, brightly lit conglomeration of geometric shapes.

Shortly after they took up their assigned position, an orbital transport detached from the station and closed on *Coronal Fire.*

"There is an Ambassador Semonov on the comm, Shipmaster," *Cor* announced via Lara's implant. "He is requesting permission to come aboard."

"Explain to him that our docking technology is incompatible with Katerinan standards."

"I already have," the computer replied. "However, I sent them specifications while we were at Gagarin. He says that his ship has been modified to mate with our shiplock."

"My, they've been busy. Tell him he has permission to approach."

The station's auxiliary was typical of vehicles designed to perform a variety of tasks in orbit. It consisted of two spheres, one fitted as living quarters and the other with the gravitic engines and consumable tanks. The exterior was festooned with grapplers and other less identifiable mechanisms.

Once again, they had to be guided in by voice. Lara listened to *Cor*'s patient stream of Novy Russky and watched the approach in the view volume.

Then came the barely detectable shudder that ran through *Fire*'s hull as the orbital ferry achieved a hard dock. That was her signal to relinquish command to Doria Teray and head down to the main airlock vestibule to greet their visitor.

"*Cor*, alert Yelena of our guests' arrival."

"No need, Shipmaster. She's already there, along with her assistants."

"I'm surprised they aren't all there."

"The rest of our passengers have been ordered to stay in their quarters. The argument during the approach was loud and greatly increased my understanding of the language."

"Glad I missed it," Lara replied.

As *Cor* had told her, the airlock suiting chamber was crowded with four anxious Katerinans and the two spacers who handled docking operations. Since the ambassador was arriving via shiplock and not the hangar bay, there was not room to assemble a Marine honor guard.

"Do you know this Ambassador Semenov, Yelena?"

Yelena laughed, one of the few happy noises she had made during her time onboard. "He is my uncle, the brother of my Mishka's mother." At the mention of her dead husband, a cloud seemed to pass through her, although not enough to completely wipe away the smile of her homecoming.

Lara turned her attention back to the airlock as the sound of rushing air died away and the light above the door turned from red to amber and then to emerald green.

After five seconds, the airlock door retracted into the bulkhead and a gray-haired man stepped across the coaming.

Lara strode forward and stretched out her hand. "Ambassador Semenov?"

"Da," came the reply. "Kapitan Sims?"

Lara nodded. "Welcome to *Coronal Fire*."

"I bring greetings from our Prezident and all of the people of Katerina and thank you for the bravery and generosity that you have shown our people," Semenov said via *Cor*'s translation.

"It is every spacer's duty to help those in distress," Lara replied as she turned toward Yelena. "And, of course, I believe you know this lady."

The two embraced and there followed a minute of rapid-fire Novy Russky. *Cor* informed her that they were having a personal conversation and declined to translate. Lara noticed that there were once again tears in Yelena's eyes and that the name *Mikhail* passed between them more than once.

After releasing Yelena, Semenov spoke to each of the other refugees briefly, before turning back to Lara.

"We are prepared to offload your passengers at your convenience, Shipmaster. Is there somewhere we can go to discuss arrangements?"

"There is, Ambassador. Follow me to our briefing room."

#

Chapter 29

The transfer of the refugees to the Kazan-tri habitat was a model of efficiency. A pair of personnel transports with modified shiplocks accomplished the task in a little over four hours. They were hours filled with sadness and joy... a period when each survivor realized that they could now get on with their lives (joy), but minus the loved ones they had lost (sadness). Mixed with these emotions was a wave of gratitude to their rescuers that produced spontaneous hugs and/or kisses for any member of the crew they met on their way to the boats.

As Lara had already seen, Katerinans were more emotionally outgoing than were the people of her home world, or much of the Morast Coordinate. Compared to Novy Russians, Envonians were cold fish.

The last refugee to board the orbital transport was Yelena Krasnova. She and Ambassador Sermenov spent the hours conferring with *Fire's* officers and expedition leaders. It was not until *Cor* announced that the last transport was ready to leave that the meeting in the conference room broke up.

Following introductions, the meeting had begun with Ambassador Semenov explaining the arrangements for taking the refugees off, after which he invited a delegation to journey down to the planet to make their wishes for Katerinan assistance known.

Teodora Voxman wasted no time in asking, "Ambassador, do Katerina's astronomers know the stellar coordinates of Sol?"

Semenov's expression went through a quick series of changes before settling into a slight frown. "I'm not competent to answer that, *Madam Akademic*. We speak of the home star in religious services, of course; but I do not remember hearing of a ship that has voyaged there. Is visiting Earth one of your expedition's objectives?"

"It is our primary objective," Lara responded. "We are studying the genetics of the core systems and need a baseline for comparison. What better standard than that of the planet on which our species evolved?"

Sermenov nodded. "I will inquire of those who study these things. It may be that the information you look for is common knowledge among our astronomers. However, it is also possible that we are as ignorant as you of the location of *Zemnoy Shar* ("Earth," *Cor* translated).

"Our colony was not founded from the home world. We were colonized from *Novi Pyetersborg* in the Sibir System, which makes us a granddaughter, at best. Nor did we voyage far from Moskva during the War Centuries."

"The same with us," Darin Mastlin said. "That is how we lost the knowledge we seek. It has only been the last few generations that order has been restored to our region. As far as we know, ours is the longest voyage attempted by the Eastern Periphery in three centuries."

"I envy you, Expedition Leader. We still have not restored full peace to our sector," Sermenov replied, "as the attack on *Aurora* proves. Life is difficult at the best of times, and more so when marauders continue to roam hyperspace. I'm afraid we have been too busy living our lives to make searching for our forebears a priority."

"That, Ambassador," Darin answered with a sigh, "seems to be a universal constant among people everywhere."

#

Three days after the departure of the last Katerinan, one of the orbit-to-orbit ferries was once again docked to the Number One airlock. The suiting anteroom was filled with expedition members en route to the surface with their kit bags. The exploratory party consisted of Lara, Darin Mastlin, Betrice Flangan, Teodara Voxman and six specialists split evenly between geneticists, technologists, and astronomers.

This time they would dispense with the military guards. The moral debt these people owed them would seem to be the greatest guarantor of their safety. Of course, as Lara had discussed with *Cor*, "would seem to be" were the operative words in that sentence.

"Everyone know their responsibilities? If so, let us get to it."

The interior of the transfer craft was typical of such vessels, except that all the inscriptions were in Cyrillic. The passenger compartment was a spherical volume transected by a meshwork deck. The usual acceleration pads were attached to the mesh. Each pad had a complete set of restraints. These floated freely in the microgravity environment.

Neither the pads nor the straps would be needed. The journey would be short and the accelerations miniscule. Instead, the ten of them stored their bags in a netted enclosure before separating into groups. They clustered around several viewports.

As soon as the ferry left *Fire*, they had their choice of planet views, Kazan-tri views, or the glowing ball that was Moskva silhouetted against the black of normal space. Fifteen minutes later, a voice announced their arrival. The voice was accompanied by a series of clanging noises, the sudden sound of rushing air, and a general popping of eardrums.

The buxom young compartment attendant, who had kept an eye on them during the voyage, directed them to a passageway opposite the one through which they had entered. Beyond was an airlock with both doors open and a swing bar marking the boundary of the habitat's artificial gravity field. A small reception committee waited just beyond.

#

"Kapitan Sims?" a gray-haired man with an aura of authority asked as Lara exited the open hatchway with her kit bag strapped to her back.

"Da," she answered.

"I am Alexi Pezhhov, Special Assistant to the Prezident," he said, extending his hand.

Lara grasped the offered hand and then introduced the members of the team. Each got a personal handshake as well. In addition to their free display of emotions, Lara had also noticed that Katerinans seemed addicted to handshaking.

Pezhkov paused after greeting Teodara Voxman and said, "Madam Akademic, Ambassador Semenov said that you are interested in the location of Earth. We have checked our current databases and must report that we could find no such information. We are delving into the historical archives. This will take some time since many of the records are still coded in their original data formats and have never been converted to our modern systems."

Teodara nodded. "That is not surprising. Following the first attack on Earth, the Galactic Survey started a program to wipe the home system from every database they could reach. Apparently, your data was among those corrupted. Since Moskva is a core star and much closer to Sol than Morast, perhaps we will be able to divine the location by indirect means."

"One would hope," Pezhkov replied. "Now, if you will all follow me, we have a winged ferry waiting to transport us to the surface."

#

The trip to the surface could have been one of hundreds of such journeys that Lara had experienced in her career. There was the lengthy period where nothing seemed to be happening, then the first keening of hypersonic winds against the fuselage, followed by the sensation of being pulled forward into her seat straps as deceleration forces built. Ambient noise in the cabin rose as the environmental system switched to maximum in a vain attempt to rid the cabin of the added heat of friction.

Pezhkov, who was seated beside her, narrated the various stages of the journey. His travelogue was abruptly cut off half an hour after departure as both *Coronal Fire* and the orbiting habitat dropped below the planetary limb astern. It took her guide several seconds to realize that his words were not being translated before he sputtered to a halt

The loss of her link to *Cor* highlighted a problem that Lara had been working since their arrival in Katerinan orbit. With *Fire* orbiting at twice geosynchronous altitude, the planet was continuously rotating out from under the ship. This was not a problem so long as they were communicating with the Katerinan government. They had worldwide comm links, both surface and in orbit.

However, the link between *Cor* and the members of the crew required an exceptionally high bandwidth, one which the Novy Russians were finding it difficult to accommodate on their domestic networks. The Katerinans had agreed to let a ship's boat place comm relays 120- and 240-degrees ahead of *Fire* in its orbit, giving them full planetary coverage save for the two polar regions.

However, it would be a few days until the relays were in place.

Until then, the ground party would be out of range of the ship for sixteen hours of the planet's twenty-seven-hour day.

Forty-five minutes after he had fallen silent, Alexi Pezhkov's communicator beeped, signifying that *Coronal Fire* was once again above the horizon. "Ah, Shipmaster, we can understand one another once more, and just in time for our landing approach."

#

The capital city was named *Pyerm*, with the last sound cut off abruptly. It was a sprawling metropolis with a hi-rise core surrounded by smaller buildings and broad stretches of vegetation. Its concentric structure and paucity of surface streets marked it as a city designed for contra-gravity transportation.

The one exception to the usual pattern was an overly broad boulevard that cut a perfectly straight diagonal from the outskirts to a large plaza at the center of the city. The tall buildings seemed to be clustered around the plaza.

"That," Alexi Pezhkov said, pointing to the complex, "is the seat of our government."

"It's a beautiful city," Lara said.

"It will become more beautiful the lower we fly. You will get a taarns' eye view on the trip in from the spaceport, Also, if you will permit, we will arrange for a parade in your honor down the Heroes' Way during your visit."

"A parade?"

"An old Russian custom. If legend is to be believed, one that comes to us from the Mother World."

Ten minutes later they were making their approach to a sprawling spaceport that bore a strong resemblance to the Morast Navy Base on Geron. It, too, was pockmarked with large hemispherical depressions, several of which held the spherical bulk of large starships.

Lara pointed out the ship a quarter-klamater from where the ferry appeared to be headed. The ship was half the size of *Coronal Fire*, but an imposing sight nonetheless as it towered above its surroundings.

"Are your ships built strong enough to land in a planetary gravity field?" Lara asked, her surprise clear in her tone.

"I'm no expert," Pezhkov replied, "but I believe they maintain partial null grav in the docks to reduce the strain so that the big ships can land."

"Aren't they afraid that a power failure will crack the ship like an egg?"

He lifted his shoulders in an expansive shrug, no mean feat while strapped in.

"I am not a constructor and am ignorant of such things."

She continued gazing at what she considered a highly dubious practice until the view was cut off as the orbital ferry touched down next to a glass-walled terminal building.

#

Chapter 30

The flight from the spaceport turned into a wide-ranging aerial tour of the city. Once airborne, the three aircars required to transport the team formed up in a classic "vee" formation and made a sweeping curve away from the city center that was their ultimate destination.

The pilots climbed into the lowest traffic zone and leisurely headed for the city's outer ring. As they flew along, Lara noted that small groups seemed to have gathered in open spaces to wave and cheer as they passed over.

"Were our arrival details advertised?" she asked.

Pezhkov smiled and nodded vigorously. "Yes, indeed. Those not able to gather in Red Square have found spots under our planned route to show their appreciation."

"Red Square? I didn't see anything red about it during our approach."

"In Novy Russky, the words 'beautiful' and 'red' are similar. Also, the name is historical and hearkens back to an almost mythical place on Earth."

The tour continued, with Pezhkov supplying running commentary, which *Cor* translated and transmitted to all team members. He waxed lyrical about various automated factories, pointed out museums and the city zoo, and generally acted like the local Minister of Commerce.

About the time Lara was thinking of asking that the tour be cut short, the pilots banked sharply and aligned with the broad boulevard they had seen from the orbital ferry. Crowds lined both sides of the thoroughfare and the cheering voices kept pace with their progress toward the square. The crowd grew larger as they swept down the Heroes' Way. It became a mob as the boulevard merged with the square. On the far side of the square, a massive black cube dominated the scene.

Pezhkov pointed at the building. "That is Parliament Megaplex, where you will be staying and where the welcoming banquet will take place this evening."

Lara nodded. She knew all about the banquet. Setting the date and time had required several hours of negotiations. The Katerinans wanted to welcome them in the early evening to give the event live news coverage with a maximum audience. Lara wanted the dinner at a time when *Coronal Fire* would be above the horizon, figuring that it was better to speak to their hosts than adhere to the local dinner hour.

The quandary had arisen because, for technical reasons, the Katerinan government had yet to approve the flight plan for emplacing more comm relays. Luckily, both requirements could be met for several hours this coming evening.

As the aircars reached the terminus of the Heroes' Way, they broke formation and maneuvered for landing. As the car banked, Lara glanced at the crowd below. Interspersed with the mass of revelers were several large holoscreens. She was surprised to see her own features clearly visible through the car window on one of them.

Each vehicle slowed as it approached the landing stage jutting out a quarter of the way up the glass megaplex. They then flared to a landing. It took a minute to retrieve their luggage and gather on the landing stage. Katerina's air was warm and humid, and carried an assortment of odors that were strange, but pleasant.

A small welcoming committee waited until they sorted themselves out and uniformed stewards took their kit bags away before advancing to greet them. A distinguished gray-haired man made straight for Lara, gave her the inevitable handshake, and then launched into what was obviously a prepared speech.

"Shipmaster, this is Anatoli Grishkin, the Mayor of Pyerm. He is bidding you welcome," *Cor* said into her implant.

The Mayor's prepared speech went on longer than just that brief outline, but the words meant the same. At the end he gestured for them to move to the silver railing that surrounded the landing stage. The noise level spiked to a level that made speech impossible as they came into view of the crowd.

So, they stood and waved.

After a minute, they were ushered away. Other uniformed

functionaries led them to a passageway leading inside the mega structure. As they passed through the environment barrier, the noise cut off so abruptly that it felt like a blow to their overloaded eardrums.

#

Parliament Megaplex was a combination hotel, convention center, government, and commercial office building, and (on the lower layers) a shopping arcade. One full floor of the hotel was reserved for their use.

The accommodations were as good as any on Bernau. Each expedition member was assigned to a suite with sitting room, bedroom, and a bathroom that could best be described as a sybarites' delight. A plate of delicacies was laid out on a table for snacking to hold them over until the evening.

Lara sampled several items and found the cuisine no stranger than at home. She spent the next few hours conversing with *Cor* via implant and exploring the relaxation settings of the power bed.

Two hours before the banquet, she took an invigorating shower and began preparations for the evening's festivities. After drying and powdering herself, she slipped into undergarments and undertook a tradition as old as humanity; namely the application of makeup... something she seldom wore at home and never aboard ship. She then slipped into a silver dress recently manufactured by the ship's autofab. En route to Moskva, Yelena had explained that dresses were traditional female garb for formal occasions on Katerina.

An hour before the big event, the other members of the team gathered in Lara's suite for last minute coordination and instructions.

When the time came, they crowded into an oversize lift (bypassing a perfectly functional nullgrav shaft because all the women were wearing skirts) and descended to the ground floor.

There they found guides in formal attire waiting for them. Each member of the ground party was approached by someone of the opposite sex.

Lara was paired with a handsome young man by the name of Boris Arkhov. He was a presidential aide. The two of them walked arm in arm down a long hallway, followed by the rest of the party in precedence order. They stopped at a doorway through which quiet orchestral music was wafting.

A large mustachioed usher stood off to one side. When Lara and her escort reached him, Archov handed over a small card. The functionary glanced at it, then turned, and in a stentorian voice, announced them to the hall beyond. They then stepped across the threshold, into the hall.

The banquet space was massive. The ceiling was ten meters above a floor of black crystalline tiles like those that covered the exterior of the building. Two side walls were floor-to-ceiling mirrors, while a third was adorned with a large mural showing a winter scene. The scene was nowhere on Katerina. There was snow everywhere, and a series of stylized people in furs working at various tasks. Behind them, a small village of low huts sat on a small hill with smoke rising from every chimney.

Hanging from the ceiling were three intricate chandeliers. Each consisted of hundreds of pinpoint lights interspersed among hanging crystals that reflected the light to every corner of the hall.

A raised platform had been set up in front of the mural. On it was a long table draped in some iridescent material in sparkling white. Arrayed across the black floor were dozens of round tables. These were draped in iridescent shades of red and blue. Most of the chairs were already occupied and Lara felt curious eyes follow her as she and Archov made their way up the wide central aisle. The two of them had gone ten paces when she heard the usher behind her call out the names of Darin Mastlin and his escort.

At the end of the aisle, and in the middle of the floor in front of the head table, a dozen people clad in resplendent suits and gowns were clustered together. A familiar figure turned and hurried to meet them. Yelena Krasnova broke into a wide smile as she approached and then folded Lara into a hug.

"Welcome to my world!"

"Thank you, Yelena."

As the two of them drew apart, Lara was struck by the contrast between this beautiful, confident, well-dressed, and well-coiffed lady and the frightened, tired, limp-haired visage in *Fire's* view volume when they had first made contact with *Aurora*. Despite the smile, she thought there a momentary hint of sadness in Yelena's gray eyes.

Yelena turned to Archov and said, "Thank you, Boris. I will take over now."

Archov bowed, pivoted, and weaved his way among the blue and red tables to where a beautiful young woman was waiting for him.

She turned back to Lara and said, "Come, let me introduce you to the Prezident and his wife.

#

Chapter 31

Yelena took her arm and guided her to the group of dignitaries. The silver-haired man she had spoken to during their long-range joint news conference turned at their approach. His features were exactly as she remembered them. However, his height had not been obvious in the view volume. He was short even by Katerinan standards, short enough to make her suddenly conscious of her own exaggerated height.

"Lara, may I present Ruslan Ivanovich Karimov, Prezident of Katerina?"

"Prezident Karimov," she said, holding out her hand, "it is good to see you again."

"And you, Shipmaster. You are probably tired of hearing it, but I want to express my deep gratitude once again for what you have done for our people." He gestured toward Yelena. "If it were not for you, I would never have seen this lovely lady again."

"We did our duty sir."

"That you did and well. My, they told me you were tall, but I had no idea!"

A woman's voice sounded from Lara's right. "Rusya, stop embarrassing the poor woman."

Lara turned to the new speaker, a middle-aged woman in an evening gown that reeked of credits and a coif that must have been produced by a human artist. No robot could have achieved the same degree of perfection.

"May I present my wife, Shipmaster? Natalya Alexandruvna Karimov. Natasha, this is Shipmaster Lara da Benthar Sims of the exploration vessel *Coronal Fire*."

"How do you do," Lara said, extending her hand. Rather than shaking it, the First Lady merely squeezed her fingers and gave her a long appraising look.

"It is very good to meet you... Shipmaster?... May I call you Lara?"

"You may."

229

"Then you can call me Natasha. That is the diminutive of my formal name. And who are these people?" she asked.

Lara turned to see Darin Mastlin and his escort standing at a respectful distance behind her, along with Betrice Flangan, Teodara Voxman, and their companions.

"My apologies, Natasha, Prezident Karimov. I would like to introduce Darin Mastlin, the leader of our expedition; Betrice Flangan, Bio/Medical Specialist for the Institute of Knowledge; and Galactician Teodara Voxman, also of the Institute."

By the time the greetings were over, the other six members of the ground party had joined them, resulting in another round of introductions.

Finally, when everyone had shaken everyone else's hand, the Prezident glanced around and said, "The other diners seem to be getting restless. Shall we begin the banquet?

"Shipmaster, Expedition Leader, you will be seated at the head table. Your specialists will be seated here on the floor. We have peopled each table with our own experts, organizing them such that people with like specialties are sitting together. The arrangement is designed to allow your people to become acquainted with their Katerinan counterparts. Is that acceptable?

"Very acceptable," Darin Mastlin replied.

"Excellent. If you specialists will follow your guides, they will make sure to get you to the proper table. Please try to keep the shoptalk to a minimum. Remember, this is a social occasion."

With that, the cluster of personages broke up. The Katerinan escorts and their charges spread out to eight different tables while the Prezident led Darin Mastlin up the steps to the dais. Yelena, serving as Lara's guide, followed them. Other dignitaries fell in line behind Lara.

Once everyone was on the dais, the other dignitaries introduced themselves. They were all high-ranking members of Parliament or the government. Then everyone took their seats.

Lara found herself sitting on the Prezident's right with Yelena to her right. Natasha sat on the Prezident's left, with Darin Mastlin in the seat beside her. She smiled at the thought that the arrangement seemed universal. It was the same as the welcoming banquet on Monmoth.

The banquet began when Karimov took his place in the center of the table. That was the signal for waitstaff to flood out of various doors carrying the first course to the tables.

First up was a salad of pickled vegetables on a bed of green leaves. When Yelena caught Lara looking at her plate with suspicion, she laughed. "This is a traditional Russian delicacy that remains unchanged from Earth, or so our academics tell us. The lettuce is unmodified from the ancestral plant, and the cucumbers and peppers are pickled because the climate of Old Russia was cold for much of the year. Obviously, we have no need of such preservation techniques, but tradition is strong among us. Try it, it tastes better than it looks."

Lara picked up one of the three forks beside her plate and tasted the concoction. It was not bad.

The next item was a bit of breaded meat eaten with fingers, followed by two different soups. A variety of dishes followed so quickly that she soon lost track.

Yelena explained that it was not necessary that she eat everything placed before her. The assortment of fried, baked, and sautéed meats on fine crystal were served communally in order that each diner had choices including one or two favorites. One bowl, Lara noted, held something slimy and moving. She gave that delicacy a pass, although Darin Mastlin did have the courage to sample it. The expression on his face convinced her that she had made the right choice.

Along with the main course(s) came a choice of wines and spirits. One was a glass filled with a clear liquid. President Yarimov watched carefully as she sipped from the glass, then stifled a cough.

"What is this stuff?" she asked in a hoarse voice.

"It's called *vodka*. Legend has it that it was originally used as rocket fuel, but that is likely just a story. I understand you come from Morast. Please tell me about it."

In between bites and sips to keep pace with the ever-changing menu, Lara explained that the Coordinate was an association of star systems, and that she herself had been born on Envon. As the Prezident seemed fascinated by her height, she explained why Envonians were blessed with so many centimeters of length and so few of breadth.

"Are you married?"

She nodded. "My husband is second-in-command aboard ship. His other wives were kind enough to give him permission to come."

The Prezident's bushy eyebrows went up, causing Lara to explain marriage customs among those who plied the blackness of hyperspace.

"Different customs for different planets," he murmured.

"Yes," Lara responded. "Just about every permutation possible is practiced somewhere in human space."

About the time the first "fish" dish appeared... something with tentacles that looked like an Envonian septopod... she and the Prezident had gotten on a first name basis. He speared one of the creatures with an instrument specifically designed for the task and segued smoothly into the 'business' portion of the meal.

"My advisors have spoken to me of this expedition of yours, Lara. I would like to hear more about it in your own words."

"Gladly, Rusya. I suppose the best place to start is at the beginning..."

She told him of their discovery of the New Hope derelict and its ten thousand mummies. Later, their find had come to the attention of the Institute of Knowledge.

"The scientists were very excited. So much so that they funded the subsequent salvage mission."

"Why?" Karimov asked. "I understand scientific curiosity, but what was it about the ship that justified the expenditure of so much credit?"

Lara laughed. "I wondered the same thing when they told me they wanted to buy Coronal Fire."

She recounted Betrice Flangan's revelation of the fertility problem during that fateful meeting at the Institute of Knowledge.

"And this flaw is found throughout the Eastern Periphery?"

She nodded. "Everywhere the Institute has looked so far. That means that whatever mistake was made is at least half-a-thousand years old."

"So, this is the reason you have come four thousand light-years to the core stars? You think that our worlds were colonized before the error was introduced into the human genome?"

"That is our working hypothesis, Rusya. We of the Periphery

branched off the main heredity tree recently. We hope to pinpoint the era when the mistake was made by mapping who has the defect and who does not."

"I am unaware of any such defect in our population, but obviously, I am no expert. However, we have experts who can find out."

"That will be most helpful," Lara answered.

"I understand that Yelena told you that we would do everything in our power to aid you in your quest."

"She did."

"Then rest assured that we will do just that. We must drink to our agreement." He picked up his vodka glass and she reached for hers.

The First Lady, who had been in conversation with Darin Mastlin, looked over to them and wanted to know what was going on.

Karimov explained what they had just agreed to. At the end of his explanation, the rest of the diners at the head table picked up their own glasses.

Up until that moment, there had been a quiet buzz of conversation from the tables below them. With the raising of glasses at the head table, the room became suddenly quiet.

Karimov scanned the expectant crowd and smiled, "I see this has gotten out of hand. Excuse me, Lara, while I explain the situation to the rest of our guests. If we are going to do this, we might as well do it properly."

He stood and spent five minutes reviewing what he and Lara had been speaking about.

"... Shipmaster Sims and I have just come to an accord. Nothing can ever repay what these people did for us in coming to *Aurora's* aid, but we can give back to our guests in some small measure."

Karimov cleared his throat and switched to his public speaking voice. "Please stand while I propose a toast." There was a general scraping of chairs as everyone at the head table and around the floor got to their feet and held their glasses high.

"Honored guests, fellow citizens of Katerina. We drink to the rapid and successful return of our rescue mission, and the swift accomplishment of our new friends' goals here on our world.

"Furthermore, may what we do here on Katerina aid them in their hunt for lost Earth!"

#

Chapter 32

Three months later, Lara was back aboard *Coronal Fire* in her conference room, attending the weekly status meeting. It had been a busy three months.

The promised parade up the Heroes' Way had taken place three days after the welcoming banquet and one day following the emplacement of communications relays in orbit.

It had been a grander version of the reception they received on arrival. A crowd estimated at two million lined the boulevard and filled Red Square while a dozen aircars flew a mere meter above the flower-strewn pavement. The cheers were a continuous roar.

Lara and Darin were in the lead car with Prezident Karimov and Yelena Krasnova. The aircars that followed carried pairs of expedition members along with local celebrities, followed by others with more celebrities and government officials. Lara's arm had been sore for two days from all the waving.

In between ceremonials, the team spent a week in meetings, planning the joint research effort. The plan that eventually emerged called for three simultaneous efforts:

Research One was the astronomy team. Teodara Voxman and the other astronomers in the crew transferred down to the surface. They planned to stay for the duration. Teodara was stationed in Pyerm, coordinating with the university there. The other team members spread out to other centers of learning where astronomical libraries could be found. In addition to modern records, some of the archives went back to the colony's founding. It was in these that they expected to find clues to Sol's location.

Research Two was the life sciences team. Betrice Flangan split her time between the ship and the planet, as did her four specialists. In one way, their effort was much easier than it had been on Monmoth. Katerina's level of technology obviated the need for mass DNA testing.

The Katerinan Ministry of Health kept records on every citizen, including detailed genomic maps. Nor were the current inhabitants the only ones on file. The Ministry of Vital Statistics kept archives going back ten generations.

Then there were scientific studies in the field of genetics and related disorders. Regardless of the subject of such studies, the backup data could prove highly useful for their current purposes.

Collecting the data had proven the easy part. The treasure trove was enormous, so massive that *Coronal Fire*'s bandwidth was insufficient to upload it in any reasonable time. Ever resourceful, the team resurrected an approach popular in the prehistoric dawn of the computer age: "sneakernet."

While local specialists dug the data out of various archives, teams worked 27 hours a day recording the information in mega-capacity memory modules. Each week, hundreds of the glittering cubes were loaded onto orbital ferries for the trip to orbit.

Research Three was headed by Izakel Vlasty, Chief Technologist. As he had on Monmoth, Vlasty and his people surveyed Katerinan industry, looking for products that would make commerce possible across 4000 light-years.

His secondary mission was to assess the level of Katerina's technology. In the last two months his team had found a few industries where Katerinan technology was more advanced than that of Morast. In general, however, Katerina was on par with the Coordinate, or lagged it by a generation.

During the weekly status meeting, the three teams rotated the lead presentation position. This week, it was *Research Three* that was up first.

Izakel Vlasty had been reporting his latest findings for a quarter hour when the hatch retracted to reveal Teo Voxman in the corridor beyond.

Vlasty paused his presentation.

"Teo," Lara exclaimed, "Welcome. We were wondering if you would make it at all."

"Me, too," the Galactician replied. "It's a shame we have to rely on our hosts for transport. Using the ship's boats would be so much more convenient."

Lara agreed. In fact, transportation to and from the surface had been a source of contention during the planning phase. The question had even been bucked up to Prezident Yarimov for a final decision.

After listening to his Traffic Czar, Yarimov turned to Lara and said, "I am sorry, but I agree with Georgi. The Inner Traffic Zone is much too crowded to allow boats not under our control free passage."

The memory of that argument momentarily took Lara's thoughts off the present. When she noticed that Teo was still waiting to be invited in, she gestured to an empty chair across the table.

"Have a seat. Technologist Vlasty is just finishing up and *Research Two* is next on the list of speakers."

The short, round astronomer placed her travel case on the table, sat down, opened it, and began arranging presentation materials in front of her.

"You may proceed, Scholar."

"I was done, Shipmaster," Vlasty replied.

"Very well. Betrice, you are up."

#

Betrice Flangan stood, moved to the holocube at the far side of the compartment, and danced her fingers across the screen of her comm. The cube's image volume illuminated to show a series of numbers in columns.

"Here is the tally so far. We have collated and filed sixty two percent of the data we have received from the surface. The third column shows the number of genomic maps in inventory. These will not be totally analyzed until after we return home, of course. However, we have compared a sample of the Katerinan data with the 2500 genomes from *New Hope* that the Institute analyzed before our departure.

"From these we have tentatively concluded that Katerinan DNA is 97% common with *New Hope* terrestrial stock."

"They've experienced a three percent mutation rate since the planet was settled? Isn't that high?" Nal asked.

"It would be if it were all caused by mutations. However, it's probably just genetic drift."

"Could you please say that in Omni?"

"Sorry, Submaster. When a new planet is colonized, only a small percentage of its parent world's population emigrates, and therefore, takes only a small subset of the planetary macro-genome with them.

"As children are born, the genetic pool is progressively homogenized through haploid combination; that is, the mother and father each contribute a random choice of half their chromosomes to the offspring. These random selections quickly transform the colony's genetic pool into a distinct set of characteristics all its own."

"But doesn't that happen on all colony worlds?" Lara asked.

"Of course. The difference between Katerina and a planet like Bernau is that Bernau's population has undergone many more cycles of genetic drift, as well as sustained artificial manipulation."

"What of Katerina's fertility? Do they have the flaw?" Lara asked.

"We have yet to see any evidence of it," Betrice replied, "and with their proclivity for large families, we should have picked up the effect, if not the cause."

"So, we now have one subset of terrestrial DNA from Katerina and another from *New Hope*, neither of which possess the flaw."

Bernice sighed. "It's not that simple. Our data may be redundant."

"What?"

"Both groups are examples of the white population of Earth. It may be that we are studying two interrelated groups, which means we only have one relevant data point. We may need to search for worlds colonized from the African and East Asian parts of the Earth to ensure we have clean data."

"Or," Nal said in his deep voice, "we could just find Earth!"

There was a moment of silence, followed by several chuckles. One of the failure points of intellectuals was that they delve so deeply into a subject that they often overlook the obvious.

Lara smiled "Yes, that would certainly solve our problem. Unfortunately..."

"I have news on that front."

#

A shocked silence permeated the conference room as every

face turned toward Teodara Voxman. The ends of her lips were tilted slightly upward. Lara had seen that expression before. It was Teo's "*I've got a secret*" smile.

Lara opened her mouth to speak, then realized she had lost the ability. She cleared her throat and tried again, "Would you repeat that?"

"I have information on the location of Sol. Two pieces of information, in fact."

"And you have been sitting there quietly without..."

"Sorry to be so mysterious," the astronomer said as her smile turned full. "I was waiting for Bernice to finish."

"I'm finished," the biologist said. "I could go on for another half hour with boring statistics, but I would rather hear what you have to report."

"All right. Let me get set up and I will give you the latest news from *Research One*. I could have just plugged into the conference from my office in Pyerm, but I thought this information is good enough to come in person. Besides, Katerinan cuisine is varied and tasty, but I was homesick for *Fire*'s auto kitchen."

Teo moved to stand where Betrice had. She fiddled with her comm. The cube's interior flickered but remained blank. She began to speak in her best lecture hall voice.

"My first bit of news comes to us from Grigor Kapinski of the Katerina Academy of Science. His team was rooting around in the basement of the big museum in Arkady Novgorad when they found a stack of nanovellum sheets wadded up into a ball and covered with dust. The few symbols they could make out appeared to be star coordinates.

"They painstakingly separated the wad into its constituent sheets. Printed on them were the coordinates of all the inhabited worlds within half a kiloparsec of Katerina. The sheets also had the logo of the Galactic Survey on them."

"You're sure it was the Survey?" Lara asked.

"See for yourself."

Teo thumbed her comm and a new image appeared. It was indeed a white sheet crisscrossed with creases. The heading was in Cyrillic, as were the names of the stars down the left column. Their catalog numbers were in column 2. In several spots, the printing was nearly obscured by cursive Cyrillic writing, showing that the printout had been someone's working copy.

The next three columns were filled with galactic coordinates, and columns 5 through 10, with hyperspace coordinates. In the lower right were several numbers separated by hyphens. The first grouping had three digits.

"What's that notation?" Lara asked.

"The date, keyed to the founding of the colony. It converts to a century after the Soldant Collective attack on Earth."

"Is Sol on this list?" Betrice asked.

Teo sighed. "That would be too easy." She thumbed her comm again and hundreds of yellow sparks materialized in the holocube. The overall pattern was spherical, but lopsided, like a partially deflated spars ball.

Lara frowned. "What caused this distortion? Shouldn't the cloud be roughly spherical?"

"It's easier to see if I highlight the boundary," Teo replied.

The view changed again. The cloud of yellow sparks was now surrounded by a translucent surface in light blue. The topology was that of a large sphere that had collided with a smaller one, leaving a perfectly spherical shallow dent in one side."

"What is that?" Nal asked.

"Grigor thinks it's the edge of the exclusion zone the Galactic Survey created when they decided to hide the Home Stars from the rest of the galaxy."

"So, some Katerinan scholar downloaded this list from the main database and just happened to intersect part of the hidden volume?"

"That is about it, Shipmaster. He also left us a clue to the location of the Home Star. If you append a family of lines perpendicular to the surface of the zone boundary, they form a cone. Assuming they centered the zone on Sol, the Earth should be at the apex of that cone."

Teo touched her comm. A translucent red cone materialized inside the dimple. A blinking star flashed at the apex.

"You said you had two pieces of information," Nal said.

"I do. I was already researching a clue from Pyerm University when Grigor commed. They found a star list in an archive. Some of the names match up with the listing in *The Earth, the Moon, and the Stars*, namely *Betelgeuse, Rigel,* and *Deneb.*

"All are bright beacon stars. When we compared the galactic coordinates with the star map from our book, we were able to triangulate Sol's position. The two calculations aren't quite the same, but close enough for government work."

For long seconds, no one said anything as the import of what Teo had said sank in. The spell was broken only when *Cor's* voice issued from an overhead speaker.

"Please look at the holocube."

A cluttered starfield appeared in the volume. After a few seconds, stars began to disappear at a rapid rate. They continued doing so until only one remained.

"Is that it?" Lara croaked.

"It is," *Cor* replied. "The spectrum matches perfectly. Ladies and Gentlemen, I give you *Sol.*"

#

Chapter 33

Lara lay cradled in Nal's arms, her body pressed tightly against his, as both contemplated the new hologram on the bulkhead opposite their bed. It was a group of stars against a black background. Star and planet holos had been popular décor items on Envon when she was growing up. This one was categorically different from those memories of her youth.

The hologram showed the view from Moskva of the Home Group, the stars that the Stellar Survey had erased from the records of everyone beyond visual range of Sol. *Cor* analyzed the spectra of several thousand stars to pick out those listed in the adolescents' astronomy book.

In the center of the holo, a bright yellow spark represented Sol. Around it were scattered glowing points of light in distinct colors. The nearest stars were the trio of the Alpha Centauri system.

Alpha Centauri A and B were both the size of Sol. One was the same spectral class. The two revolved around one another so closely that they were shown in the holo as a dumbbell shape. The third member of the system, Proxima Centauri, was a dull red and separated from its parents by a fraction of a light-year.

Then came Sirius, the brightest star in Earth's sky; and Epsilon Eridani, site of humanity's first unsuccessful interstellar colony. Procyon was another dual-star system. Its primary was a subgiant on its way to becoming a true giant, orbited by a white dwarf.

Another binary system, 61 Cygni A and B, were a pair of gravitationally bound dwarfs; Tau Ceti, a twin to Sol, was separated from its brother by 12 light-years.

These were the stars of legend. Seeing them and dozens of others displayed on their bedroom wall stirred deep emotions. The ancient names had been myths out of fairy tales. Now they were mundane points on a star map.

Lara shifted and looked at her husband's rugged features.

"Did you ever really expect to see this, Nal?"

"I never doubted it," he said with a chuckle.

243

"Never?" she asked as she moved her hand in a loving caress.

"Well, maybe once or twice. How about you?"

"Truly? It has been my greatest fear that we would stumble around until we ran out of patience and never come close to finding Earth."

"Well now that you don't have that to worry about, what will keep your brain occupied, my love?"

"I suppose we had best begin planning the next stage of our voyage. Any ideas?"

"We'll have to finish the biological surveys, of course," he answered. "I would think we could wrap those up within a month. Then, it's once more into the deep black."

"Somehow it doesn't seem real."

"What doesn't?"

"In another few months we will actually be gazing on the beautiful, blue-white Earth!"

"Assuming, of course, that it still exists," he chided.

Her response was a rude noise and a fist to his ribs, followed by a wrestling match that she had no intention of winning.

#

If Lara had thought the three months that preceded the discovery of Sol had been busy, they were placid compared to the month that followed.

As Nal had said, it took them three and a half weeks to finish data mining Katerina's genetic databases. While Betrice and her people worked long hours with little sleep, much of the rest of the crew went on holiday.

For those who had not been off the ship since Monmoth (or ever), Lara authorized a week's shore leave. Shore parties were limited to a dozen revelers at a time. They left the ship every few days on a staggered schedule, transferred to Kazan-tri and then to the planet, and returning a week later somewhat the worse for wear. No matter how tired or lacking in sleep the returnees, no one had an unkind word to say about Katerinan hospitality.

The last revelers returned to the ship at the end of the third week. The ferry that brought them also brought the last cargo of memory cubes. These were cataloged, carefully packed, and then placed into secure storage in Cargo Bay Two.

As soon as she announced their plan to leave Moskva, Prezident Karimov insisted that they have a final banquet to celebrate their success. Lara expected him to make the offer and had been mulling over who to take with her on a final visit to the planet.

She was therefore surprised when Karimov suggested that the departure celebration be held aboard *Coronal Fire*.

"I have heard so much about this marvelous ship of yours that I want to see it for myself," he explained.

"Of course, Rusya. We would be delighted to host. Of course, the attendance list will have to be pared considerably from the one at your last hurrah."

"Will a dozen guests be acceptable?"

"Of course. We'll do it a week before departure."

Playing host was something that Lara had not planned on. After five years in flight, *Coronal Fire*'s living spaces were becoming a bit dingy. At home, such mundane chores would have been handled by multi-armed cleaning mechs. A ship on an eight-thousand light-year round trip voyage had better uses for available volume, so the cleaning mechs had been left behind.

Lara set everyone not engaged in wrapping up the biological survey to work returning the ship to its usual shiny condition. The methods involved were both ancient and effective. All required the use of what had once been called "elbow grease."

On the day of the party, the ferry from Kazan-Tri brought a dozen visitors to the ship via the No. 1 airlock. In addition to Prezident Karimov, his wife Natalia, and Yelena Krasnova, there were two doctors who were instrumental in ferreting out the medical records and Grigor Kapinski of the Academy of Science. The rest of the party was fleshed out by high ranking functionaries.

Lara led the Prezident, his wife, and Yelena Krasnova on a tour. The other guests were split into groups of three and guided by Nal, Athald Daver and Doria Teray. Lara found her workload on the tour minimal. As soon as she led the party into a compartment, Yelena Krasnova took over the narration in rapid-fire Novi Russky.

The banquet itself was a rousing success. Nal and Natasha chatted for most of the meal. She was fascinated by both his physique and his color. He explained that while he had black terrestrial ancestors (everyone did), his complexion was the product of genetic manipulation to better protect him from the rays of Esther Prime's F0-class star.

As in any Katerinan banquet, there was a lot of toasting. This time they used the most popular Morast spirit: Varan rum. When it came time for Nal to toast, he raised his glass and rumbled, *"Here's to our wives and girlfriends... may they never meet!"*

There was general applause for the sentiment, among the women as well as the men. To Lara, the toast was Nal's hoary standby. Apparently, no one on Katerina had heard it before. Either that, or the rum was getting to them. There was also the possibility that they were just being polite.

The party grew even more raucous as the toasting continued. Lara was in mid-laugh at one of Prezident Yarimov's slightly off-color jokes when *Cor* activated her implant.

"Shipmaster."

"Yes, Cor?"

"The ferry pilot says he has a message for Prezident Yarimov and requests permission to enter the ship."

"Granted. Send someone to guide him to the dining facility."

"Will do."

Five minutes later, the pilot stepped over the hatchway coaming, scanned the compartment, and then hurried to Prezident Yarimov.

Yarimov received the piece of film, keyed the spot that would make the message appear, and read. He stared at the words a long time before reacting.

"Is there something wrong, Rusya?" Lara asked.

A whole gamut of emotions crossed Yarimov's features before he settled on a smile. "No, Lara, it is very good news."

He rose to his feet, signaled for quiet, and said," Ladies and gentlemen. I have important news. I will now read the message verbatim:

From:	Admiral Alexei Trudonov aboard *Prince Grigory Potemkin*
To:	Prezident Ruslan Ivanovich Karimov
Subject:	*Aurora* Rescue Mission

Sir:

1. It is my happy duty to report that we found *Aurora* after an extensive search and that all aboard are safe.

2. We were aided in this by the powerful beacon the Morast expedition placed on the liner prior to bringing word of the disaster. Without it, we would not have been successful.

3. *Aurora*'s environmental control system malfunctioned fifteen days after *Coronal Fire*'s departure. Without the donated life module, all aboard would have perished.

4. We are en route to Katerina and will arrive at Gagarin Base in ten days.

5. We have the life module aboard the Cruiser *Konstantin Tsiolkovsy* and will return it to the Morast expedition upon arrival.

Communication Ends

PART FOUR

SOL

Chapter 34

Lara relaxed in *Fire*'s control center and once again gazed upon the ghostlike topography of hyperspace. It had been two months since they bid farewell to Katerina and set out for Sol.

Their departure had been delayed three weeks while they waited for the rescue fleet to return to the inner system and *KSN Konstantine Tsiolkovsky* to rendezvous with *Coronal Fire*. The transfer of the borrowed life module had taken a full day.

Finally, Lara gave the order to break orbit.

While *Cor* negotiated the flight plan given to her by traffic control, Lara watched various hazards to navigation flow across the view volume as they climbed out of Katerina's inner traffic zone. To her surprise, she found that she was a little sad to be leaving.

By the time they reached the outer reaches of the Moskva System where gravitational curvature was flat enough to safely translate into hyperspace, her mood had changed to one of anticipation.

After two days of maneuvering, they found a hyperon stream that would carry them in the direction of Sol. The stream was a broad cyan highway in the view volume, with no splotches of red or orange out to the limits of their detectors.

Surprisingly, it stayed that way for the next three weeks. For someone used to dodging gravity infusions like the Kaligani Narrows, Lara considered this part of the voyage to be a holiday.

Nal also noticed the bland nature of the void through which they were traveling. One evening while the two of them were going over the ship's daily operations, he asked, "Do you suppose this entire region of hyperspace is devoid of gravitational infusions?"

Lara nodded thoughtfully. "It would explain why *New Hope*'s builders thought it smart to give the ship an initial shove and then trust the flow to take it the rest of the way to its destination."

"It was still a damned fool plan," Nal muttered.

"That it was," Lara agreed. "If they'd had engines, they would

251

at least have had a larger flight crew and that alone might have prevented the tragedy."

By the time *Coronal Fire* departed Bernau for the Core Stars, the Institute of Knowledge had not yet figured out the exact cause of the *New Hope* disaster. However, a thorough search of the ship did find two bodies outside the cryo tanks. They had been the totality of the flight crew while in hyper.

The prevailing theory was that something had happened to incapacitate the crew, and no one onboard was awakened in time to activate the deplaning coils. Once past their dropout point, there would have been no sense to it. Without the ability to maneuver in hyperspace, the chance of the ship ever again coming close to a star with a habitable planet were nil.

Nal's observation had come on Day 27 of the current mission. Three days later, they dropped out of hyper to take their first position reading in normal space.

The stream in which they had been immersed was aimed at a point some five degrees west of Sol. The slant course had its advantages. By not pointing directly at their destination, it allowed them to generate sufficient cross-range to obtain a parallax measurement. The new data could be used to convert their two-dimensional view of the Home Group into a three-dimensional star chart.

That had been 30 days ago. It was now Day 60, time for a second check to refine their observations. Once they had that data, they would cast about for hyperon streams that would deliver them to Sol.

"Time, Shipmaster," *Cor* said into her implant.

"All right. Make the announcement and then head downslope for null."

Twenty minutes later, *Cor*'s voice echoed again through the ship, "Prepare for breakout. Ten seconds to normal space... Breakout!"

The view of surrounding space was as it always is, a field of black punctuated by diamond-like points of light.

"All departments, begin your sweeps," Lara ordered. "Report radio contacts as you get them."

On their earlier breakout, they had detected radio signals from five planets. Many of these were garbled, but the scraps they were able to decipher proved that Standard was still the predominant language of the colonized worlds.

Within ten minutes, *Cor* confirmed they were 40 light-years from Sol. After four hours of "sniffing" vacuum, they picked up EM-radiation from seven different worlds encompassing four inhabited systems. One of the worlds was Earth. Their fears that it had been destroyed were unfounded.

"It seems to me that colonies are closer together here than at home," Lara said after receiving the computer's report. "Can that be true?"

"Based on our intercepts, I would estimate that there are 30% more inhabited worlds per unit volume here than at home," *Cor* replied.

"Are the stars denser here?"

"Negative. The star counts for the two regions are equivalent. I assume the early colonists were less exacting in their selection criteria than are we. Perhaps they did not realize how many habitable worlds there are in the galaxy."

"We'll file that as another interesting fact we probably will never figure out. How much longer before we can return to hyperspace?"

"Six hours and forty minutes."

"I will be in my quarters. Alert me ten minutes before we head back into the deep black."

#

The next morning, Lara called a conference to plan their approach to Sol. Seated around the table were herself, Nal, Darin Mastlin, Betrice Flangan, Teodara Voxman, and Legate Bas Klyster.

"Alright, people. We are fourteen days out. Your thoughts on how we make our approach."

Darin and Betrice had spent the entire voyage laying out a detailed action plan for when they reached Earth. It was based on their experiences on both Monmoth and Katerina. It called for Lara to once again handle the 'politics' of the contact, while the two of them concentrated on obtaining data on the terrestrial macro-genome.

Their unspoken assumption was that *Coronal Fire* would null out at the edge of the Solar System, announce their presence, and then follow the local traffic instructions to Earth orbit. Lara's concern was whether that was the wisest course to take.

Bas Klyster was the first to speak. "I think we need to exercise caution."

"Don't we always?" Nal asked.

Klyster smiled. "On our first contact, we knew the planet had lost its spacefaring capability and there was no possibility that it could harm us. On the second, we had convincing evidence that we would be welcomed with open arms. Neither of those situations apply to the Solar System. There are too many unknowns to just go blithely blundering in."

"How so?" Teo asked. "In a way, we are going home."

"We have all been brought up with the idea that the Solar System is our ancestral home," Klyster said. "The Earth of our imagining is a magical place inhabited by benevolent god-like beings who will be glad to share their bounty with us. It is important that we not let our illusions lead us into disaster."

"What sort of disaster?" Lara asked.

"There's no way to know until it happens. That is my point. Before we loudly announce our arrival, we need to do some reconnaissance."

The suggestion led to two hours of discussions. At the end, everyone agreed that a period of quiet study before making their presence known was in order.

Finally, Lara asked *Cor*, "Where should we drop out?"

"I have just identified Polaris from its spectrum. I suggest a quarter-light year from Sol in that direction," the computer replied. "We will be high above the ecliptic and at the point of optimum sensitivity for the sniffer array."

"Then that is what we will do."

#

"Ten minutes to breakout. All compartments report status."

As always, *Cor* had already done so, but tradition (and regulations) required it.

Lara listened to the roll call reporting readiness to return to the real universe. Finally, it was her turn.

"Shipmaster, ready for breakout. Stand by."

Seven minutes later, *Cor* took up the count.

"Two minutes... ninety seconds... one minute... 30 seconds...

Lara glanced at Doria Teray to her right who held up her right hand with crossed fingers.

A teacher had once told Lara that the gesture was at least three thousand years old. Somehow, it seemed fitting for what was about to happen.

"Ten... nine... eight... seven... six... five... four... three... two... one... Breakout!

#

Chapter 35

The view volume showed the same view as every other time they had returned to normal space... stars against an ebon background.

In this case, one of the stars was brighter than the others.

"Is that it?"

"That is it," *Cor* replied.

"Can you see any planets yet?"

Stars quickly flowed out of the boundaries of the image as the central star developed a tiny disk. There were two half-lighted circles in adjacent quadrants above the star and several other specks that were on the verge of becoming dimensional.

Quickly, the names of legend began to appear next to the various points, along with an expanded inset view of each. One half-circle was twice the size of the other, with indistinct concentric bands of mottling. A floating label in green identified it as "Jupiter." Then the other half-circle got a tag: "Saturn". That spot was fuzzy around its edges.

"What is wrong with Saturn?" Lara asked.

"Nothing. We are viewing its rings nearly face on."

The fuzzy half-blob had sixty percent of a ring around it, the ends of which were easy to see because half the planet was in darkness, as was a section of the ring itself.

Then, in quick succession, other floating tags and inset views appeared: Earth, Venus, Mars, Uranus. These were scattered randomly around the star.

Lara found that she had been holding her breath. She exhaled as the image blurred. The problem was not with the long-range scanner. It was with her eyes. They were filled with tears.

"I never thought I would live to see this day," she muttered to herself. Across the ship, the crew was having similar reactions. After a minute, the awed silence was broken by a single cheer. Suddenly, every voice onboard joined in.

Lara took a deep breath and wiped her eyes.

257

"Deploy the sniffer," she ordered.

The sensitive antenna was run out to the end of its tether, a position where it was far more sensitive than when it was stowed against the hull. It took a few seconds to orient itself. Then a box icon appeared around the dot that was Earth.

"I am happy to report, Shipmaster," *Cor* announced, "that Earth is a radio star of the first magnitude."

"What about the other worlds?"

Slowly, each of the other sparks on the screen acquired blinking icons of their own. They were coded with distinct colors to denote the level of EM radiation detected.

"I am picking up ships in interplanetary space."

"Anything else to note?"

"*Tac Seven* reports several bright radio sources that emanate in frequencies that would suggest long-range search radars."

"Orbital Fortresses?"

"Could be."

"Keep me apprised."

#

A week later, the people who had planned their arrival in the Solar System, plus Aavrom Pelot, were back in Lara's conference room. Darin Mastlin chaired the meeting.

"Teo, what have you found?"

"We are still too far out to see the continents clearly, but we have charted Earth's energy signature. The population seems to be about five billion. That is one-third of what our records give for it at the time of the Great Hegira."

Legate Klyster frowned. "Are you sure?"

Teo shrugged. "We used the standard correlation algorithm. The figure should be correct within plus or minus 30 percent. Why?"

"Because a population crash of that magnitude suggests war or plague."

"What about natural decline?" Nal asked. "The Earth did bleed population to the stars for a thousand years, you know."

"While it is true that overcrowding drove much of the exodus, the old records don't mention any significant loss of population as a result. Apparently, the maternity centers were able to keep pace with the departing starships."

"A war then. Any sign of battle damage?"

Lara shook her head. "We're too far out. To be visible, it would have to be on the order of the breakup of Luna."

"Then war is a possibility," Betrice Flangan interjected, "or possibly a plague."

"As much as I enjoy good conjecture," Darin Mastlin said, "we'll solve this problem once we make contact. We need to keep this meeting moving. Aavrom, the sniffer report, please."

Scholar Pelot cleared his throat. "I had planned a presentation around the fact that the inhabitants still speak classical Standard. Their culture must be highly traditional to have suppressed the natural evolution of their language for so long.

"However, *Cor* has found something that is going to complicate our mission." Pelot glanced up at the hidden speaker in the overhead. "*Cor*, the show is yours."

"Thank you. Since we are too far out to get a good visual, the Scholar gave me the task of mapping the EM-sources in near-Earth space using the sniffer's interferometer. I have done so.

"Most planets use a standard system for traffic control of their space-based infrastructure. Ninety percent of orbital installations are placed in precise lanes within the equatorial plane, leaving geosynchronous altitude free for communications and a few other functions that require a station to remain stationary in the local sky. Installations in polar orbit are placed very high to prevent collisions with the lower equatorial platforms.

"I expected Earth's arrangement to be the same. It is not. They use a radically different system."

The view volume lit to show the Earth surrounded by a large phantom globe marked with faint lines of longitude and latitude. The globe and planet were bisected by a horizontal plane in translucent red.

"The red represents the ecliptic, the plane in which Earth orbits. As you can see, the planet's axis of rotation is tilted at 23.5 degrees, which accounts for the seasons mentioned in the old legends. Now, watch what happens when I superimpose my discoveries onto this plot."

White diamond-like sparks began to appear, but not at

random. Each point of light lay on the surface of the phantom globe. The interior of the globe was empty save for the planet, and there was a gap where the ecliptic passed through the globe's surface.

Cor continued. "There are twelve thousand dots in all. Each is a truly gigantic structure. Taken in toto, these small points of light represent a significant percentage of Earth's industrial base; possibly all of it."

"How large is that globe?" Lara asked.

"Two hundred thousand klamaters in diameter."

Lara frowned. "How do they prevent all those orbits from clashing?"

"Very simply. None of the installations is in orbit about Earth. All share the planet's vector around Sol. The arrangement is known as a 'free-flying shell'."

"Known by whom?"

"The initial inventor, for one. The concept is an offshoot of an idea first postulated by an ancient philosopher named Freeman Dyson and predates the invention of star travel. Its advantage is that there is no near-planet crowding like that we encountered at Katerina and it allows a nearly unlimited volume for the placement of infrastructure."

"Don't forget the fact that it violates every known principle of orbital mechanics," Nal muttered.

"Only if you assume the various stations are in free flight, Submaster. They are not. They keep their formation by continuous thrust from their gravitic engines. At the shell's altitude, Earth's gravitational pull is only three-thousandths of a standard gee, which is probably the reason that particular altitude was chosen."

"Aren't they afraid that one of their behemoths will suffer a power failure and crash into Earth?" Lara asked.

"If a station loses propulsion, it will revert to its naturally inclined heliocentric orbit. Rather than crashing down, it will drift up and clear of the formation. It will return to the formation six months later and on the opposite side of Sol. That should be long enough to repair the engines or push the station into a different orbit."

"So, how does this unorthodox arrangement complicate our mission?" Lara asked.

Cor almost sounded apologetic when she answered. "Once we

make contact, we will undoubtedly be directed to one of the shell habitats. As at Katerina, the ground party will have to rely on local transportation to complete the journey to the surface."

"So?"

"With the ship one hundred thousand klamaters above Earth, speed-of-light delay will be too great for me to provide you with simultaneous translations.

"The ground party will have to learn to speak Standard."

#

Chapter 35

Lara woke from a fitful sleep. She was still groggy as she opened her eyes and took inventory of her surroundings. She was in her own bed with the cabin gravity turned down to ten percent. The only illumination came from the standard emergency lights required by regulation. The soft sound of wind blowing through trees emanated from the overhead. In other words, all was normal.

Except it was not.

She could not escape the feeling that had plagued her as she slept. Despite the evidence of her eyes and ears and the cool tingle on her skin where a thin film of sweat evaporated, she felt that she was somewhere else. Her brain seemed sluggish, filled with echoes of memories not her own. She lay there for minutes trying to shake the feeling that something was wrong with the universe.

Finally, she gathered her strength, sat up in bed and reached out with her right hand to break the beam that shut off her tormentor. The feeling of 'otherworldliness' subsided but did not totally go away. She tried to swallow, but her mouth was dry, and the attempt provoked a spasm of coughing. When it was finished, her left hand moved up of its own accord to pull the skullcap crowded with electrodes from her head.

In the holoplays, mnemonic training is presented as being fast and easy. If only it were like that in real life.

The electric currents that triggered her synapses caused all manner of symptoms. Coming out of the artificial trance was like waking to the fading memory of a bad dream.

This had been the sixth session in which *Cor* force fed her the language of Earth. Even as she stared blankly around her, she felt a hint of relief that it was finally over.

Nor was she alone in her torment. All over the ship, the dozen other victims who would soon set foot on Planet Earth were coming out of their crash course in speaking the ancient language known as Standard.

\#

Cor's news about the arrangement of Earth's exo-atmospheric infrastructure had been a surprise. So, too, the consequences of that arrangement.

It had not occurred to Lara that there were any limitations as to the computer's ability to monitor a hundred different conversations and then respond to each instantaneously.

She should have known better.

Computers are not magic, no matter how much they might project the impression. They have their limitations. They had experienced one such on Katerina. Until the comm relays were placed in orbit, they were forced to schedule events at times when *Cor* was above the local horizon.

The link that allowed *Cor* to do her translation trick required a very high bandwidth. The one-third second delay inherent in communications between Earth and its shell of fellow flyers was too great to support simultaneous translation, especially when the round-trip delay was twice that long.

That did not mean that *Cor* could not handle translations. For millennia, translators had successfully handled far longer delays with aplomb. A person spoke, the translator translated, and the listener listened. In fact, the inherent delay in serially converting information from one language to another had its advantages. It gave each participant time to gather their thoughts while awaiting their turn to speak.

But *Cor* had been right. The archaic system was not as efficient as understanding in real time. And so, Lara and the rest of the ground party suffered through six days of discomfort.

When her feelings of disorientation subsided, Lara prodded her memory to see how well this latest inoculation had taken.

"Fuck!"

She blinked. Had she said that out loud?

What a strange word, she thought. For some reason, monosyllables of four letters held power in Standard, as they had in the earlier Anglic, and the word she had just mouthed was the most powerful of all.

"Did you say something, Shipmaster?" *Cor* asked from the overhead. The computer's voice had an amused tone.

"Just practicing my linguistics," she replied in her most innocent voice.

#

Following their arrival on the outskirts of the Solar System, *Tac Seven* had found eight installations radiating radar and lidar beams of immense power. Two weeks later, six of those sources were positively identified as Planetary Defense Fortresses. These were positioned at the cardinal points of the free-flying shell and could engage foes inbound from any direction with overlapping lanes of fire.

The remaining two were nowhere near Earth. They orbited in the gap between Saturn and Uranus and were on opposite sides of Sol. Their distance from the system primary put them too far out to aid in Earth's defense. That fact alone made their function obvious.

Einstein's great contribution to human knowledge was his insight that the "force" we perceive as gravity is not a force at all. It is curvature of the local space-time continuum. The degree of curvature in normal space is affected by the presence of a nearby mass (such as a star).

Hyperspace is different. While hyperon flows are driven by gravitational differentials emanating from infusions from other universes; the region known as "null," where hyperon velocity asymptotically approaches light-speed, is devoid of such disturbances.

"Thus, the transition from normal space to hyperspace (or the reverse) involves a discontinuity in the mythical force known as gravity; a 'jolt' as a starship disappears from one domain and materializes in the other. If the transition takes place far from a star, the jolt is indiscernible. However, if the ship jumps into a region of normal space close to a star, the instantaneous change in local curvature can knock the jump engines out of calibration. To repair the damage requires the services of a major shipyard.'

That is the reason ships en route to or from a star make their transition beyond the Destarte Limit, the range at which it is safe to jump.

For a typical main sequence star like Morast or Sol, the DL is approximately 1.5 light-hours from the system barycenter (the point in space around which the star and its planets mutually rotate; also known as the system's center of gravity).

Theoretically, an arriving ship can safely drop out of hyper anywhere beyond the DL. In practice, however, most systems establish acceptable zones for arrivals and any vessel appearing somewhere else is classified as a potential invader. Heavy fines are levied against violating ship owners to teach them not to make the mistake again.

In the Solar System, that meant they would have to officially arrive within five light-minutes of one of the two fortresses between Saturn and Uranus.

#

Lara was once again in Control, Nal was in Engineering, and Legate Klyster was at his duty station in the Combat Information Center. The rest of the crew were at their stations and the scientists in their cabins.

"Everyone report readiness to jump," Lara ordered.

The roll call continued to its conclusion without pause. When it was complete, she linked to *Cor* via implant. "Are you sure you know where we are going?"

"Very sure, Shipmaster. Total pseudo-distance will be two light-years and elapsed voyage time, a day-and-a-half."

Their plan was to officially enter the Solar System via the closest approved gateway, which was currently one-quarter light-year distant. Even so, it would take 36 hours to reach it traveling at high multiples of the speed of light.

Like the sailing ships of old, starships cannot always take the straight-line course from Point A to Point B. *Cor* had charted the hyperon streams as *Fire* dropped towards null during their first approach. She used this information to plot a roundabout course to arrive in the target zone.

The voyage would take a day and a half.

Lara sighed and remembered an ancient saying: *"That which cannot be cured must be endured,"* before releasing the ship into *Cor's* expert, if immaterial, hands.

"You may jump when ready."

#

Chapter 36

"Breakout!"

Cor's announcement had an echoic quality as Lara watched the unbroken black of hyperspace suddenly change to the speckled black of normal space. The reason for the echo was that *Cor* had made the announcement both via ship's annunciator and implant.

The view was the same as it had been 36 hours earlier, with the exception that the bright central star was now a tiny round ball. The human eye can give dimension to an object one arc-second in width. Lara estimated Sol was now about twice that size.

"Where are we, *Cor*?"

"We are three hundred thousand klamaters above the ecliptic and five hundred thousand out-orbit from the fortress. We were just painted by both radar and lidar pulses. They should notice us right about..."

"Unknown ship, identify yourself"

"... now."

"Go ahead," Lara said.

"This is the Scientific Research Vessel *Coronal Fire*. We are four years and seven months out of Bernau, the capital world of the Morast Coordinate, in the Eastern Periphery of the Orion Arm. We are here to seek Earth's aid in a scientific study and request permission to approach your position."

Speed-of-light delay to the fortress was 1.5 seconds, which meant that the computer to whom they were speaking could have responded within 3 seconds. There was no reply for more than five minutes.

Finally, an identifiable human voice sounded in Lara's implant and from the overhead speakers. "This is Sentinel Alpha Prime. Please repeat your identification and include your registry number."

The words issuing forth from the speakers were in Omni. However, *Cor* fed the original signal to Lara via her implant. She was pleased that she could understand the request without translation.

"I'll take it *Cor*."

"You have control, Shipmaster."

"This is Shipmaster Larath da Benthar Sims in command of the Scientific Research Vessel *Coronal Fire*. We have come 4000 light-years to Sol to seek your help on a matter of importance. We do not have a registration number because we have never been here before. We request approach instructions to your station where we will submit to inspection."

"Stand by, *Coronal Fire*. Approach instructions follow."

There was a brief whining sound, after which *Cor* responded. "Instruction received. We will arrive in 40 hours."

#

Sentinel Alpha Prime was not the single monster fortress that Lara had envisioned; or it was, but it did not orbit Sol alone. It was a veritable city in space. There were more than one hundred large habitats, workshops, shipyard berths, power stations, consumables tanks, and other collections of geometric shapes whose function was not obvious. It reminded Lara of the much smaller facility in the Morast System.

There were also the other ships inbound for Earth. Small intra-orbit transports flitted between the ships and the floating city in vacuum.

The two days that it had taken to close the distance had not been idle ones. Fortress personnel peppered them with questions concerning their identity and mission. They were especially interested in what and where the Morast Coordinate was and the overall astropolitical situation in the region.

Several scholars were kept busy explaining the history of the Eastern Periphery and the current political structure at home. Teo Voxman spent a long afternoon showing them star maps and other data on the far-off colony worlds.

Nor was the information flow in one direction. The first thing *Cor* requested were specifications and design models for the construction of terrestrial-standard docking mechanisms. Engineering then got to work designing and fabricating a mod kit for the Number One Airlock.

When they had closed the distance to two hundred thousand klamaters, *Cor* reported that radar and lidar beams were continuously playing across the hull. Lara ordered that their own fire control systems stay unpowered to not disturb their soon-to-be hosts.

Lara spent the final eight hours listening to the conversations between *Cor* and Sentinel Alpha's computer. The station controllers vectored them to a point thirty klamaters out-orbit of the fortress, with a clear view of Sentinel Alpha Prime.

"Any idea why the want us there?" Lara asked Nal in Engineering.

"To give them a clean shot in case we don't meet their standards for admission?"

After an interminable time, *Cor* finally announced: "We have matched velocities and are ready to receive inspection teams."

"Stand by, *Coronal Fire*. Our customs and health officials will rendezvous with you in thirty minutes. There will be medical inspections and Ambassador-at-large Isaac Smythe Sarcoff will conduct your entry interview. Please answer all questions truthfully and fully."

"*Coronal Fire* is standing by."

#

The intra-orbit ferry that approached could have come from any of a dozen star systems. In fact, the ferry looked strikingly like the double sphere design they had seen at Katerina save that the curves were smoother and the protruding equipment not as obvious.

"*Coronal Fire*, this is Transport 735. Docking instructions."

"Seven-Three-Five. You will be docking to the Number One Airlock. Guide lamps are coming on now."

"We see it, *Fire*. Any special instructions?"

"Come in slow. Maintain pressure integrity until we are certain we have hard dock. The mechanism is new and untested. We finished it last night."

"Understood. We are inbound."

Everyone aboard *Fire* watched as the transport made a sweeping turn to align itself with the airlock. The latching mechanism at 735's nose disappeared into the new cylindrical appendage. Lights on the exterior turned from red to green.

"We have capture and hard dock," *Cor* reported, followed by, "the transit tunnel is now pressurized. You may disembark when ready. Be careful transitioning from the tunnel into ship's gravity."

Lara, Nal, and Darin Mastlin hurried to the suiting anteroom just inside the airlock and waited for the visitors. Unlike earlier welcoming parties, there were no Marines in evidence.

The first figure to exit the airlock tunnel was a man in an armored vacsuit. He floated into view, rotated to put gloved hands on the overhead grab bar, and pivoted expertly into ship's gravity.

When his boots were on the deck, he moved to place his back against the bulkhead next to the airlock and uncradled a projectile weapon. Two more soldiers followed, spreading out to adjacent bulkheads.

Their suits were black with unfamiliar insignia. Their visors, silvered as a defense against lasers, hid their features. None of them spoke.

After a brief pause, a fourth man exited the airlock. He was in head-to-toe white isolation garb marked with a caduceus. He carried a rectangular container of the sort that had replaced the doctor's black bag back before the first starship left Earth.

Unlike the soldiers, his visor was clear. He looked around for a few seconds before his voice sounded through external speakers on his suit: "Who is in charge here?"

"I am," Lara replied, stepping forward. "Shipmaster da Benthar Sims."

"I am Medtech Josiah Bartwell. I am here to perform a health inspection. First, there are several standard questions to be answered. Afterward, I will need blood samples from six members of your crew. I understand you come from a stellar nation called the Morast Coordinate?"

"We do."

"How many planets are in your group?"

"Sixty-three full voting members and twenty-seven associates."

"Then, if it is possible, I would like test subjects from different planets."

"Certainly. We three are from different worlds and we will get you three more. *Cor*, please have Teo, Doctor bin Sool, and Aavram

Pelot report to the suiting chamber."

"They are on their way, Shipmaster."

"Let us get the standard questions out of the way," Bartwell said. "You have been en route nearly five years. Is that correct?"

"It is."

"I'll need a complete record of the sicknesses you have treated during the voyage."

"No one has been sick," Lara replied. "We spent four years in cold sleep with only a small operating crew. All crew members have had full spectrum inoculations."

"Have you visited any worlds before arriving here?"

"Two. Monmoth in the Inis-Afallon System and Katerina in the Moskva System."

Bartwell paused as he checked his database. "I'm afraid we have no record of either of those. Please describe them."

Lara gave a brief recounting of their visit to the two planets, noting that Monmoth was recovering from war damage and Katerina had been settled by ethnic Russians from Novi Pyetersborg. She then assured the medtech that no one had been sick during or after the visits.

The questioning went on for another ten minutes. Finally, Bartwell said, "I'll take those blood samples now. I note that you and this black man are of widely varying genotypes. Are your differences due to genetic manipulation?"

"They are. My home world's gravity is about thirty percent higher than Earth. Nal's home world has gravity twice standard and orbits an F0 star."

"Do you have any idea of the divergence quotient between your two genotypes?"

"No," Lara replied.

"It doesn't matter. The blood tests will measure it."

The other three 'specimens' arrived as the medtech set up his apparatus. Their presence made the suiting chamber crowded. Once personal information had been taken, the blood draw was done quickly and painlessly.

Bartwell put his instruments and equipment away, closed his kit, and said, "That is it for my needs. We will have your results tomorrow in time for your official interview aboard Sentinel Alpha

Prime."

With that, he turned and made his way back through the airlock, falling forward as he reached the gravity interface line and kicking off expertly when most of his body was in microgravity.

The soldiers remained statues in the corners of the compartment.

A minute later, a second man in isolation gear appeared in the airlock. His suit had an insignia that Lara did not recognize. He swung aboard the ship, then turned and moved directly toward Lara.

"I am Ambassador Isaac Smythe Sarnoff. Welcome to the Solar System. I understand that you are requesting assistance from Earth for some sort of scientific study."

"We are."

"Is there somewhere we can go to discuss your needs and Earth's concerns with newcomers from beyond our borders?"

Lara felt a moment of worry at the mention of 'concerns'. She hid her feelings behind a smile and said, "Follow me to our briefing room."

#

Chapter 37

The quorum in the conference room consisted of Lara, Nal, Darin Mastlin, Betrice Flangan, and Legate Klyster. The latter was in a standard shipsuit rather than his uniform. Ambassador Sarnoff semi-reclined at the end of the conference table. His environment suit made it impossible for him to sit in a standard chair, but a sturdy storage chest gave him a modicum of comfort.

After introductions, Sarnoff began the formal meeting.

"I was not on duty today, but when I heard that you are from the far reaches of human space, I asked to be assigned. Earth has been cut off from our colonies for centuries. All we hear are vague stories of wars and destruction. Has the bloodletting finally stopped in your region?"

Darin Mastlin nodded. "Quite some time ago," he said in Standard. "We have been rebuilding for several centuries. Our region of the periphery has six star-nations and dozens of smaller associations. We had heard similar stories about the Core Stars. We are pleased to discover that Earth survives."

"Your message said that you need our help. What is so important that you crossed four thousand light-years to seek us out?"

Darin turned to Lara, "That would be your cue, Shipmaster."

Lara began her usual recounting of how *Coronal Fire* discovered *New Hope*. She spoke in Standard while *Cor* translated her words into Omni via implant for Nal and Legate Klyster. Her delivery was not as smooth as it usually was, but she found she could converse in the new language.

Midway through her tale, the Ambassador held up a gloved hand and told them he would be back shortly. After that, his lips moved intermittently, but without sound penetrating his helmet. Two minutes later, his external speakers again came alive.

"I was speaking to Control. They did a quick check of our history archives. There was a colony ship of that name launched late in the twenty eighth century, headed for the Grisham System. It never arrived. Do you have records of your discovery?"

"We do."

"The station archivist would be very appreciative if you can provide him a copy."

"Certainly. *Cor*, pull up the records of both *New Hope* encounters and translate them into Standard for the Ambassador."

"It will take a few days, Shipmaster. I will need to learn the local data conventions, and the records are voluminous."

"Will that be acceptable?" Lara asked.

"No hurry," Sarnoff replied. "Obviously, your visit doesn't fall into the usual categories. It will take a few days to figure out what to do with you. I can provide a standard record cube if that will help."

"Are you suggesting that we will be held in the outskirts of the Solar System for an extended period?"

"You will have to clear medical inspection, of course. But I was referring to the time it will take to arrange for a team to help you. The preliminaries can be completed while you are heading in-system."

"And what sort of payment will Earth need for this assistance?" Nal asked.

Sarnoff shifted his gaze to the Submaster. "At a minimum, we'll want full copies of your historical databases to fill the gaps in our own records. As to further payment, how can I answer that until we know the extent of the assistance?"

"Fair enough," Darin replied. "What other questions have you for us?"

"I need a description of this science study of yours."

"Betrice, give the Ambassador an overview of what we hope to accomplish. We'll provide our written proposal before he returns to the fortress."

"Gladly," she answered, turning to Sarnoff. "The Eastern Periphery has a severe problem, Ambassador. Our many genetic modifications seem to have introduced a flaw into our DNA. Our birth rate has been dropping for generations and seems to have accelerated lately. In addition to the Coordinate, two other star-nations report the same decline. We suspect others are keeping quiet about it."

"That sounds serious," Sarnoff replied. "How can we assist

you?"

"We have a major research effort going at home. We salvaged *New Hope* because it contains ten thousand examples of human DNA that predate the flaw. We will be using that information as a benchmark, a calibrated sample to which we can compare our various worlds' macro-genomes.

"It's a start, but we will need a much larger sample if we are to complete the work within our own lifetimes. We are here to obtain that larger sample."

"That is something even I can understand," Sarnoff said. "We will probably want more information during your interview aboard Sentinel Alpha Prime tomorrow. I will pass my layman's explanation and your written proposal to my superiors. They will get genetic specialists involved to help you when you arrive at Earth. I do have a quick assessment if you are interested."

"We are very interested," Betrice replied.

"Offhand, I can think of one obvious roadblock to implementing your plan."

"Roadblock?"

"You have to understand, Dear Lady, that Earth is a very old world..." He halted in mid-sentence, then emitted a barking laugh. "That sounded profound in my head but came out rather trite. Let me begin again... Earth is the *oldest* world. I imagine you people have romanticized the old rock during your long separation."

Lara laughed. "You mean the streets aren't paved with gold and the inhabitants don't walk around with halos over their heads?"

"I'm afraid not. We are people, just like you. We go about our lives immersed in our own concerns, we strive to acquire credit, and we are moderately honest... at least, most of us are. Unfortunately, some of us are not. Every society back to the beginning of time has had its liars, thieves, and con artists, and we are no different.

"We have relatively few police because our methods of preventing crime have been honed over the millennia to a remarkably high degree of sophistication. Still, there are those who live outside the bounds of society, and they are very sophisticated, too. Do you know about identity hoaxers?"

"We call them identity thieves," Darin Mastlin responded. "Our computer systems have elaborate safeguards to catch them, but some always seem to get through."

"Ours, as well. There was a time when people used numbers issued by the government to identify themselves. Those proved too easy to counterfeit, as did fingerprints, retina scans, and every other form of biometric identification. Finally, we found a biometric trait that cannot be counterfeited and adopted that as our standard means of identification."

"What is that?"

"We use each individual's DNA code; all three billion units. To say that those codes are jealously guarded is to engage in galaxy-scale understatement."

"Are you saying that we will be unable to gain access to Earth's heredity data, even if we strip identifying details from it?"

"I'm saying it will be difficult. The courts may not see the fact that a whole Sector may be dying as reason enough to allow such information to be copied. For one thing, you would need permission from each individual before their record could be accessed."

Nal asked, "What do you do with these records when a person dies?" There was a pause while *Cor* translated his Omni into Standard.

"Their code is transferred to the Registry of the Dead."

"How many generations has this system been in place?" Betrice asked.

"I'm afraid I don't know," Sarnoff responded. "More than a thousand years, I suppose."

Betrice laughed. "That will fill our needs. In fact, it may be better than getting data from the living. We are interested in the primal human macro-genome. Do you think your courts will allow a data dump of your Registry of the Dead?"

"I don't know. All we can do is ask."

#

Chapter 38

As Ambassador Sarnoff had told them, a delegation consisting of Lara, Darin Mastlin, and Betrice Flangan was summoned to Sentinel Alpha Prime the following day and presented with a clean Bill of Health. They also went before a tribunal convened to pass judgement on whether they should be allowed to continue to Earth.

The tribunal consisted of two men and a woman seated behind a long table. The three expedition members sat in chairs before them.

"My name is Ramses Bartha," the silver-haired man in the center said. "I am Prime Councilor here. It is my responsibility to judge whether a ship with no previous history can be allowed to enter the inner Solar System. I have been briefed on your mission and you have my sympathies. However, there are certain other questions that must be answered first.

"Starting with, 'What weapons do you have aboard your ship?'"

"The sort needed to fight off pirates," Lara answered. "In fact, we fought a battle with one en route." She went on to describe the upgrades the Morast Navy had built into *Coronal Fire*, and, at Bartha's insistence, events leading up to the battle.

"We will need to see these weapons, Shipmaster."

"You are welcome to."

"An inspection team will be dispatched next watch. You can expect them in..." He checked his comm. "... six hours. If we allow you to visit Earth, we expect your offensive systems to remain dormant for the length of your visit. Is that acceptable to you?"

Lara did not hesitate. "It is."

She could answer so quickly because they had discussed how they would respond during the three days they had maneuvered to arrive at Sentinel Alpha Prime. They had not discussed trying to hide the fact that *Fire* was a Q-ship. Even if they could conceal the missiles and beam projectors, their oversize power generators, missile magazine, and combat control center could not be disguised as anything other than what they were.

"I take it that it is not unheard of for an armed freighter to drop out of the deep black and request entry into the Solar System," Darin Mastlin said.

"About one-third of the ships that call have weapons onboard," the middle-aged woman next to Bartha replied. "We understand your need to defend yourselves. However, you must understand that we are well equipped to defend ourselves as well, Expedition Leader. Sentinel Alpha Prime is, to all intents and purposes, a Planetary Defense Fortress. We had the capability to destroy you the moment we detected you."

"As we surmised," Lara responded.

"Because we have no experience with your people, we will require you to conduct yourselves in accordance with our directives when you reach Earth.

"The first of these is that one of our people will accompany you on your voyage to the inner system. He will check in with us at irregular, but precisely scheduled, times. If we do not hear from him on schedule, we will assume that you have abrogated our agreement. Is this acceptable to you?"

"It is."

"Ambassador Sarnoff has requested the duty. Is he acceptable to you?"

"He is."

"When you reach Earth, you will be directed to parking orbit near one of the planetary PDFs. We find that calms the most warlike temperament."

"Message received and understood."

"You do realize, Shipmaster, that you will not be in Earth orbit and will have to station-keep for the duration of your visit?"

"We analyzed your... shall we say, unique... habitat configuration and understand the orbital mechanics involved."

"When did you do this?"

Lara explained that they had dropped through null a quarter-light-year out to scout the Solar System. The three inquisitors exchanged looks at the news. Whatever their reaction, they did not show it in their expressions.

The rest of the meeting involved discussions as to what

mutually beneficial arrangements could be made to pay if the Registry of the Dead were made available. The problem would be the universal one that occurs when strangers meet for the first time: What is it that one party wants that the other has?

#

"Welcome aboard," Lara said to Isaac Sarnoff as he swung across the gravity boundary. He had a lanyard clipped to his belt that stretched back across the interface to a cargo sled piled high with a vacsuit and several travel bags. As soon as he steadied himself in *Coronal Fire*'s gravity field, he pivoted and pulled the sled across as well.

"Good to be aboard, Shipmaster."

Without an environment suit, Sarnoff was a fit young man with sandy hair and a ready grin. He was about 180 centimeters tall. He looked around the suiting antechamber with an appreciative gaze.

"The inspection team was impressed by your level of technology, Shipmaster. I understand that some of your equipment is more advanced than our own."

"You can call me, Lara."

"Isaac," he replied.

"Like Sir Isaac Newton?"

"I'm surprised you know that, Lara. Do they teach Earth history on your home world?"

"They teach it everywhere in the Periphery. As you surmised yesterday, ever since we were cut off, the Mother of Men has been a near mystical place to us. Here, let us help you with your bags."

Lara turned to Spacer Kice Coxander, who was hovering in the background. "Please take the Ambassador's luggage to his cabin, Kice."

"Will do, Shipmaster."

Sarnoff surrendered the sled to the spacer, who disappeared into the main circumferential passageway with it. Sarnoff watched him go. When he turned back toward Lara, she handed him a small rectangular device.

"What's this?" he asked.

"Communicator. Hang it around your neck. You will be able to talk to anyone onboard. *Cor* will handle the translations in real time."

Sarnoff stared at the comm for a few more seconds, then slipped the scarlet cord over his head.

"Can you understand me?" Lara asked in Omni. The Standard translation came out of the comm just as she finished speaking.

In their adventures, she had gotten used to hearing the comms respond to one side of a conversation so often that she had learned to tune them out. This time she could understand both ends.

Sarnoff nodded. "That brings up something that is the subject of much curiosity aboard the Fortress. How is it that many of you speak Standard, Lara, while most of you do not?"

"When *Cor* realized that she wouldn't be able to provide real-time translation when we reach Earth, she taught those of us slated for the ground party to speak the local language."

"Taught you how?"

"Mnemonic education," she answered. Sarnoff's expression showed lack of comprehension. "You know, where you lay in your bed and the computer pumps the words directly into your brain?"

After a few seconds, he said, "I am sorry, but we have nothing like that. This must be one of those things where you are more advanced than we are. Could you teach me your language the same way?"

"I don't see why not. I must warn you; the process can be disconcerting. Why do you want to learn a tongue you will have no use for when we leave?"

"I am a diplomat by trade. To do my job, I need to learn all I can about you.

"*Cor.*"

"Yes, Shipmaster."

"How long to teach Ambassador Sarnoff Omni?"

"Conversational or Technical?"

"The former," Sarnoff said. "After all, we only have ten days before we reach Earth."

"Three four-hour sessions administered twenty-four hours apart."

Once again, Lara saw a flash of wonder cross her guest's features. It started her to thinking. Could it be possible that ordinary old Bernau could be significantly more advanced than fabulous

Earth?

It was a thought that shocked her to the core.

#

Chapter 39

The Earth and Luna were three-quarters in shadow in the view volume. The Earth filled the center region while Luna was to its left. Sol was a white ball to the right of the planet. Surprisingly, both the moon and the star were the same size.

"Home, sweet home," Isaac Sarnoff muttered from beside Lara.

"How long has it been since you were home?" she asked.

"Two years."

The thing that might have interested Sarnoff's masters was that they were conversing in Omni. The Ambassador had tolerated mnemonic teaching sessions better than Lara, or so he claimed.

The Ambassador was a popular man aboard *Coronal Fire* after the nine-day voyage into the inner Solar System. He was a skilled raconteur and had entertained the crew during third meal with his tales of Earth.

During the day, *Fire*'s scientists took turns quizzing him about Earth's government and history. However, try as he would, Sarnoff had difficulty explaining the system by which the Solar System was administered. The best analogy Lara could come up with was a council of deep thinkers directing a coterie of professional bureaucrats, aided by a vast computer network that gave advice to the citizenry, who were not obliged to follow it, but nearly always did.

In the words of an ancient philosopher, it was a puzzlement.

One thing Sarnoff had made clear was that Earth did not rule a star-nation, and especially not a galactic empire. The years of warfare had convinced the caretakers of humanity's first home that their safety lay in keeping their independence. They traded with a dozen star-nations and thirty or more individual systems, but owed allegiance to none of them.

"Traffic Control has cleared us for final approach," *Cor* announced. "We should start to see the various habitats any minute."

Even as *Cor* spoke, there was a sparkle on the screen several diameters below the planet, a pinpoint of white tinged with violet. Over the next fifteen minutes, the volume was pockmarked with many similar sparks.

"What are those?" Lara asked.

"Heat rejection towers, or rather their radiators."

The first object took on dimensional form half an hour later. It was a sphere large enough to be a small moon. It was covered by violet-white sparks. It also resembled Sentinel Alpha Nine.

"Is that a PDF?" Lara asked, extending her arm to point.

"It is indeed," Sarnoff said. "That is Bastion Sirius Three, named after the battle that turned back an invasion fleet about five hundred years ago. We caught them gathering around the Dog Star's third world and wiped them out.

"You will be orbiting a thousand kilometers to the west at Grand Terminus, the main transfer point for this section of the cosmic sphere."

Lara smiled. "You slipped there, Ambassador."

"How so?" he asked.

"You mispronounced klamater."

"So, I did."

They watched as more large structures appeared in magnified inset views around the view volume's periphery. There were fusion generators, shipyards, factories, orbital farms, storage tanks, and things she could not classify. Sarnoff identified one peculiar object as an iceberg from the outer system that had been wrapped in reflective foil and which served as a water and oxygen source for the habitats.

Despite their lack of uniformity, the objects in the formation Sarnoff called "the celestial sphere" had one thing in common: They were gigantic. They had to be to be seen at this range, even when magnified.

Nor were they particularly close together. A sphere two hundred thousand klamaters in diameter has a surface area of 5 x 10^{11} square klamaters, which leaves plenty of empty space between the various orbiting structures. The fact that they were in solar orbit meant that the formation was static while Earth rotated within it.

Another twenty minutes went by before *Cor* announced that

their destination was in sight. The view changed to show a large rotating habitat. One end wore a crown of heat rejection radiators while the other was topped by a transparent dome. Several ships floated beside it, including one oversize warship.

"Is that Grand Terminus?" Lara asked.

"It is," Sarnoff answered.

"It's rotating. Surely they aren't using spin gravity like the ancient space stations."

"No, they do that for thermal control. For a habitat that size, you do not want to let one side get significantly hotter than the other. The thermal-induced bow could seriously damage the hull."

"And the warship?"

"That is the *Terrestrial Space Navy Cruiser Excalibur*, your nursemaid for this visit."

"We are flattered that you think so highly of us to devote an entire cruiser to keep an eye on us," Lara said.

"The inspectors' report concerning your weapons indicated that you might be able to take anything smaller."

"What about Bastion Sirius Three?"

Sarnoff laughed. "That's our backup. Do not let it worry you, Lara. Considering our history, the TSN is paid to be paranoid."

#

Grand Terminus was a city with the population of Capital packed into one-tenth the volume (if Capital's volume was measured out to the city limits and down to the lowest subterranean transport stratum).

It was a cylinder two klamaters in diameter and six klamaters long. The upper half ("upper" being defined by artificial gravity polarity) had one hundred residential and commercial decks and an Earth-like park beneath the dome. Vast volumes were devoted to life support, spaceport, warehouses, and all manner of industry in the lower half.

Three days later, Lara and the rest of the ground party were housed in the Grand Terminus Hotel while they underwent orientation and education before they boarded winged ferries for the trip down to the planet. The orientation sessions were hosted by Isaac Sarnoff and Nozomi Frye, a decorative Asian woman who had been assigned as official host and unofficial minder for the duration of their visit.

During the morning session, Nozomi announced that they were invited to a welcoming dinner in one of the habitat's banquet halls that evening. Having come aboard with just her kit bag, Lara expressed concern that she had nothing to wear.

"They have shops on the Main Concourse," Nozomi answered.

"Nothing will fit me. We Envonians are a strange shape compared to the rest of humanity."

"No problem. The garment is cut to your personal measurements. It will be delivered within the hour."

"How can I pay for it?"

"The diplomatic corps has arranged drawing accounts for each of you for the length of your stay."

"How do we access them?"

"Here, let me assist you," Nozomi said, taking out her comm. She asked Lara for her full name and planet of birth, then manipulated the screen for a few seconds before handing the instrument to her. "Here, touch your finger to the sensor and hold it there for ten seconds."

Lara did as she was told. There was a quiet beep. Nozomi took the instrument back, glanced at the screen and smiled.

"You now have an identity in the planetary registry. Your DNA is on file and you can purchase anything you want merely by touching the sensor in the shop."

"How will I know if I've been overcharged?"

This brought a gentle smile and a kindly look from two brown eyes that bore a strong resemblance to Teo Voxman's, and to a lesser extent, Lara's own eyes. "You can't be overcharged. The computer will not allow it. And if the shop owner somehow manages to do so, he or she will be getting a visit from the diplomatic corps. We can't have people *zyloing* the tourists, you know."

This was not the first time Lara had come to realize that *Cor's* mnemonic teaching program was not as complete as it could have been.

#

The three female members in the ground party ... Lara, Betrice, and Teo ... accompanied Nozomi Frye to the hotel shops and the four of them spent an enjoyable third period examining clothes in a holographic fitting chamber. They each chose three outfits for their visit. Nozomi assured them that they could add more if the occasion arose.

The male members of the party went with Isaac Sarnoff to a different shop but did not seem to have enjoyed themselves to the same extent when they all met back in the commons that served their hotel rooms.

At 20:00 hours, they were escorted to the dining facility, the outer wall of which was curved and transparent, with the vacuum of space beyond.

The expedition members hurried over to gaze out at the black sky sprinkled with moving stars. The habitat's rotation period was ten minutes. Just as they reached the compartment periphery, Earth climbed into view from spinward.

Half the leading hemisphere was bright with daylight and painted with white clouds and blue sea, with a hint of land poking over the planet's limb. The trailing three-quarters of the globe were in darkness decorated by sprawling fields of bright lights that marked the location of great cities and small towns. Across the face of the darkness, quick flashes revealed a scattering of thunderstorms.

They watched as Earth swept across their field of view and disappeared to anti-spinward in thirty seconds. Three minutes later, Luna appeared for the same period, followed five minutes after that by Sol. The star's rays were heavily filtered, allowing them to gaze in comfort at the collection of sunspots sprinkled across its face. Two minutes later, Earth made its reappearance.

"It's beautiful," Betrice exclaimed just before the planet dropped from view behind the habitat's hull.

"It was, wasn't it?" Lara said. "I wonder if the fact that it's our ancestral home makes us more sensitive to that beauty than if it were another world?"

Betrice was to Lara's right and Teo Voxman to her left. The echo of her comment had not died away when she heard the astronomer mutter to herself: *"Never in my life did I ever expect to see this."*

The words were more prayer than observation.

They would all have gladly watched through another revolution but were interrupted by Isaac Sarnoff's voice in Omni.

"Ladies and gentlemen, come meet your colleagues up from Earth. Tonight, we get acquainted. Tomorrow we go down and begin our work.

#

Chapter 40

The ground-to-orbit ferry was crowded with two hundred passengers. The visitors from the Morast Coordinate sat in a block of nine rows on the starboard side where they could gaze out at the planet that was growing perceptibly below.

To Lara's surprise, there was no wing obscuring their view. When she first sat down and strapped herself in, she had noticed the absence, turned to Isaac Sarnoff, and asked, "Where's the wing?"

He had laughed. "Aha, we have a technology that you don't. Good, I was beginning to develop an inferiority complex."

"That doesn't answer the question."

"Our ferries don't use them. That's one advantage of the Cosmic Sphere."

Her expression made him laugh again. He then went on to explain the physics of travel between ground and sphere, and back again. The principle was so obvious that Lara felt stupid for not thinking of it herself.

Ground-to-space launches everywhere else in the galaxy involve transports accelerating to planetary orbital velocity to catch up with the habitats and other satellites passing overhead. Then, upon their return, reentry vehicles use aerobraking to shed most of the orbital energy before switching to powered flight for the landing. It was the system developed at the dawn of the space age.

Earth had developed a different system.

The Celestial Sphere was in orbit about Sol, not Earth. Thus, the only differential velocity between the heliocentric orbits of the habitats and the heliocentric orbit of Earth was the 1600 klamaters per hour delta associated with Earth's rotation.

With contragravity propulsion, a ship need only expend the energy required to climb out of Earth's gravity well, and to shed whatever rotational speed had been imparted to it by the spaceport from which it departed. The energy required was less than ten percent that of a "normal" launch to orbit.

Nor was the reentry the usual artificial-meteor-trailing-

289

plasma-fire light show. Before diving into atmosphere, the ferry synchronized its speed with Earth's rotation before dropping into atmosphere on a slant course toward its destination.

The process was less harrowing than the reentries Lara was familiar with, but also less interesting. During the four hours it took to cross the gulf between the Sphere and the upper atmosphere, she drifted off to sleep.

The banquet had kept all of them up late.

When Ambassador Sarnoff peeled them away from the view-wall, he introduced four specialists assigned to help them with their problem.

The first was Dr. Hiram Gordon of the Institute for Reproductive Science. He was an elderly white-haired man with a full beard who was short even by Earth standards.

The second terrestrial was Sonya Baraka, a computer specialist with the Registry of the Dead. She was good-looking and young. Her hair was reddish-brown and worn in an asymmetric style that flattered her features. From Darin Mastlin's reaction when he was introduced, Lara wondered about terrestrial attitudes toward casual liaisons. She made a mental note to check into it at her earliest opportunity.

The other two newcomers were Fredrich von Hollander and Kwame Yahaya. Hollander, like Isaac Sarnoff, was in the Terrestrial Diplomatic Service. Yahaya was a computer expert who specialized in interfacing different operating systems. His hair was close-cropped and dense, hugging his head like a skull cap. His skin was almost as dark as Nal's, but his face had more angular features.

The banquet consisted of four round tables near the view-wall set apart from the other diners in the compartment. The newcomers divided themselves between the tables, as did the expedition members. Ambassador Sarnoff sat with Darin, Lara, Betrice, and Dr. Gordon at the "head table" where they talked about the expedition's goals and how to complete them.

Nozomi Frye circulated among the other three tables to facilitate social interaction between her charges and the terrestrial specialists. She must have been successful, Lara noted, because by the end of the evening, the attendees were swapping dirty jokes in Standard. She also noted (from her vantage point at the serious table) that Sonya Baraka was holding her own in the contest.

#

"Wake up! We're beginning our approach."

Lara stirred, opened her eyes, and then took a moment to orient herself. She then sat bolt upright when she remembered where she was.

"Did I miss anything?"

"No," Isaac Sarnoff answered. "We entered atmosphere twenty minutes ago and are letting down toward Sahara Spaceport. Look over the side. There is a sight to remember."

Lara twisted in her seat and pressed her nose to the viewport. The sun was high, without a cloud in sight. Far below lay a checkerboard of green fields that stretched to the blue band of the horizon. There were machines working in some of the fields, looking like tiny Envonian clutterbugs.

The fields were variegated. One plot was filled with trees spaced in precise geometric rows. The next field was a smooth sea of green. Beyond were two side-by-side plots of golden yellow.

A threadlike shape came out of the mist in front of them and ran parallel to their flight path. Directly below, it revealed itself to be a large diameter pipe that crossed the fields on a diagonal. Every klamater or so, smaller pipes branched to the right or left before splitting several times into a web of ever smaller pipes.

Interspersed among the fields were houses of glass and shiny metal that glittered in the sun. Most had landing pads on their roofs.

"Beautiful, but I've seen farms before," Lara replied. "We have them on Envon."

"Not like these," Sarnoff said. "This was once the bleakest desert on Earth. About a thousand years ago, our ancestors tamed it with desalinization plants and those pipes you see. Now it is the breadbasket of Europe and North Africa."

The ferry continued to fly over the agriculture belt for ten more minutes before the blue of a sea peeked over the curved horizon ahead.

"That's the Mediterranean," Sarnoff said. "The Romans called it *Mare Nostrum*, Our Sea."

"I've heard of the Romans. Soldiers in skirts, right?'

"I don't think the Centurians would have appreciated that description, but yes. Our flight path parallels the coast until we get to the Gulf of Sidra where we turn south for the spaceport. We're high enough that you may see Sicily and the tip of the Italian boot off to the right if the atmosphere is clear enough."

The reference to a boot did not make sense to Lara, but she was too busy to ask for clarification as she watched the world of legend slip beneath her. Judging from the awed comments drifting forward from behind her, she was not alone in her enjoyment.

Ten minutes later, the ferry turned left, banking like a plane, and then began to drop quickly toward an immense span of concrete. From her vantage point, she could only see one edge of their destination. Most of it was blocked by the body of the ferry.

As the ground continued to expand below her, Lara's heart began to beat faster, and her breathing became shallow. She could feel her pulse in her temple. To the right, a midsize city came into view. It was built in concentric circles. The center was dominated by two- and three-story buildings whose whitewashed walls gleamed in the sunlight. The periphery was dominated by needle-like towers of glass and steel.

Then they were over the expanse of concrete. The ferry altered course toward a large building, moving no faster than a groundcar. It slowed and then came to a halt before rotating ninety degrees left. The ship hovered for several seconds before dropping down into a pit filled with machinery and boarding bridges.

The landing was so smooth that she did not detect the moment of touchdown. The quiet hum of the contragravs grew quiet and her eardrums popped as pressure equalized. A chime filled the cabin.

This was the signal for the terrestrial passengers to stand up and extract their luggage from the overhead. The sight made Lara homesick. They were indistinguishable from a crowd on Bernau or Envon queuing for departure at the end of a journey.

She sat quietly while the terrestrials filed past. Some looked the visitors over, but never stared at their different physiques. When the last of the other passengers had filtered out of the forward airlock, Isaac Sarnoff signaled it was time for the expedition to leave.

At the front of the craft, they reached the open airlock through which a warm breeze was flowing. The portal was only wide enough to pass single file. Lara stepped in front of Sarnoff, hefted her bag over her shoulder, and passed out into the open air and direct sunlight. She walked to the end of the boarding bridge before turning to look out across the expanse of concrete toward the city beyond.

She inhaled deeply, closed her eyes, and turned her face up to the yellow-white star overhead. She held her breath as long as she could and then exhaled with a whoosh.

A shiver ran down her spine. She luxuriated in the sensation. She had breathed her first lungful of the atmosphere that had sustained ten thousand generations of her ancestors.

There had been no odor to the air. In fact, it smelled like a dozen other spaceports she had visited. Still, it exhilarated her. Although she was an elongated freak from a star invisibly distant, a momentary contentment washed over her.

Some primeval instinct within told her that she was home.

#

Chapter 41

From Sahara Spaceport, an aircraft flew them to Buenos Aires, where they were put up in a hotel that made the one aboard Grand Terminus look like a hostel snack bar. There the group broke up into its constituent functions.

Lara and Darin Mastlin accompanied Freidrich von Hollander and Isaac Sarnoff to a large building in the center of the city where the offices of the Earth Non-Government were housed. They were introduced to many functionaries with titles selected to impart minimal information as to their actual jobs and participated in a long and sumptuous working lunch hosted by the ministry's Chief Counselor.

The terrestrials, having received the report of the border inspectors aboard Sentinel Alpha Prime, had a good grasp of the purposes of the expedition. They explained in more detail than Ambassador Sarnoff had that it would be impossible to obtain a database holding Earth's current macro-genome.

Not only was there the problem of the fetish against revealing one's own DNA code, but one of Expedition's initial assumptions was wrong. Back on Bernau, Betrice Flangan pointed out that evolution shaped humans to inhabit a specific niche in the terrestrial biosphere. Since the inhabitants of Earth had no need to change their heredity, they would not have done so, and a vast reservoir of the original human genetic code could still be found on the Mother of Men.

Betrice had not considered the human penchant for vanity.

Since time immemorial, parents have always wanted what is best for their children. This includes the best possible set of genes their parents can provide. Thus, as soon as gene manipulation became possible, prospective mothers and fathers used the technology to reengineer their offspring. The result was that the pure human heredity for which *Coronal Fire* searched was not to be found on Earth, or anywhere else in the galaxy.

This did not mean that their search had been for naught, the

Chief Councilor assured them. The purpose of their quest was to compare the genetics of the Periphery with a sample that had not been tainted by the genetic flaw. That, the Earth could supply.

Thus, a large sample from the Registry of the Dead would serve as a basis for their research, especially since the taint of genetic tinkering lessened the farther back in the Registry one looked.

Lunch dragged on as several different 'deals' were discussed. It was finally agreed that Earth would be willing to supply DNA maps of those who had been dead for at least two centuries, including the oldest records on file.

At the conclusion of the meal, they all moved back to the offices and began to discuss price. The haggling continued through third meal and was not complete when the Chief Councilor called a halt at 22:00 hours.

#

The rest of the team had not been idle in their absence. Betrice and her team of biologists sat with other medical and genetic specialists to explore the form in which the decedents' DNA data was filed in the Registry. As expected, there had been several changes in format down through the centuries. That was Kwame Yahaya's specialty.

He and Betrice found that they worked well together as they designed a common format into which the data could be translated. That format would have to be capable of being converted into something Morast computers could read. Yahaya referred to what they were trying to create as a *Rosetta Stone* program. Betrice was curious as to the source of the term, but even *Cor* came up empty after she transmitted a query on the long-range circuits to the Cosmic Sphere.

Teodara Voxman and her two astronomers met with their counterparts at a ministry that still bore the name Stellar Survey. It was not the original survey, of course; but the terrestrials were interested in obtaining astrographic data on the Eastern Periphery, as well as the hyperspace plots *Cor* had collected en route.

Each working group labored late into the evening and it was not until the next morning that the team was able to get together for first meal, which the locals called "breakfast."

"So, what are we going to have to give the terrestrials to get their genetic codes?" Betrice asked as she spread a purple substance on a tasty, if oddly shaped, pastry called a croysant.

"They seem especially interested in our hyperspace maps between here and the Periphery," Teo said. "An already mapped path extending four thousand light-years into the unknown would seem to be highly marketable."

Darin nodded. "Also, they have expressed interest in our technology. Perhaps that interest is sufficient to justify establishing an active trade route between here and the Coordinate."

"How long will it be before we actually have our hands on the data?" Lara asked. She was sipping from a cup with a steaming hot confection called cocoa.

"Betrice?" Darin asked.

"We will probably have the data converted within the month."

"Teo?"

"We spoke of trading stellar databases yesterday. They claim to have astrographic and hyperspace data on ten thousand colony worlds and would like to add the Eastern Periphery to their records. Once we agree to a swap, it should not take more than a week to get everything organized."

Darin nodded. "As for Lara and me, we've been invited to New York in about ten days to meet with the General Council. Apparently, the city was completely rebuilt after the attack by the Soldant Collective.

"I guess it is time for us to get back to work. We will get together and compare notes each morning. After that, I will assign someone to compose the daily report for transmission to the ship. Teo, you have the duty this morning. If anyone has anything pressing, let me know and I will call us together as needed.

#

"Did anything come out of this morning's confab?" Isaac Sarnoff asked Lara when he showed up at her door an hour later.

"Confab?" she asked.

"Meeting, conference, jaw-session..."

"No, we were just getting organized. Weren't you eavesdropping?"

"No, of course not," he said before hesitating. "Or rather, I wasn't. I cannot guarantee that the security services were not. Even so, I presume you spoke Omni, so if they want to know what you said, they will run it past me."

"It was fairly boring," Lara said with a smile, which turned into an expression of curiosity. "What are you doing here this morning? Did we have an appointment?"

"No. I thought you might like to see Chichén Itzá."

"What's that?"

"A Mayan city that is almost four thousand years old."

"Mayan?"

"The original inhabitants of Central and South America. Their descendants, the Aztecs, greeted Cortez when he and his men waded ashore."

Lara laughed. "I'm sorry, but while Earth history is taught on Envon, the details are a bit spotty prior to the invention of star travel."

"No problem. I can fill you in on the way. If you are interested, of course."

"Wait a second. I'll check in with Darin Mastlin."

Onboard ship, Lara would have silently linked with Darin via their implants. With *Cor* out of range, she was forced to do it the old-fashioned way. She extracted the communicator the terrestrials had given her and spoke his name.

"Yes?" he said when his face appeared on the device.

"Anything I have to do today, boss?" She was speaking Standard and the last word seemed right for the leader of their expedition.

"No, why?"

"Ambassador Sarnoff wants to take me to see an archeological site." She looked at Sarnoff and said, "It is an archeological site, isn't it? A four-thousand-year-old city would not still be occupied, would it?"

He shook his head. "No, long dead. Although, we do have cities older than that. Rome, for instance. There was a big festival there four years ago to celebrate the fifth millennial anniversary of the founding of the city."

Mastlin heard the answer and said, "You are free to go if you like. What do you think he is up to?"

Lara smiled. "I think he is trying to get to know me better."

"Have fun. Report in when you get back."

"Will do."

#

Chapter 42

The aircar Isaac Sarnoff requisitioned for the trip was a superpowered speedster. The contragravs were capable of speeds up to Mach 2. Even so, it took three hours to fly from Buenos Aires to Chichén Itzá on the Yucatan Peninsula.

They took the direct route straight across South America. The car's bubble canopy gave them a panoramic view of the continent and Sarnoff kept up a running travelogue.

The car was equipped with a bar and finger food, as well as a sound system. The ride was so luxurious that Lara suspected the Ambassador had an ulterior motive for this trip (other than the obvious one).

By the end of the first hour and the third drink, she was more relaxed than she had been since they had last pulled her out of cold sleep. She rested in the comfortable embrace of the fully reclined seat and watched the world go by.

Isaac in the other seat said, "Enough travelogue for one day. Let us talk about you."

She smiled. She had been expecting this for some time.

"What do you want to know?"

"Your husband, Nal, seems a formidable man. Would he object if I made romantic advances to you?"

"I am Nal's ship-wife. He has two others at home, you know."

He nodded. "I had heard that."

"What about you? Are you married?"

"Not at present. Being in the Diplomatic Corps and assigned to a Sentinel Station is not conducive to family life."

"Then I would say that we are both free at the moment, Mr. Ambassador," Lara answered.

"Call me Isaac," he whispered before leaning across the narrow divide between the seats and planting his lips on hers. The kiss was tentative and gentle. Lara did all she could to cooperate.

When their lips parted, he moved to slide over into her side. She put a restraining hand to his chest, stopping him.

301

He raised his eyebrows in query.

"Maybe on the way home. Your description of Chichén Itzá intimated that we will be doing a lot of hiking today. I need to conserve my energy. Besides, I am interested in learning all I can about Earth. You have no idea how much being here means to all of us."

He sighed and powered his seat into a sitting position. "All right, ask away."

They spent the next two hours in conversation, interspersed with kisses of increasing ardor to keep the blood flowing. The blood flowed well enough that Lara was considering relenting on postponing their encounter when a tone sounded from the aircar's autopilot.

"What was that?"

"Time to begin our descent. If you will look at that bit of land just coming into view ahead on the right, that's Yucatan."

#

Chichén Itzá was a contrast of ancient and modern sights. The city was surrounded by green vegetation out of which had been hacked a clearing on the dirty white limestone bedrock. Modern hotels surrounded the ruins with aircar parking, restaurants, and locals hawking their wares.

The central site included a large stepped pyramid to the southeast and an even larger stadium-like pile of masonry to the northwest. Both were covered by transparent weather bubbles to protect the ruins from erosion. A sign next to the weather bubble at the entrance to the pyramid said that the original had been constructed in the 30th century and that the current bubble was the twelfth to stand on the site. A sign next to that one explained in considerable detail the penalty for defacing any part of the monument or collecting unauthorized souvenirs.

The stadium had indeed been a sports arena; the site of a particularly bloody form of sparsball. An automated recording relayed the information that the game was played with a heavy rubber ball that was bounced off a player's hip. The intention was to pass the ball through one of the stone rings mounted high on each of the two vertical walls of the court.

Hip ball was played all through the Mesoamerican culture, but the games in the giant stone stadium had religious significance and involved human sacrifice. Tradition told of the losing team being killed and thrown into the nearby sacrificial well.

Lara and Isaac next visited El Castillo, the stepped pyramid of Kukulcán. Lara insisted on climbing the 91 steps to the pyramid's flat top on which sat a temple. The pyramid top was 24 meters above the limestone plain. There the sweaty, panting pair rested while they took in the view, which, despite the bubble, was unobstructed.

A late afternoon lunch in one of the hotel restaurants completed their visit. All through the tour, sexual tension had been building between them. When Isaac suggested they skip desert, Lara readily agreed, and they took a taxi back to where they had left the aircar in a distant parking area.

Once airborne, Isaac set the autopilot to return them to Buenos Aires and then turned to Lara.

"Shall we get out of these sweaty clothes?"

There followed a race to see who could disrobe first. Isaac reclined his seat and Lara climbed over the divide to join him... her length made that the logical choice. There followed a prolonged period of questing hands and lips exploring sensitive flesh, and after a suitable pause, a joining of two souls from different worlds in that most human of all acts.

#

"Well, that was worth the wait," Lara said sometime later. She was still nude, but back in her own seat.

"Yes, it was," Isaac agreed. "Would milady care to go another round?"

"In a while," she replied. "I need to catch my breath and, you sir, need to recuperate."

"I resent that," he said with a leer.

"Resent it or not, it's still a fact."

"I suppose so. Drink?"

"Yes, please."

They lay back and watched South America pass beneath them at 2400 klamaters per hour. The sun was low in the west. On the ground, the sun was setting, casting long black shadows across the land; but up where they were, it was still bright.

"I just thought of something that has been bothering me since before we arrived," Lara said.

"What?"

She explained how *Coronal Fire* had dropped through null while still a quarter light-year out from Sol to spy out the territory. That initial survey had revealed that Earth's energy signature placed their population at only five billion. Lara described the speculation aboard *Fire* as to how Earth could have lost two-thirds of its population after the Great Hegira.

She ended her explanation by saying, "From the condition of the planet, it is obvious that it wasn't war. Tell me about the plague."

Isaac had been admiring her form while she talked. The question caused his eyes to shift from her body to her face. His brow furrowed. "What plague?"

"The one that cost Earth two-thirds of its population."

"I don't know what you are talking about. There wasn't any plague."

"Then how did you manage to shed twelve billion people?"

He laughed. "On purpose and very, very carefully."

"I don't understand."

"After we beat off the attacks from our onetime colonies, our ancestors decided that the planet was overpopulated. They embarked on a program of population control designed to reduce our numbers without destroying our civilization. It took three centuries and there were times when we were on the brink of civil war, but we managed it."

"How?"

"If you want the technical details, you will have to ask the geneticists. Babies on Earth are almost never produced in the manner we just attempted. When a couple want a baby, they go to a reproduction clinic. The clinicians extract half-a-dozen eggs from the mother and a sperm sample from the father, and then analyze them to obtain the best possible genetic outcome. And, of course, they select for the desired sex of the child and repair any obvious defects. We've done it that way since before star travel."

"How does that regulate the population?"

"I wasn't finished. They also check for Thorson-Nakuta factor.

If it is not present, they add it to the zygote's DNA. Of course, these days it always is."

Lara blinked. She found she could not control her voice for a dozen seconds. When she finally regained her power of speech, she asked, "And this controls the mother's fertility?"

"Of course," Isaac replied. "In the beginning, they limited every fertile female to a single offspring. Later, they upped it to two. It is not that simple, of course; but that is the idea. To keep Earth's population within optimum limits, the geneticists modify the factor's potency every generation to make necessary adjustments."

Lara gulped and reached for her clothes. She could feel her face turning hot. She managed to get out a strangled, "Get dressed."

"Why?" Isaac asked.

"Because I have to make a call and I don't want Darin to see us naked."

#

Chapter 43

Once again, Darin Mastlin's features appeared on her comm unit. "Are you back?"

"No, I'm calling from the aircar."

"Did you have an enjoyable time?"

"I did, and it was educational. That is why I am calling. Isaac and I were just discussing how Earth trimmed their population after the Hegira. It wasn't a plague."

"What was it?"

"They limited each mother's fertility so she could only have one child at first, and then increased it to two children when they reached their current population level."

"Interesting," Mastlin said. "Betrice will want to know all about it. Why the phone call?"

"I thought it sounded a lot like our genetic flaw."

There was silence on the other end of the call for half a minute. It was as though she could follow his train of thought through his changes of expression. Finally, he cleared his throat and hesitantly asked, "Do you think the two are related?"

"I don't know. I do think we ought to explore the possibility."

"Agreed. When are you arriving?"

Lara turned to Isaac, who flashed two fingers twice.

"Twenty-two hundred hours. Alert the team. We need to plan."

#

The whole team was gathered in the commons when Lara arrived with Isaac in tow. She asked him to repeat what he had told her, then explained her supposition that it sounded a lot like what was happening at home.

"How could it be related?" a rumpled Teo asked. Her team had worked all day at the Stellar Survey, and she had been asleep when Darin rousted her out. "Earth didn't begin their program until after we lost contact with them. Isn't that correct, Ambassador?"

"When did you lose contact?"

"Some time after the Stellar Survey erased Sol's coordinates from the master database seven centuries ago."

"Our fertility control program began about that time. We will have to ask one of the specialists for an exact date."

"So, I kept all of you up for no reason?" Lara asked.

"Not necessarily," Betrice said. She had been quiet since Lara made her announcement. "It's true that Morast ceased trading with Earth, but we really never traded with them anyway. The distance between us is just too great. That does not mean that we were completely isolated, however."

She turned to Isaac. "Ambassador, I assume that this fertility regulator in your genes did not take effect immediately."

"Why would you assume that?" Darin asked.

"Because if every female were limited to a single child upon inoculation, it would have been impossible to spread it. And it defies common sense to expect all nine billion women on Earth at the time to volunteer for the treatment. To infuse the full population, you would inoculate a subset of women and then let the fertility inhibiter remain dormant for three or four generations before activation."

"That is correct," Sarnoff said. "To be effective, a woman must inherit both parts of Thorson-Nakuta from her parents; obviously, one from each. During the initial 'seeding', each zygote was given two copies of T-N-Alpha or T-N-Beta, but never one of each.

"The mother then passed on one-half of the full factor to her children, and they passed it on to their children. Eventually, men carrying Alpha found women carrying Beta, or the reverse, and their offspring ended up with the full factor.

"Obviously, it makes no difference if males carry the full treatment. We don't have babies. However, when a female receives both halves during conception, the hormonal changes late in her first pregnancy activate the active components of the T-N genetic code. Specifically, it changes her biochemistry to stop embryos from attaching to the uterine wall."

Bernice nodded. "Which brings us back to how Thorson-Nakuta could have reached the Eastern Periphery. Infected spacers and immigrants have been streaming outward from Sol for fifteen centuries. Just as the sixteenth century sailors left their genetic mark on every continent they touched, so too their thirty-sixth century counterparts carrying Thorson-Nakuta.

"Once a planet is infected with the T-N genetic code, the infection grows generation by generation until the loss in fertility becomes bad enough to affect the birth statistics. On Earth, the reduction in fertility is a positive; everywhere else it is a plague. Nor is the plague limited in time or space. It expands until it reaches the borders of human space. That is how the Periphery might have become infected."

The compartment was quiet for a long time before Darin Mastlin cleared his throat and, in a hoarse voice, said: "An interesting theory. How do we go about proving it?"

#

The next day, Lara met Isaac for second meal. She expected a quiet tête-à-tête repast after which they would return to her room for light gymnastics.

Instead, he showed up with a man and a woman in tow. He embraced her and gave her a quick kiss on the cheek, then whispered, *"Sorry, but the boss insisted. Business before pleasure."*

He turned to his companions and in a normal voice, said, "Lara, I would like to introduce two members of the Terrestrial Board of Trade and Industry: Garth Baldwin, Chairman; Isabel Morales, Senior Member. They have expressed an interest in meeting you to discuss matters of mutual interest."

"Hello," Lara said, shaking their hands.

"Let's get a table and drinks," Isaac said, gesturing toward the hotel dining room.

When all of them were seated, Isaac turned to Baldwin. "Chairman, the floor is yours."

"Shipmaster, I cannot tell you how good it is to meet you," Baldwin said. He was one of those gray-haired executive types whose voice seems louder than it is and who is obviously used to being the most important person in any conversation.

"Thank you, Mr. Chairman. How may I be of service?"

"We of the Board of Trade have been looking over the report concerning your ship. The inspectors were impressed with some of your technology. The fact that you were able to teach Ambassador

Sarnoff your language so effortlessly is startling.

"We have been assigned to evaluate the possibility of trade between Earth and the Eastern Periphery star-nations."

"And what have you concluded?"

Baldwin sighed. "I'm afraid that nothing either of our realms produce has sufficient value to justify setting up a trade route involving an eight-year round trip."

Lara nodded. "That has been our conclusion at each of the two planets where we stopped en route."

"Our secondary mission is to put a price on the information you look to gain from us. Put simply, Shipmaster, we are trying to figure out whether you can pay us a fair price for our data in any currency we value. It turns out that there is a special case that allows both of us to get what we want. I will let Board Member Morales explain."

The woman was middle aged, with lustrous black hair. She was typical of the people Lara had seen since her arrival in Buenos Aires.

She leaned forward and said, "Those areas where your technology is more advanced represent value to us."

"I fail to see how," Lara replied. "We can describe what the technology does, and how it is operated and maintained. But we cannot tell you how to manufacture it. That data doesn't exist aboard *Coronal Fire*."

"Your government launched an expedition to Earth to obtain genetic information you require for your studies. Why can't we do likewise?"

"You are suggesting an expedition to the Coordinate?" Lara asked.

"Why not? The cost is much less than that of setting up a permanent trade route. Your need for our DNA records justified the cost of a ship and ten years of lifespan from its crew. The same may be said of our need for your technology."

Lara thought about it. It seemed logical. Theoretically, the ship dispatched to Morast could return with treasure more valuable than anything the ancient mariners obtained from the 'spice islands' on Earth.

"I see your point," she said, nodding. "This is the 'currency' that you will accept in payment for the data from the Registry of the

Dead?"

"It is," Isabel Morales replied. "However, we will need guarantees that your people will honor the agreement when we show up to collect. Do you have the authority to sign a binding contract?"

"We are chartered by the Morast Coordinate to find Earth and negotiate for data. The authority comes with the charter."

#

Chapter 44

The meeting with the geneticists happened two days later. Betrice, Darin, and Lara attended. Teo begged off, explaining that her team was designing a translation program for the hyperspace route data.

The meeting was to be held at the Biology Center of the University of Antarctica, the same institution where Alain Destarte made his breakthrough that opened the stars. Isaac Sarnoff went with them.

Once again Lara found herself flying high above South America, but south this time. They were in a chartered commercial transport. Isaac sat next to her and narrated as he had done two days earlier. He did so loud enough that Darin and Teo could hear him from across the aisle.

Twenty minutes after leaving Buenos Aires, the green countryside gave way to brown desert. To the west, tall snow-covered mountains could be seen on the distant horizon, their white flanks softened by blue haze.

At the end of an hour, they reached a region of waterways, with the ocean to the east. Isaac pointed out a long inlet that penetrated deep inland. "That," he explained, "is the Strait of Magellan through which the 16th century European explorers first reached the Pacific Ocean."

Ten minutes later, they reached the tip of South America and headed out over an expanse of sea named after another famous mariner of the Age of Exploration. It was not long before a wall of white appeared before them and Earth's southernmost continent came into view.

Soon they were flying over ice for as far as the eye could see. The forbidding landscape was dotted with artificial installations and small cities beneath weather domes.

It was near noon and three weeks from the southern summer solstice when they approached Shackleton, the capital city of Antarctica. The sun was 23 degrees above the horizon behind them and cast shadows even at "high noon."

There was nothing small about Shackleton. A huge weather dome dominated the center of the city. A ring of smaller-by-comparison domes circled it, and hundreds of other structures dotted the dazzling landscape for dozens of klamaters in all directions.

The central domes were connected by glittering transport tubes that arched high above the ice to keep them from being buried by snow during the winter storms. Long depressions in the ice radiated out from the central dome, marking the location of under-ice transportation links.

Isaac leaned close to point through the view window. "The University is under that dome in the ring at 3 o'clock."

Lara intentionally pressed her body to his. It was the closest the two of them had been since they had arrived back from Chichén Itzá. As pleasurable as the sensation was, she once again became aware of the holes in her mastery of Standard. While his comment was intelligible in the linguistic sense, she had no idea what time had to do with locating the university.

The transport dropped down toward a dome a quarter-circle around from the University dome and slowed to a near hover as it floated a few meters above the ice. A large hatch opened, and the transport slipped through into the cavernous interior. The hatch closed behind them as the aircraft settled to the concrete floor.

Isaac climbed to his feet and announced, "Everyone, welcome to Antarctica."

#

Despite snow and ice to the horizon, the temperature inside the dome was optimized for comfort. Isaac led them to a station where they boarded a transport pod that whisked them through one of the glittering tubes that connected to the central dome. They were inside the big habitat for thirty seconds before the pod turned to enter a second tube.

Shackleton's city center was a cluster of tall towers, one of which acted as a support for the weather dome, and a grid of footpaths with apartment buildings packed closely together. There were a few individual homes interspersed between the taller buildings. Some of these had patches of what looked like grass in front of them.

Overhead, suspended from the dome, banks of floodlights substituted for the sun during the winter months and helped the plants grow all year long. Their brief glimpse of the metropolis gave the impression of something one would see in a museum diorama or a little girl's bedroom.

They entered the second tube. There was a momentary flash of ice and snow as they crossed to another dome, and then decelerated into a station in which a large illuminated sign proclaimed *University of Antarctica, Home of the Penguins.*

"We're here," Isaac said. "Time to disembark."

The four of them climbed out onto a pedestrian platform. Isaac led them through a maze of tunnels. Finally, they reached a hallway lined with identical doors on both sides, identified only by numbers.

He stopped at one and ushered them inside. There they found a conference room decorated in a style common to universities throughout human space. Seated in the middle of a long, polished table was a white-haired woman flanked by a middle-aged man and a young woman.

The trio rose to their feet as Isaac crossed the room and introduced himself. He then gestured for his charges to approach.

"Professor Anastasia Crowley, may I introduce our visitors from the Eastern Periphery? This is Shipmaster Larath da Benthar Sims of the Starship *Coronal Fire*; Darin Mastlin, Expedition Leader; and Betrice Flangan, Biologist. Both Darin and Betrice represent the Institute of Knowledge on Bernau in the Morast Coordinate. The Institute is an organization with similar functions to our own universities."

Professor Crowley introduced her companions and a general shaking of hands ensued. She then gestured for the guests to take seats on the other side of the table. When everyone was situated, Isaac continued:

"Our guests have come four thousand light-years to solve a problem in your field of specialization, Professor. They have some questions regarding the Thorson-Nakuta Factor."

"I will be glad to impart any information that I can," she said. "Let us begin with you telling me about this problem."

Betrice spent ten minutes relating the history of dropping birth rates in the Eastern Periphery and how the Institute of Knowledge had approached the problem to date. She then explained how the idea to compare the current macro genome of the Periphery with the terrestrial original had come about.

"And so, we came here to obtain DNA records from a time before the extensive genetic tinkering that accompanied the Great Hegira."

Professor Crowley nodded. "It seems a sound plan. I understand it has not gone as you had hoped. What brings you here today?"

"Lara learned of your population control program and thought it resembled our problem with birth rates. We have been cut off from Earth for seven centuries. However, there is a possibility that the two are related, so we came here to learn more."

"Yes, Ambassador Sarnoff mentioned the possibility when he commed me. We will begin with our standard introduction. Katerina will do the honors."

The young woman, who had been introduced as Katerina Witt, stood up and moved to the front of the room where a holocube sat. The lights dimmed, the cube came alight, and she began to speak.

#

"As you can well imagine, the Hegira put a considerable strain on Old Earth. Yet, no matter how many headed off to the stars, our population continued to expand. By the time the Interstellar Wars began, Earth's population was 18 billion.

"If that seems a lot, let me assure you that we had the resources to house and feed all of them. Even in those days, Earth had a robust orbital infrastructure, including massive fusion plants, factories, and all manner of industry. Furthermore, we had nine planets, 250 moons, and tens of thousands of asteroids and comets from which to draw resources.

"However, the attacks changed our outlook. Our intellectuals grew worried about a general collapse and mass starvation.

"And so, we decided to reduce our population. Eric Thorson and Hijoro Nakuta collaborated to come up with the Thorson-Nakuta Factor."

Katerina Witt paused in her recitation and let her gaze sweep over her audience. "That is the history. Are there any questions?" After a general shaking of heads, she said, "Then let us proceed to a description of the way the Factor works."

The explanation mirrored that which Isaac Sarnoff had given them but was more technical in nature. There were long interruptions as Betrice asked questions and Katerina or Professor Crowley answered.

When this occurred, the two lapsed into a strange language filled with jargon. Despite the interruptions, Katerina Witt finally reached the end of her presentation and said, "That concludes the background on our population control program. Now Professor Crowley will get into the actual mechanics of how the Thorson-Nakuta works."

#

Chapter 45

Professor Crowley rose from her seat and stood beside the holocube. She manipulated the controls, causing a new image to appear in the volume. It was the familiar double helix of the human DNA string. Two long strands wrapped around one another like a tightly wound helical staircase held together by base pairs acting as "treads."

The DNA molecule in the cube was red, with occasional green specks along its twisted length.

"As I am sure all of you know, the helical outer strands of DNA are the structural part of the molecule. They are composed of nitrogen and phosphate molecules known as polynucleotides and are held together by base pairs composed of various nucleic acids. Thus, DNA's name: *deoxyribonucleic acid*.

"Considering the complexity of the molecule, you would think that there would be thousands of nucleotides, but there are only four: *Adenine, Guanine, Cytosine*, and *Thymine*. Thymine always attaches to Adenine and Cytosine with Guanine. Are you with me so far?"

Lara laughed. "About every third word dissolves into static in my brain."

"Never mind," Betrice said. "Some of us are following along better than others."

Crowley nodded. "It's not important that everyone understand the intricacies. The general outline is what is important for our discussions. We have color-coded this illustration to make a point. Most DNA base pairs, shown here in red, are noncoding. That means that they have nothing to do with the production of proteins. The green sections are the protein producers, and at its most basic, the source of life.

"When scientists first mapped the DNA molecule, they were surprised to discover that 98 percent of its contents had no clear function. They dubbed this 'junk DNA.'

"In fact, they were very wrong. This noncoding part is integral to the functioning of cells, particularly the control of gene activity. Noncoding DNA has sequences that act as regulatory elements, that decide when and where genes are turned on and off as proteins are manufactured.

"If your problem is caused by Thorson-Nakuta, it is not surprising you have not yet identified the source. We purposely hid it in the noncoding DNA."

Betrice frowned. "Why would you need to hide it?"

The corner of Professor Crowley's lips curved upward at the question, but not in a smile. It was more of a grimace.

"Seven hundred years ago, Earth's politics were riven by factions. The information I am giving you today was classified as a state secret at the highest level. They worried that if the details became widely known, one faction might use the knowledge to out-breed the others. Luckily, political enthusiasms work on a much shorter time scale than human genetics. The fears proved baseless."

"So where do we tell our people at home to look?" Lara asked.

"That is a simple question with a complex answer," Crowley replied. "Each half of Thorson-Nakuta takes up more than one hundred thousand base pairs, many of which are not contiguous. We can provide you with maps, but the analysis is not easy."

Betrice nodded. "So, when we get home, we start looking for Thorson-Nakuta in our people's DNA. If we find it, we have proven that our genetic flaw is actually your population control system."

Professor Crowley agreed. "Yes, that is one strategy to pursue. It is not absolute proof, you understand. You may be suffering from Thorson-Nakuta *plus* something else. However, the probabilities are high that you will have found your problem."

She paused and looked thoughtfully at her guests before continuing: "However, there is another strategy you may want to try first. Why wait until you get home? Why not begin the search at once?"

It took a moment for Lara to process the question. "I beg your pardon?"

"You have a shipload of your citizens in the Cosmic Sphere. Why not sample their DNA?"

"Wouldn't it be the wildest bit of luck if one of us possessed the factor?"

"Perhaps," the Professor agreed. "Although, if this 'flaw' of yours is widespread enough to show in your statistics, then it has penetrated your gene pool much more extensively than you realize.

"Remember, preventing conception after the first child is the final stage of the process. Before that can happen, Thorson-Nakuta must be sufficiently widespread that breeding pairs with complementary halves become commonplace.

"How many people are there on your expedition?"

"Two hundred and thirty-four," Lara replied.

"It's a long shot, but hardly a waste of time. If we test each of your expedition members and find nothing, then it only means that you will have to wait until you get home to begin your survey.

"If, on the other hand, we find Thorson-Nakuta in your crew, the hypothesis is confirmed."

And so, Lara called the ship and explained the situation to Nal and *Cor*. Her ship husband agreed to begin preparations for testing the blood of everyone onboard. Unfortunately, the usual methods of sample collection would not work. Professor Crowley insisted on special collection ampoules and other equipment.

Therefore, the University of Antarctica supplied the test kits and Lara volunteered to transport them. Two days later, she and Isaac Sarnoff were aboard a transport bound for the Cosmic Sphere.

#

Chapter 46

"Have you told your husband about me?" Isaac asked during the long climb out to the Cosmic Sphere.

"Of course," Lara said. "We don't keep secrets from each other."

"Is he going to punch me in the nose when I step out of the airlock?"

She smiled. "Like all women, I have an atavistic desire to see two big males fight over me, but no. We are both free individuals with free will."

He sighed. "That takes away one worry... I think."

"If you are really afraid, you didn't have to come, you know."

He shook his head. "Orders. I am your liaison officer and the boss wants to make sure everything goes well. We are about at the point where the haggling begins."

She raised her eyebrows in an unspoken question.

His light manner turned serious. "The powers-that-be think the data you are seeking must be very valuable to you, especially now that you suspect Thorson-Nakuta."

"Of course," Lara replied. "We have never tried to hide that fact."

"But will you meet our price once we give it to you?"

She shrugged. "How can I answer that until I hear what it is you want? We have various trade goods in our holds that are examples of our technology. Take your pick."

Isaac laughed. "I think we will want more than a few samples. The price will be in the form of technical data for technologies where you are definitely ahead of us."

Lara nodded. "Just as we told Garth Baldwin and Isabel Morales. You are welcome to the technical details of any technology that interests you... within reason, of course. All you need do is come to the Periphery to collect. In fact, we are counting on you to do just that."

"Really? I had not heard that. Why?"

323

"Because we want you to bring a second copy of whatever data you give us when you come. That will ensure that the information gets through if something happens to us on the way home. It will also guarantee any deal we make. If *Coronal Fire* suffers a mishap en route, you can offer our government the same data that we failed to deliver and thereby enforce your demands for payment."

"What do you think will happen to you?" Isaac asked, suddenly concerned.

Lara shrugged. "Who knows. We could run into an uncharted gravity infusion or another pirate. Nal and I were discussing the possibilities last evening. Because of our last encounter with a pirate, we are going to increase our duty crew from four to twelve on the way home.

"That way we won't have to crash anyone out of cryo if we run into trouble. And we are increasing our stock of consumables to make sure we can feed everyone for the full four years."

"Do you have any idea when you will be pulling out?" Isaac asked.

"As soon as we can prepare the ship. It has been almost five years since we headed into the deep black and will be another four to get home again. One good thing. We will not be stopping to ask directions en route. Now I have a question to ask you."

"Ask away."

"Were you ordered to make love to me by your bosses?"

"Of course not," he said in a scandalized tone. "Encouraged, maybe, but never ordered. Besides, the whole thing was my idea in the first place. You aren't offended, are you?"

She put on her most stern expression and held it for ten seconds before bursting into a smile. "No, not offended, just sad that we haven't had another chance."

"What about aboard..."

"No," she replied. "I will be renewing my vows to Nal aboard *Fire* for the next couple of days. If you feel lonely, I am sure there are any number of women aboard who would jump at the chance to sleep with a real, live Earthman.

"Now, when we head back down to Buenos Aires, it will be a different situation. Perhaps you can show me the sights of Earth again..."

#

Nal was waiting when they swung into *Fire*'s artificial gravity field. He quickly folded Lara into his embrace and tilted her head down for a kiss. If she thought he held it longer than was necessary, she kept her opinion to herself.

When he released her, he turned to Isaac and extended his hand. Isaac took it. The handshake also seemed to take longer than necessary. From the expression on both men's faces, she suspected they were having one of those games of dominance men are so fond of.

While they tried to crush each other's hands, she turned and pulled on the lanyard attached to her belt. A large white box slid from the airlock into the ship, emitting the usual "clunk" that went with the passage from zero gee to gravity.

"Is Dr. bin Sool ready for this, Nal?" she asked, turning back to her husband, who was surreptitiously flexing his fingers.

"Standing by, Shipmaster." The use of her title signaled that he was back on duty.

"Did he get the instructions Earth sent up?"

"He did. *Cor* translated them."

At the computer's name, Lara sent a signal via her implant. After relying on her vocal cords for so long, it felt strange.

"Anything to report, Cor?"

"Everything is fine, Shipmaster. The crew has been alerted and the current shore party recalled. The last man came aboard about an hour ago."

"Sober?"

"More or less."

While Lara and the ground party had been busy on Earth, Nal had started a program of giving 48-hour passes for crewmen to visit Grand Terminus. It had proved as popular as the shore leaves on Moskva.

"Shall we join the crew?" Nal asked.

"Let's go," Lara replied. She led off, followed by Isaac Sarnoff, followed by Nal, who carried the sample box.

Save for crewmen on duty, the entire crew was gathered in the dining facility. It was a tight fit. The ambient noise level was moderate when they arrived but fell to a hush in a few seconds.

Lara strode to the end of the compartment where the food dispensers were located.

"Welcome back, Shipmaster," a voice called out. Several others seconded the sentiment.

She smiled. "Has Submaster Taryn been working you too hard?"

From the ensuing rumble, she suspected the answer was 'yes.' While she and the scientists were on Earth, *Coronal Fire* had been on a continuous test-repair-replace cycle to get everything ready for the trip home.

She signaled for silence. "All right. Settle down and I will explain what is going on."

When the compartment quieted, she briefed the crew on Earth's population control system and the suspicion that it had made its way to the Eastern Periphery. She emphasized that the idea was just a theory at the moment.

"We will, of course, attempt to prove or disprove the theory when we get home. If we find no trace of Thorson-Nakuta in our population, we will continue with our original plan using the data from the Registry of the Dead. If, however, we find that this product-of-Earth is widely spread, then we will be able to formulate a plan to get rid of it."

"What sort of plan would that be?" a voice called from the back of the compartment.

That was the same question she had asked Professor Crowley.

"The plan will essentially be to reverse the process by which Earth created it. Reproduction specialists will remove the offending sequences from each zygote before implanting it in the mother."

"So, we won't know for four more years?" Yarin Delnost, the Chief Astrogator asked.

"Perhaps not. Professor Crowley, Earth's leading expert on the subject, suggested that there was something we can do at once. That is why Ambassador Sarnoff and I returned to the ship today.

"Some of us may carry the suspect genetic code. Dr. bin Sool will use the terrestrial equipment we brought with us to sample the blood of everyone onboard. Don't worry, it doesn't hurt. I and the other members of the ground party have already been tested.

"If we do not find a trace of Thorson-Nakuta in any of us, that proves nothing. However, if we find even one of us is infected, then our hypothesis is confirmed, and we will have succeeded beyond the wildest dreams of those who organized this expedition. Are there any questions?"

#

Chapter 47

Lara stirred and slowly traded her dreams for reality. She felt safe with Nal's arms wrapped around her. When she opened her eyes, he was looking at her.

"Good morning," she mumbled.

"And to you. Did you sleep well?"

"Yes."

"How was last night? Better than your visit to that ruin with the unpronounceable name?"

"Infinitely," she said. "You haven't made love to me like that since we were first married. Were you trying to prove something?"

"Maybe."

She laughed. "Ah, male vanity. You don't have to worry, darling. Last night, I was with the one I love, not just engaged in light exercise."

That earned her a kiss.

"I've lost track. How did Isaac make out last night?"

Nal chuckled. The deep rumble in his chest sent chills through her body. "I believe Doria Teray won the bidding."

"That should have made him happy."

"What are your plans for today, my love?"

"I want to review your progress getting the ship ready. We will have to do that this morning. I had hoped to spend another night aboard, but now that we have our samples, we will be heading back down to Earth this afternoon. They seem to be in a rush on the ground," Lara replied. "Now, get your lazy ass out of bed."

"Yes, Shipmaster," Nal said in a meek tone that belied his current expression, which said that he would much rather remain in bed... with her.

Half an hour later, the two of them were enjoying their meal in the dining facility when Isaac Sarnoff walked in. He saw them and hesitated until Lara signaled that he should approach. He did not look the worse for wear.

Her expression was deadpan as she said, "Good morning. How

was your night?"

"Not bad," he said, mirroring her expression. "Not bad at all."

"And how is Doria?"

"I believe she is of the same opinion," he replied. "I asked her to breakfast, but she claims she has the watch this morning. I am hungry. I presume the food dispenser operates the same way it did on our voyage in from Sentinel Alpha Prime."

"The very same."

She and Nal watched him navigate between tables to the dispensers. He came back with a tray loaded with gantha juice, a well-done bisonoid steak, root bulbs, and samosen toast.

When he had drained his juice, he asked, "What is the schedule for today?"

"Nal and I are going to review progress toward getting the ship ready for hyperspace. You, I, and our sample case have an appointment aboard Terminal Station at 15:00 hours. We are on a special ferry flight direct to Shackleton Airport. Apparently, we will be the only two passengers."

Isaac nodded. "I talked to the Boss this morning. He says they are standing by to analyze the samples as soon as they get them. You should feel honored. I've been in the diplomatic service for twenty years and this is the first time they've ever treated me to a special flight."

"What about the samples from the ground party?" Lara asked. "Have they been analyzed yet?"

"No word, I'm afraid," he said as he stuffed a large piece of bisonoid into his mouth. He did not bother to look up when he answered.

Lara had gotten to know Isaac well enough that his response seemed off, like he had been expecting the question and spit out his answer too quickly.

She thought, *Did Isaac just lie to me?*

The rest of the meal consisted of small talk. Lara slowly dropped out of the conversation and listened. Somewhere deep inside, she felt slightly irked that these two men seemed completely comfortable around one another.

#

The transport that awaited them at Terminal Station was a small executive-class ferry. It had seats for twelve passengers, of which, only two were occupied. They were alone save for the pilot, whose duties consisted of waiting for the autopilot to fail, and a comely young cabin attendant who plied them with refreshments.

"This is definitely first-class treatment," Lara said as she lay back and scanned the empty compartment. Isaac was beside her and the sample case strapped into a seat in the next row forward.

"Yes," Isaac agreed. "This sort of transportation is reserved for high ranking officials and people with large credit ratings. Also, the descent will be a treat for you."

"How so?"

"We are en route to Antarctica. After we leave the Cosmic Sphere, we will enter the atmosphere directly over the South Pole. After that, it is simply a matter of descending straight down until we reach traffic control altitude and head for Shackleton. This will be the quietest reentry you have ever experienced."

And so, it was.

Isaac fell asleep shortly after they left Terminal Station and did not wake until just before they hit atmosphere.

"I take it Doria kept you up quite late last night," she said, trying to keep a smirk out of her voice.

Isaac rolled his eyes and sighed loudly but said nothing.

"Since you are awake, I thought we could talk some business."

"Talk away."

"What's going on?"

"What do you mean?"

"Why the hurry? We were going to spend two days aboard *Fire*, and now we are rushing back to Earth."

Isaac paused for several seconds, considering his response. Then he nodded.

"You are perceptive. Something has changed. We have an appointment with the System Council Executive Committee in Toronto four days from now. That does not leave much time for the scientists to do their work."

"Who is this committee and what do they want?"

"The committee consists of the decision makers. They will listen to your request for data and decide what we ask for in return.

As I told you, the time for haggling is nigh."

Isaac again tried to explain how Earth's "government" worked and though Lara nodded along, she still was not sure she understood. After a while they lapsed into silence and Lara contented herself with looking over the side as the planet grew below her.

Deep inside, excitement was stirring.

She had devoted five years of her life to first getting ready for this expedition and then casting about the galaxy, searching for Earth When finally, the Moskvans had dredged up the data that led to Sol, a great weight lifted from her shoulders. The fear of failure that had nagged at her since she came out of cryo was gone.

Now, a different weight was about to lift. Not only were they about to receive the genetic data, but they had found a likely culprit for their low birthrate problem.

She chided herself even as the thought popped into her head. True, Thorson-Nakuta would cause a similar problem to the one they were experiencing, but so would any malady that resulted in low birth rates.

They continued the descent in silence. Then, as scattered habitations began to appear amidst the fields of ice, the ferry halted its descent, banked right, and headed for the capital city.

Since the South Pole is on the same time as the space habitats, they touched down in the airport dome just before third meal. Gathering their sample case and kit bags, she and Isaac transferred to the city's tube system and arrived at University Station a few minutes later. They found Katerina Witt waiting for them on the platform. As soon as they exited the transport car, she relieved Isaac of the sample box.

"Pardon me while I get this to the lab. Professor Crowley wants to see you. Conference Room 226."

With that, she turned and disappeared down a tunnel.

Isaac turned to Lara and held out his arm. "Shall we follow at a more leisurely pace, Milady?"

"We shall."

#

Room 226 was the same conference room where their earlier

meeting had taken place. Anastasia Crowley rose as they entered and met them halfway to the door.

"It's good to see you again, Lara. You, too, Isaac. I suppose you have heard about our command performance on the twenty-third?"

"We have," Isaac replied. "What changed?"

"Scheduling constraints. The ExComm had a cancelation and we are taking the slot. We will fly to Toronto on the twenty-first and get the preliminaries out of the way."

"Preliminaries?" Lara asked.

"Briefings for you and your people. They will go over the draft agreements. If you request changes, they will make them so we can go before the full committee on schedule."

"Have you gotten any results from the ground party DNA analyses, yet?"

"We have."

"What did you find?"

"I'm afraid I can't tell you. Sorry, orders from above. The powers-that-be want us to present our full findings at the same time."

"Why?"

The Professor looked sheepish and shrugged. "Who knows? It may be a negotiating strategy to wring the best deal out of you, or some executive flaunting his position. Don't worry about it. You'll have all the data soon enough."

Like most such advice, Professor Crowley's admonition was wasted.

Lara worried.

#

Chapter 48

The next day, Lara and Isaac returned to Buenos Aires to reunite with the team. Darin Mastlin was as perturbed about the sudden silence about test results as Lara. Betrice Flangan was more than perturbed. She was ready to commit violence. Only Teo Voxman remained calm.

Lara admired her stoicism but could not mirror it.

"How goes the translation, Teo?"

"It is compete, Shipmaster. We have not let the terrestrials test it yet, of course; so, there may be some tweaks when we finally hand it over. Once we prove our program, they will have a direct map to Bernau any time they want to use it."

"And your team, Betrice?"

"We've done test runs on sample data from the Registry of the Dead. We can read complete DNA codes back about eight hundred years. Prior to that, the records have a lot of holes in them."

"Are they of any use?"

"Some. About a quarter of the files are complete, and the ones we have tested show only superficial changes to what we believe is the original genetic code. What about this big meeting? Is the whole team going?"

Lara shook her head. "Isaac says the four of us are sufficient. Darin will be our spokesman. We three will act as subject matter experts. Have we finalized our negotiating position?"

"We have."

"Is anyone going to let me in on it?"

No one spoke for what seemed like forever but was two seconds. When the answer came, it was from an unexpected source.

"We have a new capability," Darin said. Except he did not say it aloud. His voice was inside her head. "We requested a high bandwidth connection to the ship and *Cor* got the implants working."

"Hello, Shipmaster."

"Hello, *Cor*. How did you manage this?"

Two second delay.

"It wasn't difficult once Darin thought of it. I sent down a neural relay while you were away, and we got it working yesterday. It gives us a secure channel of communication on which the terrestrials cannot eavesdrop."

"Surely they must know what you are doing."

Two second delay.

"They know we are transferring data to and from the ship, but they don't know what that data is."

So, what is our negotiating strategy?" Lara asked.

Two second delay.

"We will give them anything they want and make a few requests of our own," Darin said via relay through *Coronal Fire*. "The most important is that the ship they send to Bernau carry duplicates of the data we receive... just in case."

"That's not much of a negotiating strategy."

Darin shrugged and his voice arrived in her head two seconds later. "We hope they will take 'yes' for an answer."

#

The following morning, they lifted off from Buenos Aires and headed north. Their route, which was more easterly than the flight to Yucatan, took them across the Caribbean Sea. They flew over a large island and then a smaller island chain surrounded by shallow water. The water was aquamarine shading to light blue, with cities-on-stilts jutting out from the islands and underwater domes clearly visible from the air. They could even see individual fish swimming lazily in the shallows.

Lara pointed out the window and asked, "What are those fish called?"

Isaac leaned close, pressing his body against hers. He searched for a few seconds until he located the fish, then sat back and smiled. "Those are sharks. Too bad we don't have time for that tour. I would have taken you diving. Sharks are bigger than you are and carnivorous."

A little while later, land came into view and then slid beneath them as they crossed into North America.

The land looked to be one vast residential preserve. Clusters of dwellings surrounded by green spaces transitioned to tracts of farmland, which in turn gave way to small cities. The whole scene reminded Lara of a public park back home.

Finally, the transport descended toward a string of large lakes. One specific lake continued to grow until they passed low over its surface and touched down at an airport on its shore.

"Welcome to Toronto, North American Directorate," Isaac said to his four guests. "Those tall buildings in the distance are our destination, the seat of our 'non-government,' as Lara calls it. That is where we will meet the Executive Committee of the Planning Council."

#

The hotel was one more in a line of luxury hostels. Teodara made a comment about becoming blasé about their upscale accommodations. "I'm not sure I will be able to adjust when we go back aboard ship."

"Don't worry," Lara assured her. "You will be in cold sleep."

Sol was dipping below the horizon when they arrived and after thirty minutes, they found themselves in their rooms with a couple of hours before the first social event – another in a long line of dinners. This one was informal and with some of the Executive Committee members.

In exploring her hotel room, Lara found a closet filled with terrestrial clothing in her size. She spent her time luxuriating in a hot bath until it was time to get ready. Finally, an annunciator announced that the rest of party was standing by. She joined them in the hallway.

The dinner was in a private room off the restaurant at the top of the hotel. Isaac once again did the introductions.

"Darin, Lara, Betrice, Teo, may I introduce Chief of Council Ulrich von Neumann, Councilor Melinda Price, and Councilor Jose Muñoz, all of the Executive Committee of the Terrestrial Planning Council.

"Councilors, Lara da Benthar Sims of the starship *Coronal Fire*; Darin Mastlin, Expedition Leader; Betrice Flangan, Biologist; Teo Voxman, Cosmologist."

Von Neumann was an elderly, balding man with a harried look

and a nasal voice. Melinda Price was a blonde middle-aged woman in an elegant gown and Jose Muñoz was darkly handsome with a well-trimmed mustache.

When Melinda Price shook Lara's hand, she said, "I had heard you were very tall. They weren't exaggerating."

"Yes, we Envonians all look like products of the ancient torture machine that stretched people. The form keeps our weight down and gives us strength against Envon's gravity."

"That is the reason for your visit, I understand. A problem with the genetic modifications that allow you to better survive on your worlds?"

"It is indeed. Not just Envonians, but most people of the Eastern Periphery. We began this expedition because we thought the geneticists had made a mistake during the Time of Chaos. That is still the most likely explanation, but we have another possibility we are exploring."

"Yes, I know," Price answered. "Shall we sit down and have dinner? You must be hungry after your long journey."

The party sat around a long table served by four waiters. Von Neumann proclaimed there would be no business until after the desert course, and final drinks were in hand.

When the last of the dishes had been cleared, he used a spoon to tap on a glass to gain everyone's attention. When the various conversations subsided, he said, "I hope you enjoyed your meal. In addition to meeting you, we arranged this dinner to give you a preview of tomorrow's proceedings and the days that follow.

"We will convene at 09:00 in a conference room off the Hall of Delegates where we will present Earth's various proposals. The first will involve the transfer of DNA data from the Ministry of the Dead; the second, actions to aid you in the survey of your populace for Thorson-Nakuta. We will also tell you what we expect to receive in return for this data.

"After our presentation, we will listen to your proposals of what you want from us. If there are no major disagreements, we then turn our proposals into a formal Memorandum of Agreement.

"The following day, we will go before the full Executive Committee at 10:00. The members will ask you questions until they are satisfied that everyone understands what each of us is willing to do in support of the agreement."

"What sort of questions?" Darin Mastlin asked.

"One thing they are interested in is your authority to bind your government to our agreements. After questions, the full Council will vote. If a majority is in favor, then we will proceed to the signing."

"Signing?"

"Part of the ceremony involves each of you swearing, in a recorded statement, that you were under no duress.

"We will then have a formal dinner at which long speeches will be made before adjourning for the night. The following day, we will meet again to create a detailed Action Plan toward readying your ship for its return voyage."

"What if we cannot come to an agreement?" Darin asked.

Von Neumann's smile was the sort diplomats wear to hide their inner thoughts. "Then we will enter into extended negotiations to resolve our conflicts and the meeting with the full Executive Committee will be postponed. I warn you, if that happens, it could take months to get back on the schedule.

"Are there any questions?"

"I have one," Betrice said. She was still irritated about the silence regarding DNA test results. She had kept herself under control all evening, but her tone showed that was over.

"Go ahead."

"We asked for the results from the ground party DNA testing. Your people said they had orders not talk about it. What the hell is going on?"

Melinda Price leaned forward and said, "I will take this one, Ulrich."

Von Neumann nodded. "I yield the floor."

Price sighed and said, "Last night, as you noted, we had only the results from your people here on Earth. We were hesitant to generalize from such a small sample. However, the academics in Antarctica reported their full results only one hour before your aircraft touched down.

"We planned to lead off tomorrow's activities by giving you a detailed briefing on the results. I see no reason why we cannot give you a preview here tonight."

Price locked eyes with each of the expedition members in turn;

then, in a quiet voice said, "We discovered traces of Thorson-Nakuta."

Those words sent a lightning bolt through Lara's body. The sudden rush of adrenaline momentarily cost her the power of speech. The other members of her party were reacting similarly.

Darin Mastin was the first to recover. He managed to croak out, "How many and who?"

Melinda Price took out her comm and scrolled down the screen.

"We have found definite Thorson-Nakuta traces in two individuals. One is a spacer named Frelan Cartwell. He has a complete set of Thorson-Nakuta Factor. Of course, being male, that has no effect on him. However, if he has any sisters, they will likely be limited to one offspring each."

"And the other?" Lara asked.

Melinda Price turned to her. There was something in her expression that did not seem right. It was her eyes…

"The second individual is you, Shipmaster."

"*Me?*"

"Yes. You are a special case. The scientists found fragments of Thorson-Nakuta Alpha in your genome. Specifically, there are three strings of more than one thousand base pairs at widely separated spots along your DNA strand."

"Is there any chance that they are just a coincidence?" Lara asked.

"About as much chance as all of the stars going dark in the same second."

\#

Chapter 49

The following day went exactly as Ulrich von Neumann had outlined it. In the morning, the terrestrials laid out the full results of the DNA testing.

Save for Spacer Frelan Cartwell in Engineering and Lara, every other member of the team was clean of any trace of Thorson-Nakuta.

Even so, the discovery that two out of two hundred thirty-four individuals tested positive had far reaching implications. Because Thorson-Nakuta is dormant until enough of the population carries it to produce a complementary breeding pair, a one percent "hit" rate was astounding. Professor Crowley's geneticists estimated there were several billion infected individuals in the Eastern Periphery.

However, *estimating* does not equate to *knowing*.

What they knew for sure was that Cartwell's home world, Phoebe, was heavily infected, and Lara's World, Envon, was infected to an unknown degree. The other worlds of the Eastern Periphery were *terra incognita*, unknown territory. As a couple of ancient cosmologists once remarked, "The absence of evidence is not evidence of absence," a principle known as the Ignorance Fallacy.

And so, the relative importance of the two research projects flipped in an instant. The need to map Thorson-Nakuta was now more pressing than the retrieval of humanity's primal macro genome.

At the end of the presentation, Darin Mastlin turned to von Neumann. "All right, what's the price?"

Von Neumann once again smiled in that way that did not signify mirth

"A good question, Expedition Leader, and one without a simple answer. We have information that is obviously of immense value to you; yet you have no direct means to pay us what it is worth. So, of necessity, both parties will have to proceed on faith."

"And what is this 'faith' going to cost us?"

"Our price for the Thorson-Nakuta information is four Morast

Coordinate technologies."

"Which four?"

Von Neumann shrugged. "We have no current idea. However, when we visit Bernau, we will study your technical prowess and make our choice."

"What if we don't have anything you consider sufficiently advanced?" Darin asked.

"Then we will have made a fool's bargain. However, we already know of your language educator, and your ship is surprisingly well armed for a converted freighter. We will take our chances."

Darin nodded. "Point taken. What about the Registry of the Dead data?"

"We want two additional unique technologies for that, also to be chosen by us."

Darin made a show of thinking about it, while conducting a poll by implant via the neural relay in Lara's luggage. The vote, including *Cor*, was unanimous.

He sighed theatrically. "Very well. It's a deal. Anything else?"

"Yes," von Neumann replied. "We want all of the trade goods your ship carries in its holds. They are examples of your technology and examining them may give us ideas."

"Agreed."

Von Neumann sat back as his face broke into a genuine smile. "Well that was easy. Now, I believe it is your turn. What are your demands?"

#

The rest of the morning and afternoon went smoothly. This was the fastest agreement in the history of galactic negotiations. The expedition's demands were few. It was important, they explained, as a safety measure, that the terrestrial expedition to Bernau carry all the information that *Coronal Fire* would be taking home.

Then came their lesser demands. In addition to receiving all available information on Thorson-Nakuta, they requested three DNA analyzers and all technical data on their construction and use.

And, almost as an afterthought, Lara reminded them that her ship had come a long way and needed replenishment. Von Neumann readily agreed to having the Terrestrial Space Navy provide them with everything they needed.

Composing the Memorandum of Agreement took most of the afternoon. In the process, Lara learned that Formal Standard used a lot of phrases and language that dated back centuries. The final document had the feel of having been written on parchment.

It was a tired group that returned to the hotel. Lara did not return alone. Isaac Sarnoff convinced her that this was the last opportunity to renew their relationship and that they should not let it go to waste.

They didn't.

#

The Hall of Delegates was a massive auditorium-style space with seating for five hundred. In front was a stage on which the Executive Committee sat behind a raised structure resembling a judge's bench. Three polished tables for witnesses were arrayed at the foot of the stage, with curved rows of lush workstations behind them for use by spectators, of which there were none.

A massive holocube was suspended from the ceiling over the committee members' heads. At the moment, the cube displayed a real-time view of the Earth projected from somewhere in the Cosmic Sphere.

Upon entry, the expedition members were ushered to the center witness table while Isaac Sarnoff and other members of the diplomatic services sat to their left. Isaac was in the seat closest to his charges. The table to the right had ornate papers laid out on it along with archaic writing instruments. The sound damping field gave the hall the curious dead-air ambience common to fog-shrouded nights yet did nothing to interfere with voices.

Upon taking her seat, Teo looked around and said, "This hall reminds me of Parliament Building on Invorna."

Isaac Sarnoff, upon hearing that, laughed. "The design harkens back to an ancient building in New York that was destroyed in the Soldant Collective's attack. It is possible your parliament used the same inspiration for their design."

Lara was about to comment on her disappointment that she had not had a chance to see New York when a disembodied voice emanated from somewhere overhead.

"All rise for the Executive Committee of the Terrestrial Planning Council."

Everyone got to their feet as twelve robed councilors filed onto the stage from their right. Each halted when he or she reached their seat. They stood for a few seconds, then sat in unison. Ulrich von Neumann sat in the center of the stage. His robe was more lavish than those of his colleagues, and his seat a bit higher. Melinda Price sat two places to his left while Jose Muñoz anchored the line on the right.

After a few seconds, von Neuman intoned in what Lara realized was his official voice, "This committee welcomes our esteemed visitors from the Morast Collective in the Eastern Periphery of the Orion Arm. Please raise your right hands for the administration of the oath."

Darin, Lara, Betrice and Teo, having been forewarned, promptly raised their right arms with palms facing forward.

The oath asked them to attest that their answers today would be truthful, without reservation or attempt to mislead, and that they would not withhold any pertinent details relating to the matters at hand.

The expedition members said, "I do," in unison.

"Very well, be seated. This hearing regarding the ship from the Morast Coordinate is in session."

For more than an hour, the Committee peppered them with questions and comments. As predicted, Darin Mastlin was asked to explain by what authority he could bind the Morast Parliament to the promises they were making.

Another Councilor asked Lara to recount her discovery of *New Hope* and the later expedition to retrieve the ship. Then Betrice was questioned about the genetic flaw that was destroying fertility in the Eastern Periphery. One committee member asked about hyperspace conditions between Bernau and Earth, with an emphasis on their battle with the pirate en route to Katerina.

Then there came a lengthy period when each of the witnesses was grilled about the various terms of the agreement and their understanding of their duties under those terms. Finally, they were asked to stand individually and swear that they were in their right minds and under no duress.

When the Committee ran out of questions, Ulrich von Neumann intoned, "All questions having been answered, the Committee will now retire to vote."

All twelve stood and filed out of sight. The team sat passively and waited for fifteen minutes before a tone sounded and the disembodied voice asked them to stand once more. The Committee members marched back in to resume their seats.

After some shifting around, a sound like banging on wood emanated from the speakers and Ulrich von Neumann's amplified voice said:

"The Committee has considered the proposal before us in closed session and has voted on the proposition before us. A majority of members having voted in favor, the Memorandum of Agreement is adopted.

"Petitioners are requested to approach the table on which the agreement is displayed, and individually affix their signature, thumbprint, and DNA sample to memorialize their concurrence with the Memorandum of Agreement."

Each of them did as asked. The DNA was collected by placing their thumb onto a small black box. There followed a pinprick, then they pressed thumbs below their signature to leave a drop of blood.

Lara was second to sign. As she wiped her thumb over a piece of wet fabric that stopped the bleeding, she wondered how far back in history this custom had originated.

A hush fell over the auditorium while Committee members conferred. Then, the sound of wood being hammered was again heard and von Neumann intoned what was obviously a ceremonial phrase.

"All matters before this Committee having been successfully concluded, I hereby proclaim that these proceedings are at an end.

"This meeting is adjourned!"

#

Chapter 50

Lara was in *Coronal Fire*'s control room and contemplated the hectic activity that had filled the last month. At times she thought they would never get the ship ready for the deep black.

The banquet that followed the Executive Committee's approval was epic. No one in the ground party was sober when they finally staggered back to their hotel. Isaac Sarnoff once again went with Lara to her room, but neither of them had the energy for lovemaking. Rather, they cuddled as they slept the rest of the night.

They remedied that oversight the next morning. Then Isaac kissed her and left to return to Sentinel Alpha Prime. Lara cleaned up, got dressed and contacted Nal aboard *Coronal Fire* to tell him that she loved him.

A new functionary named Kyle Zagni arrived at the hotel to take them to the Hall of Delegates. There they met an entirely new team which consisted of specialists, technicians, experts in logistics, and a naval officer. The latter's task was to coordinate the reprovisioning of *Coronal Fire*.

The Action Plan they developed over the next week was a project planning exercise. Each action was time-phased to produce the desired result at the right time. Coming up with the plan was straightforward. Executing it was not.

One major effort was the transfer of DNA data from the Registry of the Dead to *Coronal Fire*. Luckily, Earth had some truly high-speed data links and it was not necessary to resort to memory modules as they had at Katerina.

The full compendium was massive. Each descriptor had three billion coded entries to describe the individual's genetic code. That was multiplied by the number of people who had died over a span of seven hundred years. The volume of data was worsened by the fact that Earth's population during the Age of Chaos had peaked at 18 billion.

It fell to *Tac Seven* to transform the data into something Morast computers could read. Test runs had been ongoing since they landed on Earth. But test runs are limited in size and complexity and several problems arose and had to be resolved before the data was stored safely in *Fire's* memory vaults.

The second major effort involved translating the data on Thorson-Nakuta from Standard to Omni. Problems arose because *Cor's* understanding of the local language was centuries out of date and lacked the specialized vocabulary associated with bio-genetic science. The task might have been impossible had *Cor* not spent her time in the Cosmic Sphere eavesdropping on Earth's communications. Among the data transferred were several techno-dictionaries covering every specialty associated with genetic science.

Teo's team had similar problems in the other direction. They were transferring the hyperspace map data recorded en route to the Terrestrial Space Navy. Despite her team's tests, they encountered many glitches.

To Lara's surprise, the various bottlenecks had eventually been resolved and each party's data was safely in their respective data vaults within ten days.

Then had come the exchange of hardware. A TSN ship rendezvoused with *Fire* to offload three DNA analyzers and take aboard several thousand items the expedition had carried for trade goods.

When the exchange was complete, a second ship docked with *Fire* to offload food, deuterium-enriched monatomic hydrogen, cryogenic oxygen, water, and other consumables.

Finally, *Fire* was ready for space. After a brief ceremony, Lara ordered *Cor* to power gravitics and they left the Celestial Sphere behind.

#

Lara's reverie was interrupted by *Cor's* voice in her implant.

"We are approaching our jump point, Shipmaster."

"How long?"

"Ten minutes."

"Is everyone at their station?"

"All accounted for."

In the view space before her, Sol was once again just the

brightest star in the sky. Earth had shrunk to a misshapen dot with an even smaller dot floating beside it.

It had been ten days since they left Earth and they were outside the Destarte Limit. While ships entering the Solar System were constrained to enter near an approved gateway, there was no such requirement for departing craft. Thus, *Fire* was well below the ecliptic, pointed toward a star their children's astronomy book labeled Rigel.

The ten days following departure from Earth had been less hectic than the month preceding, but there had still been plenty to do. The first member of the science team had gone into cryo twelve hours out, and a steady stream followed. Five days later, the first crewmember went into the tanks.

She and Nal had made the most of their time together. They made love every night and, in between bouts, held discussions about what it had all meant.

Perhaps it had been the realization that their time together was limited (she would spend the next six months awake and he in cryo), but Lara fell into a contemplative mood.

"This foray seems to have been successful," she began one night in his arms. "Isn't there something to be learned from our experiences?"

"Like what?" he'd asked as he tweaked a nipple in an attempt to distract her.

"Stop that! I'm serious."

He sighed. "All right, my love, you have my attention. What did we learn?"

"At Monmoth, we searched for anything to justify trade between their system and ours. We found nothing. At Katerina, we did the same and came to the same conclusion. Likewise, Earth."

"Yet, the Terrestrials are coming to Bernau anyway. Why?"

"To obtain those parts of our technology that are more advanced than theirs," Nal replied.

"Precisely. During the whole trip, we were searching for the wrong thing. Galactic distances are too great and ships too slow to ever build a workable trade route between Earth and the Periphery. But that assumes a continuous flow of ships carrying physical cargo. We forgot there is one cargo with a credits-to-mass ratio of infinity."

"Data?" he asked.

She nodded. "Before the Age of Chaos, knowledge in the galaxy was distributed widely. Then the wars destroyed much of what any particular world knew. Recovery has been spotty, leaving wide variance in technological levels from system to system. We saw that at Inis-Afallon, Moskva, and Earth. There are twenty-five thousand human colonies in the Orion Arm, yet we only interact with a few hundred of them."

"Are you suggesting we turn *Fire* into a peddler of technical data?"

She paused, furrowed her brow, then said, "I hadn't thought of it. Why not?"

"Did you have something else in mind?

She nodded. "Something on a grander scale. What if the Institute of Knowledge sought out lost colonies and exchanged data with them for payment? They have the infrastructure and resources to buy and maintain the ships. It would be a reborn Stellar Survey. Not only would the exploration ships bring back wealth, but they would bind lost colonies together in an expanding *Pax Galactica*."

Nal thought about it, then said, "You might be on to something. We will discuss it with Darin Mastlin after we uncork him at the end of the voyage. Now, if you don't mind, I have to go into cryo in two days and my time is short. I would like to get back to the business at hand."

"Yes, dear."

He silenced her with a kiss as he moved into full body contact. Lara filed the idea in her head, resolving to expand on it over the next six months.

Cor's voice interrupted her thoughts and brought her back to the present.

"It's time, Shipmaster."

"Very well. Call the roll."

Almost at once, the voices echoed in her physical ears as eleven duty personnel informed *Cor* that they were ready to jump. Every two months, four members would be replaced, giving those still awake fresh faces to look at. The expanded crew should be able to fight the ship and would make life more interesting for those awake than it had been on the trip to Earth.

The roll call finished with, "Shipmaster, ready to jump."

"The ship is ready to jump," *Cor* announced formally.

"Very well, jump when ready."

Ten seconds went by while Lara stared at the shrunken Sol and the tiny dot that was the Mother of Men. Then the stars went out and the hazy cyan fog of null filled the view volume.

"Beginning upfreq to 1000 lights," *Cor* announced.

Lara lay back in her couch, eyes scanning for red splotches of gravity infusions ahead. There were none.

A feeling of wellbeing descended on her as she began to hum. The ship was back in its natural element...

... and they were headed home.

\#

The End

Author's Biography

Michael McCollum was born in Phoenix, Arizona, in 1946, and is a graduate of Arizona State University, where he majored in aerospace propulsion and minored in nuclear engineering. He is recently retired from Honeywell in Tempe, Arizona, where he was Chief Engineer in the valve product line. In his career, Mr. McCollum has worked on the precursor to the Space Shuttle Main Engine, a nuclear valve to replace the one that failed at Three Mile Island, several guided missiles, Space Station Freedom, and virtually every aircraft in production today. He was involved in an effort to create a joint venture company with a major Russian aerospace engine manufacturer and traveled extensively to Russia in the decade after the fall of the Soviet Union.

In addition to his engineering, Mr. McCollum is a successful professional writer in the field of science fiction. He is the author of a dozen pieces of short fiction and has appeared in magazines such as Analog Science Fiction/Science Fact, Amazing, and Isaac Asimov's Science Fiction Magazine. His novels (originally published by Ballantine-Del Rey) include *A Greater Infinity, Life Probe, Procyon's Promise, Antares Dawn, Antares Passage, The Clouds of Saturn,* and

The Sails of Tau Ceti. His novel, *Thunderstrike!*, was optioned by a Hollywood production company for a possible movie. Several of these books have subsequently been translated into Japanese, German, Russian, and the Queen's version of English.

Mr. McCollum is the proprietor of Sci Fi - Arizona, one of the first author-owned-and-operated virtual bookstores on the INTERNET, which first published *Gibraltar Earth, Gibraltar Sun, Gibraltar Stars, Antares Victory,* and *Euclid's Wall*. He also runs Third Millennium Publishing, an INTERNET site that supplies web and publishing services to independent author/publishers.

Mr. McCollum has been married to a lovely lady named Catherine for 40 years, and has three children: Robert, Michael, and Elizabeth. Robert is a financial analyst for a software company in Massachusetts. Michael is a computer technician, having completed a stint as a Military Police Specialist with the Arizona National Guard. He served for a year in the lovely land between the Tigris and Euphrates Rivers. Elizabeth is married and living with her husband, Brock, a computer programmer, in Washington, D.C. She works for the Department of Health and Human Services.

Sci Fi - Arizona

A Virtual Science Fiction Bookstore and Writer's Workshop
Michael McCollum, Proprietor

WWW.SCIFI-AZ.COM

If you enjoy technologically sophisticated science fiction or have an interest in writing, you will probably find something to interest you at Sci Fi - Arizona. We have short stories and articles on writing– all for free! If you like what you find, we have full length, professionally written science fiction novels in both electronic form and as hard copy books, and at prices lower than you will find in your local bookstore.

Moreover, if you like space art, you can visit our Art Gallery, where we feature the works of Don Dixon, one of the best astronomical and science fiction artists at work today. Don is the Art Director of the Griffith Observatory. Pick up one or more of his spacescapes for computer wallpaper or order a high-quality print direct from the artist.

We have book length versions of both Writers' Workshop series, "The Art of Writing, Volumes I and II" and "The Art of Science Fiction, Volumes I and II" in both electronic and hard copy formats.

So, if you are looking for a fondly remembered novel, or facing six hours strapped into an airplane seat with nothing to read, check out our offerings. We think you will like what you find.

NOVELS

1. Life Probe

The Makers searched for the secret to faster-than-light travel for 100,000 years. Their chosen instruments were the Life Probes, which they launched in every direction to seek out advanced civilizations among the stars. One such machine searching for intelligent life encounters 21st century Earth. It isn't sure that it has found any...

2. Procyon's Promise

Three hundred years after humanity made its deal with the Life Probe to search out the secret of faster-than-light travel, the descendants of the original expedition return to Earth in a starship. They find a world that has forgotten the ancient contract. No matter. The colonists have overcome far greater obstacles in their single-minded drive to redeem a promise made before any of them were born...

3. Antares Dawn

When the supergiant star Antares exploded in 2512, the human colony on Alta found their pathway to the stars gone, isolating them from the rest of human space for more than a century. Then one day, a powerful warship materialized in the system without warning. Alarmed by the sudden appearance of such a behemoth, the commanders of the Altan Space Navy dispatched one of their most powerful ships to investigate. What ASNS Discovery finds when they finally catch the intruder is a battered hulk manned by a dead crew.

That is disturbing news for the Altans. For the dead battleship could easily have defeated the whole of the Altan navy. If it could find Alta, then so could whomever it was that beat it. Something must be done...

4. Antares Passage

After more than a century of isolation, the paths between stars are again open and the people of Alta in contact with their sister colony on Sandar. The opening of the foldlines has not been the unmixed blessing the Altans had supposed, however.

For the reestablishment of interstellar travel has brought with it news of the Ryall, an alien race whose goal is the extermination of humanity. If they are to avoid defeat at the hands of the aliens, Alta must seek out the military might of Earth. However, to reach Earth requires them to dive into the heart of a supernova.

5. Antares Victory – First Time in Print

After a century of warfare, humanity finally discovered the Achilles heel of the Ryall, their xenophobic reptilian foe. Spica – Alpha Virginis – is the key star system in enemy space. It is the hub through which all Ryall starships must pass, and if humanity can only capture and hold it, they will strangle the Ryall war machine and end their threat to humankind forever.

·   It all seemed so simple in the computer simulations: Advance by stealth, attack without warning, strike swiftly with overwhelming power. Unfortunately, conquering the Ryall proves the easy part. With the key to victory in hand, Richard and Bethany Drake discover that they must also conquer human nature if they are to bring down the alien foe ...

6. Thunderstrike!

The new comet found near Jupiter was an incredible treasure trove of water ice and rock. Immediately, the water-starved Luna Republic and the Sierra Corporation, a leader in asteroid mining, were squabbling over rights to the new resource. However, all thoughts of profit and fame were abandoned when a scientific expedition discovered that the comet's trajectory placed it on a collision course with Earth!

As scientists struggled to find a way to alter the comet's course, world leaders tried desperately to restrain mass panic, and two lovers quarreled over the direction the comet was to take, all Earth waited to see if humanity had any future at all...

7. The Clouds of Saturn

When the sun flared out of control and boiled Earth's oceans, humanity took refuge in a place that few would have predicted. In the greatest migration in history, the entire human race took up residence among the towering clouds and deep clear-air canyons of Saturn's upper atmosphere. Having survived the traitor star, they returned to the all-too-human tradition of internecine strife. The new city-states of Saturn began to resemble those of ancient Greece, with one group of cities taking on the role of militaristic Sparta...

8. The Sails of Tau Ceti

Starhopper was humanity's first interstellar probe. It was designed to search for intelligent life beyond the solar system. Before it could be launched, however, intelligent life found Earth. The discovery of an alien light sail inbound at the edge of the solar system generated considerable excitement in scientific circles. With the interstellar probe nearing completion, it gave scientists the opportunity to launch an expedition to meet the aliens while they were still in space. The second surprise came when *Starhopper's* crew boarded the alien craft. They found beings that, despite their alien physiques, were surprisingly compatible with humans. That two species so similar could have evolved a mere twelve light years from one another seemed too coincidental to be true.

One human being soon discovered that coincidence had nothing to do with it...

9. Gibraltar Earth – First Time in Print

It is the 24th Century and humanity is just gaining a toehold out among the stars. Stellar Survey Starship *Magellan* is exploring the New Eden system when they encounter two alien spacecraft. When the encounter is over, the score is one human scout ship and one alien aggressor destroyed. In exploring the wreck of the second alien ship, spacers discover a survivor with a fantastic story.

The alien comes from a million-star Galactic Empire ruled over by a mysterious race known as the Broa. These overlords are the masters of this region of the galaxy and they allow no competitors. This news presents Earth's rulers with a problem. As yet, the Broa are ignorant of humanity's existence. Does the human race retreat to its one small world, quaking in fear that the Broa will eventually discover Earth? Or do they take a more aggressive approach?

Whatever they do, they must do it quickly! Time is running out for the human race...

10. Gibraltar Sun – First Time in Print

The expedition to the Crab Nebula has returned to Earth and the news is not good. Out among the stars, a million systems have fallen under Broan domination, the fate awaiting Earth should the Broa ever learn of its existence. The problem would seem to allow but three responses: submit meekly to slavery, fight and risk extermination, or hide and pray the Broa remain ignorant of humankind for at least a few more generations. Are the hairless apes of Sol III finally faced with a problem for which there is no acceptable solution?

While politicians argue, Mark Rykand and Lisa Arden risk everything to spy on the all-powerful enemy that is beginning to wonder at the appearance of mysterious bipeds in their midst...

11. Gibraltar Stars – First Time in Print

The great debate is over. The human race has rejected the idea of pulling back from the stars and hiding on Earth in the hope the Broa will overlook us for a few more generations. Instead, the World Parliament, by a 60-40 vote, has decided to throw the dice and go for a win. Parliament Hall resounds with brave words as members declare victory inevitable.

With the balance of forces a million to one against *Homo sapiens Terra*, those who must turn patriotic speeches into hard-won reality have their work cut out for them. They must expand humanity's foothold in Broan space while contending with a supply line that is 7000 light-years long.

If the sheer magnitude of the task isn't enough, Mark and Lisa Rykand discover they are in a race against two very different antagonists. The Broa are beginning to wonder at the strange two-legged interlopers in their domain; while back on Earth, those who lost the great debate are eager to try again.

Whoever wins the race will determine the future of the human species... or, indeed, whether it has one.

12. Euclid's Wall – First Time in Print

A century after civilization fell in a day and a night of tectonic cataclysm, scattered communities have regained a fraction of what humanity lost on that Day of Destruction. One such is the Duchy of Hampshire on the southern tip of England.

Hampshire is at war with the Califat de Normandie. It is a war that has been profitable for merchant sea captain Ethan Scott of the Sailing Barque *Hellespont*. Despite the money to be made, Scott prays for the war to end. Each time he puts to sea, he risks his ship and the lives of his crew on his ability to evade the Norman raiders in the Channel and the Eirish Sea. It is a gamble he will inevitably lose if he keeps at it too long.

The Duke of Hampshire has problems of his own. War is expensive. If he doesn't find additional resources soon, he will be defeated. The Duke plans to send an expedition to North America to discover whether the fabled wealth of old still exists there. For that, he needs a ship.

Scott's chance meeting with a beautiful woman presents both men with the solution to their respective problems. Soon *Hellespont* sets sail for America and the mysterious Wall that scholars believe precipitated the fall of civilization, and which may yet destroy the world.

13. Lost Earth

A GALAXY REBORN

It is the 43rd century and humanity occupies a substantial chunk of the Orion Spur, the small galactic arm in which Sol is located. Homo sapiens Terra has become Homo sapiens Galactica.

Following the invention of faster-than-light travel in 2530, the Great Hegira went from a trickle to a flood as human-occupied space expanded at an exponential clip. Over the centuries, rivalries grew, as did star system navies. When widespread war finally came, it raged across entire sectors.

Mass bombardments of enemy planets took their toll. Much that had been built during the preceding thousand years was smashed in flashes of nuclear fusion.

A dark age descended. Eventually, a new Pax Galactica took

hold. The return of stability brought with it a renaissance. Much knowledge that had been lost was regained.

Much, but not all.

On worlds across human space, parents told their children stories of a place where once dwelt knights and princesses, magicians and dragons, where bold warriors sallied forth to victory or defeat.

What the children did not learn was where this magical place could be found. The years of chaos had robbed them of that information. The stellar coordinates of Sol were lost.

And with them, the location of Planet Earth.

14. A Greater Infinity

Duncan MacElroy was an ordinary engineering student before he went out for a six-pack of beer one night and never came back. Instead, he found himself embroiled in a war for the dominance of Paratime, as well as defending our own particular version of Earth from predators on both sides of the battle lines. For he quickly discovered that "parallel universes" aren't, and that a single individual can make all the difference in the worlds!

15. Gridlock and Other Stories

Where would you visit if you invented a time machine, but could not steer it? What if you went out for a six-pack of beer and never came back? If you think nuclear power is dangerous, you should try black holes as an energy source — or even scarier, solar energy! Visit the many worlds of Michael McCollum. ! guarantee that you will be surprised!

NON-FICTION BOOKS

16. The Art of Writing, Volume I

Have you missed any of the articles in the Art of Writing Series? No problem. The first sixteen articles (October, 1996-December, 1997) have been collected into a book-length work of more than 72,000 words. Now you can learn about character, conflict, plot, pacing, dialogue, and the business of writing, all in one document.

17. The Art of Writing, Volume II

This collection covers the Art of Writing articles published during 1998. The book is 62,000 words in length and builds on the foundation of knowledge provided by Volume I of this popular series.

18. The Art of Science Fiction, Volume I

Have you missed any of the articles in the Art of Science Fiction Series? No problem. The first sixteen articles (October, 1996-December, 1997) have been collected into a book-length work of more than 70,000 words. Learn about science fiction techniques and technologies, including starships, time machines, and rocket propulsion. Tour the Solar System and learn astronomy from the science fiction writer's viewpoint. We don't care where the stars appear in the terrestrial sky. We want to know their true positions in space. If you are planning to write an interstellar romance, brushing up on your astronomy may be just what you need.

19. The Art of Science Fiction, Volume II

This collection covers the *Art of Science Fiction* articles published during 1998. The book is 67,000 words in length and builds on the foundation of knowledge provided by Volume I of this popular series.

20. The Astrogator's Handbook – Expanded Edition and Deluxe Editions

The Astrogator's Handbook has been very popular on Sci Fi – Arizona. The handbook has star maps that show science fiction writers where the stars are located in space rather than where they are located in Earth's sky. Because of the popularity, we are expanding the handbook to show nine times as much space and more than ten times as many stars. The expanded handbook includes the positions of 3500 stars as viewed from Polaris on 63 maps. This handbook is a useful resource for every science fiction writer and will appeal to anyone with an interest in astronomy.